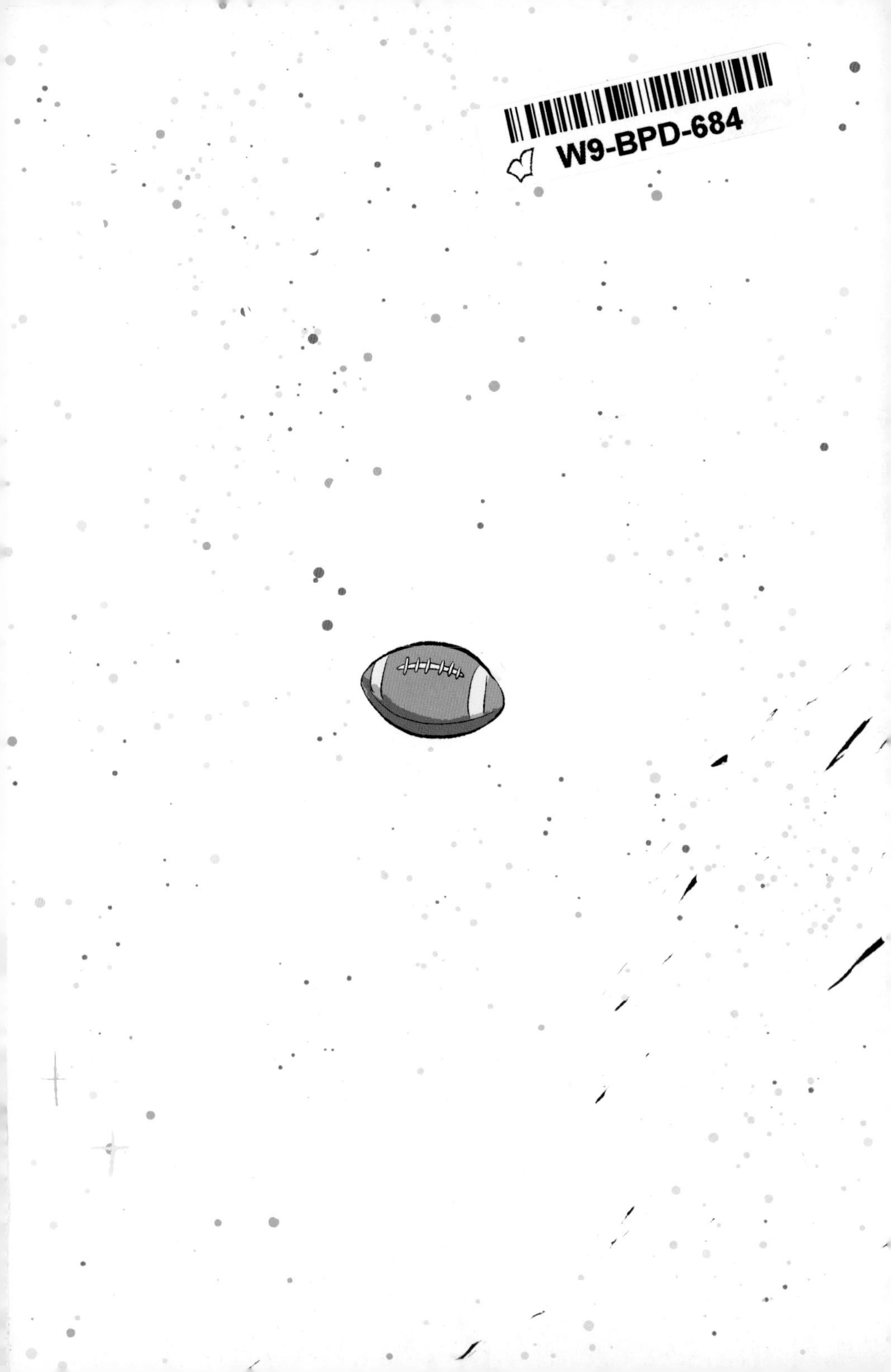

Stephen McCranie's

# SPACE BOY

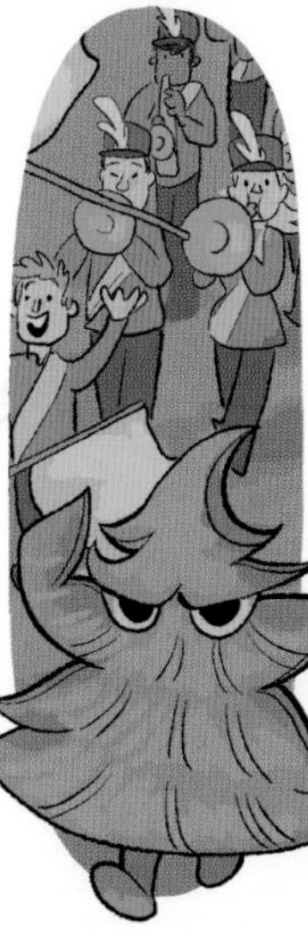

## VOLUME 7

Written and illustrated by
**STEPHEN McCRANIE**

DARK HORSE BOOKS

President and Publisher **Mike Richardson**
Editor **Shantel LaRocque**
Assistant Editor **Brett Israel**
Designer **Anita Magaña**
Digital Art Technician **Allyson Haller**

STEPHEN McCRANIE'S SPACE BOY VOLUME 7
Space Boy™ © 2020 Stephen McCranie. All rights reserved. Dark Horse Books® and the
Dark Horse logo are registered trademarks of Dark Horse Comics LLC. All rights reserved.
No portion of this publication may be reproduced or transmitted, in any form or by
any means, without the express written permission of Dark Horse Comics LLC. Names,
characters, places, and incidents featured in this publication either are the product of the
author's imagination or are used fictitiously. Any resemblance to actual persons (living or
dead), events, institutions, or locales, without satiric intent, is coincidental.

This book collects Space Boy episodes 95–110, previously published online at
WebToons.com.

Published by Dark Horse Books
A division of Dark Horse Comics LLC
10956 SE Main Street | Milwaukie, OR 97222
StephenMcCranie.com | DarkHorse.com

To find a comics shop in your area, visit comicshoplocator.com

First edition: June 2020
ISBN 978-1-50671-401-1
10 9 8 7 6 5 4 3 2 1
Printed in China

Names: McCranie, Stephen, 1987- writer, illustrator.
Title: Space Boy / written and illustrated by Stephen McCranie.
Other titles: At head of title: Stephen McCranie's
Description: First edition. | Milwaukie, OR : Dark Horse Books, 2018- | v. 1:
"This book collects Space Boy episodes 1-16 previously published online at
WebToons.com."--Title page verso. | v. 2: "This book collects Space Boy
episodes 17-32, previously published online at WebToons.com."--Title page
verso. | v. 3: "This book collects Space Boy episodes 33-48, previously
published online at WebToons.com."--Title page verso. | v. 4: "This book
collects Space Boy episodes 49-60, previously published online at
WebToons.com."--Title page verso. | v. 4: "This book collects Space Boy
episodes 61-75, previously published online at WebToons.com."--Title page
verso. | v. 6: "This book collects Space Boy episodes 76-92, previously
published online at WebToons.com."--Title page verso. | Summary: Amy lives
on a colony in deep space, but when her father loses his job the family
moves back to Earth, where she has to adapt to heavier gravity, a new
school, and a strange boy with no flavor.
Identifiers: LCCN 2017053602| ISBN 9781506706481 (v. 1 ; pbk.) | ISBN
9781506706801 (v. 2 ; pbk.) | ISBN 9781506708423 (v. 3 ; pbk.) | ISBN
9781506708430 (v. 4 ; pbk.) | ISBN 9781506713991 (v. 5 ; pbk.) | ISBN
9781506714004 (v. 6 ; pbk.) | ISBN 9781506714011 (v. 7 ; pbk.)
Subjects: LCSH: Graphic novels. | CYAC: Graphic novels. | Science fiction. |
Moving, Household--Fiction. | Self-perception--Fiction. |
Friendship--Fiction.
Classification: LCC PZ7.7.M42 Sp 2018 | DDC 741.5/973--dc23
LC record available at https://lccn.loc.gov/2017053602

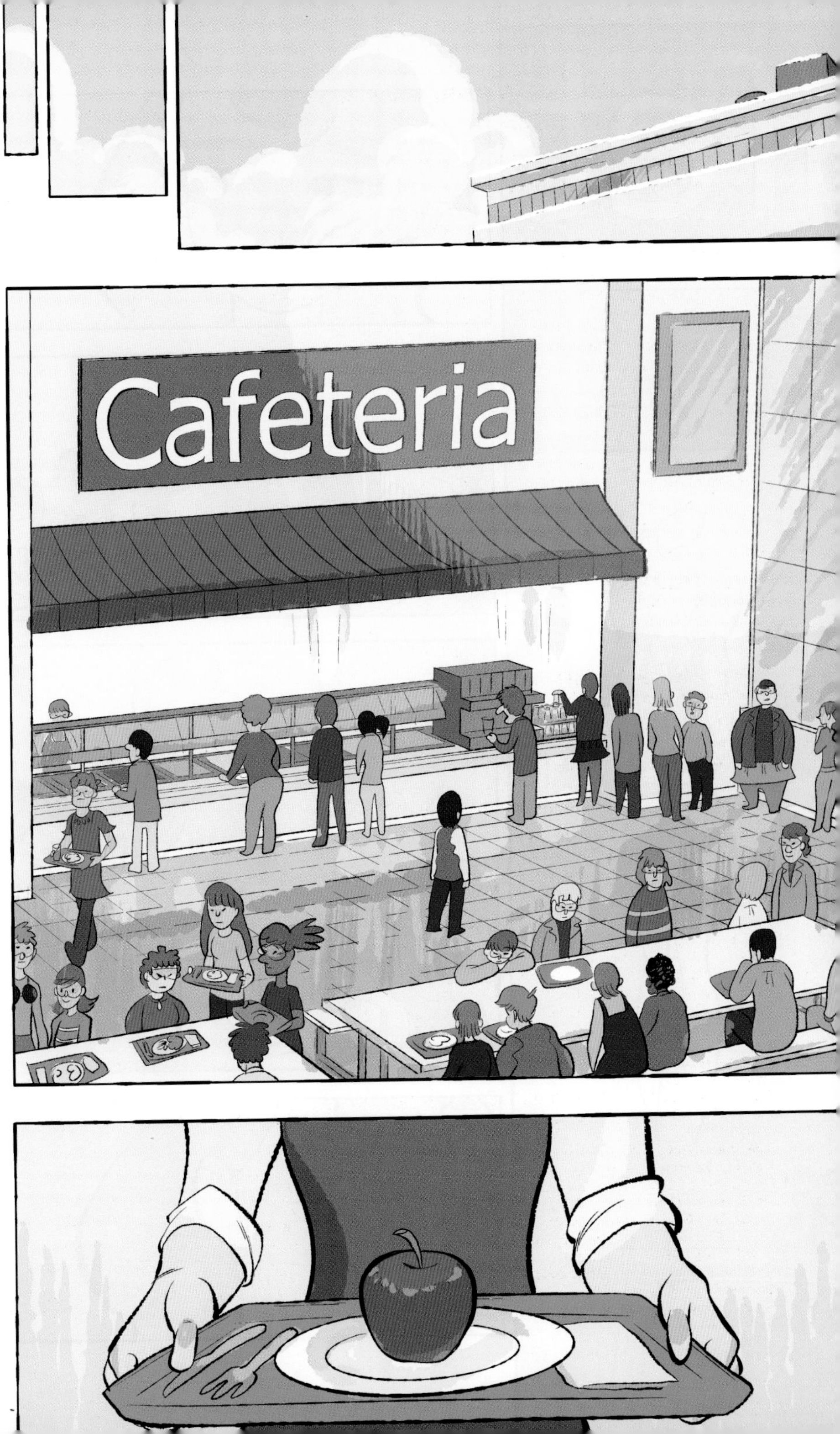
Cafeteria

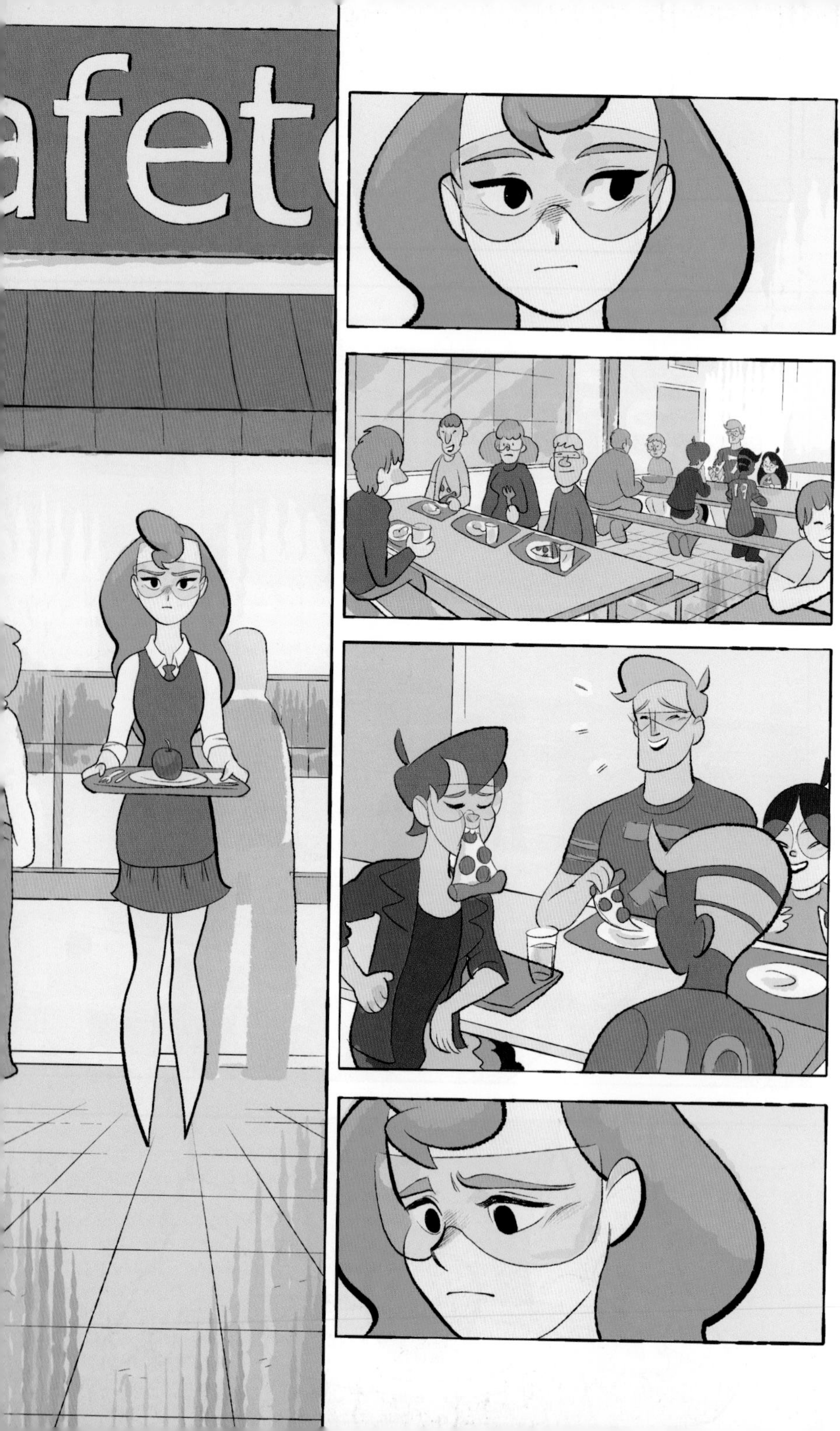
afet

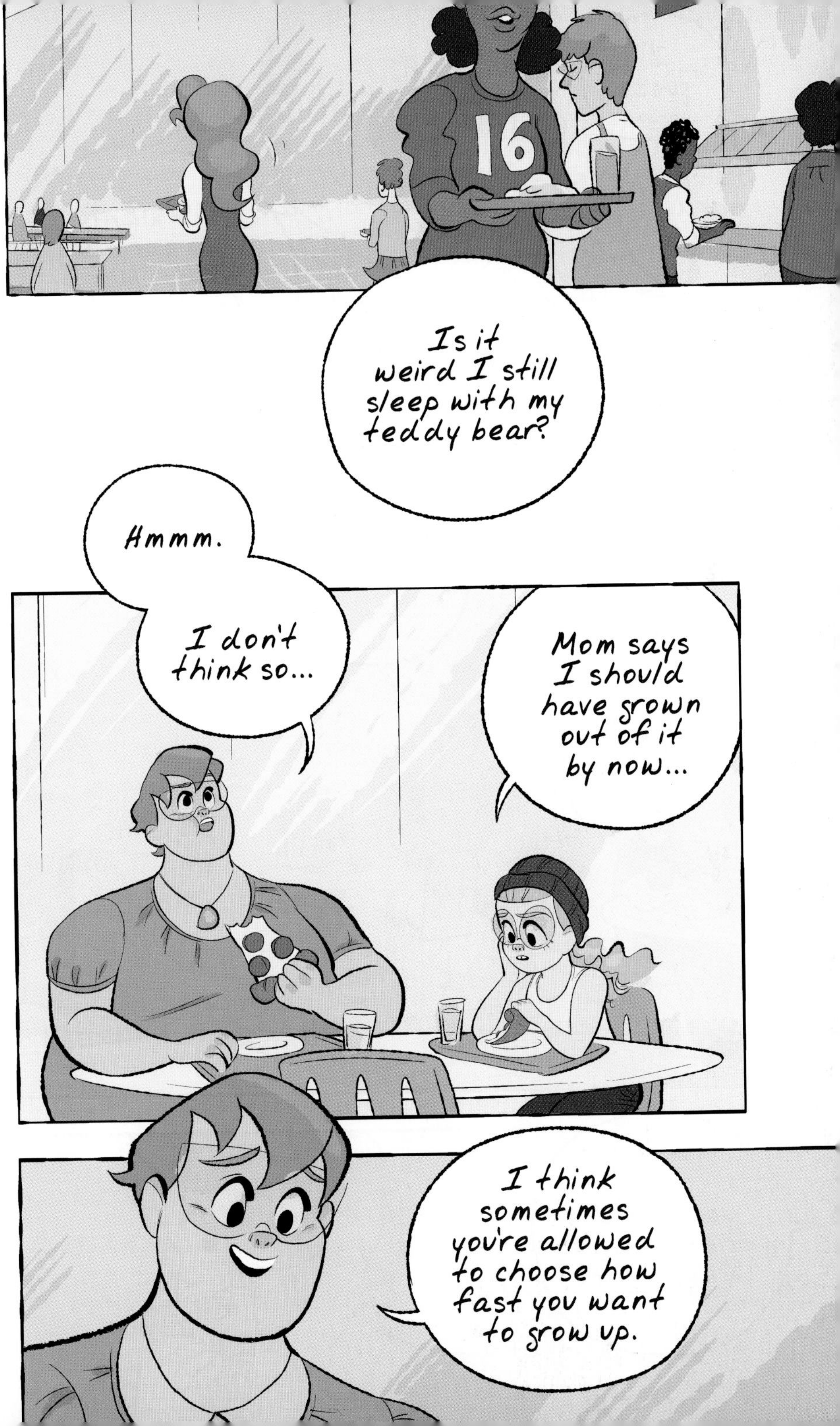
Is it weird I still sleep with my teddy bear?
Hmmm.
I don't think so...
Mom says I should have grown out of it by now...
I think sometimes you're allowed to choose how fast you want to grow up.

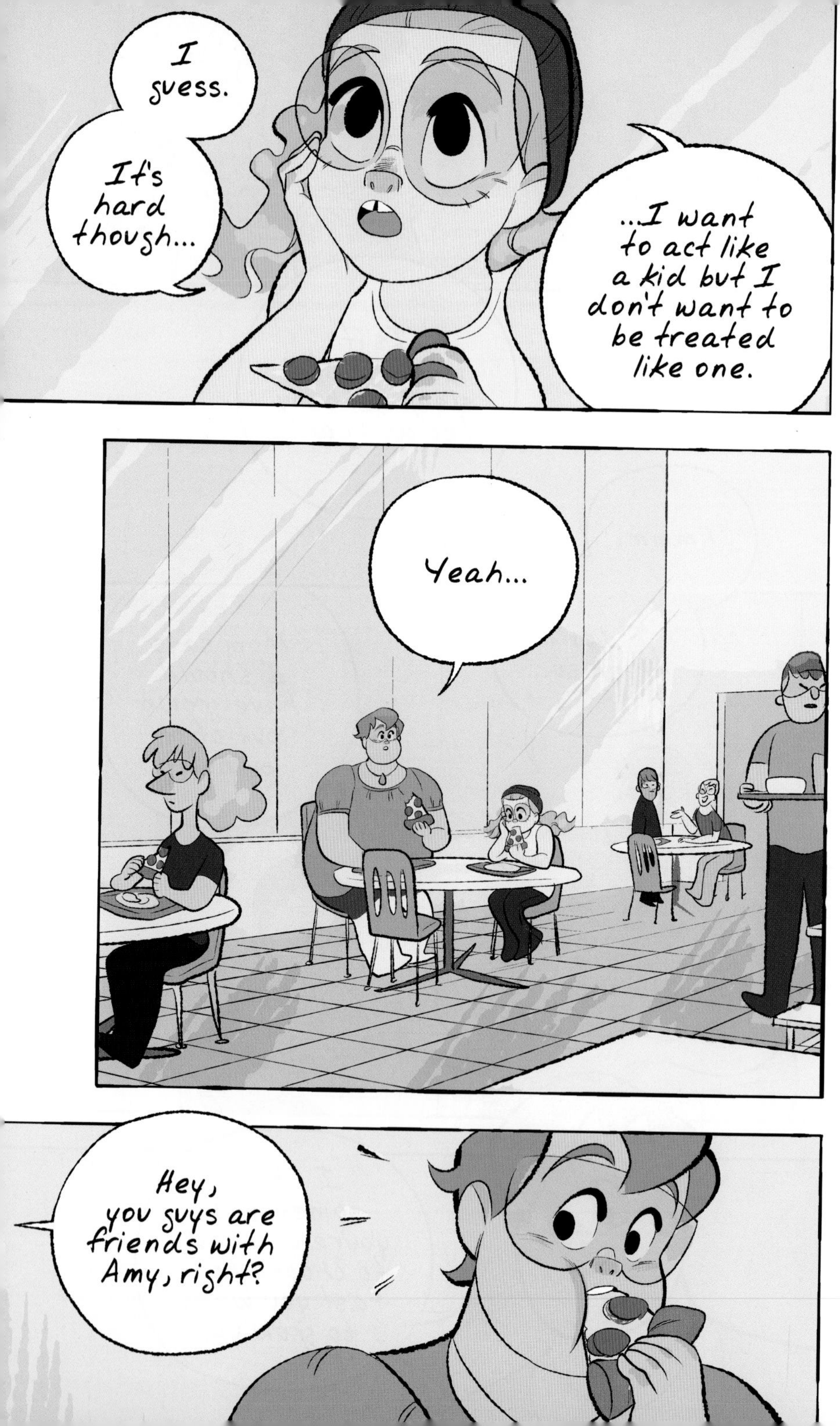
I guess.
It's hard though...
...I want to act like a kid but I don't want to be treated like one.
Yeah...
Hey, you guys are friends with Amy, right?

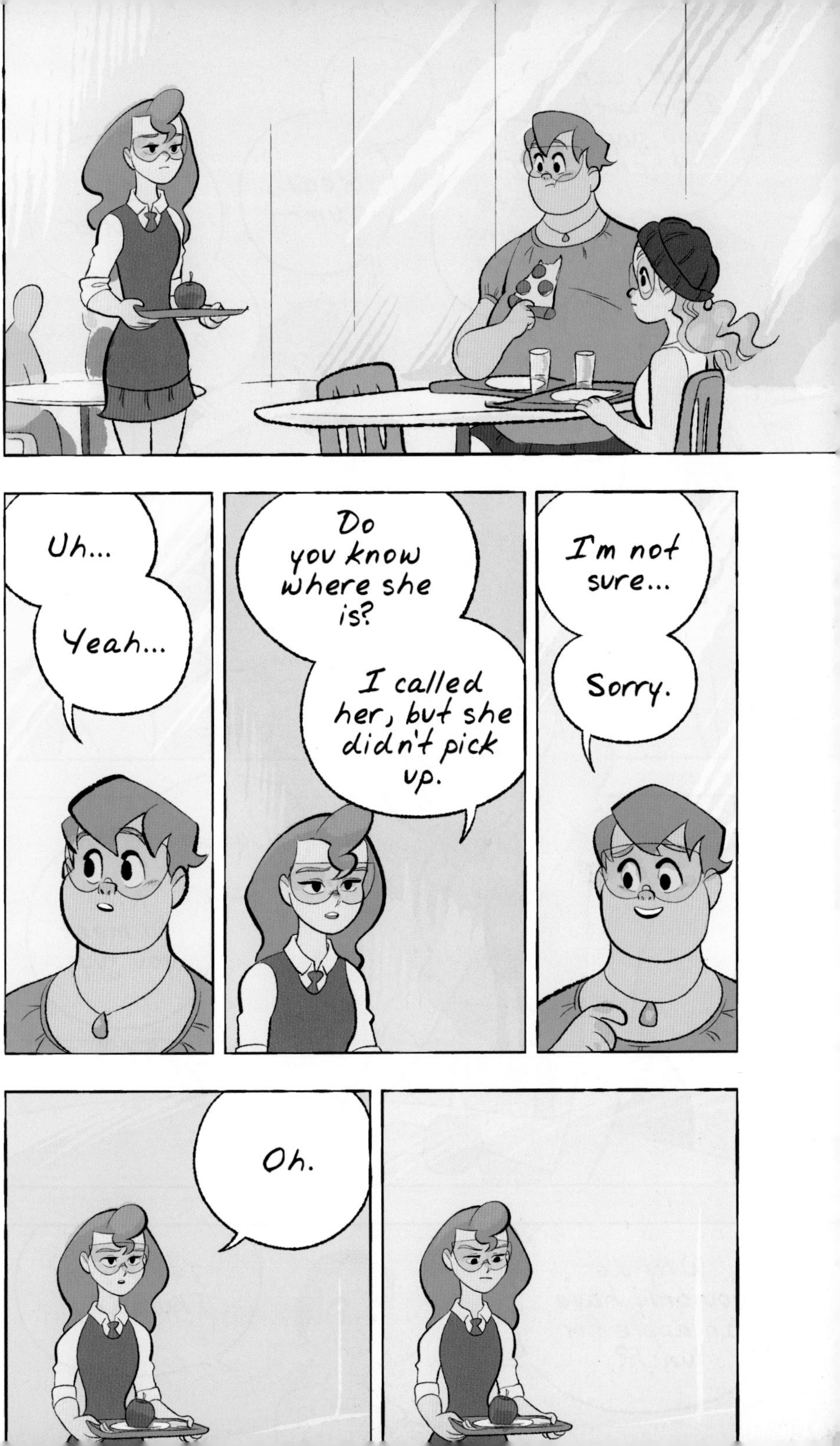
Uh...
Yeah...
Do you know where she is?
I called her, but she didn't pick up.
I'm not sure...
Sorry.
Oh.

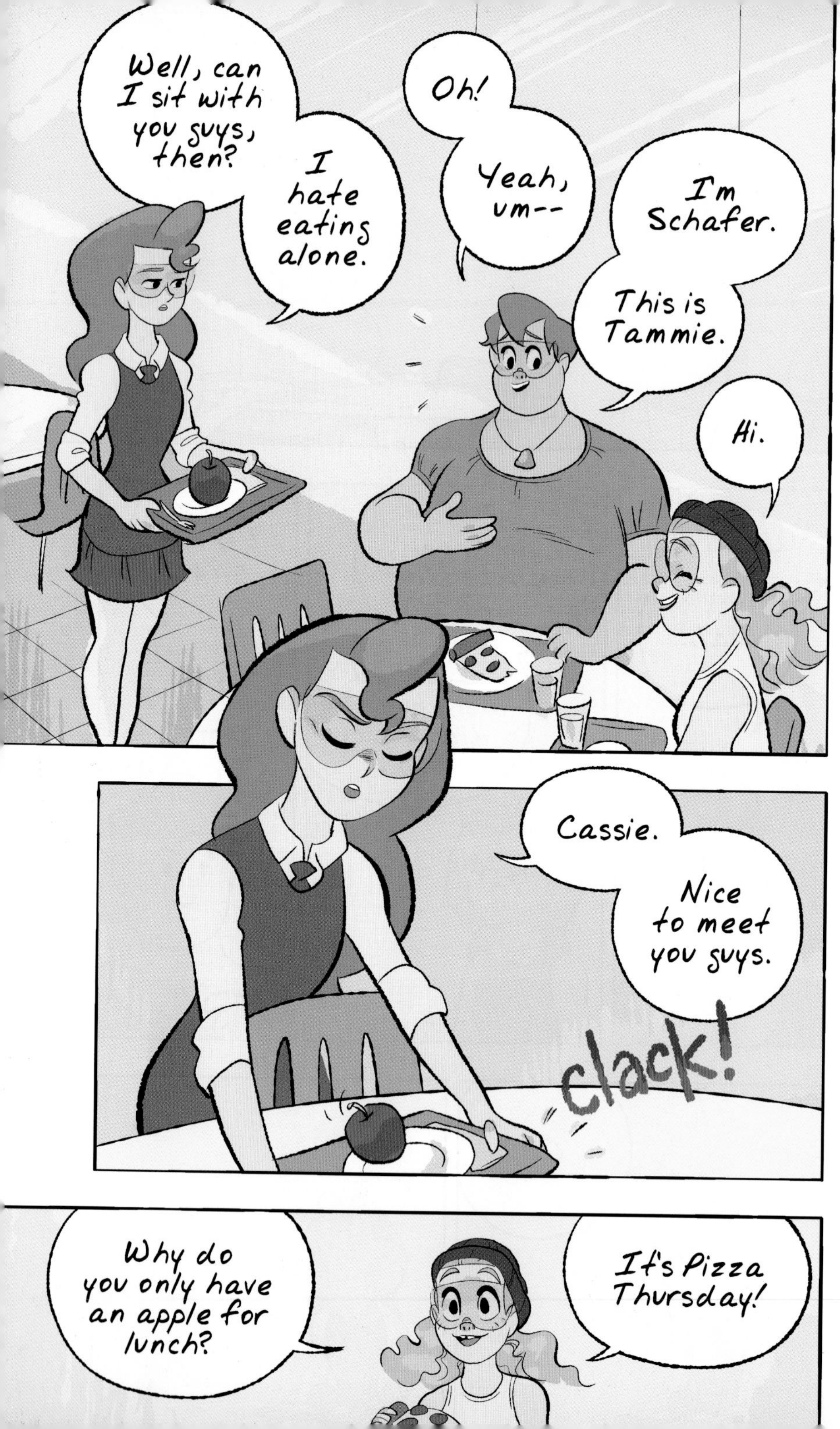

Well, can I sit with you guys, then?
I hate eating alone.
Oh!
Yeah, um--
I'm Schafer.
This is Tammie.
Hi.
Cassie.
Nice to meet you guys.
clack!
Why do you only have an apple for lunch?
It's Pizza Thursday!

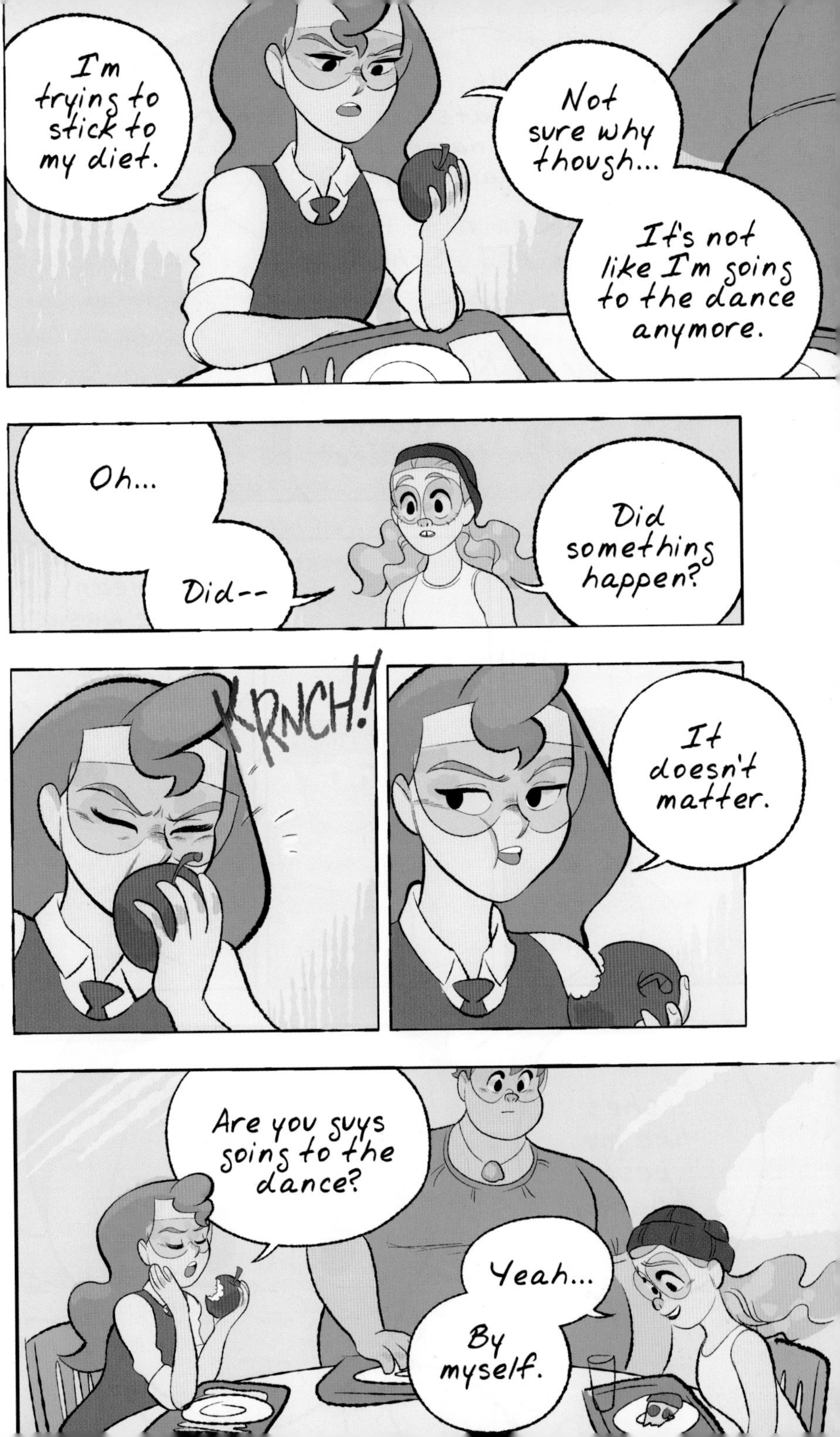
I'm trying to stick to my diet.
Not sure why though...
It's not like I'm going to the dance anymore.
Oh...
Did--
Did something happen?
KRNCH!
It doesn't matter.
Are you guys going to the dance?
Yeah...
By myself.

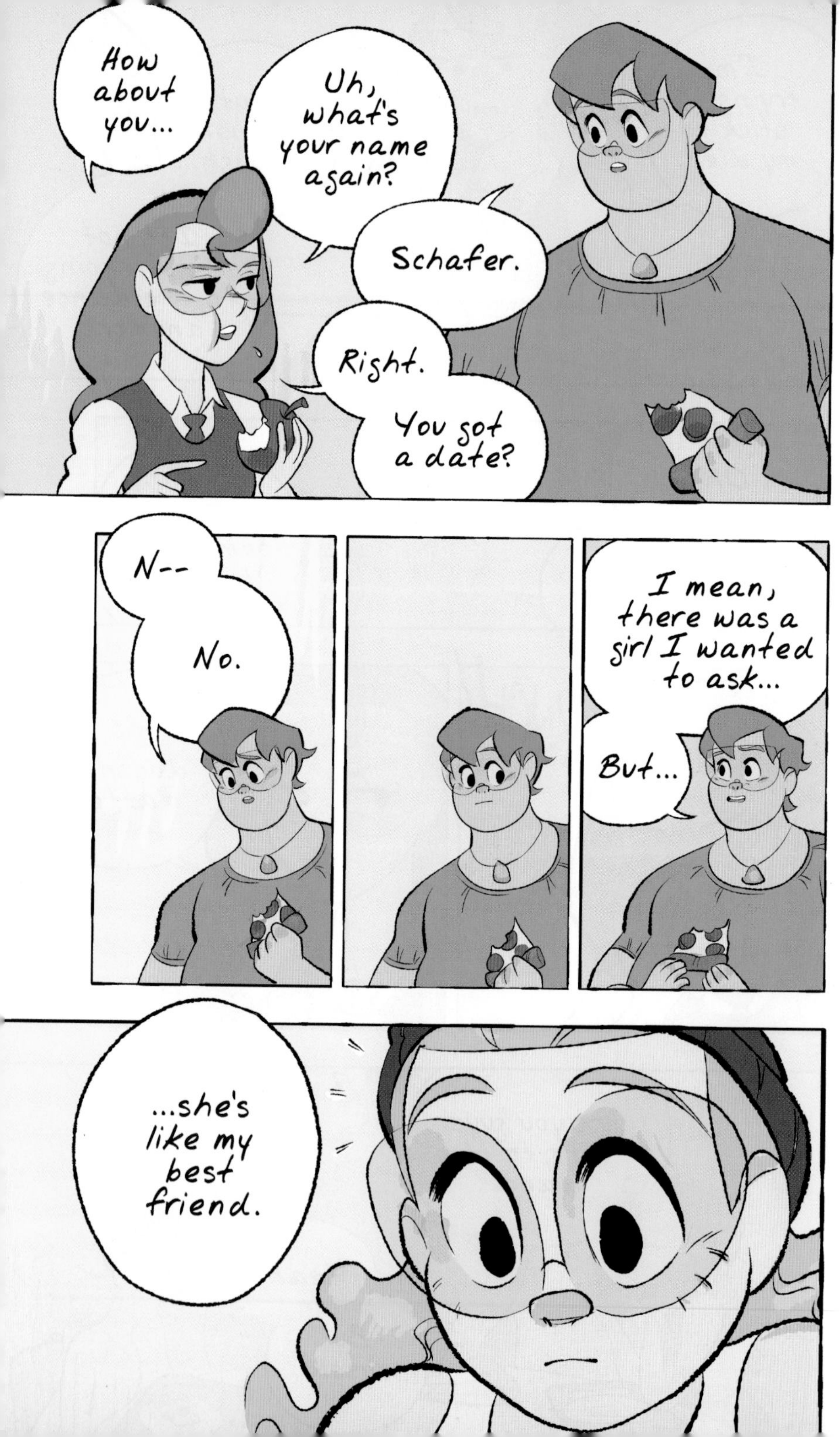
How about you...
Uh, what's your name again?
Schafer.
Right.
You got a date?
N--
No.
I mean, there was a girl I wanted to ask...
But...
...she's like my best friend.

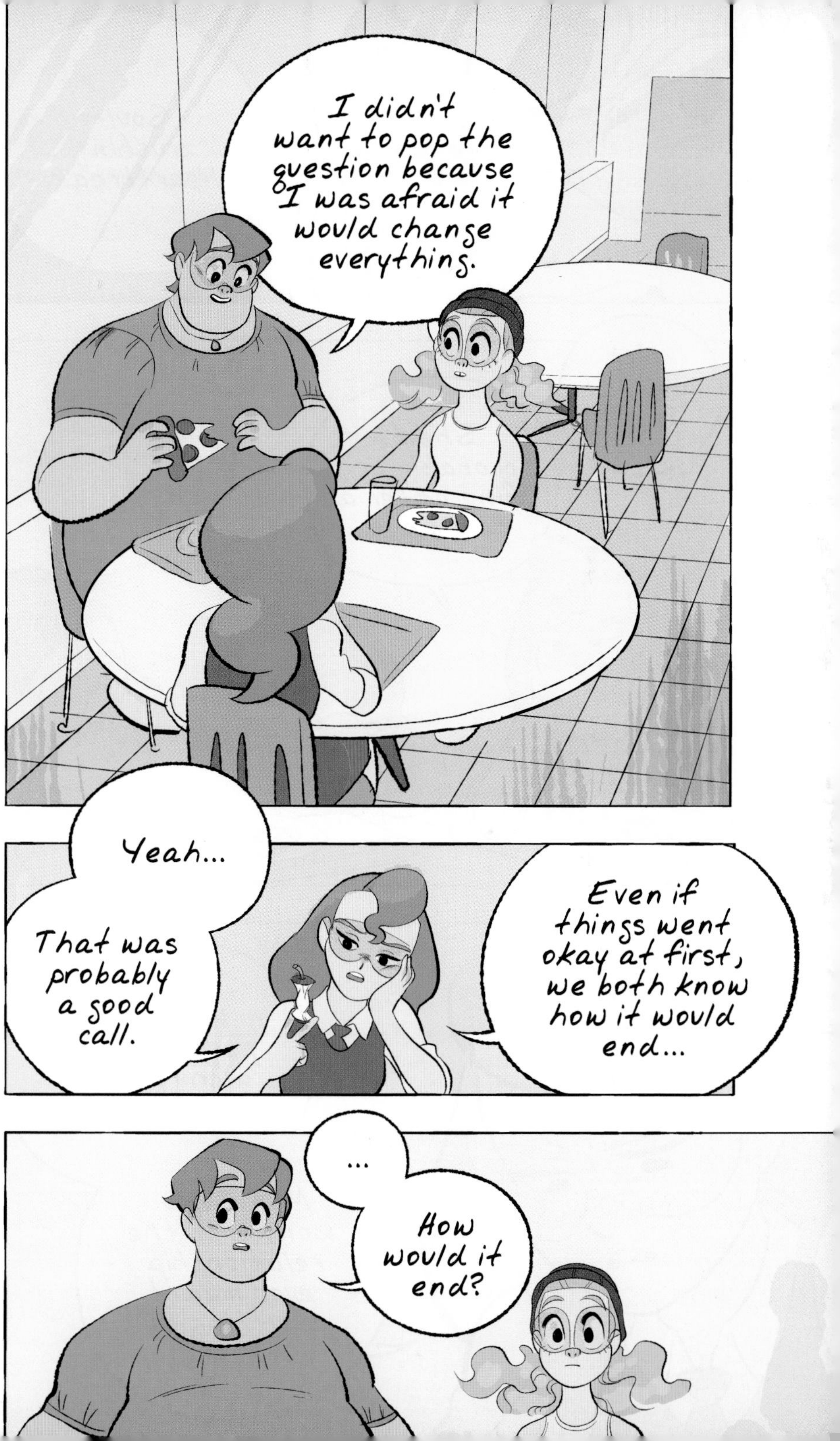
I didn't want to pop the question because I was afraid it would change everything.
Yeah...
That was probably a good call.
Even if things went okay at first, we both know how it would end...
...
How would it end?

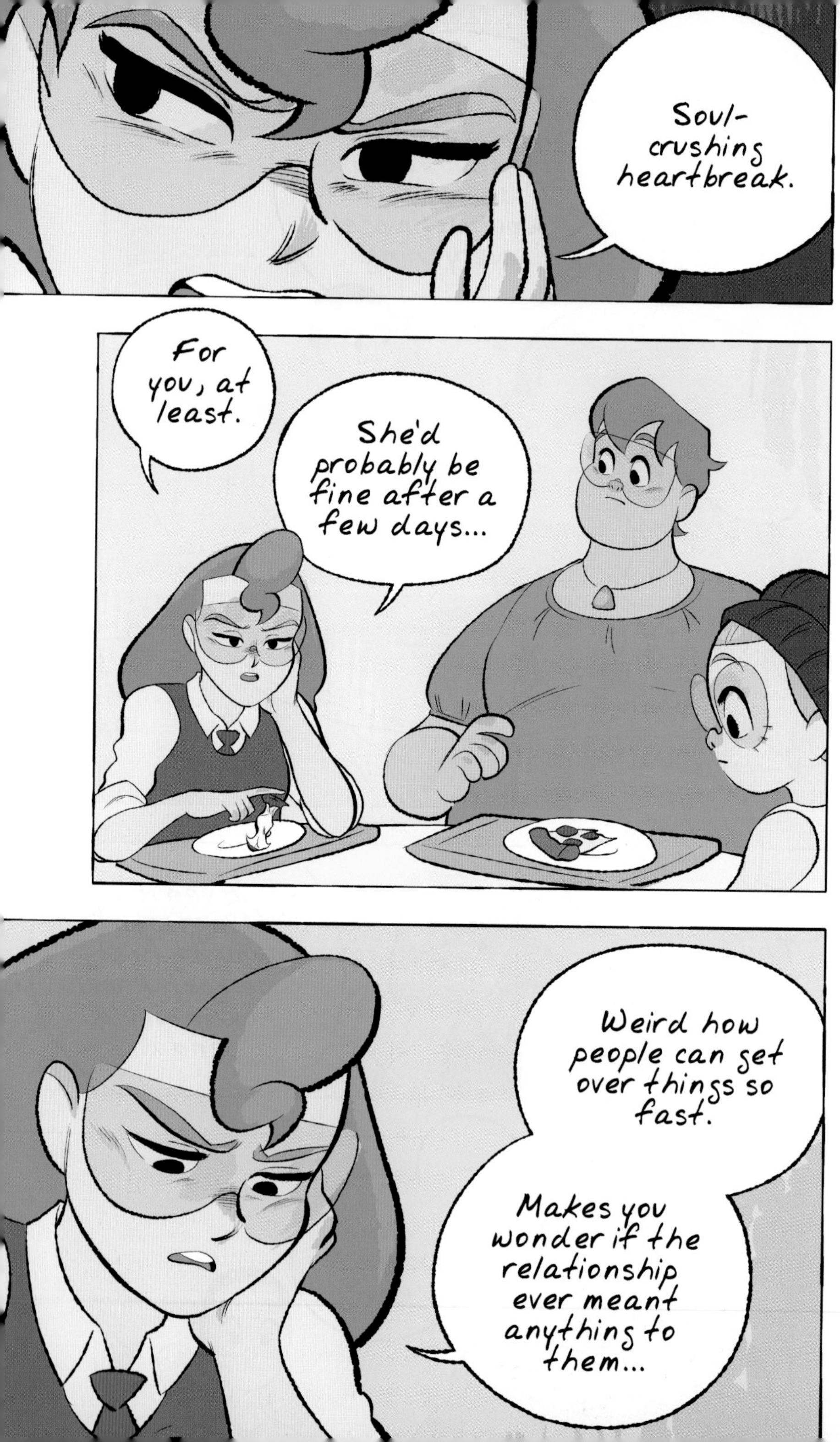
Soul-crushing heartbreak.
For you, at least.
She'd probably be fine after a few days...
Weird how people can get over things so fast.
Makes you wonder if the relationship ever meant anything to them...

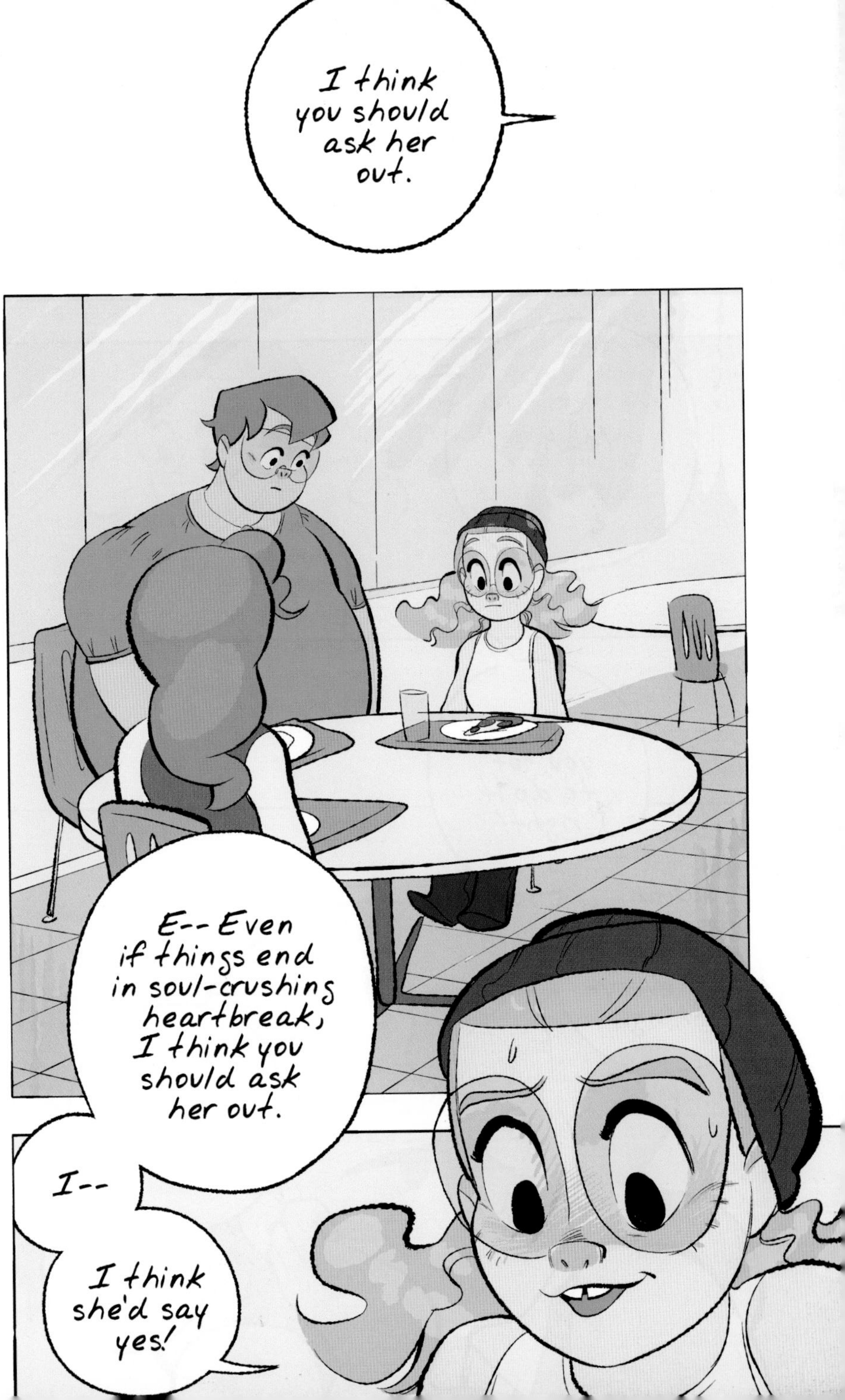
I think you should ask her out.
E--Even if things end in soul-crushing heartbreak, I think you should ask her out.
I--
I think she'd say yes!

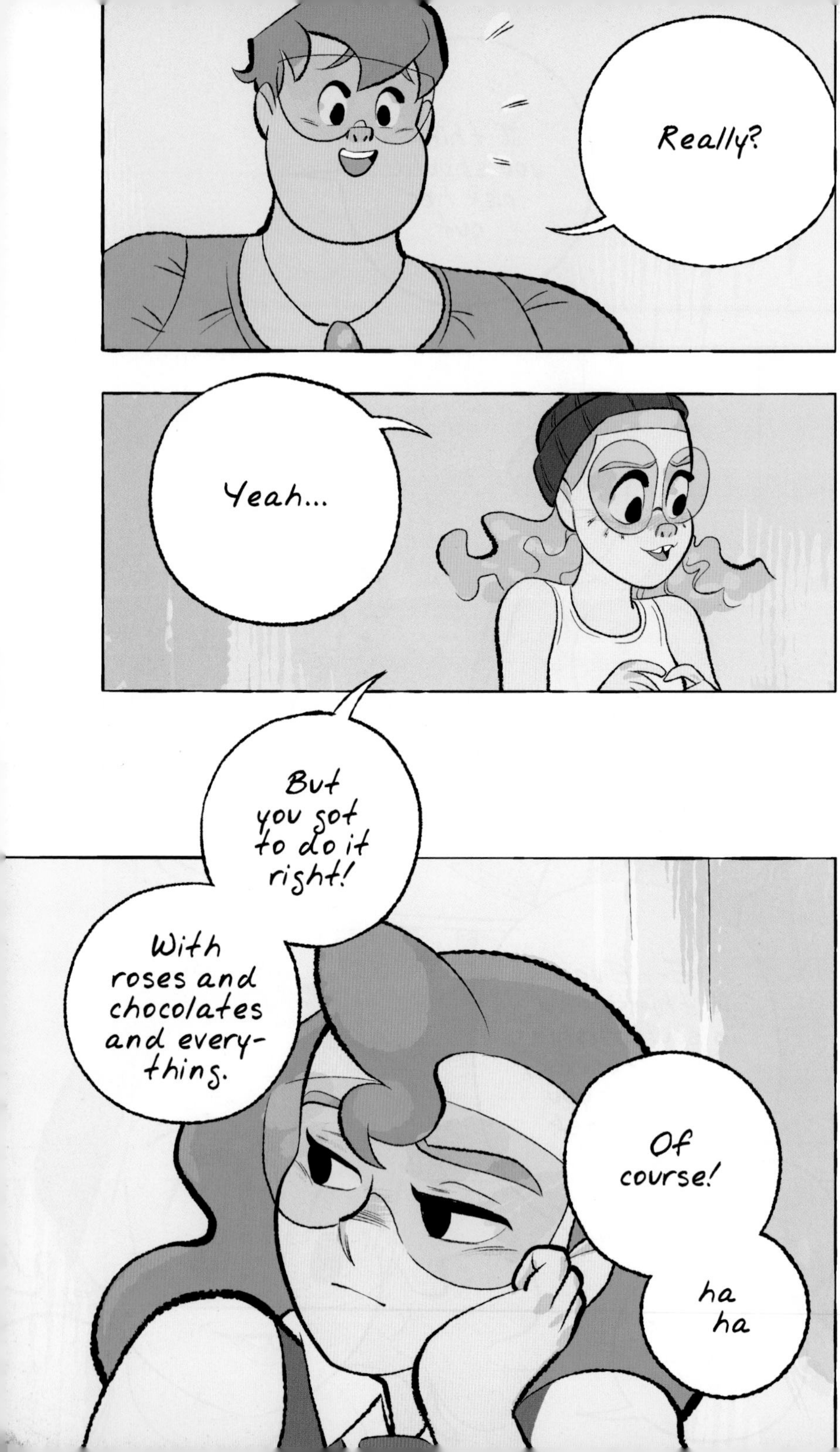
Really?
Yeah...
But you got to do it right!
With roses and chocolates and everything.
Of course!
ha ha

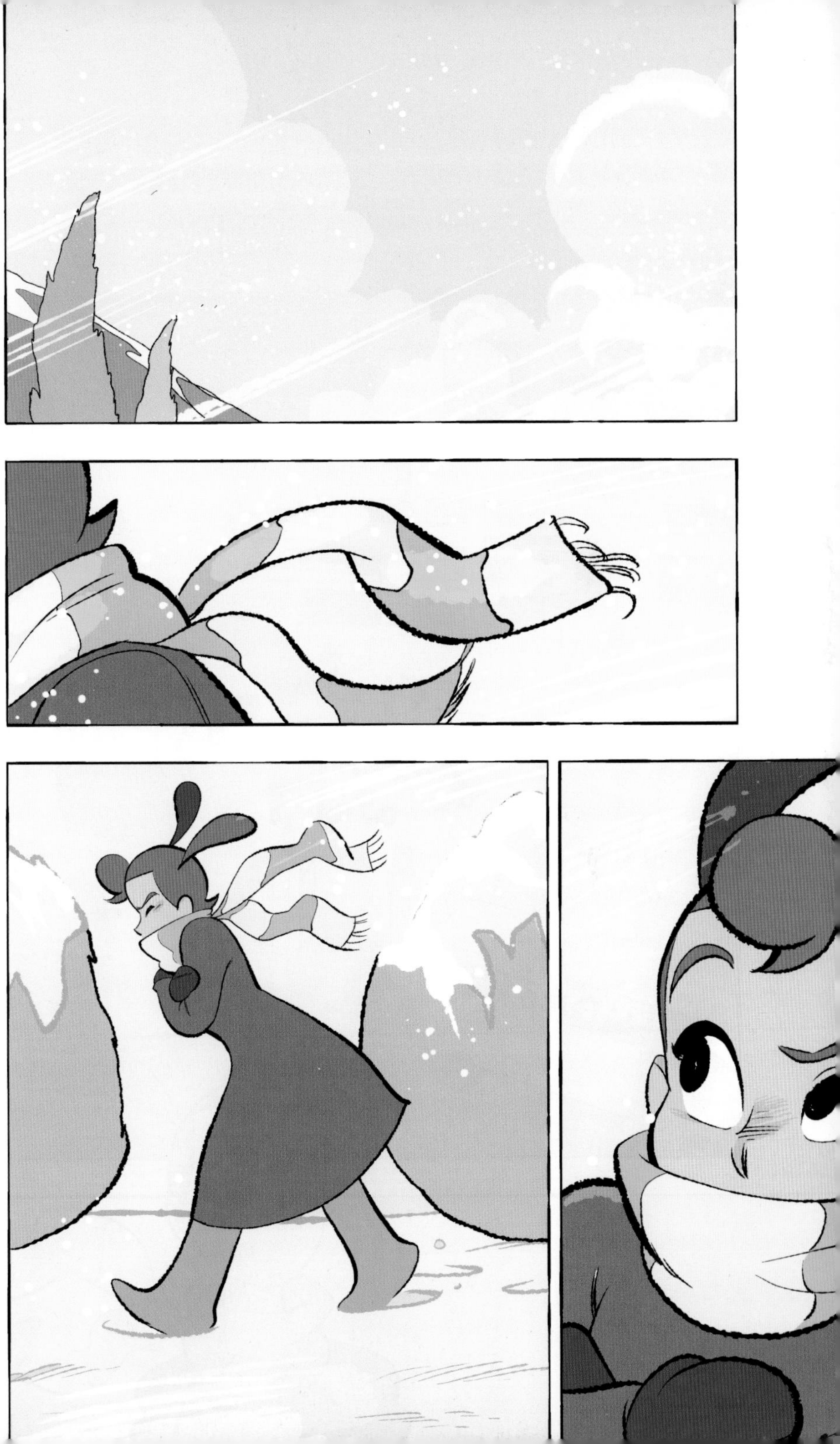

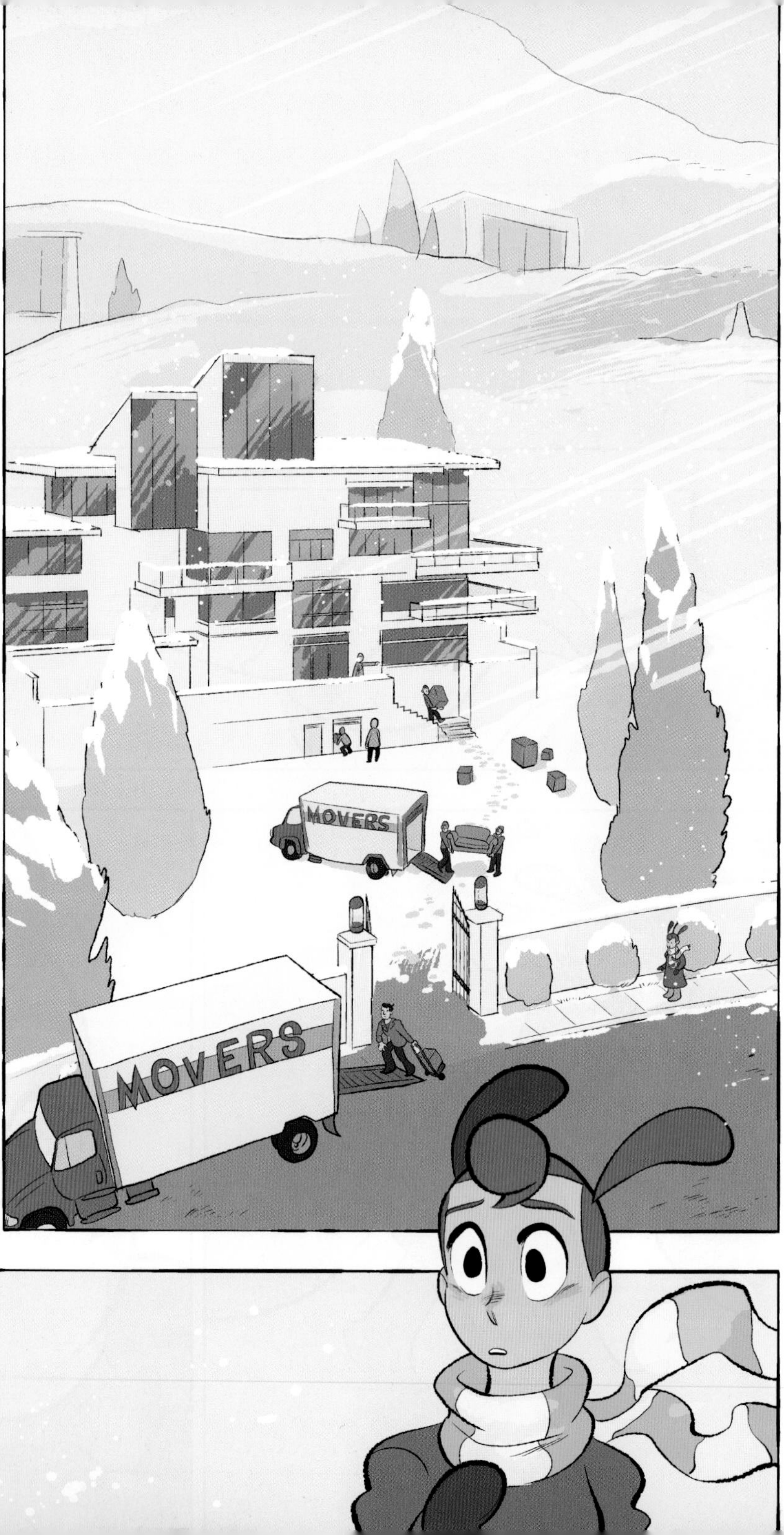
MOVERS
MOVERS

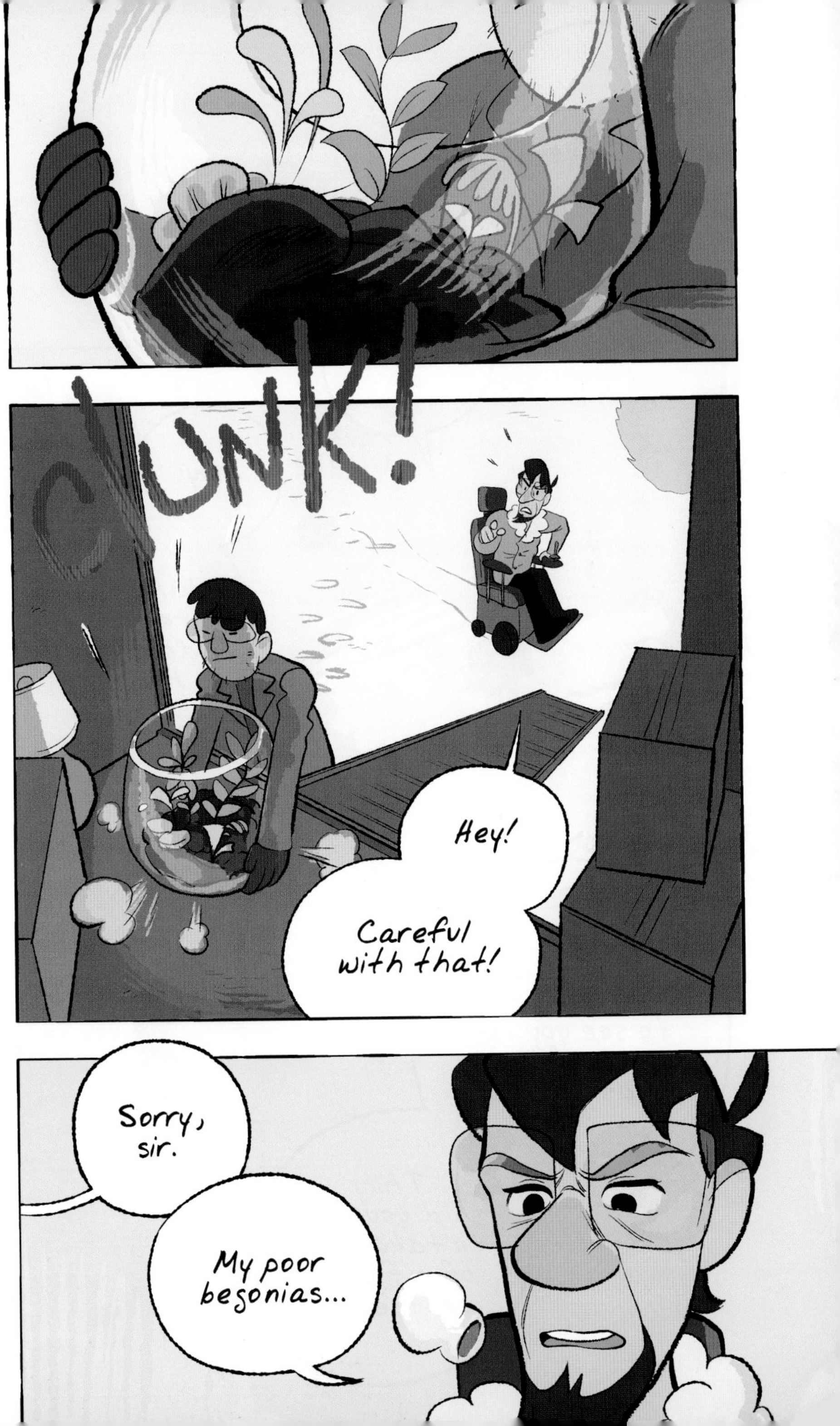
CHUNK!
Hey!
Careful with that!
Sorry, sir.
My poor begonias...

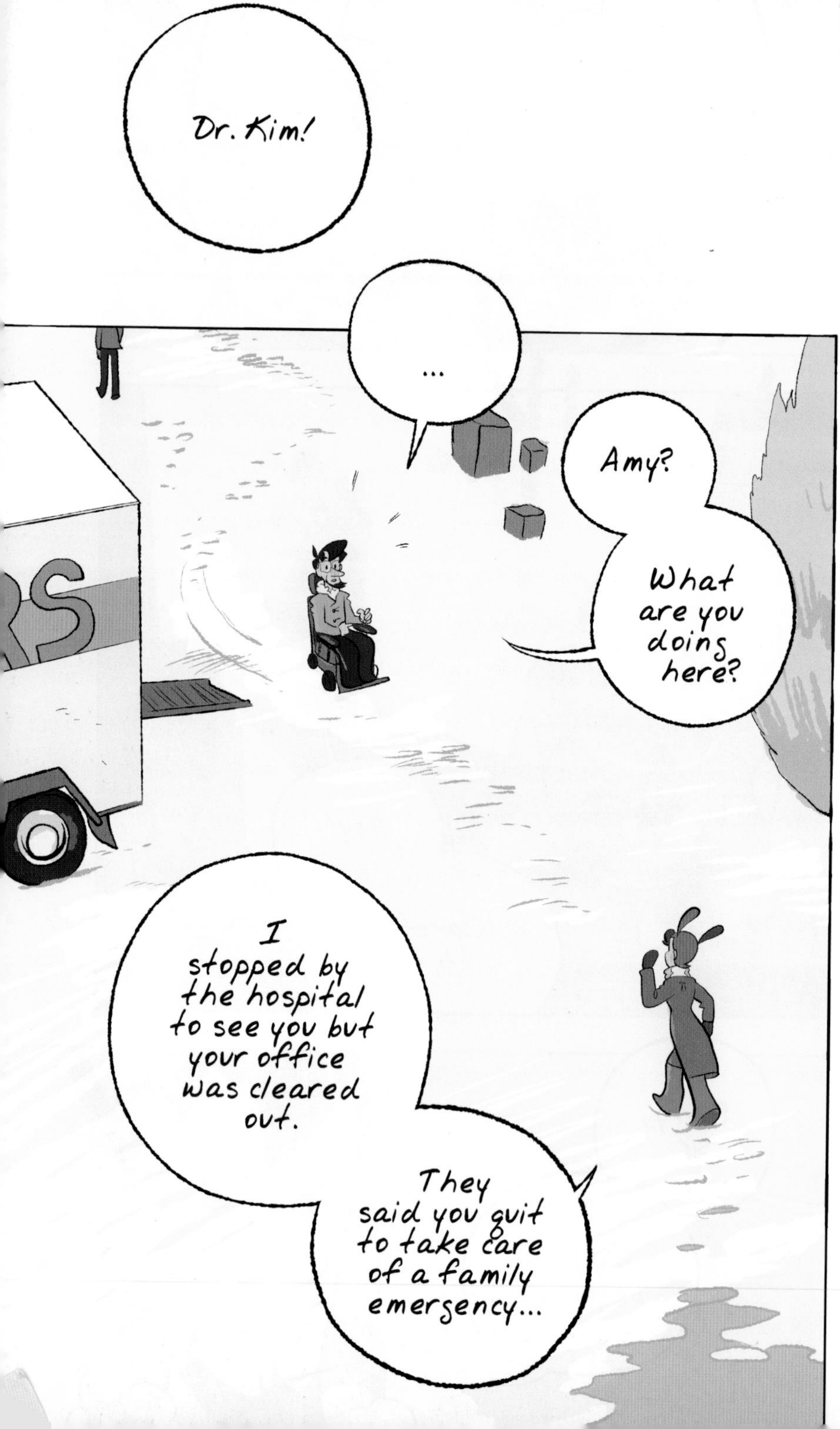
Dr. Kim!
...
Amy?
What are you doing here?
I stopped by the hospital to see you but your office was cleared out.
They said you quit to take care of a family emergency...

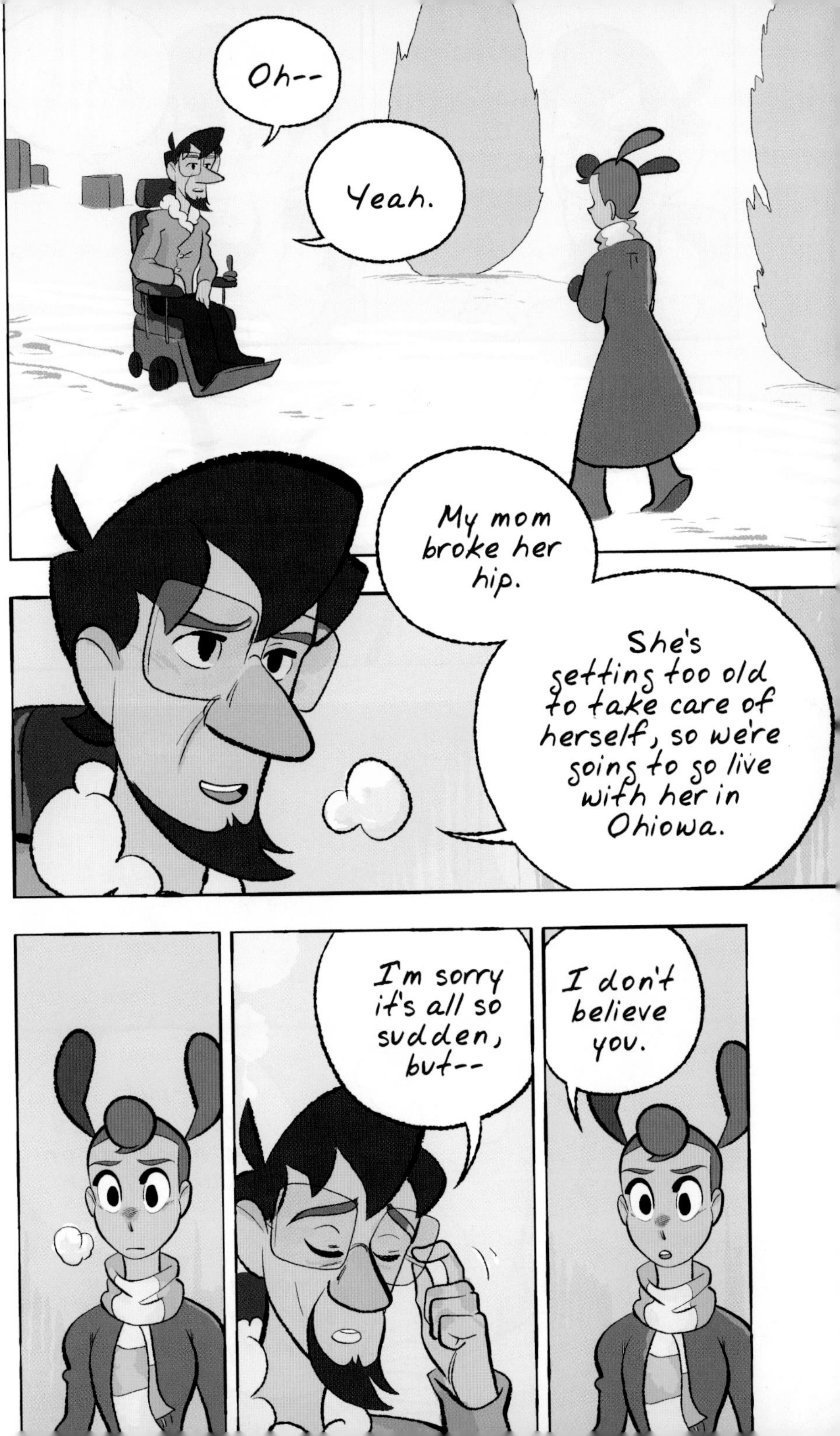

Oh--
Yeah.
My mom broke her hip.
She's getting too old to take care of herself, so we're going to go live with her in Ohiowa.
I'm sorry it's all so sudden, but--
I don't believe you.

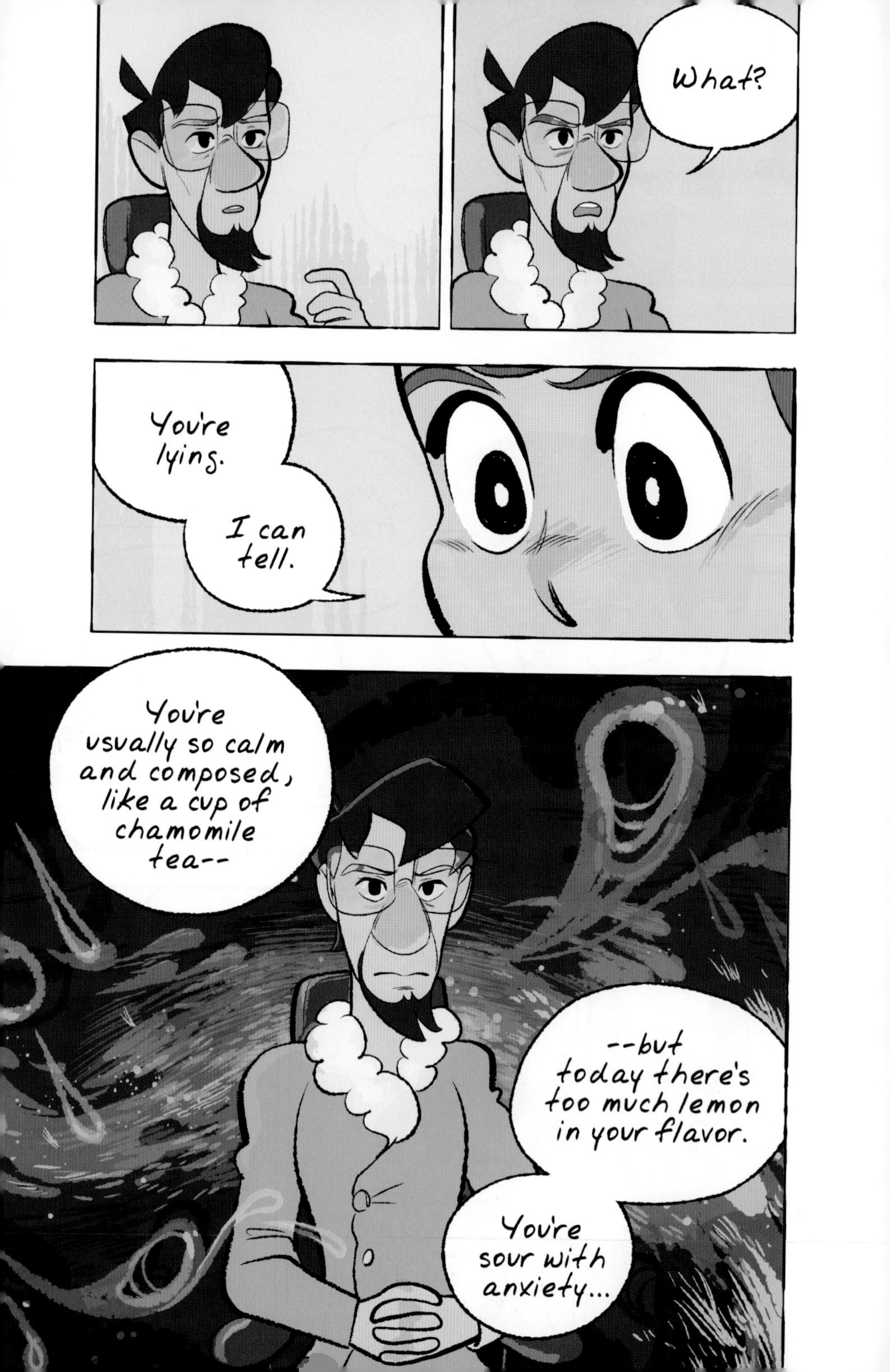
What?
You're lying.
I can tell.
You're usually so calm and composed, like a cup of chamomile tea--
--but today there's too much lemon in your flavor.
You're sour with anxiety...

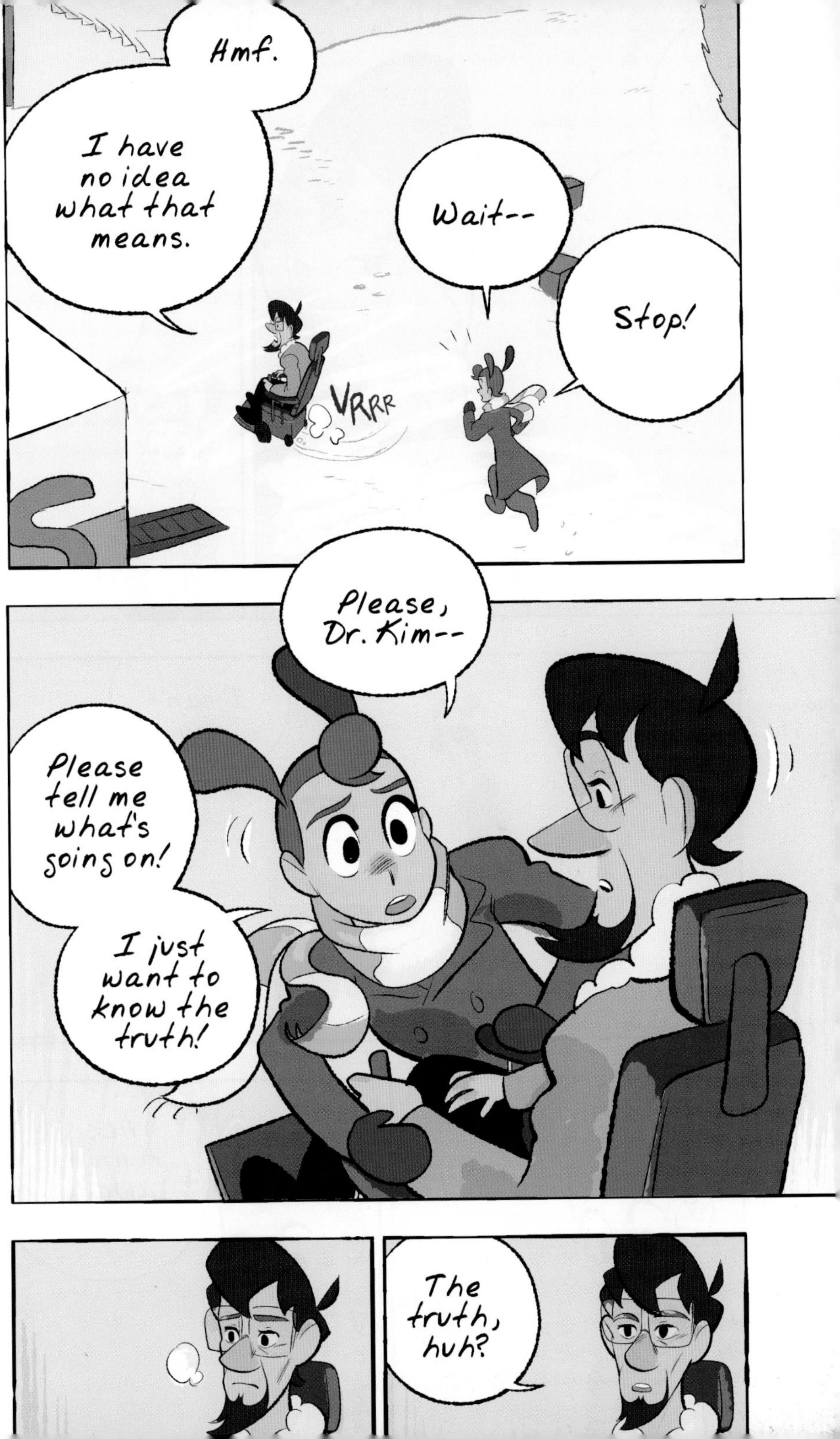
Hmf.
I have no idea what that means.
Wait--
Stop!
VRRR
Please, Dr. Kim--
Please tell me what's going on!
I just want to know the truth!
The truth, huh?

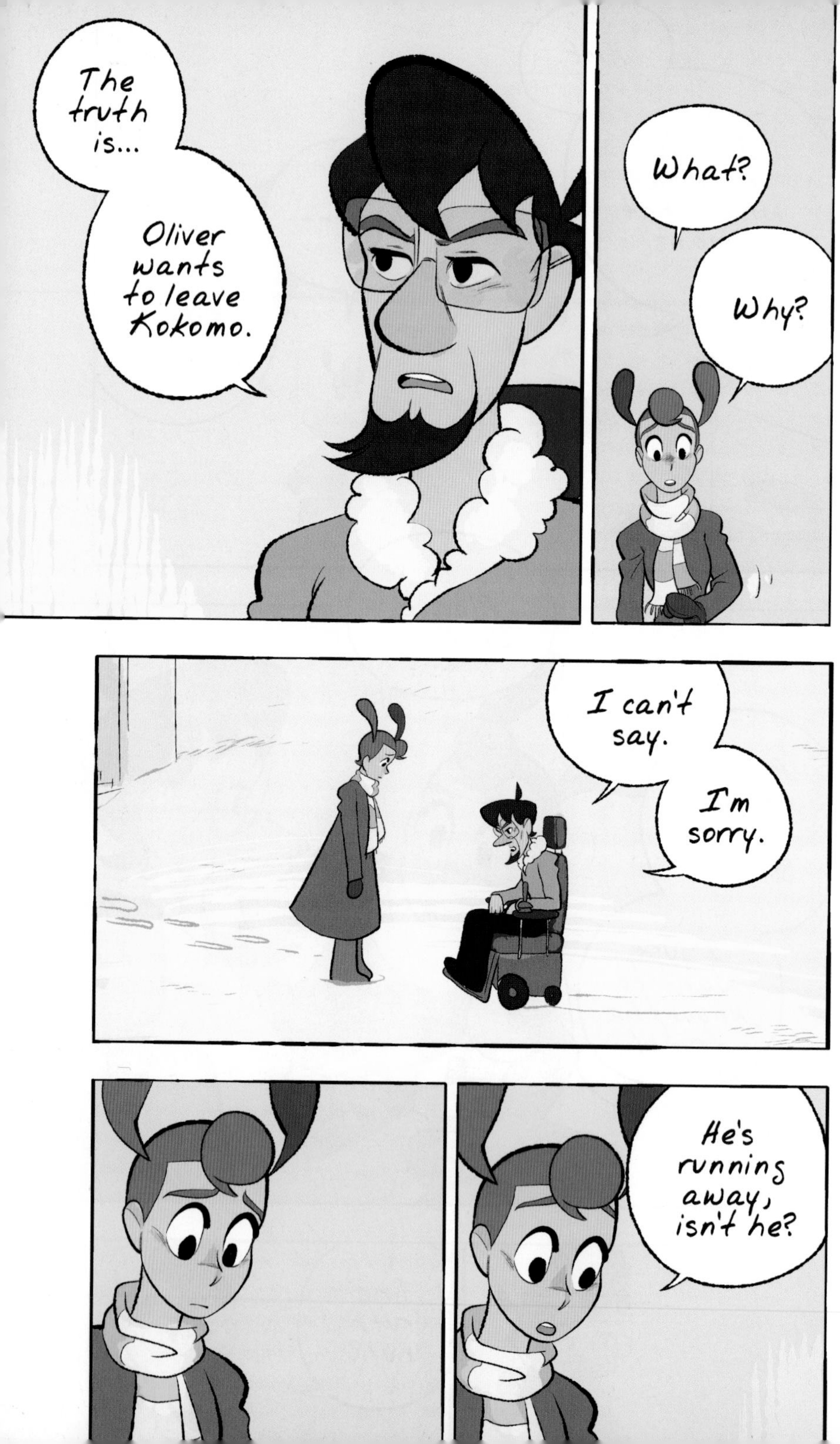
The truth is...
Oliver wants to leave Kokomo.
What?
Why?
I can't say.
I'm sorry.
He's running away, isn't he?

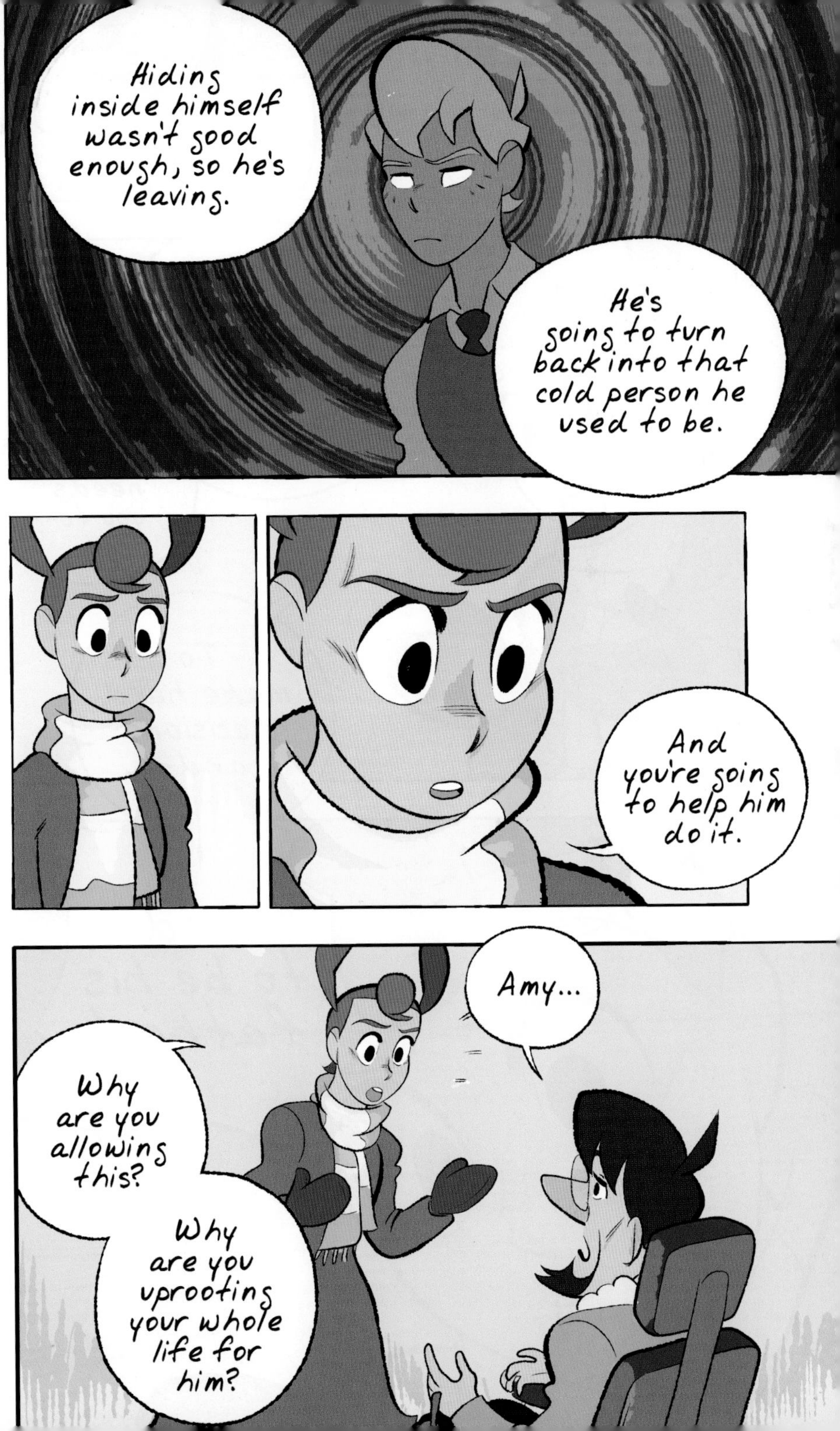
Hiding inside himself wasn't good enough, so he's leaving.
He's going to turn back into that cold person he used to be.
And you're going to help him do it.
Amy...
Why are you allowing this?
Why are you uprooting your whole life for him?

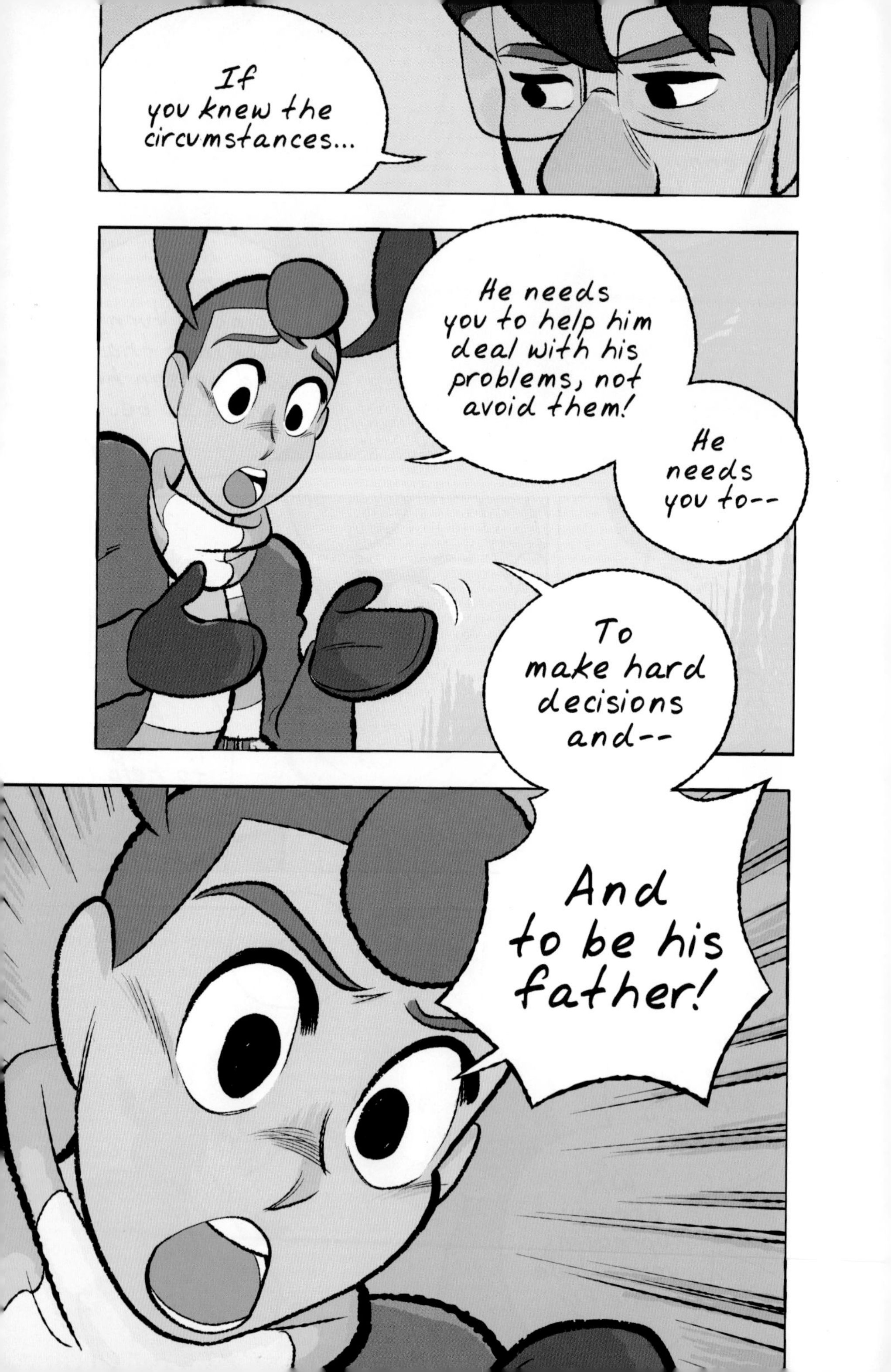
If you knew the circumstances...
He needs you to help him deal with his problems, not avoid them!
He needs you to--
To make hard decisions and--
And to be his father!

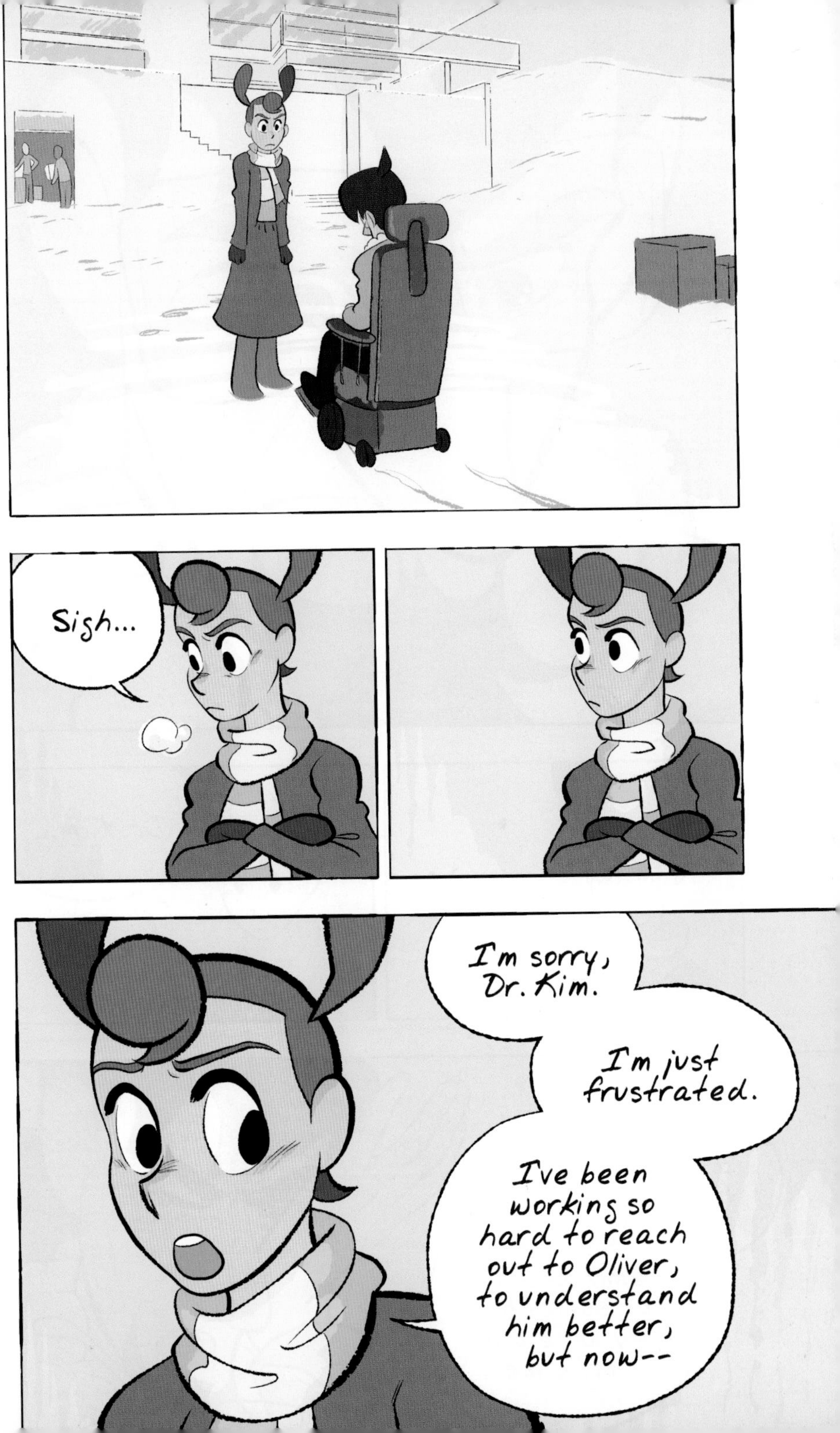
Sigh...
I'm sorry, Dr. Kim.
I'm just frustrated.
I've been working so hard to reach out to Oliver, to understand him better, but now--

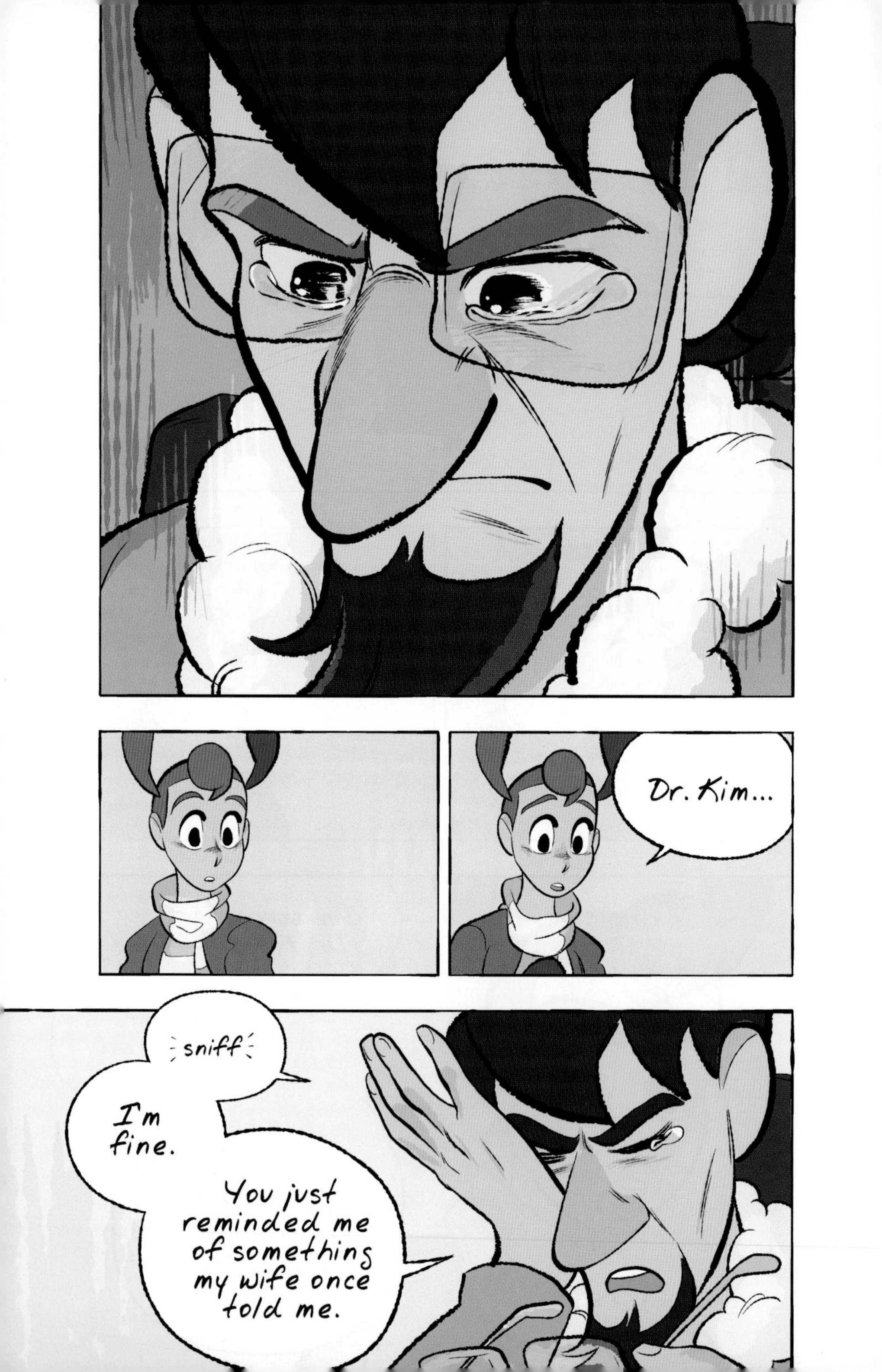
Dr. Kim...
sniff
I'm fine.
You just reminded me of somethins my wife once told me.

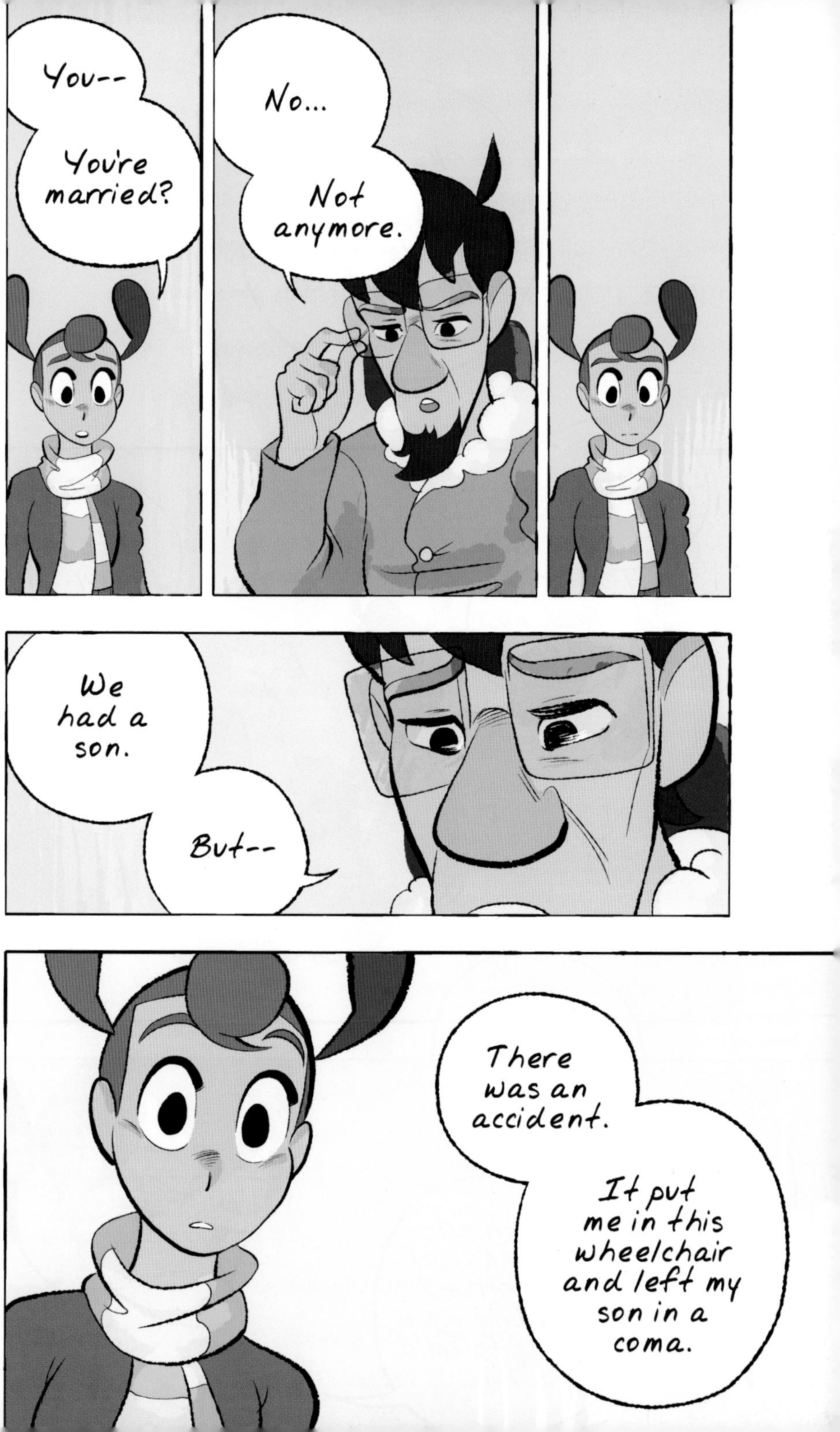
You--
You're married?
No...
Not anymore.
We had a son.
But--
There was an accident.
It put me in this wheelchair and left my son in a coma.

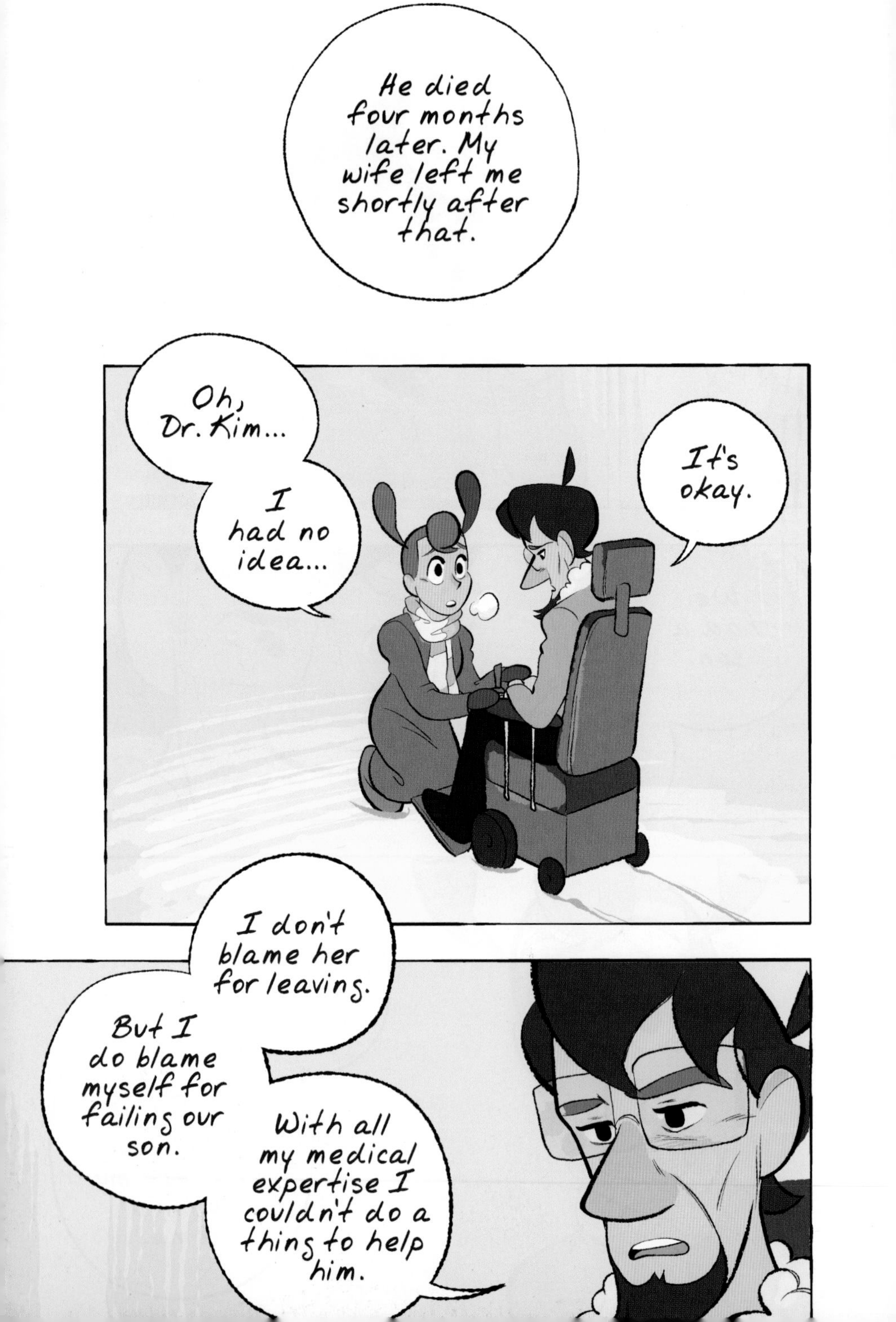
He died four months later. My wife left me shortly after that.
Oh, Dr. Kim...
I had no idea...
It's okay.
I don't blame her for leaving.
But I do blame myself for failing our son.
With all my medical expertise I couldn't do a thing to help him.

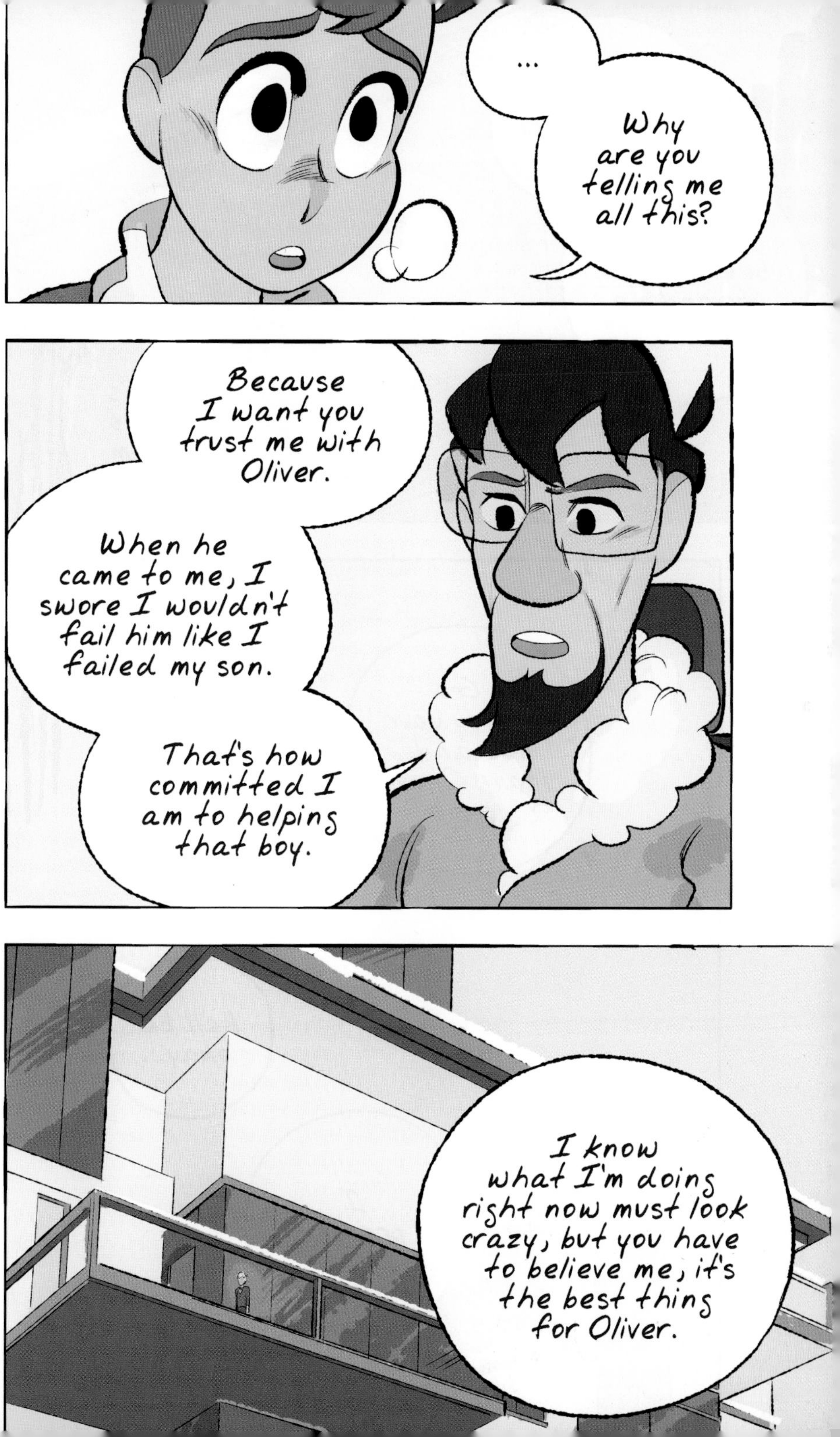
...
Why are you telling me all this?
Because I want you trust me with Oliver.
When he came to me, I swore I wouldn't fail him like I failed my son.
That's how committed I am to helping that boy.
I know what I'm doing right now must look crazy, but you have to believe me, it's the best thing for Oliver.

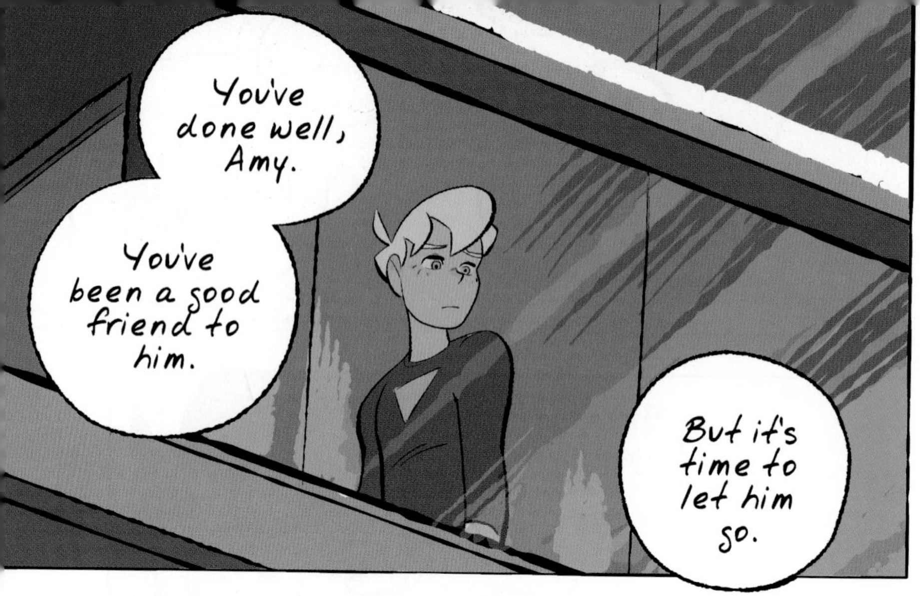
You've done well, Amy.
You've been a good friend to him.
But it's time to let him go.
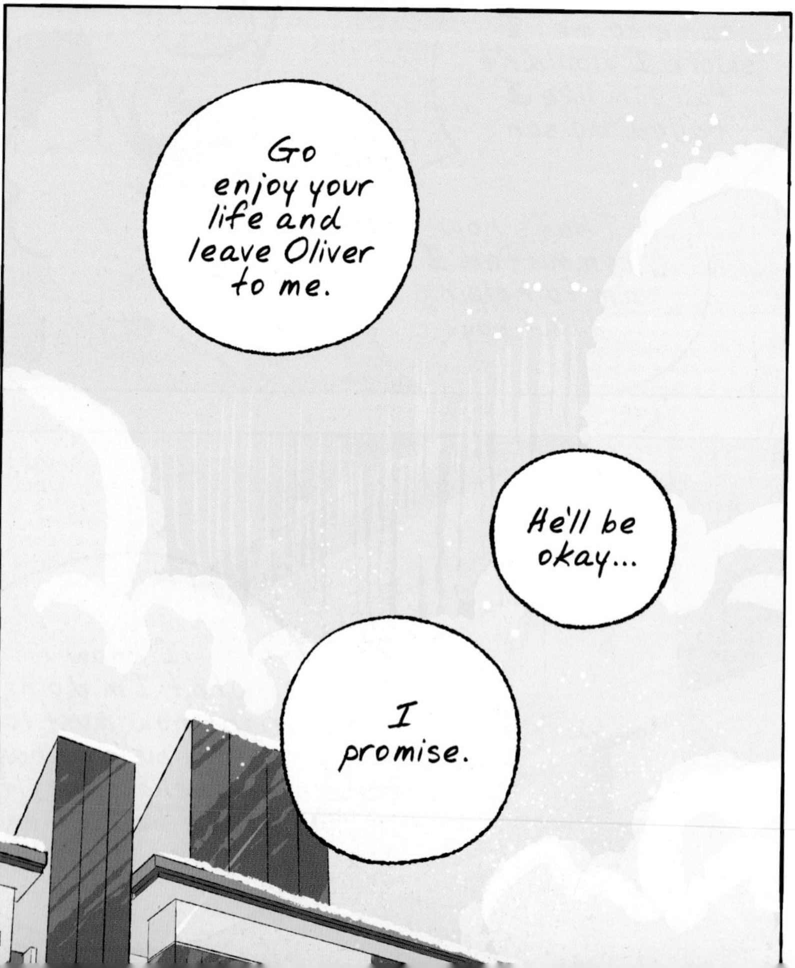
Go enjoy your life and leave Oliver to me.
He'll be okay...
I promise.

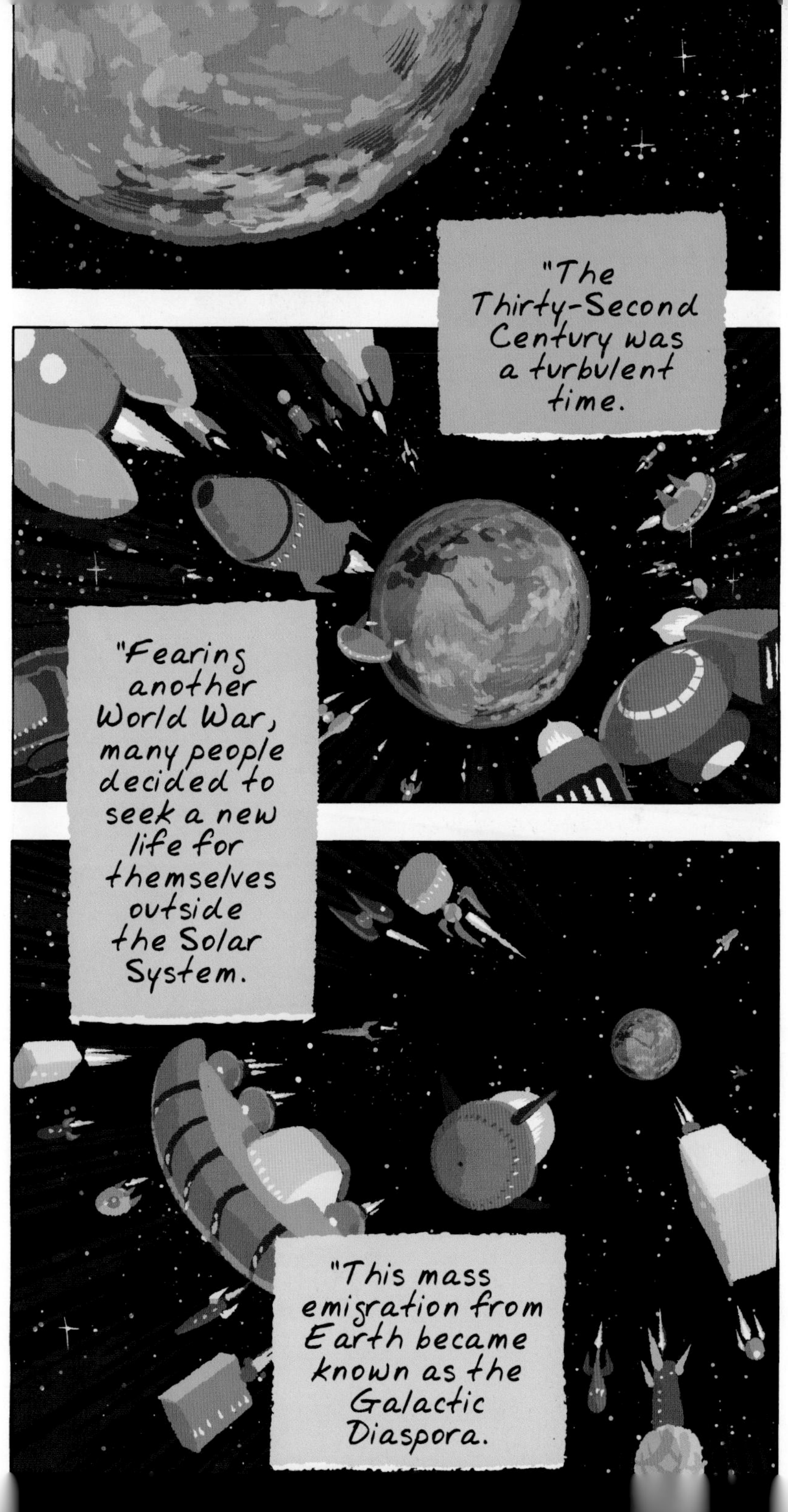
"The Thirty-Second Century was a turbulent time.
"Fearing another World War, many people decided to seek a new life for themselves outside the Solar System.
"This mass emigration from Earth became known as the Galactic Diaspora.

"Three technologies made the Diaspora possible.

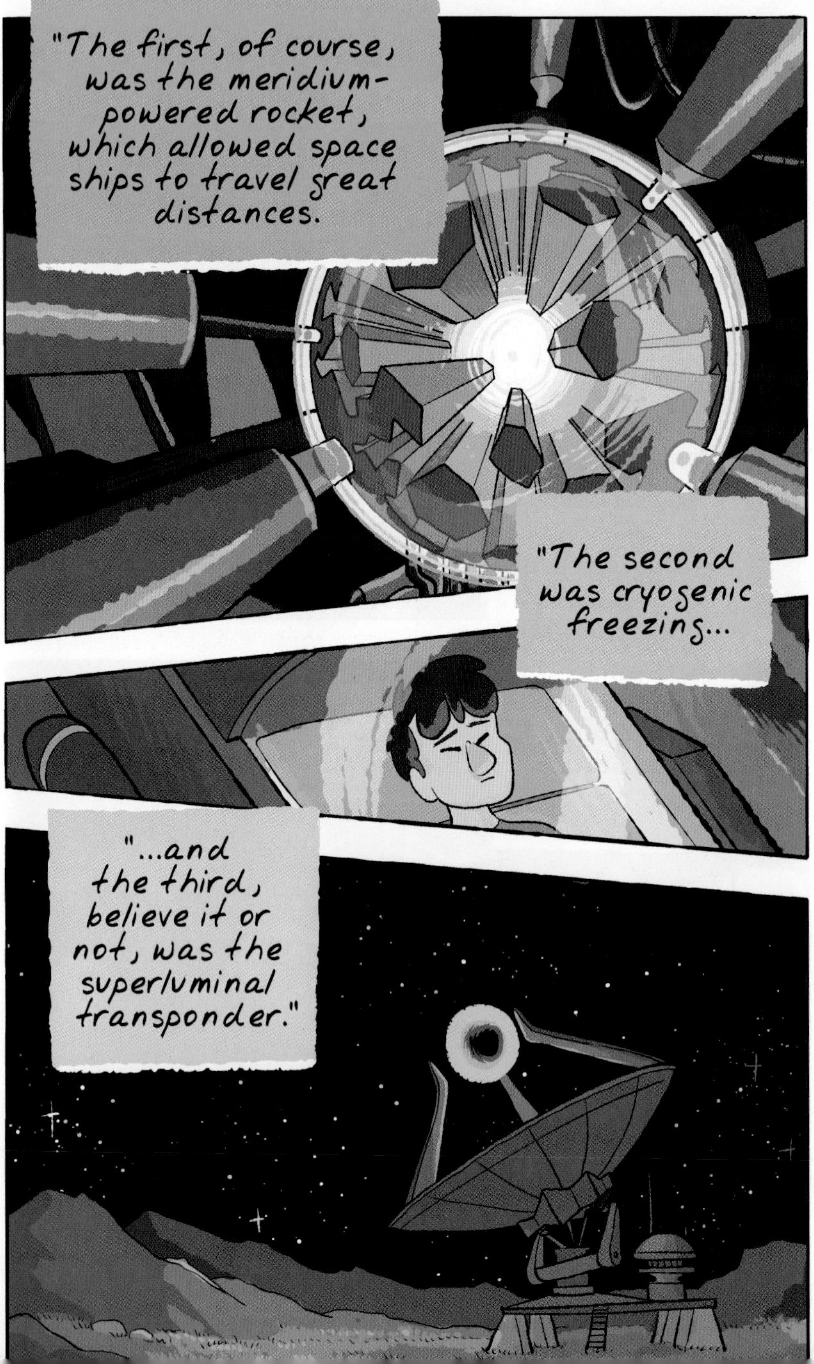
"The first, of course, was the meridium-powered rocket, which allowed space ships to travel great distances.
"The second was cryogenic freezing...
"...and the third, believe it or not, was the superluminal transponder."

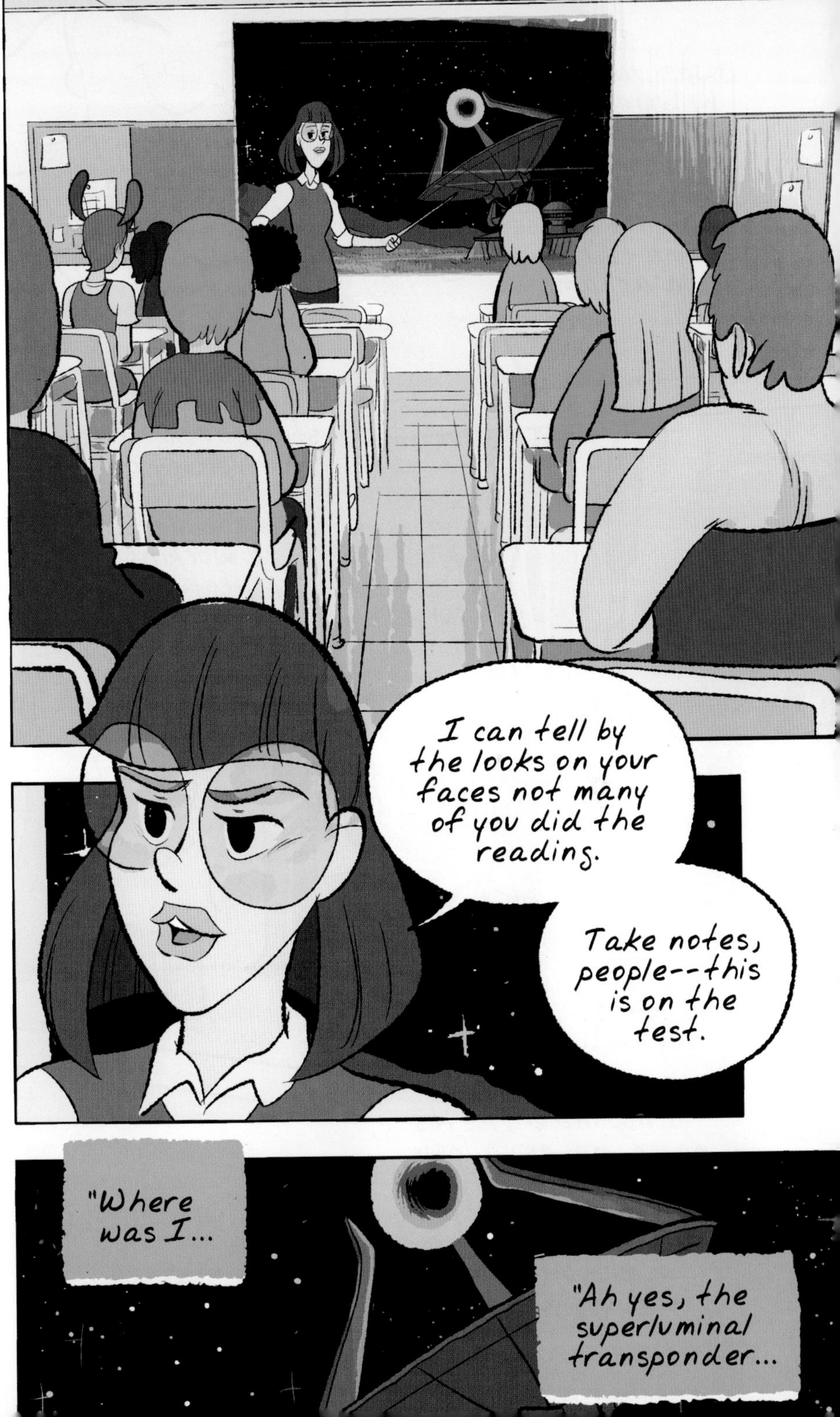
I can tell by the looks on your faces not many of you did the reading.
Take notes, people--this is on the test.
"Where was I...
"Ah yes, the superluminal transponder...

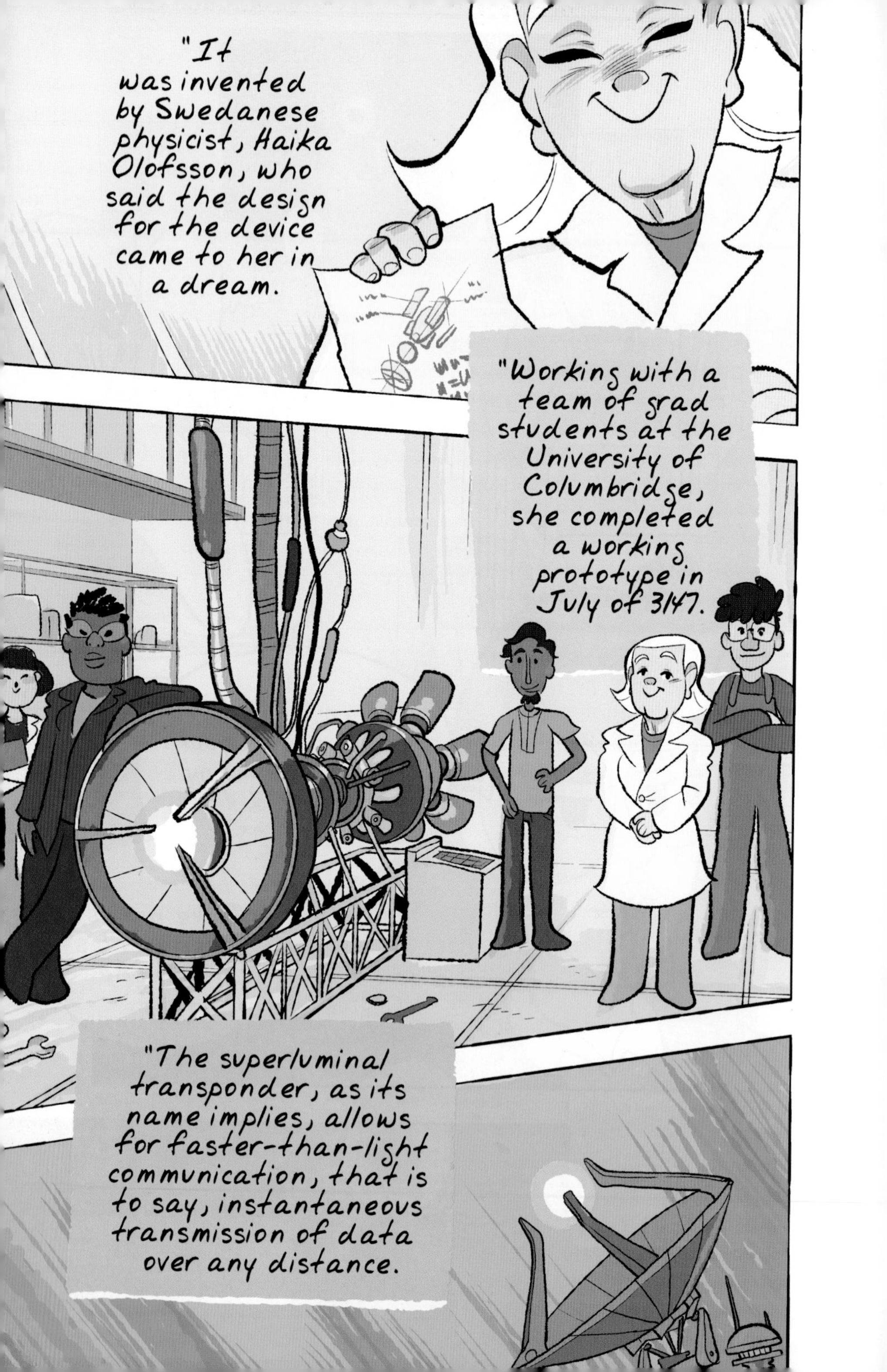
"It was invented by Swedanese physicist, Haika Olofsson, who said the design for the device came to her in a dream.
"Working with a team of grad students at the University of Columbridge, she completed a working prototype in July of 3147.
"The superluminal transponder, as its name implies, allows for faster-than-light communication, that is to say, instantaneous transmission of data over any distance.

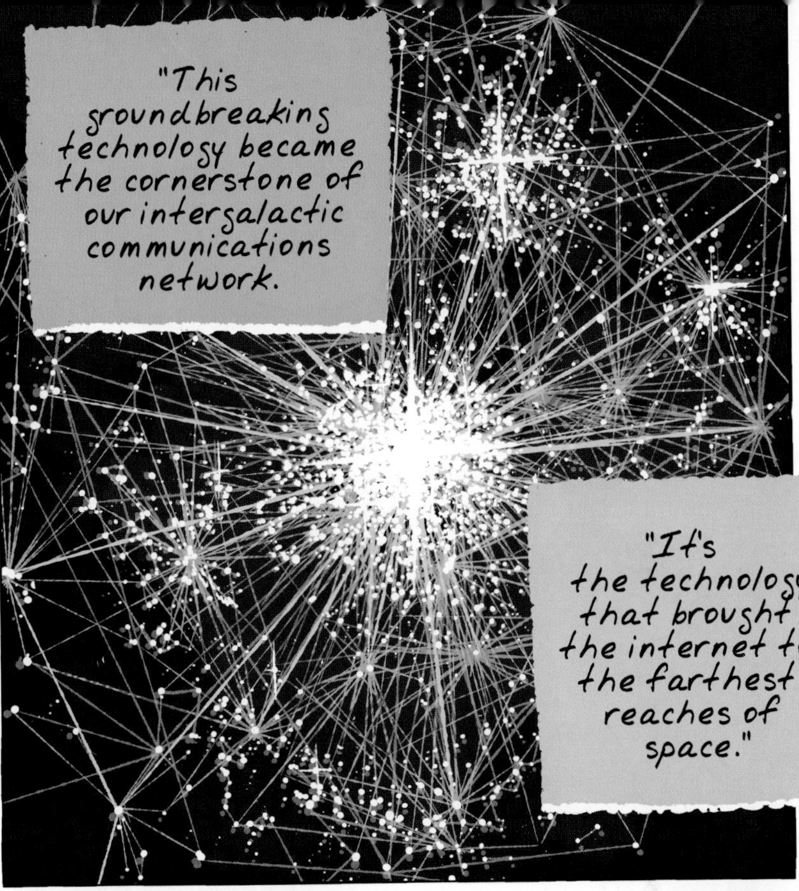
"This groundbreaking technology became the cornerstone of our intergalactic communications network.
"It's the technology that brought the internet to the farthest reaches of space."

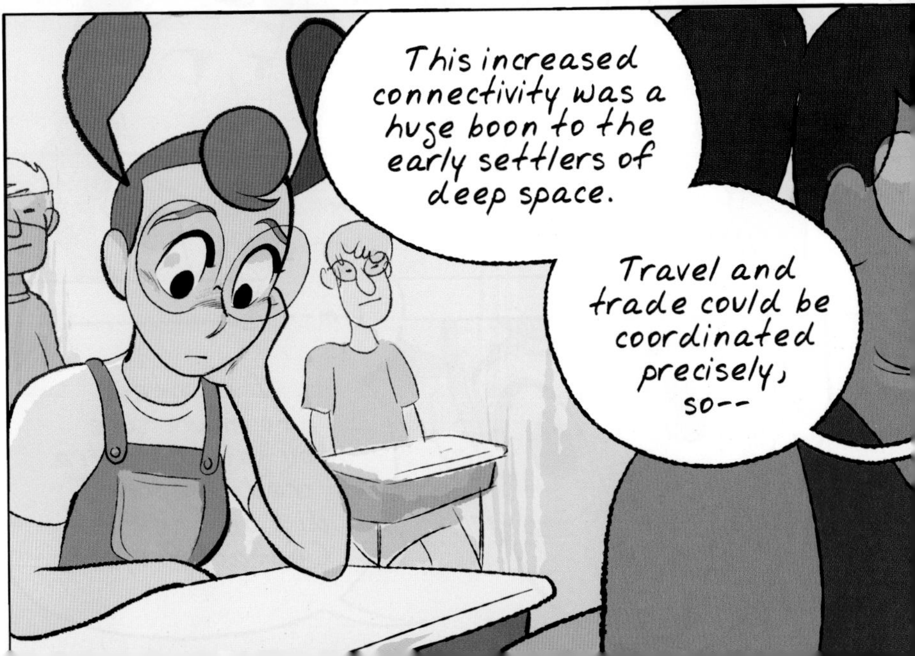
This increased connectivity was a huge boon to the early settlers of deep space.
Travel and trade could be coordinated precisely, so--

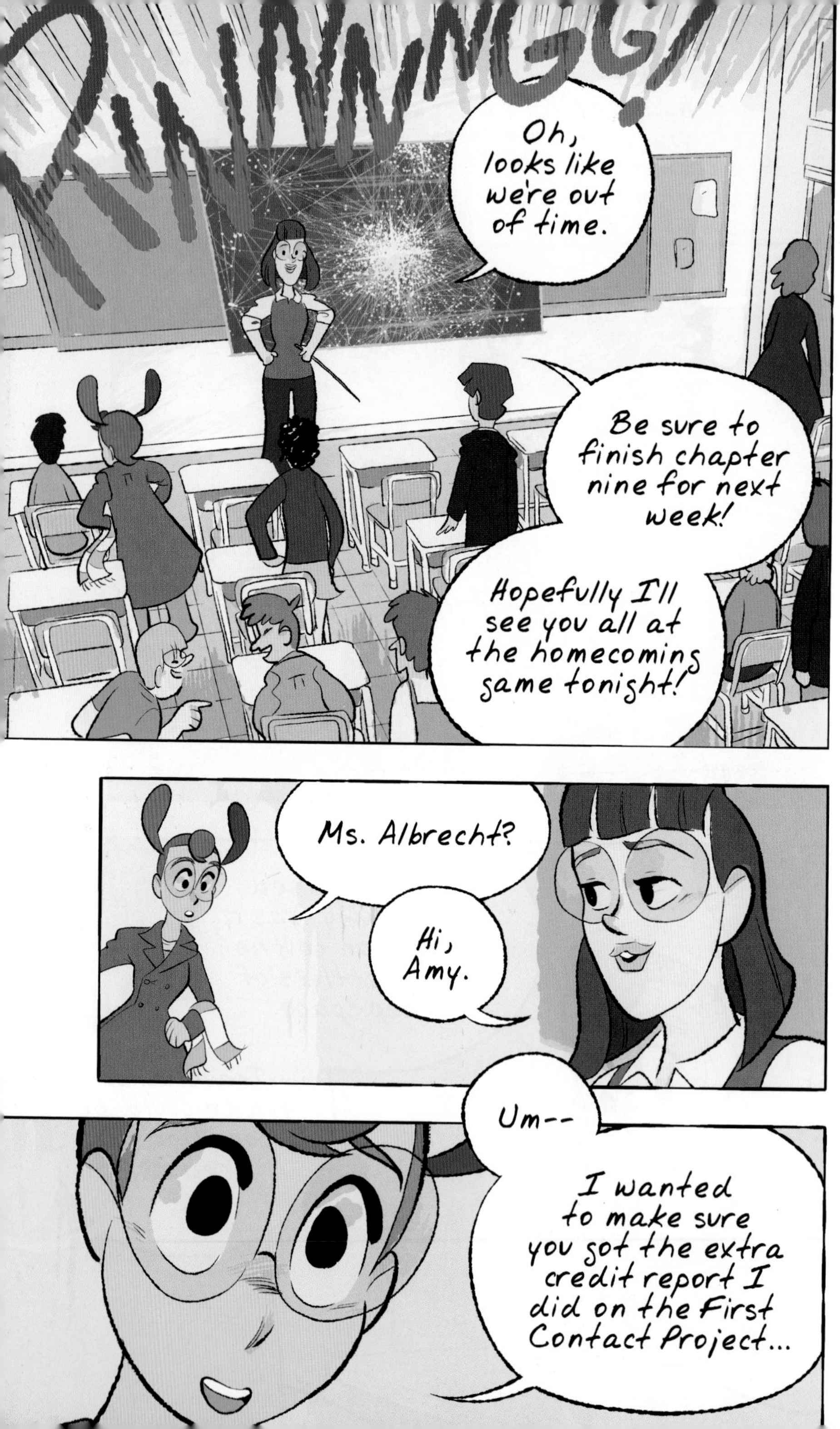

RIIINNNGG!
Oh, looks like we're out of time.
Be sure to finish chapter nine for next week!
Hopefully I'll see you all at the homecoming game tonight!
Ms. Albrecht?
Hi, Amy.
Um--
I wanted to make sure you got the extra credit report I did on the First Contact Project...

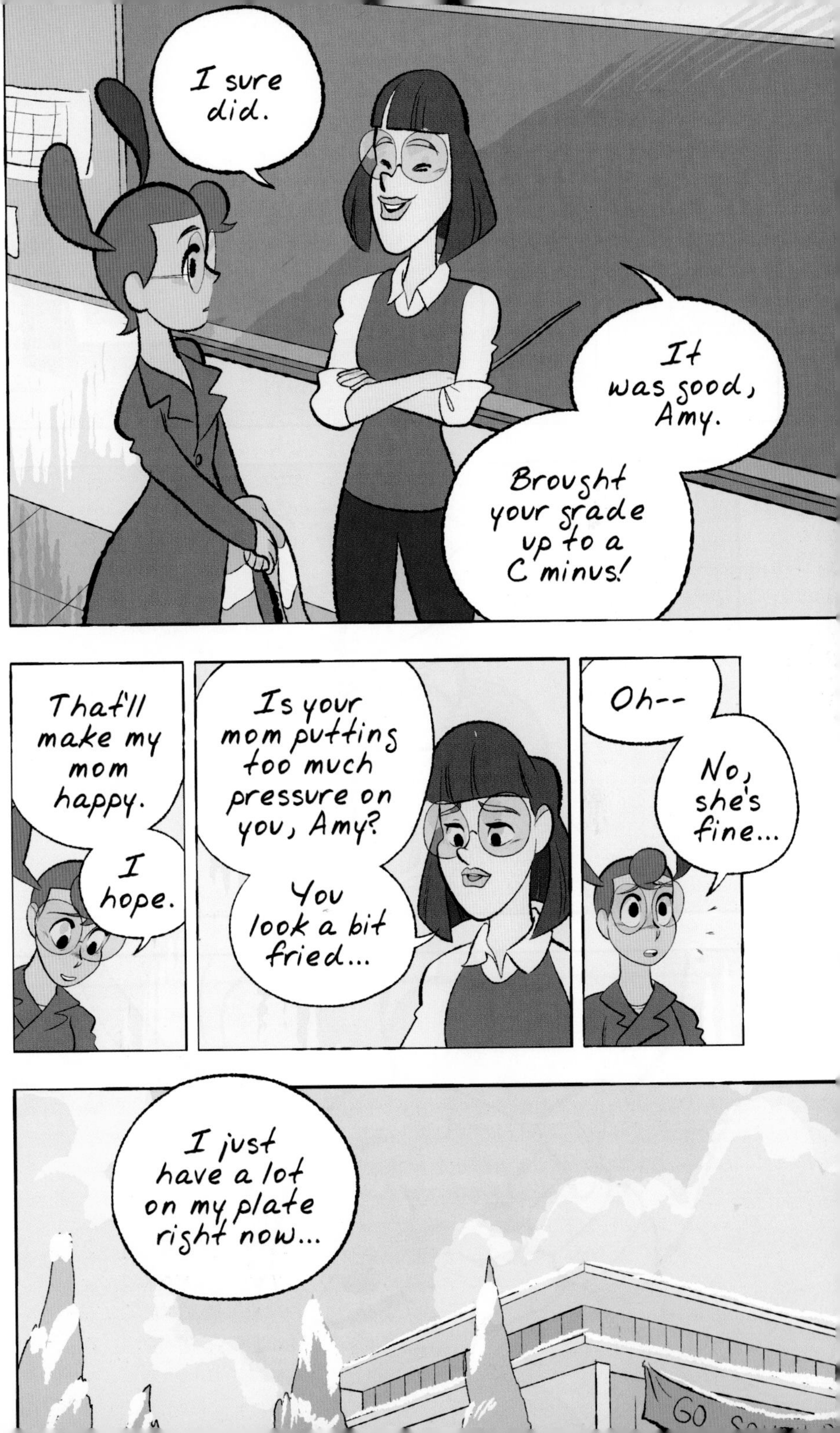
I sure did.
It was good, Amy.
Brought your grade up to a C minus!
That'll make my mom happy.
I hope.
Is your mom putting too much pressure on you, Amy?
You look a bit fried...
Oh--
No, she's fine...
I just have a lot on my plate right now...
GO

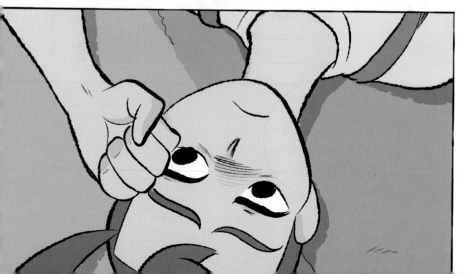

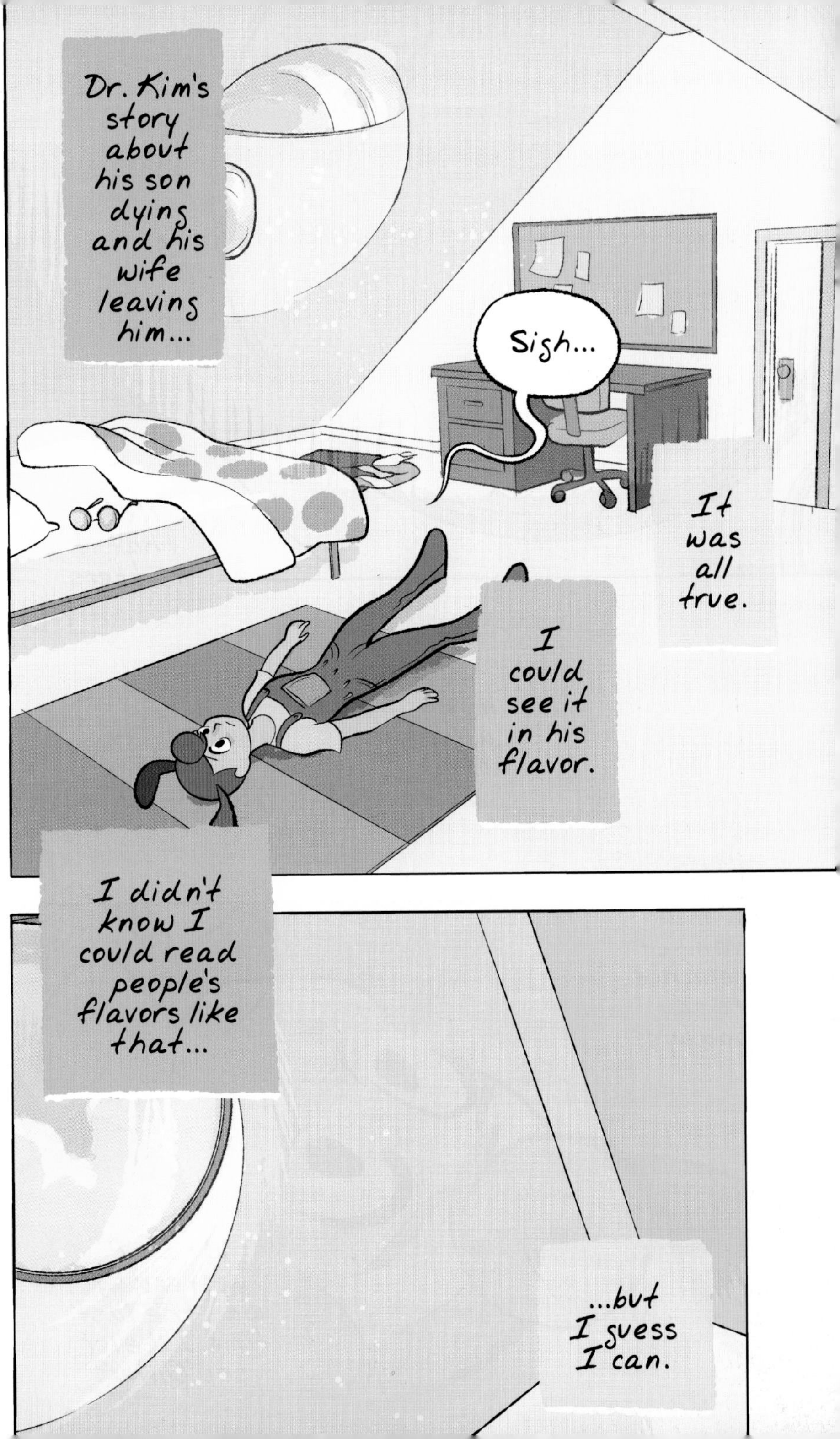
Dr. Kim's story about his son dying and his wife leaving him...
Sigh...
It was all true.
I could see it in his flavor.
I didn't know I could read people's flavors like that...
...but I guess I can.

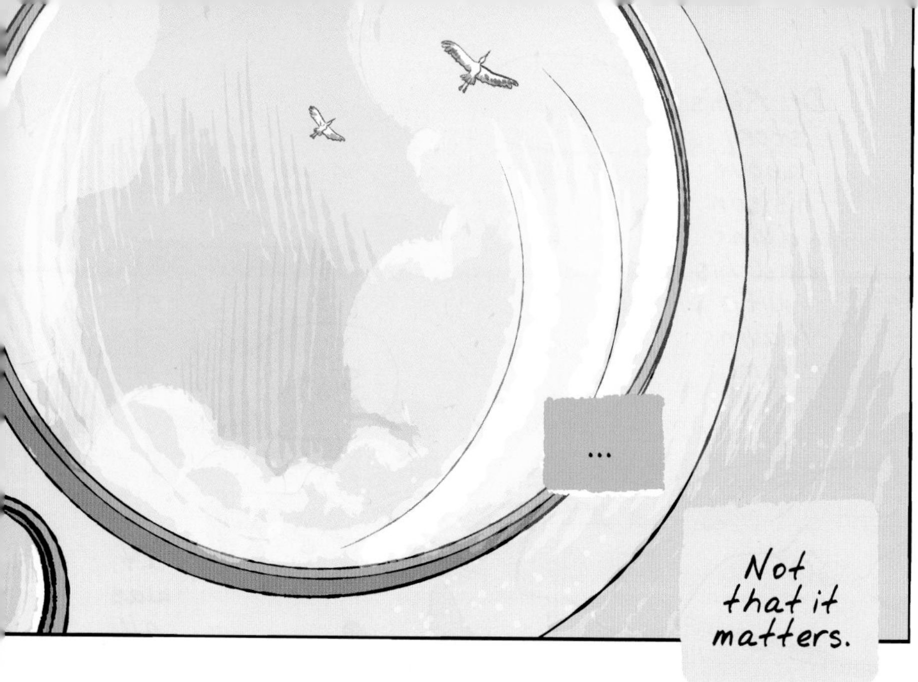
...
Not that it matters.

Oliver's moving away and there's nothing I can do to stop it.

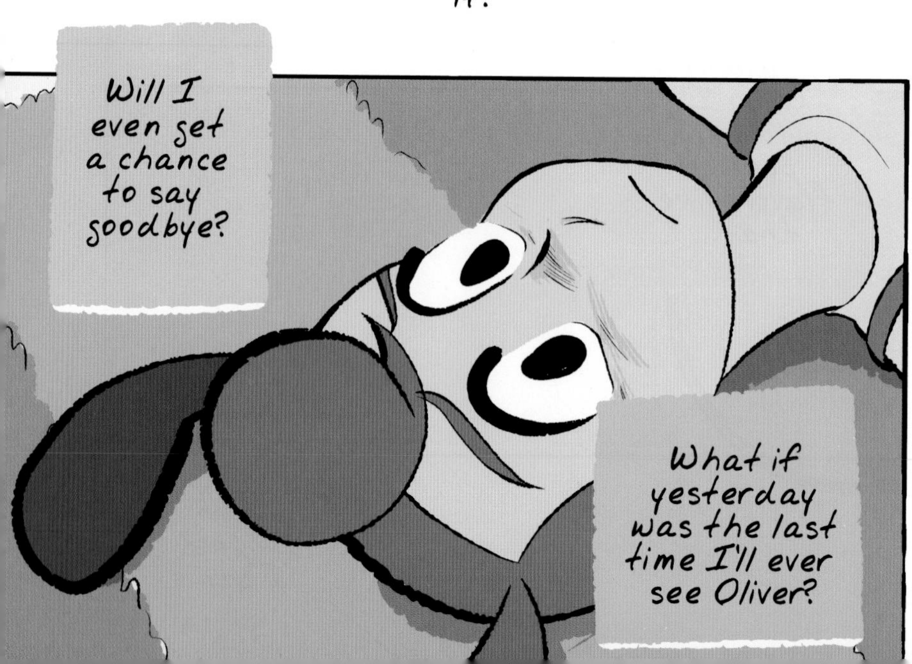
Will I even get a chance to say goodbye?
What if yesterday was the last time I'll ever see Oliver?

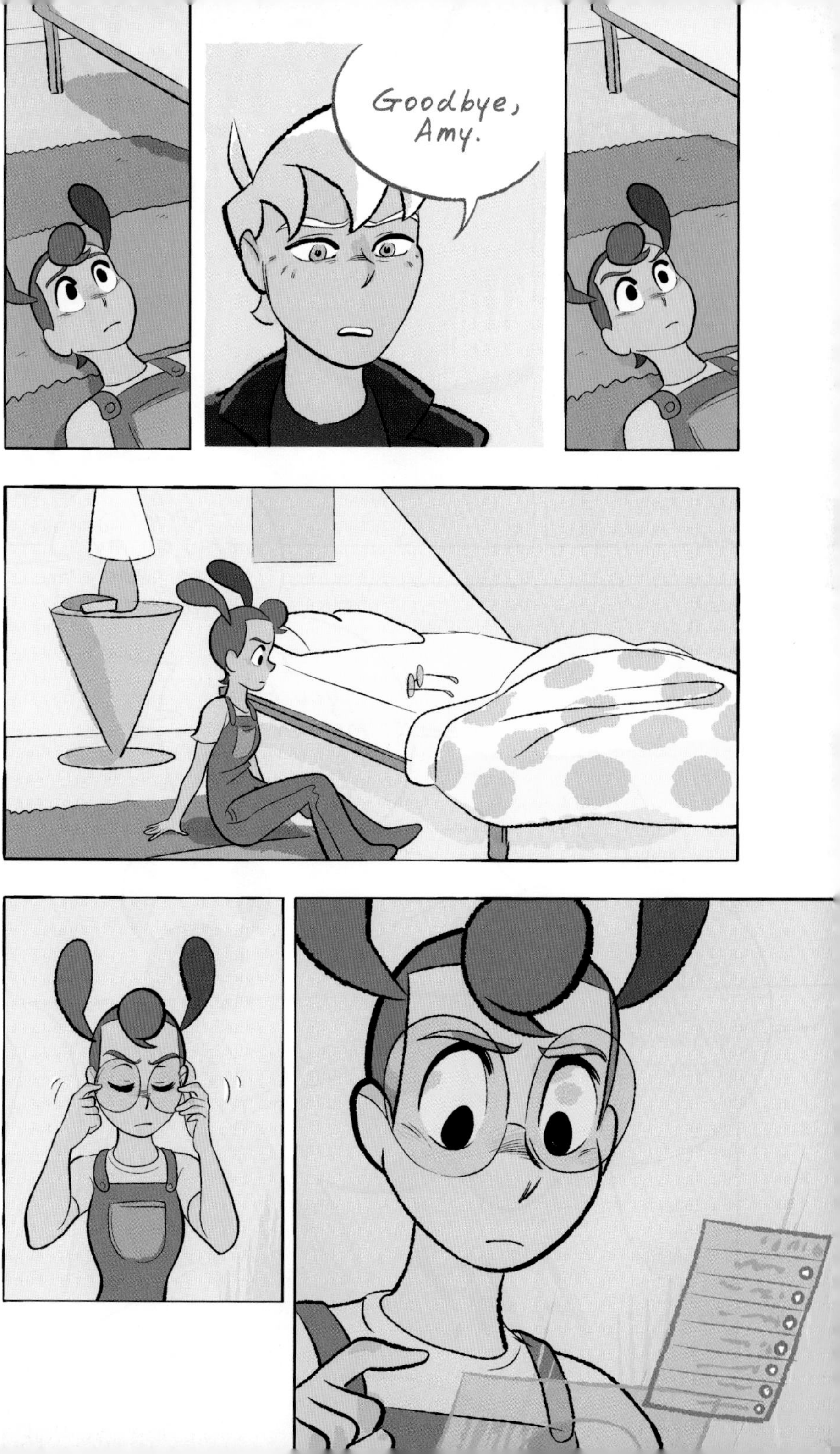
Goodbye, Amy.

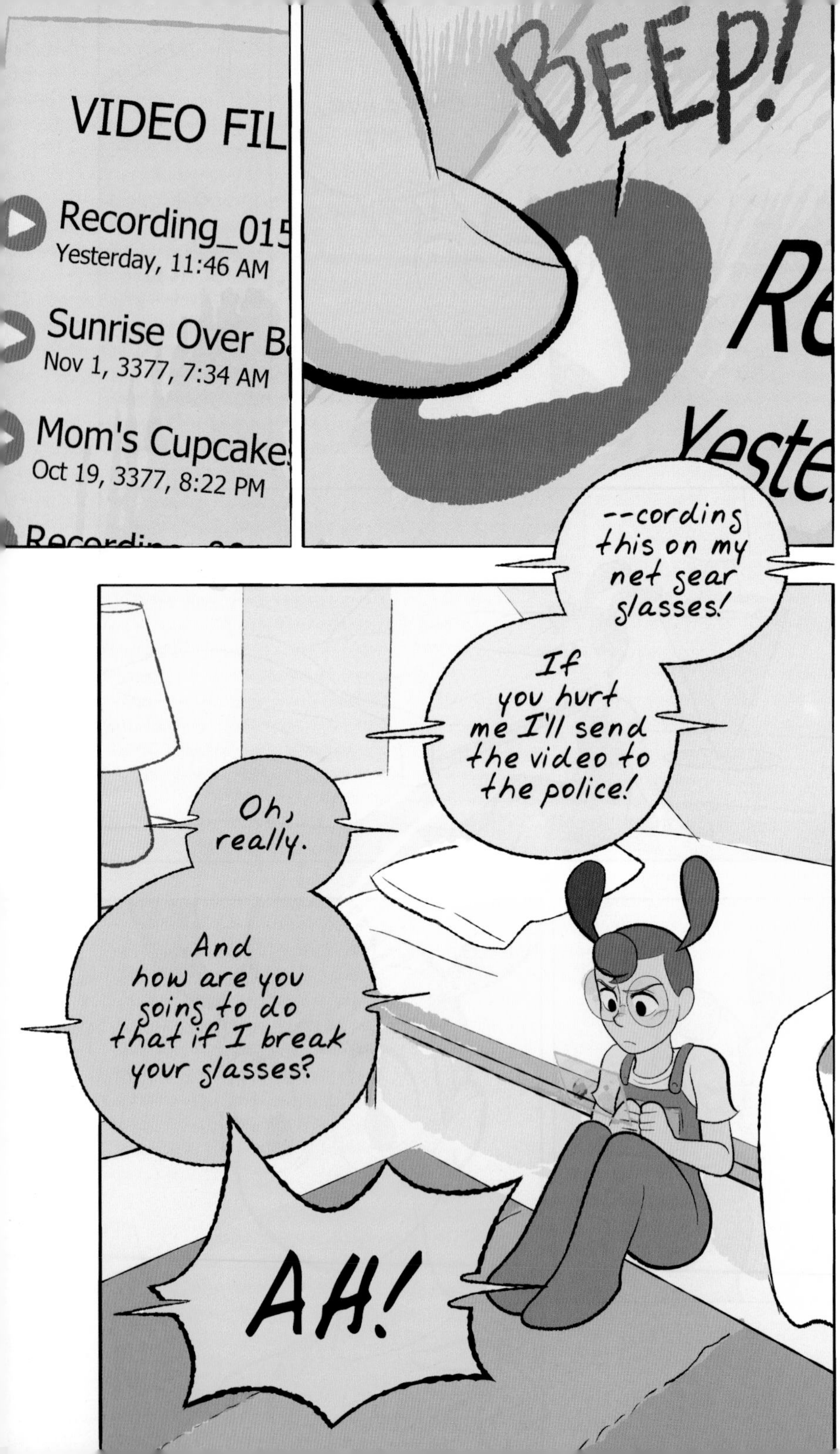
VIDEO FIL
Recording_015
Yesterday, 11:46 AM
Sunrise Over B
Nov 1, 3377, 7:34 AM
Mom's Cupcake
Oct 19, 3377, 8:22 PM
BEEP!
Re
--cording this on my net gear glasses!
If you hurt me I'll send the video to the police!
Oh, really.
And how are you going to do that if I break your glasses?
AH!

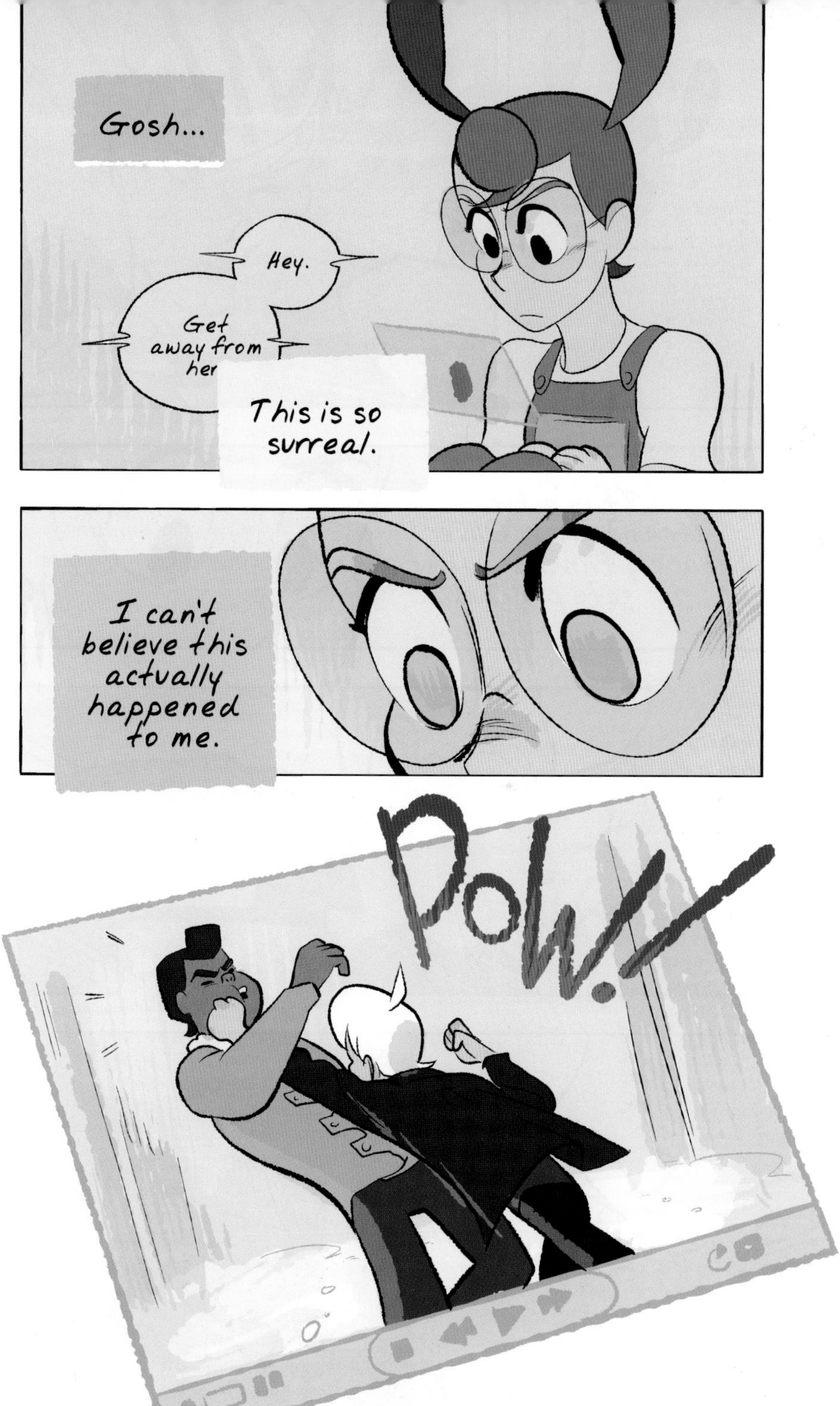
Gosh...
Hey.
Get away from her
This is so surreal.
I can't believe this actually happened to me.
POW!!

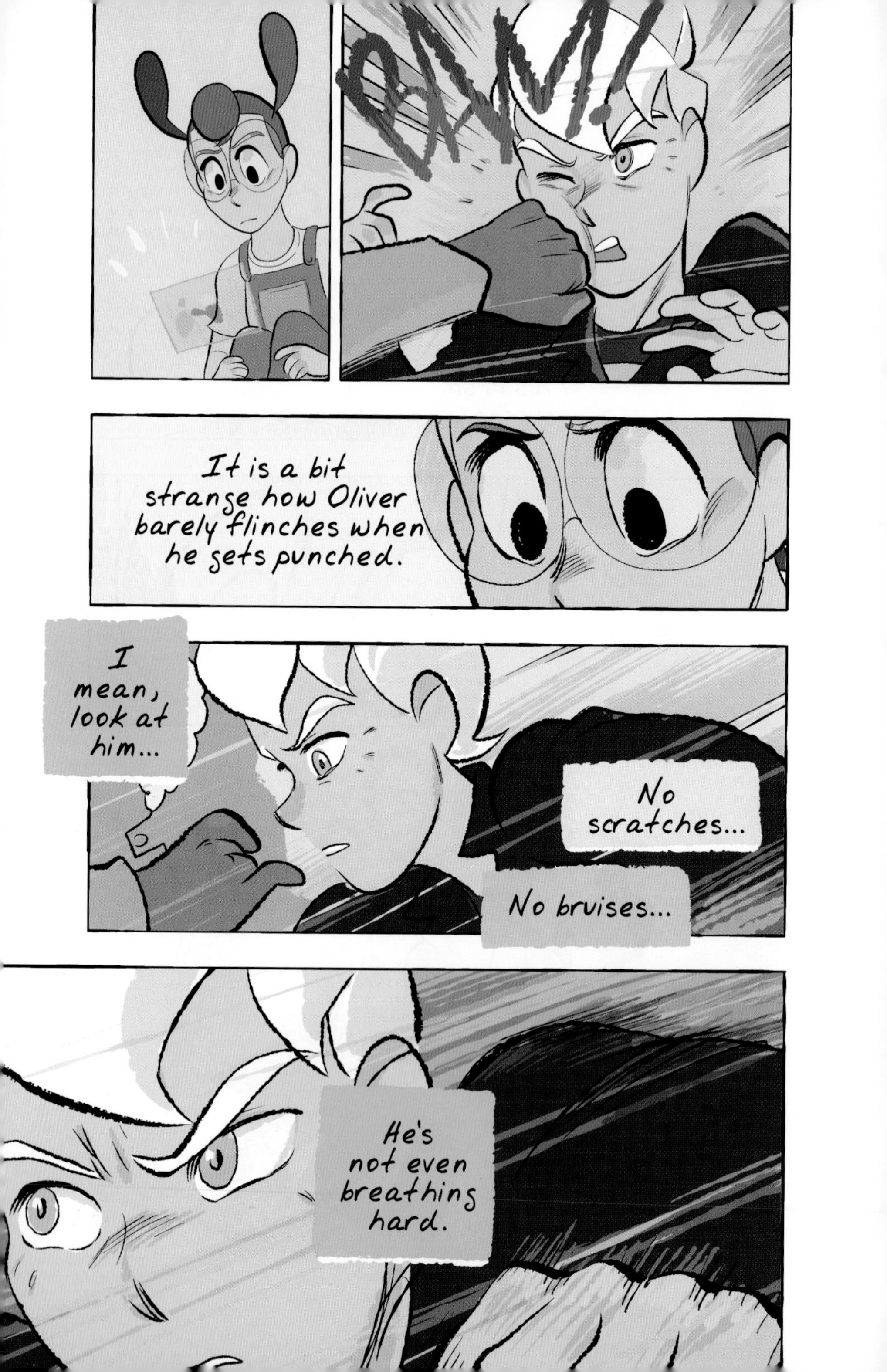
BAM!
It is a bit strange how Oliver barely flinches when he gets punched.
I mean, look at him...
No scratches...
No bruises...
He's not even breathing hard.

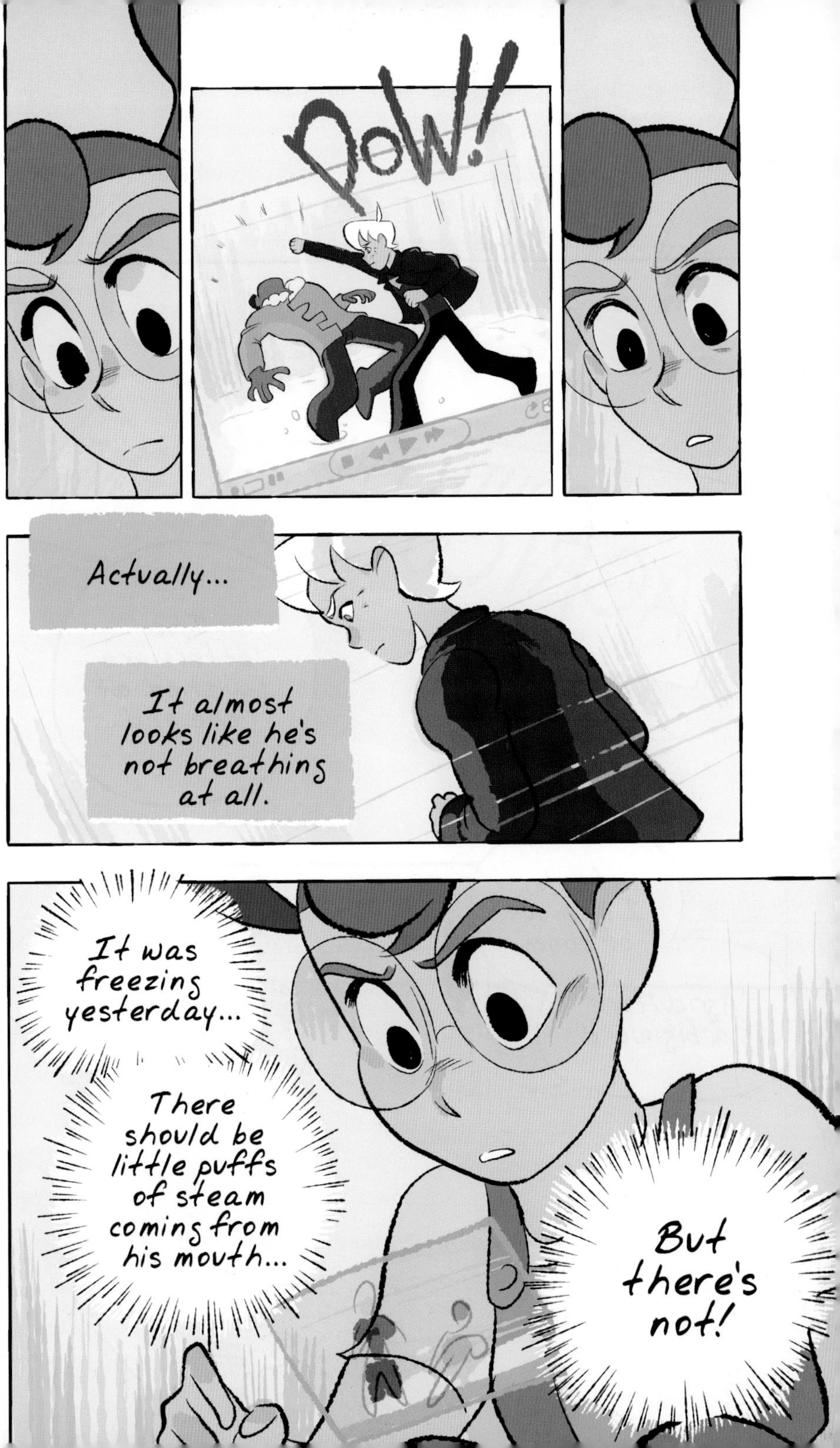
POW!!
Actually...
It almost looks like he's not breathing at all.
It was freezing yesterday...
There should be little puffs of steam coming from his mouth...
But there's not!

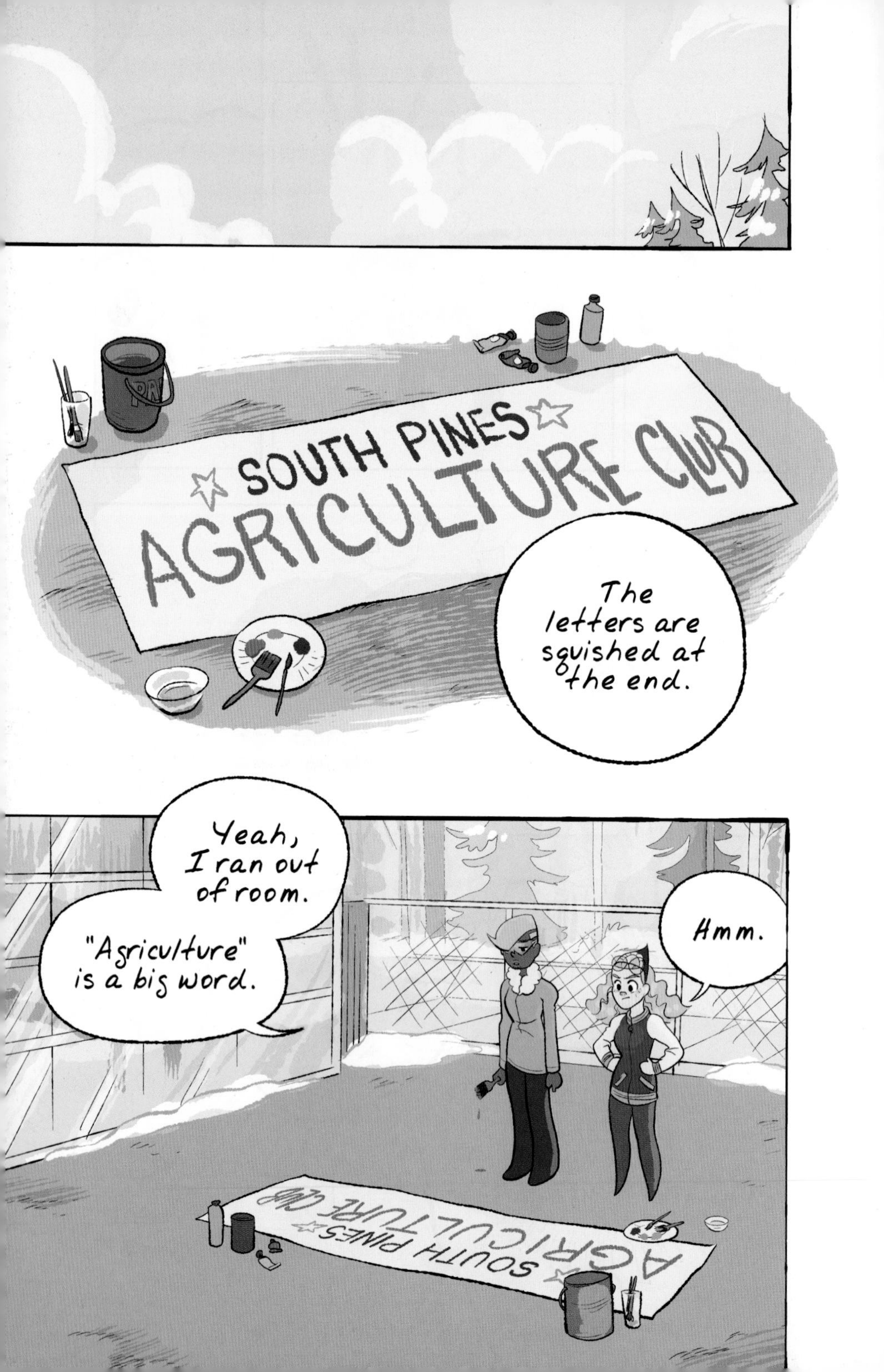
SOUTH PINES AGRICULTURE CLUB
The letters are squished at the end.
Yeah, I ran out of room.
"Agriculture" is a big word.
Hmm.

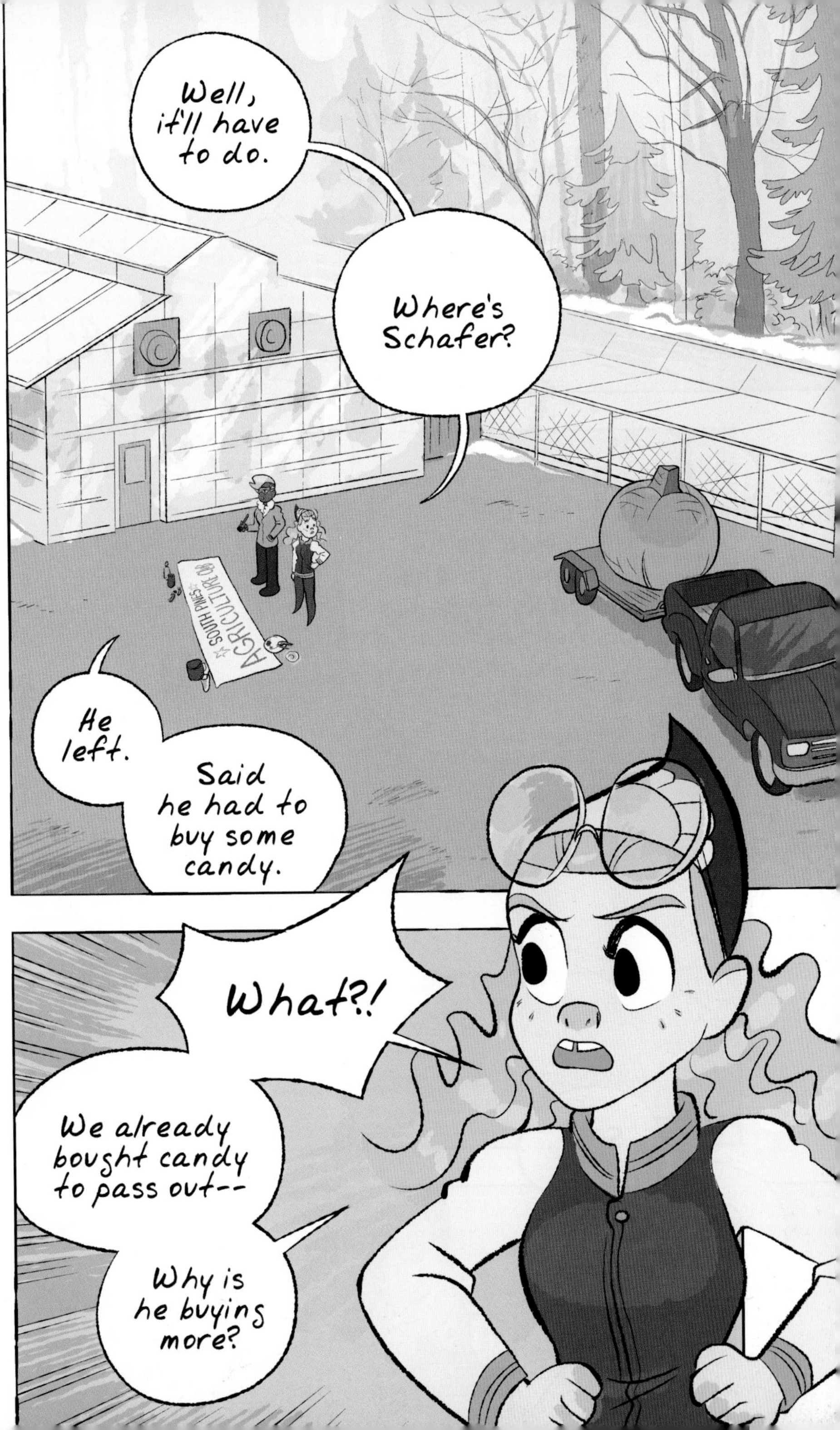

Well, it'll have to do.
Where's Schafer?
SOUTH PINES AGRICULTURE CLUB
He left.
Said he had to buy some candy.
What?!
We already bought candy to pass out--
Why is he buying more?

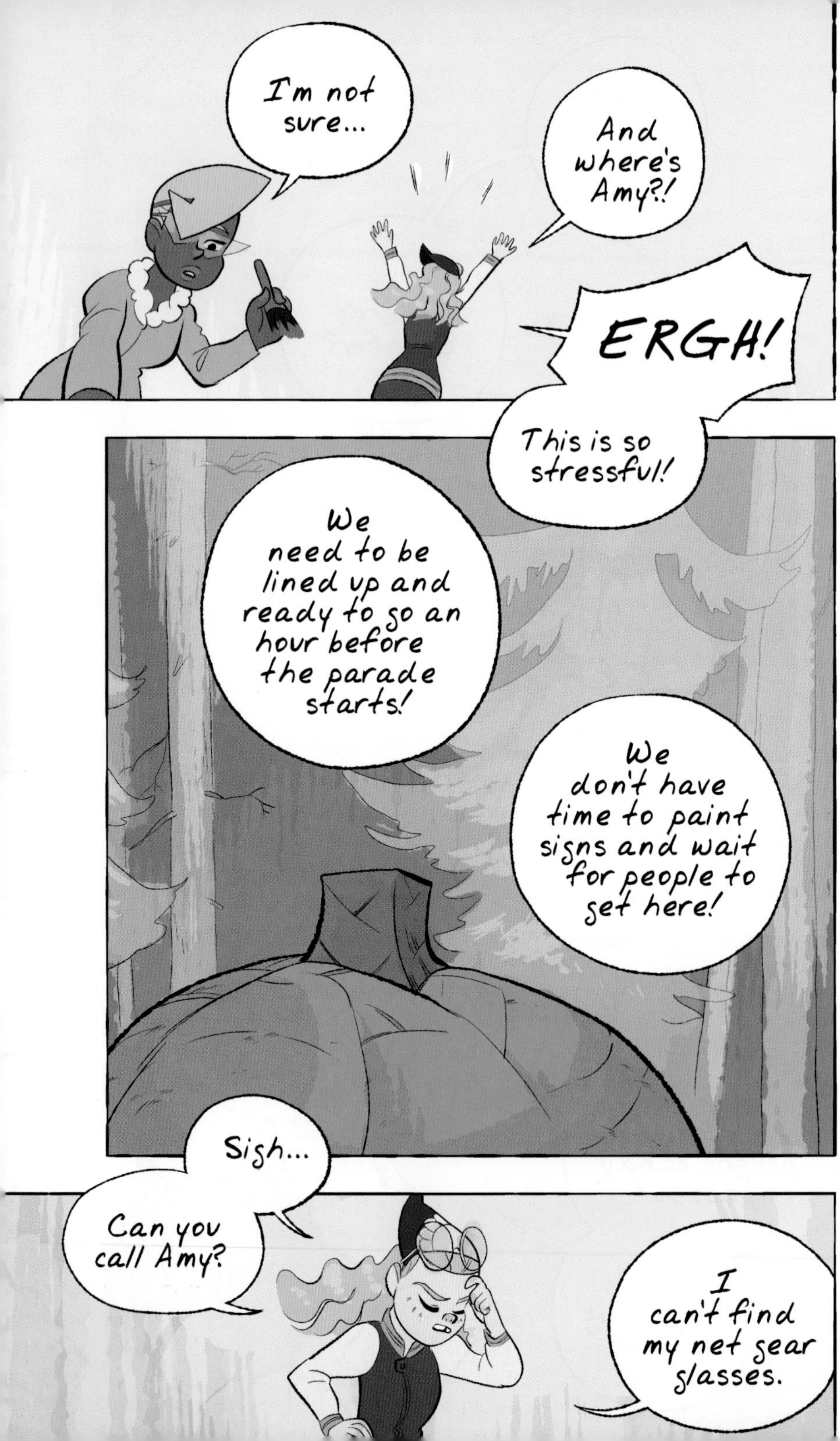

I'm not sure...
And where's Amy?!
ERGH!
This is so stressful!
We need to be lined up and ready to go an hour before the parade starts!
We don't have time to paint signs and wait for people to get here!
Sigh...
Can you call Amy?
I can't find my net gear glasses.

They're on your--

I know!

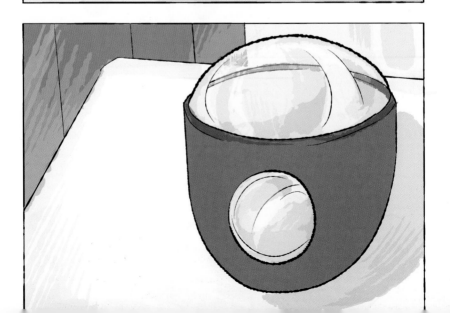

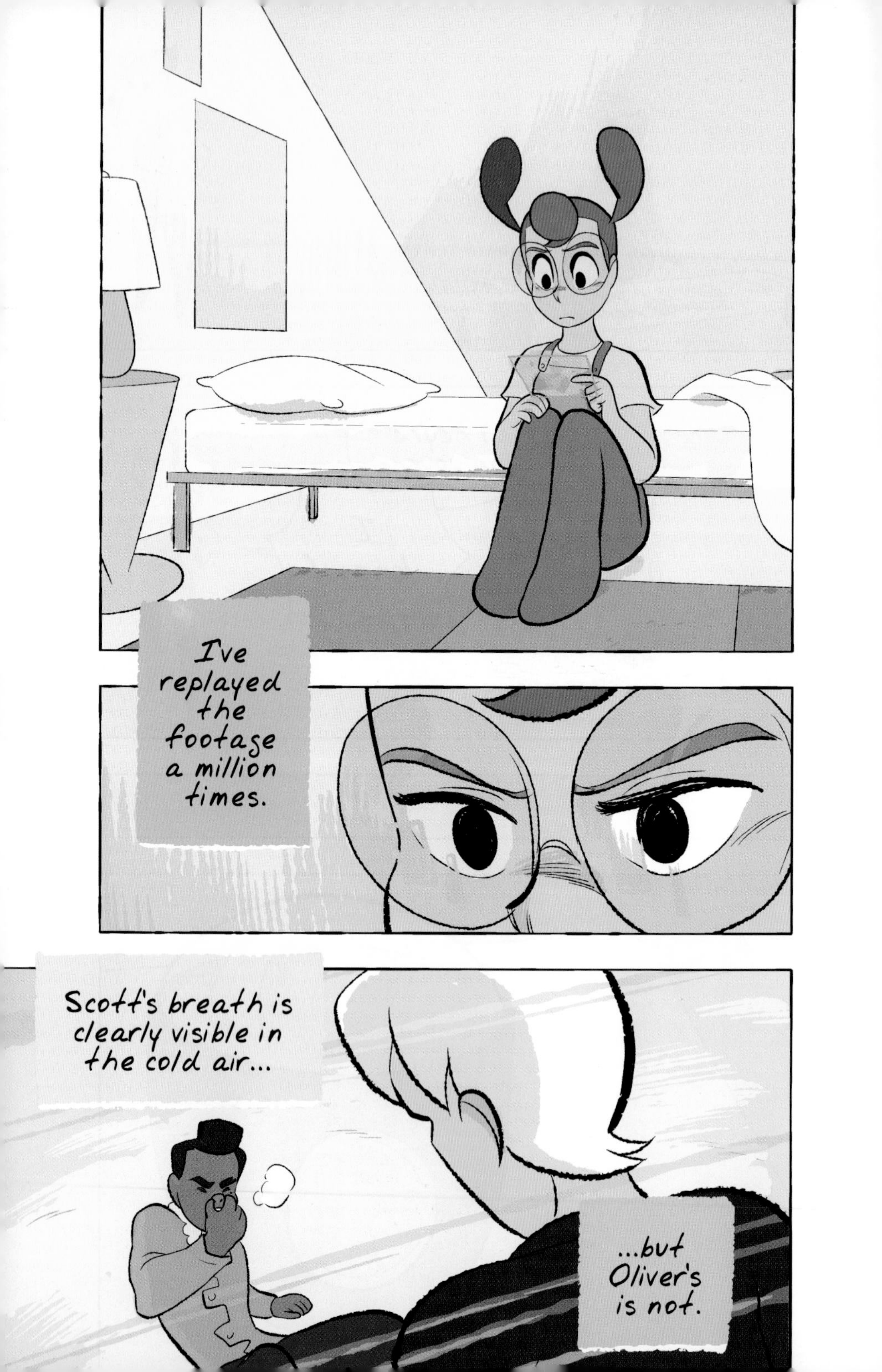
I've replayed the footage a million times.
Scott's breath is clearly visible in the cold air...
...but Oliver's is not.

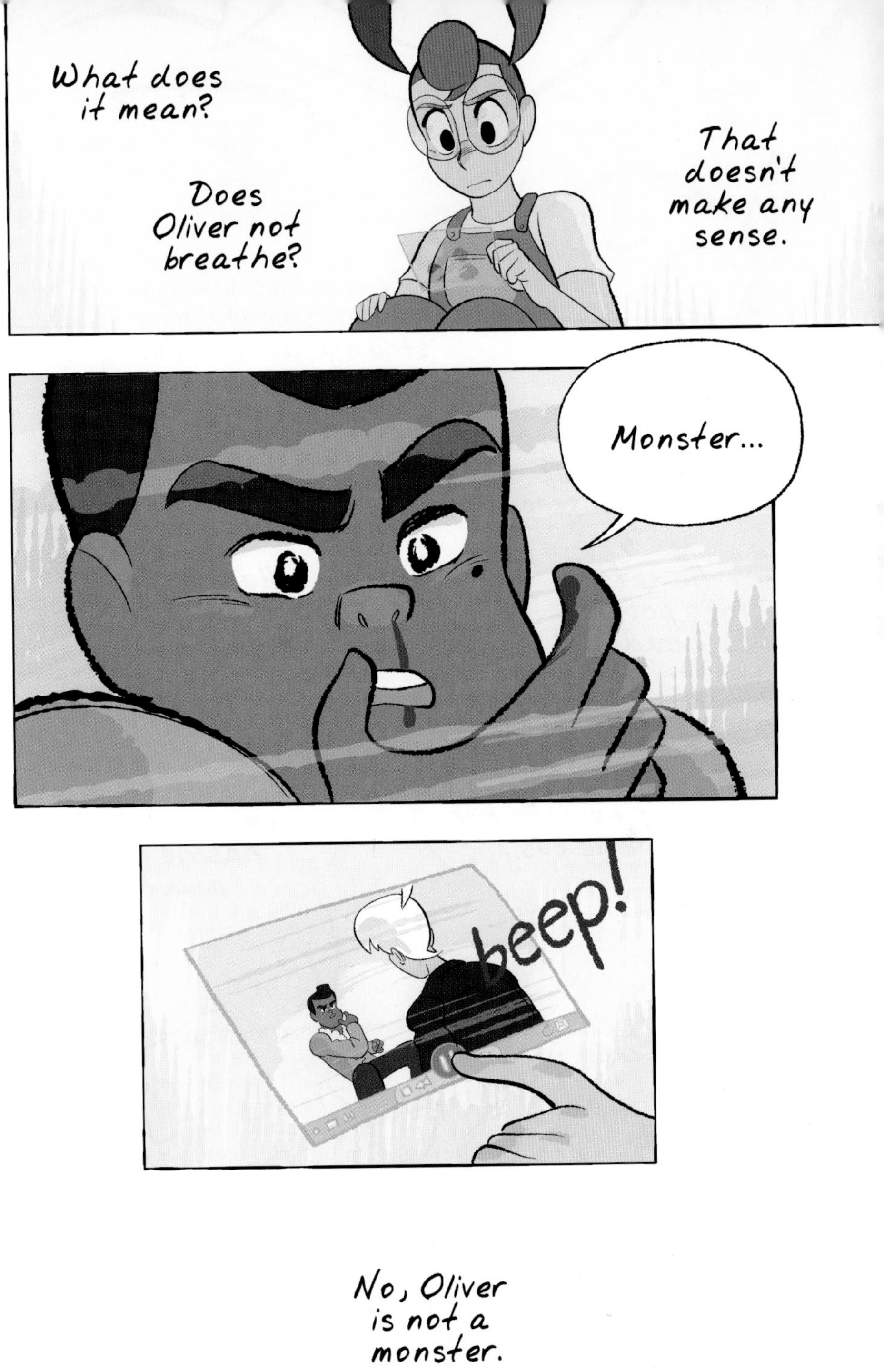

What does it mean?
Does Oliver not breathe?
That doesn't make any sense.
Monster...
beep!
No, Oliver is not a monster.

But...

...there has always been something strange about him.

He's dangerous.

He gets into people's heads.

He once save my friend nightmares just by sitting next to her on the bus...

He lied to you, Amy.

And if he's willing to lie about his own name, what else has he lied about?

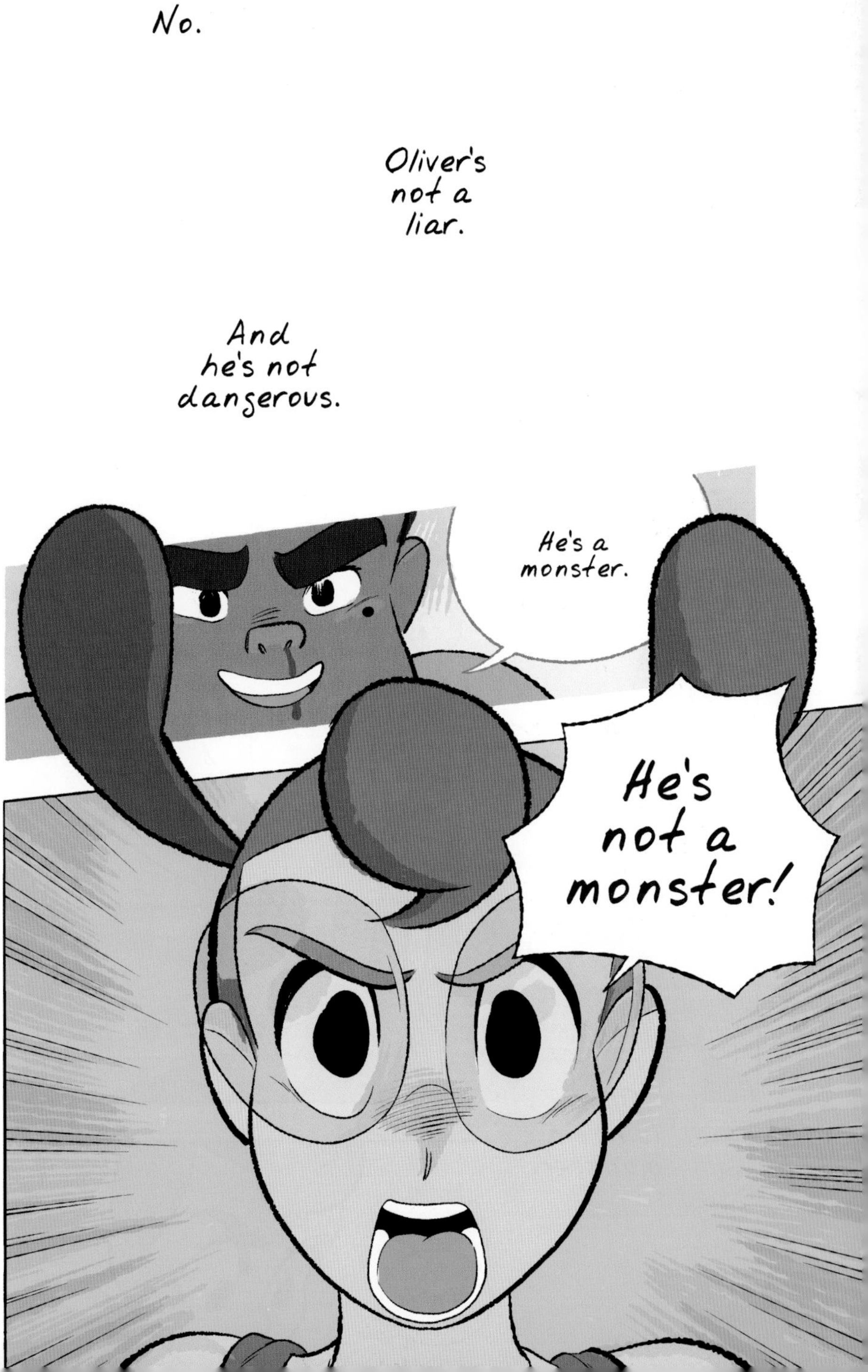
No.
Oliver's not a liar.
And he's not dangerous.
He's a monster.
He's not a monster!

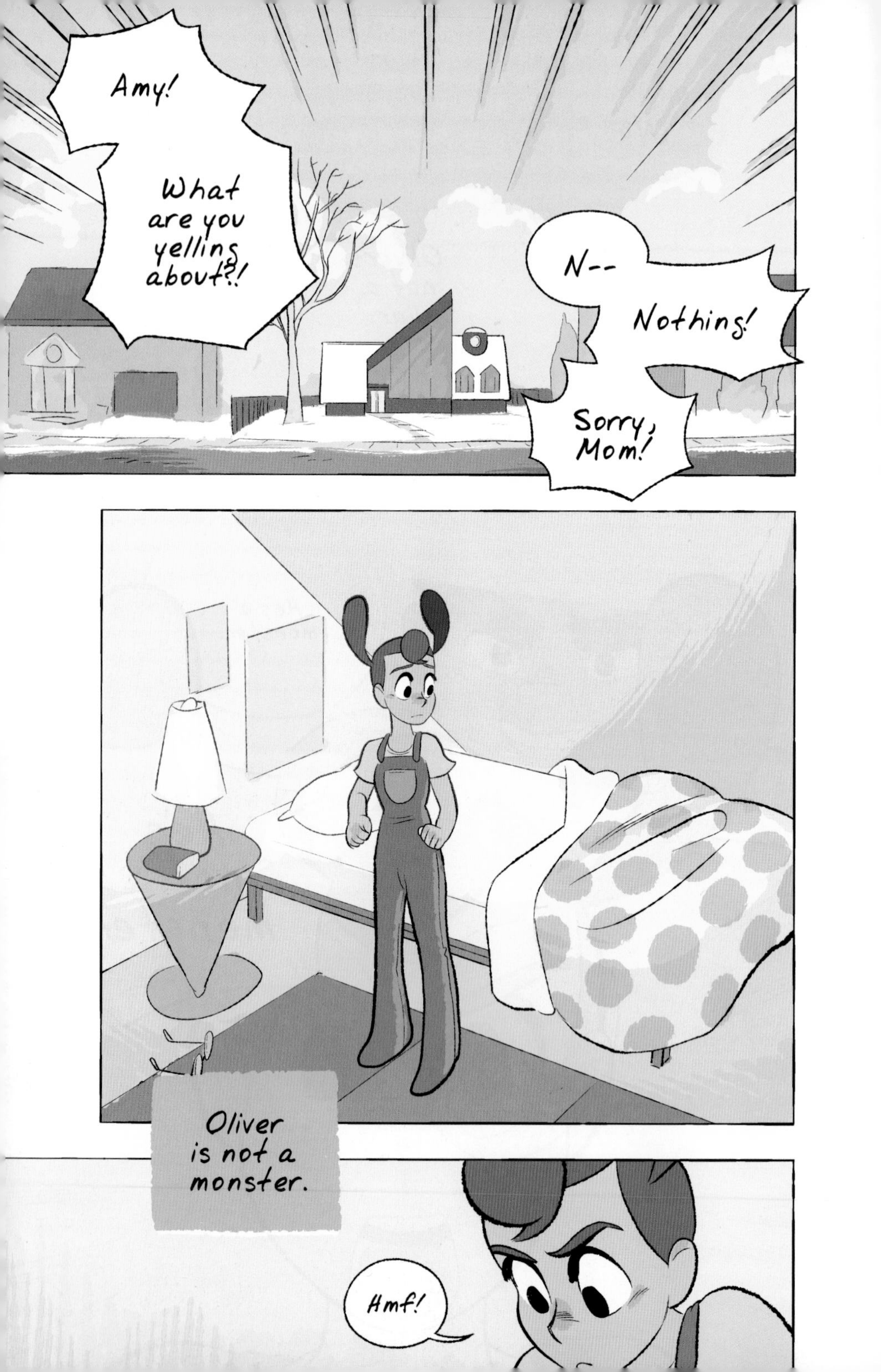
Amy!
What are you yelling about?!
N--
Nothing!
Sorry, Mom!
Oliver is not a monster.
Hmf!

Oliver
is a...

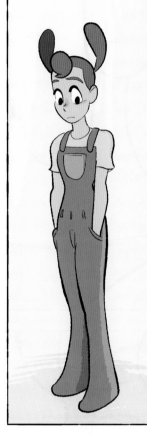

A...

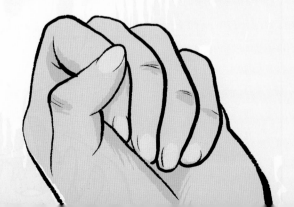

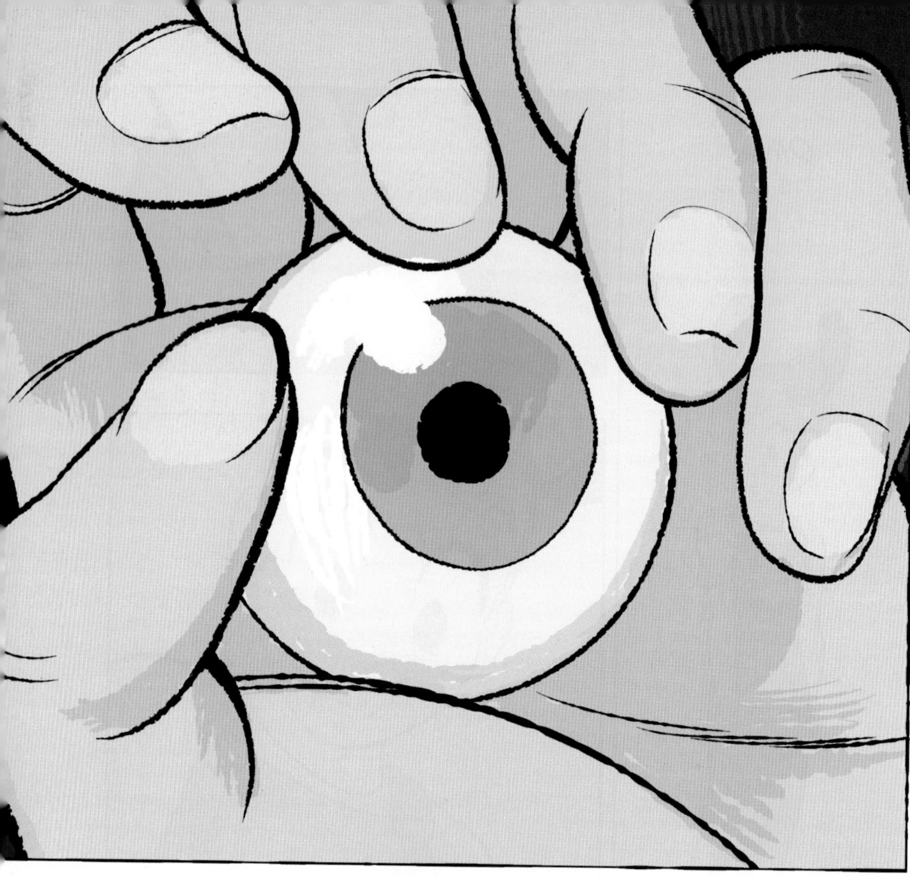

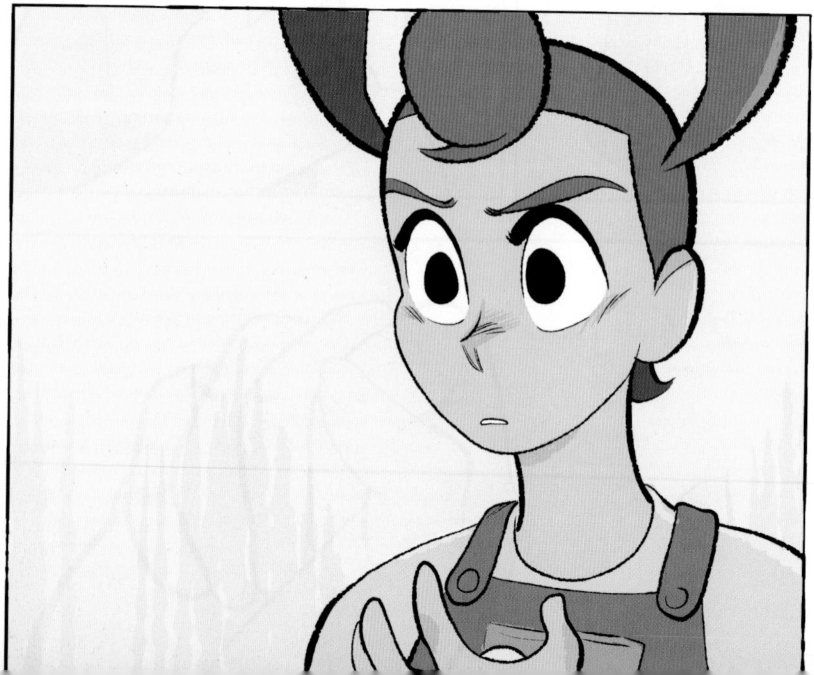

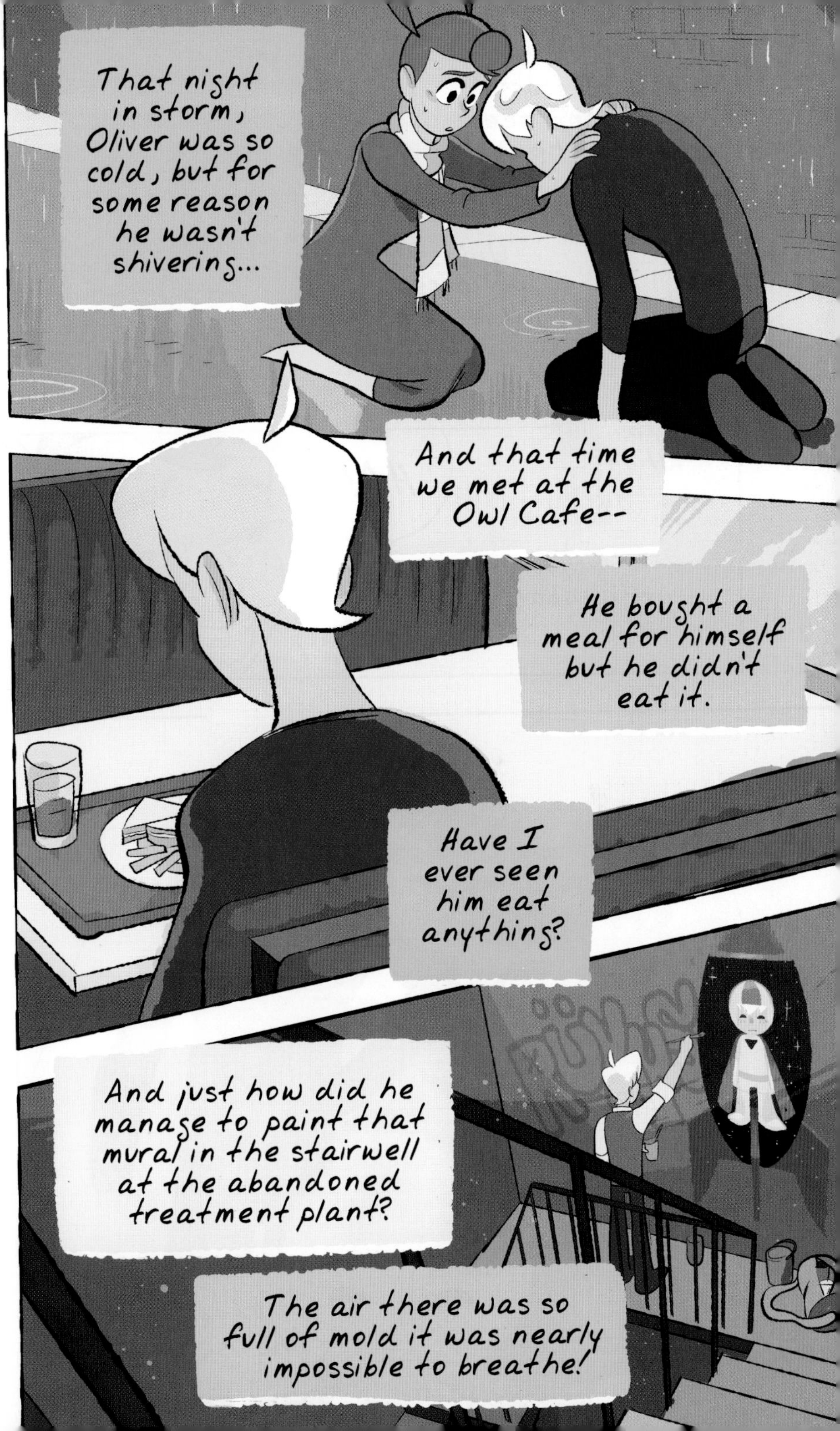
That night in storm, Oliver was so cold, but for some reason he wasn't shivering...
And that time we met at the Owl Cafe--
He bought a meal for himself but he didn't eat it.
Have I ever seen him eat anything?
And just how did he manage to paint that mural in the stairwell at the abandoned treatment plant?
The air there was so full of mold it was nearly impossible to breathe!

Unless, of course,
Oliver doesn't need
to breathe...

Unless,
of course,
Oliver is a...

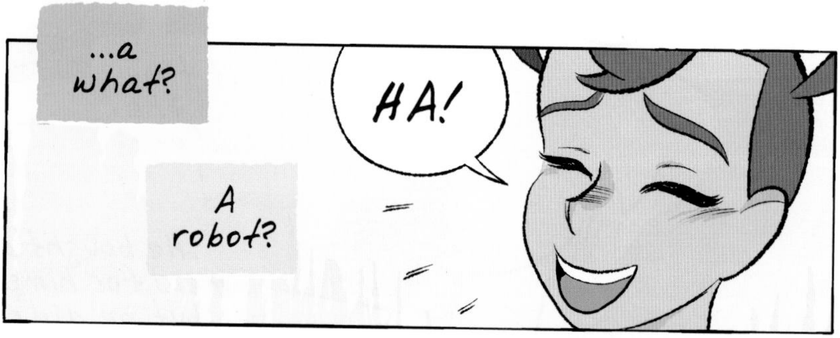
...a
what?
HA!
A
robot?

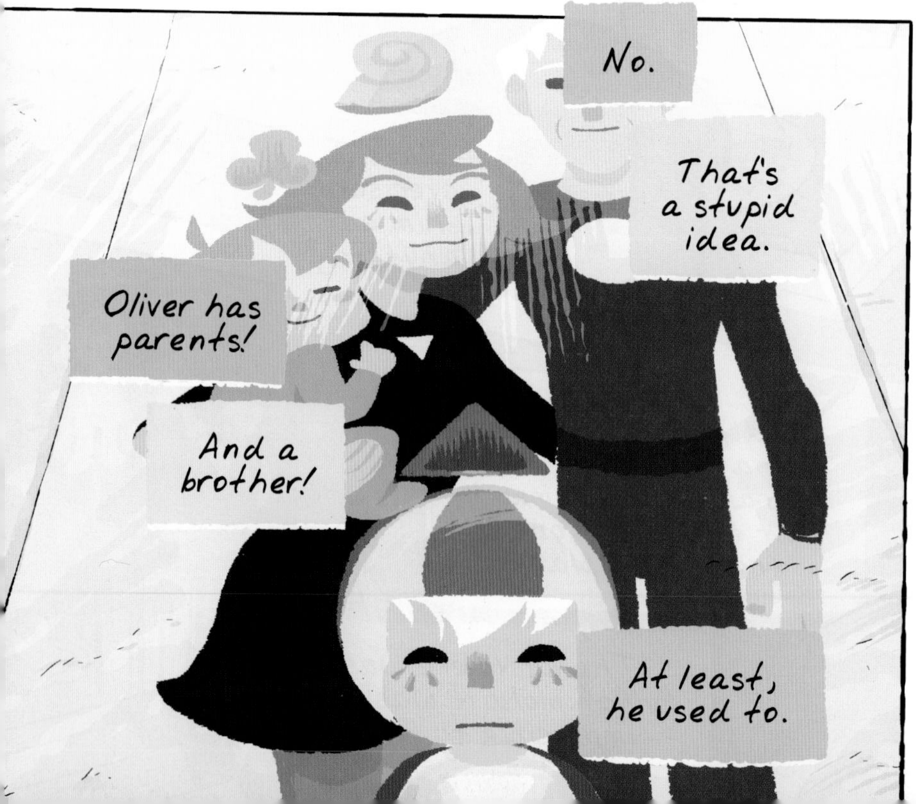
No.
That's
a stupid
idea.
Oliver has
parents!
And a
brother!
At least,
he used to.

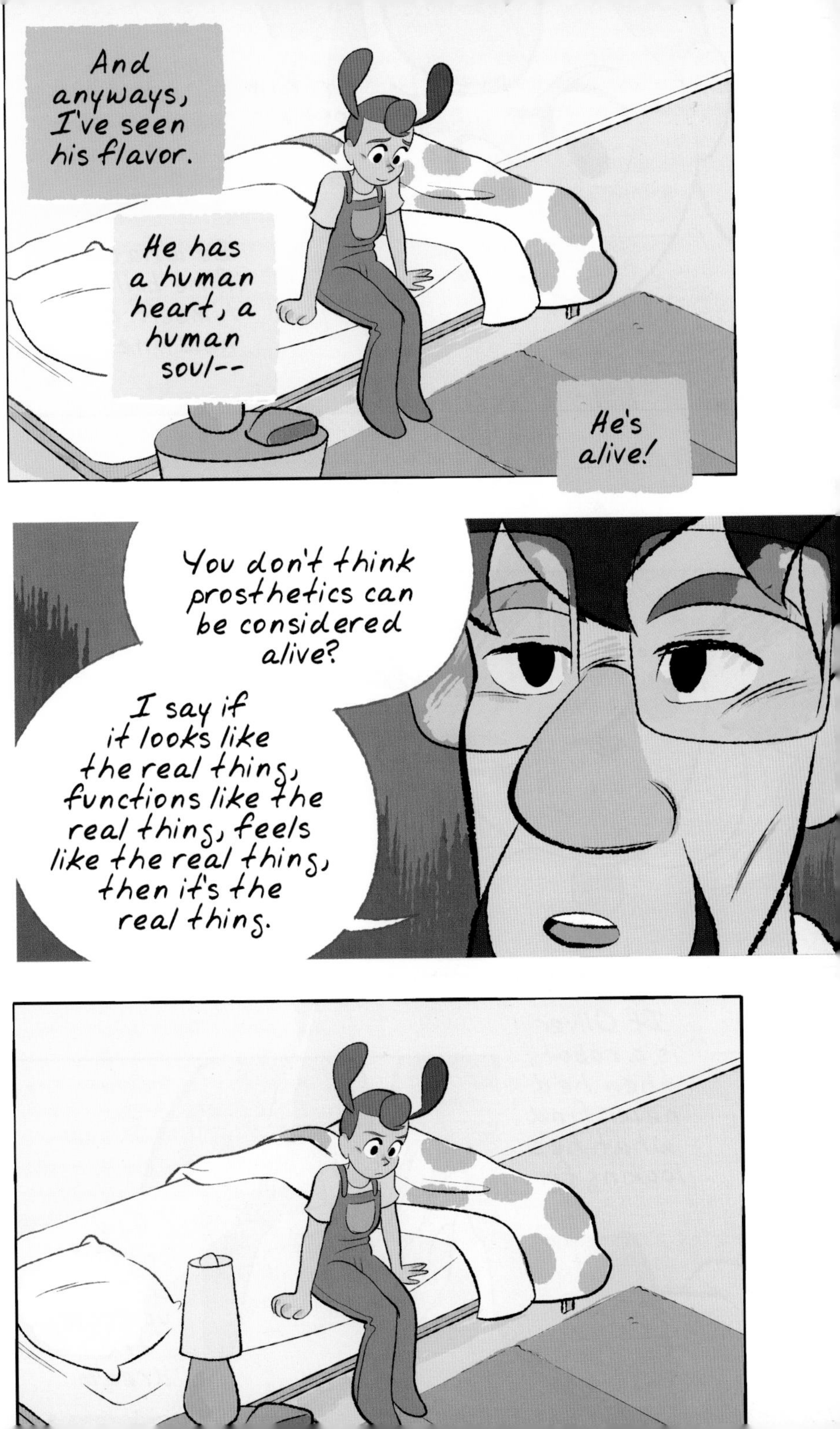
And anyways, I've seen his flavor.
He has a human heart, a human soul--
He's alive!
You don't think prosthetics can be considered alive?
I say if it looks like the real thing, functions like the real thing, feels like the real thing, then it's the real thing.

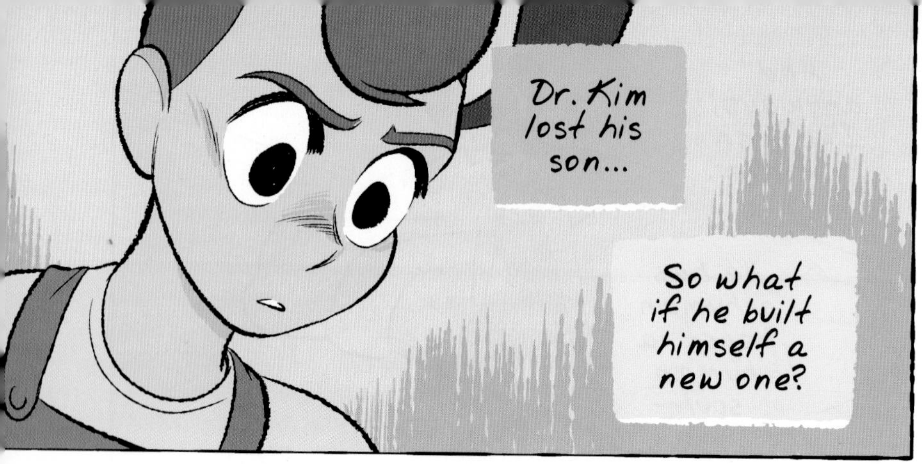
Dr. Kim lost his son...
So what if he built himself a new one?

No.

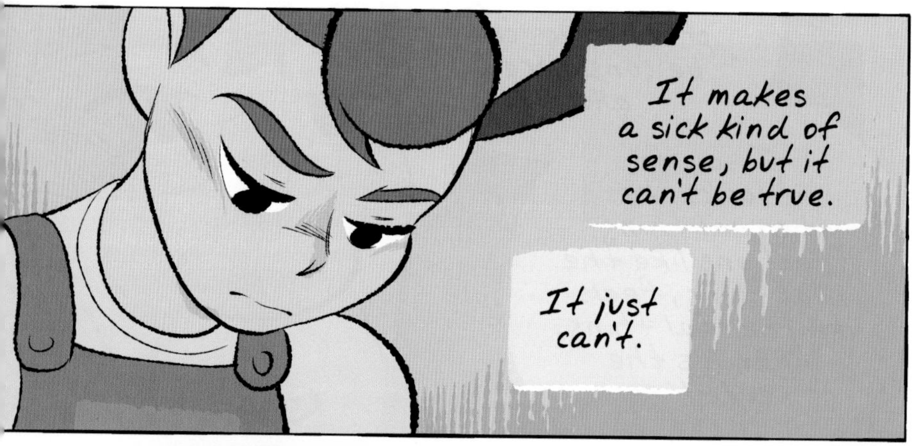
It makes a sick kind of sense, but it can't be true.
It just can't.

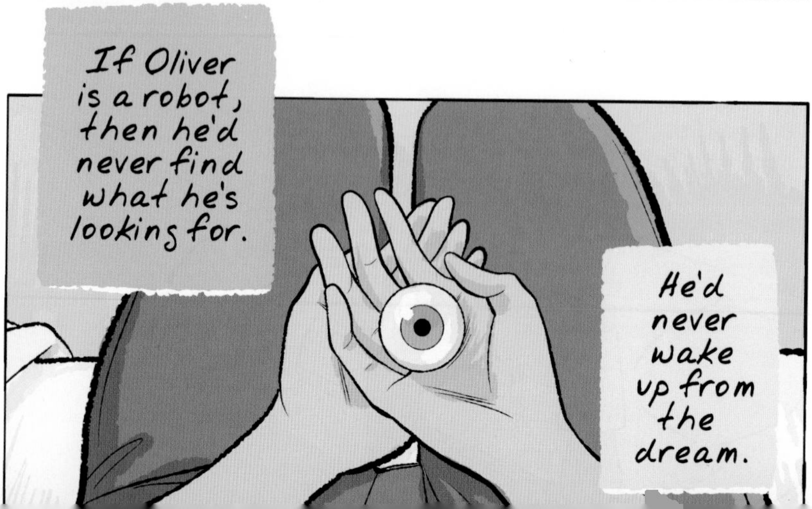
If Oliver is a robot, then he'd never find what he's looking for.
He'd never wake up from the dream.

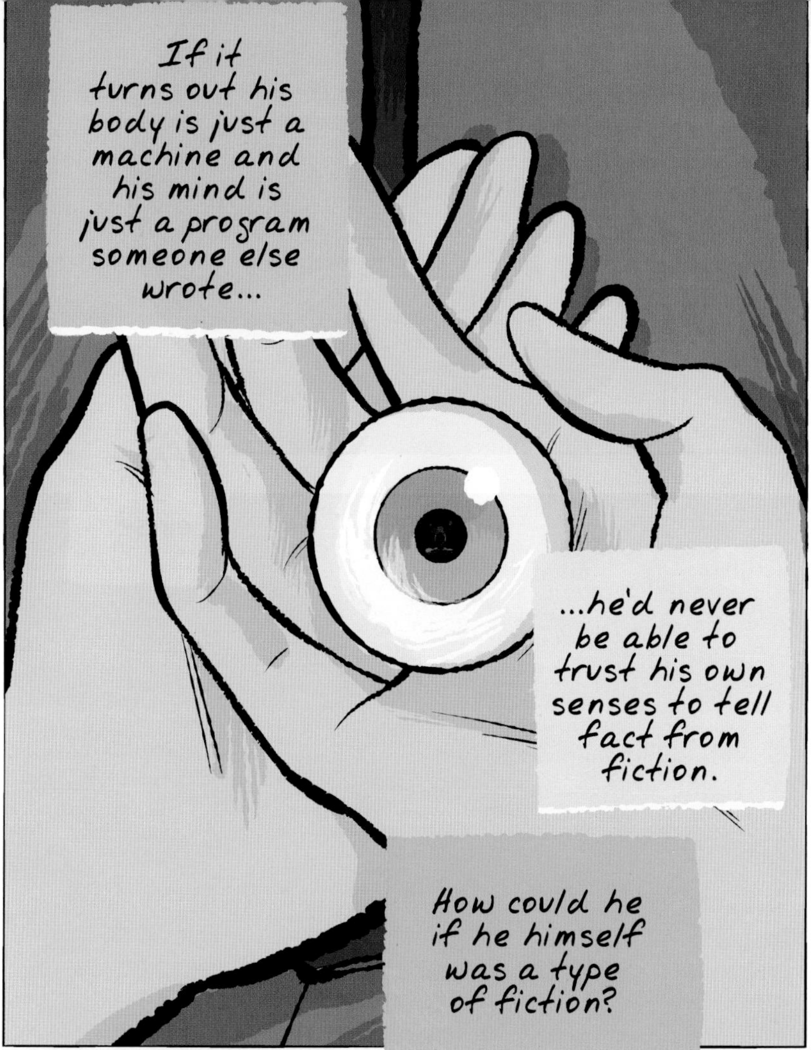
If it turns out his body is just a machine and his mind is just a program someone else wrote...
...he'd never be able to trust his own senses to tell fact from fiction.
How could he if he himself was a type of fiction?

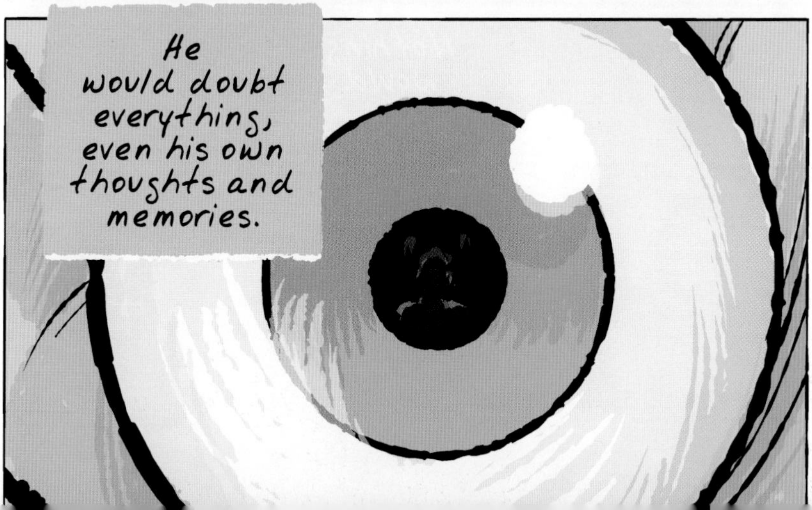
He would doubt everything, even his own thoughts and memories.

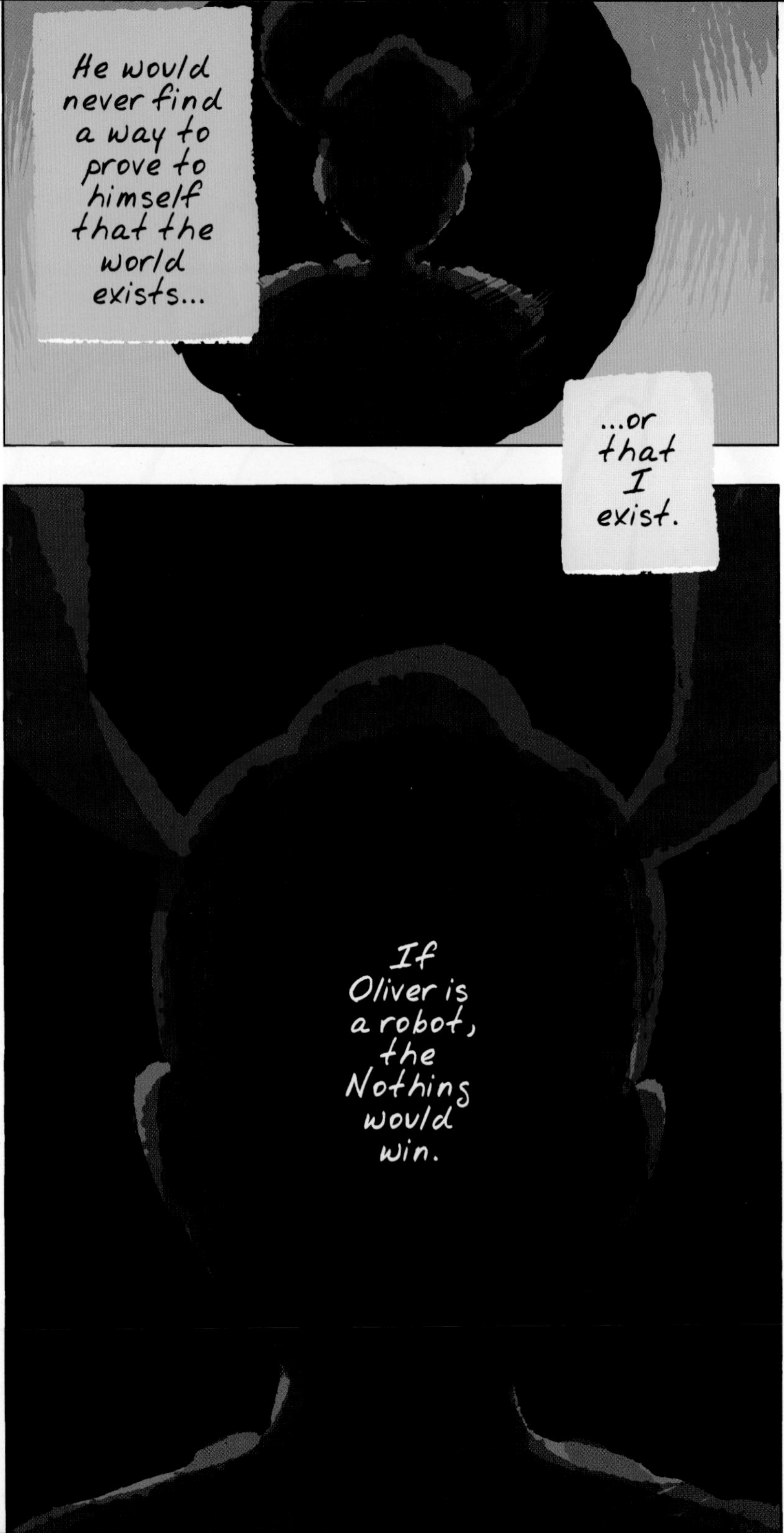
He would never find a way to prove to himself that the world exists...
...or that I exist.
If Oliver is a robot, the Nothing would win.

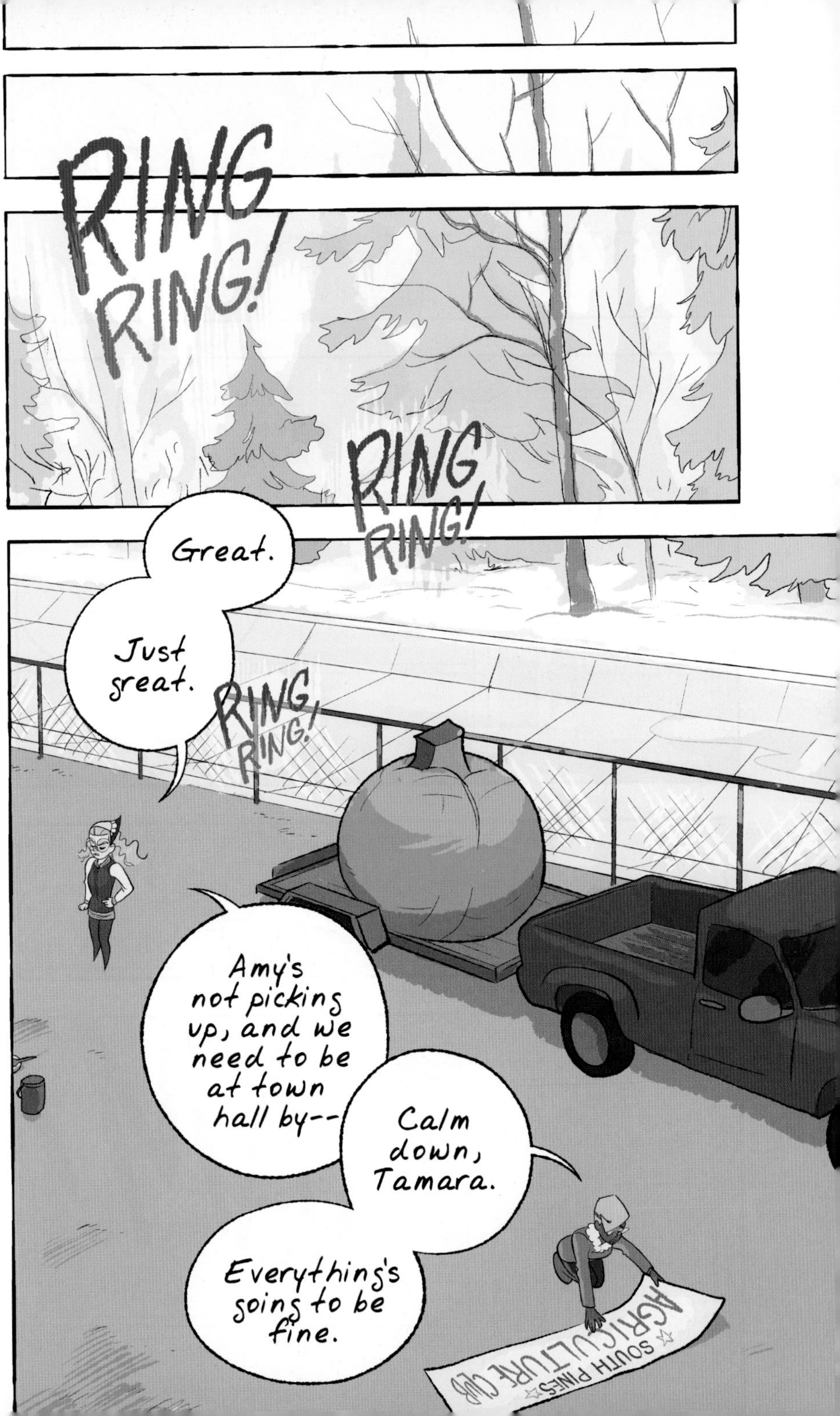
RING RING!
RING RING!
Great.
Just great.
RING, RING!
Amy's not picking up, and we need to be at town hall by--
Calm down, Tamara.
Everything's going to be fine.
SOUTH PINES AGRICULTURE CLUB

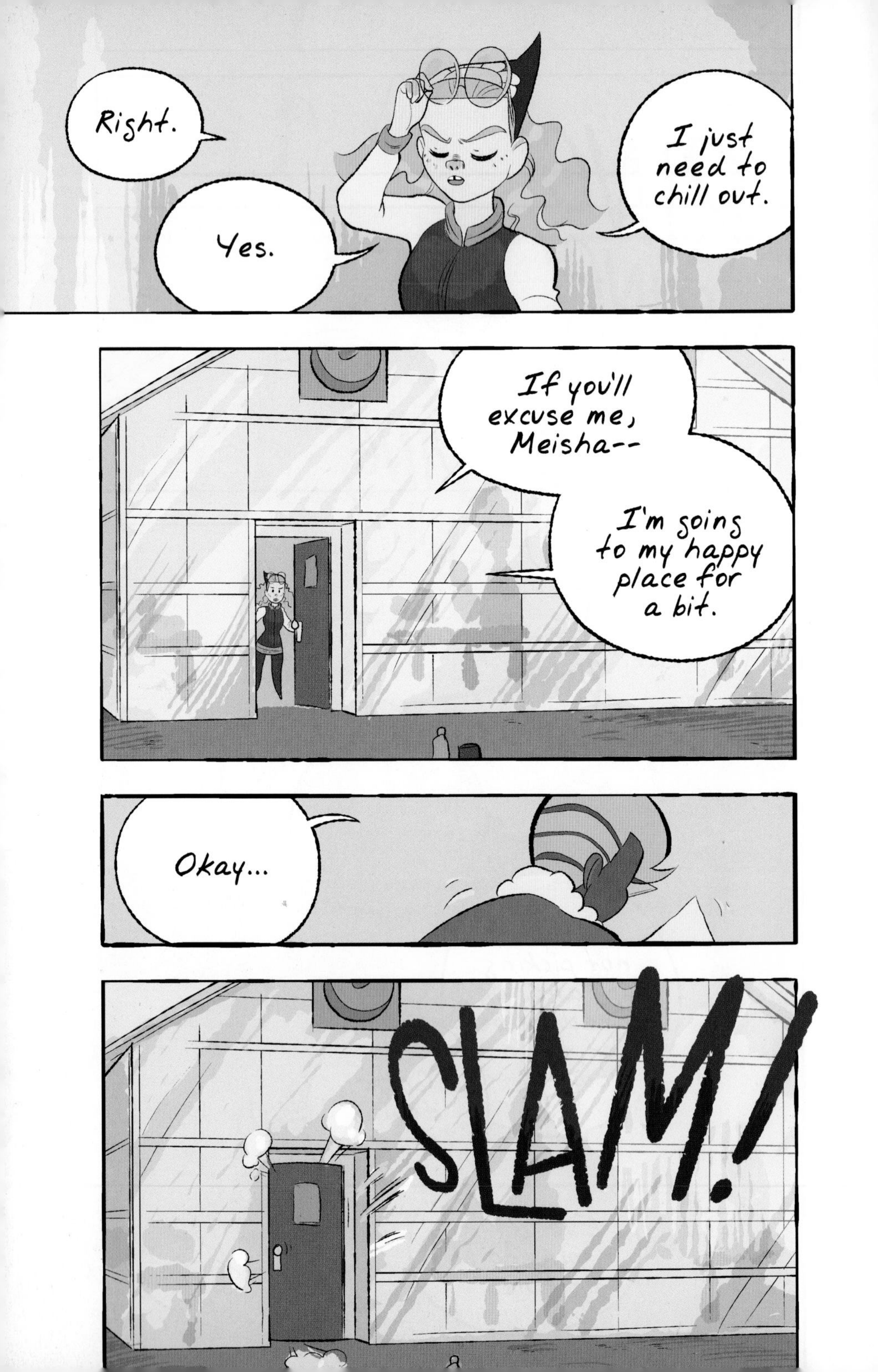
Right.
Yes.
I just need to chill out.
If you'll excuse me, Meisha--
I'm going to my happy place for a bit.
Okay...
SLAM!

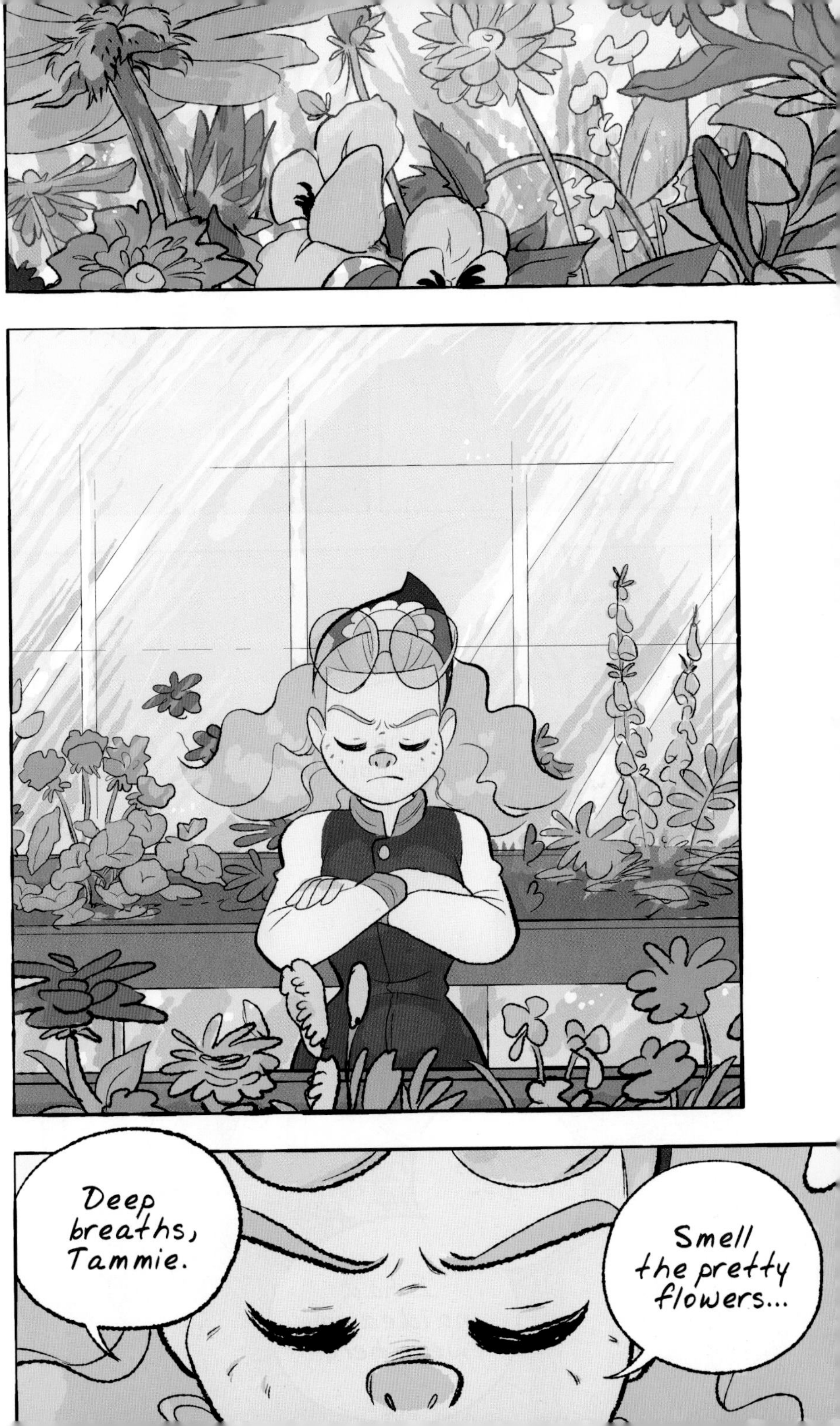
Deep breaths, Tammie.
Smell the pretty flowers...

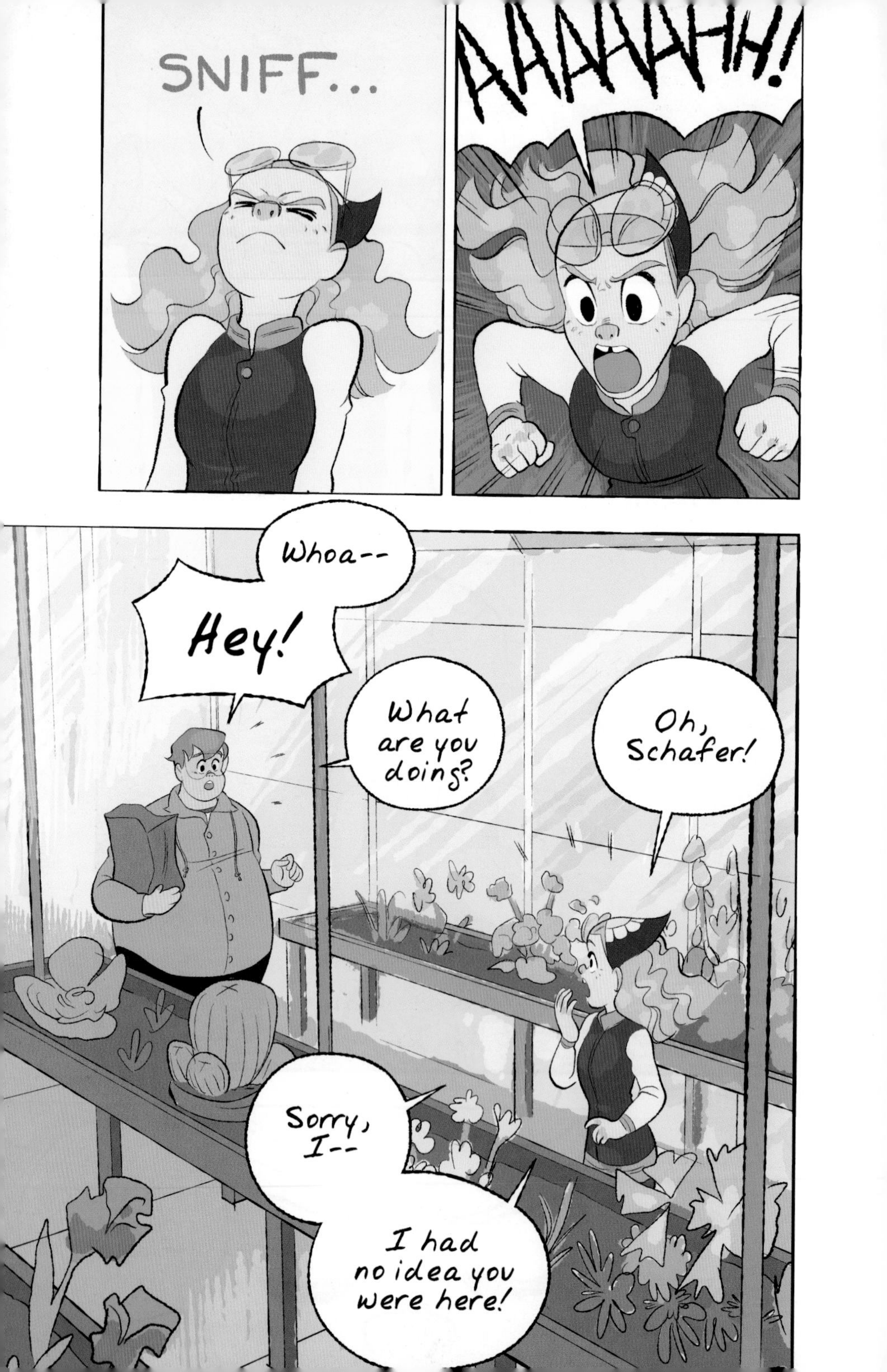

SNIFF...
AAAAAHH!
Whoa--
Hey!
What are you doing?
Oh, Schafer!
Sorry, I--
I had no idea you were here!

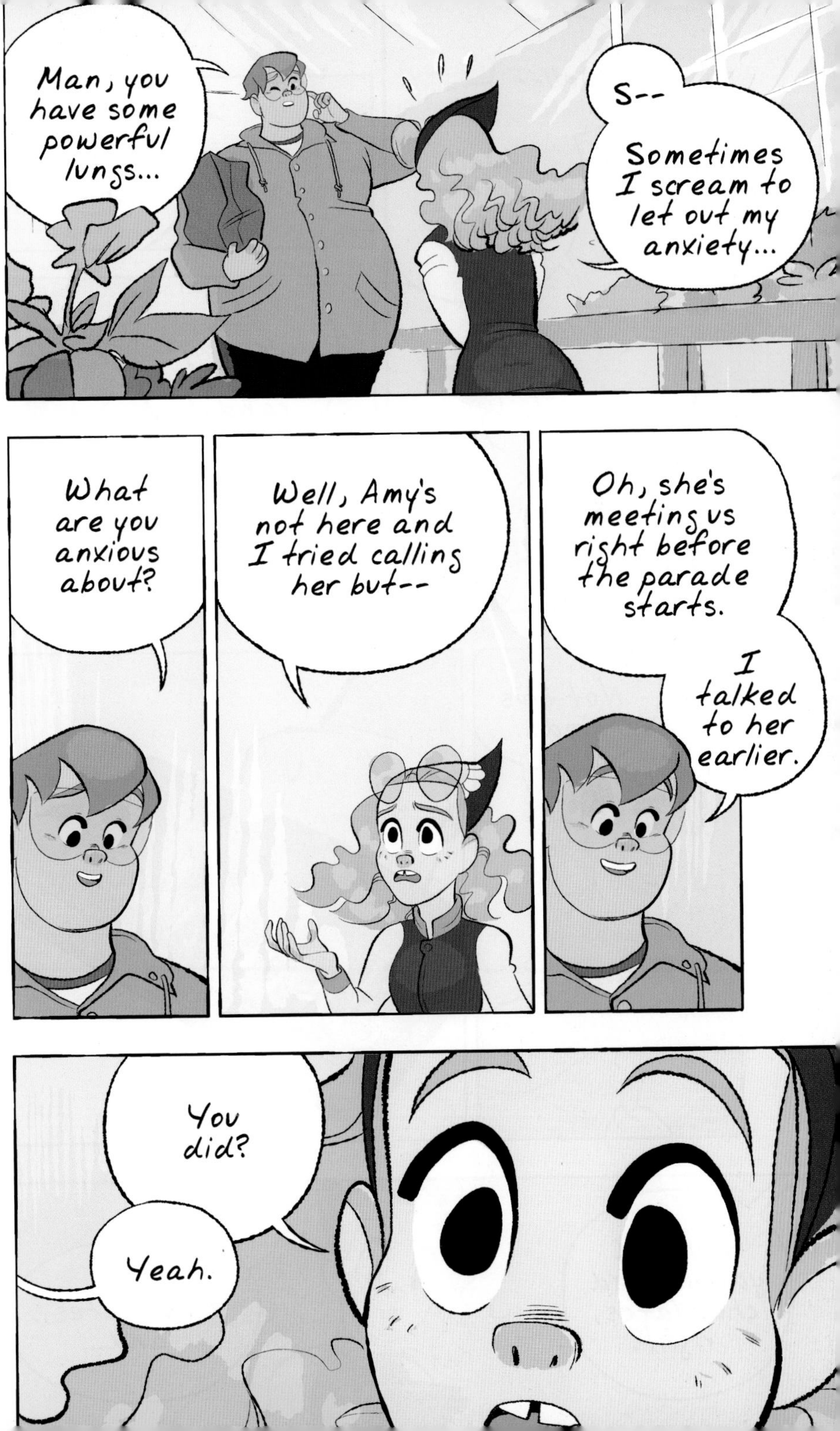
Man, you have some powerful lungs...
S--
Sometimes I scream to let out my anxiety...
What are you anxious about?
Well, Amy's not here and I tried calling her but--
Oh, she's meeting us right before the parade starts.
I talked to her earlier.
You did?
Yeah.

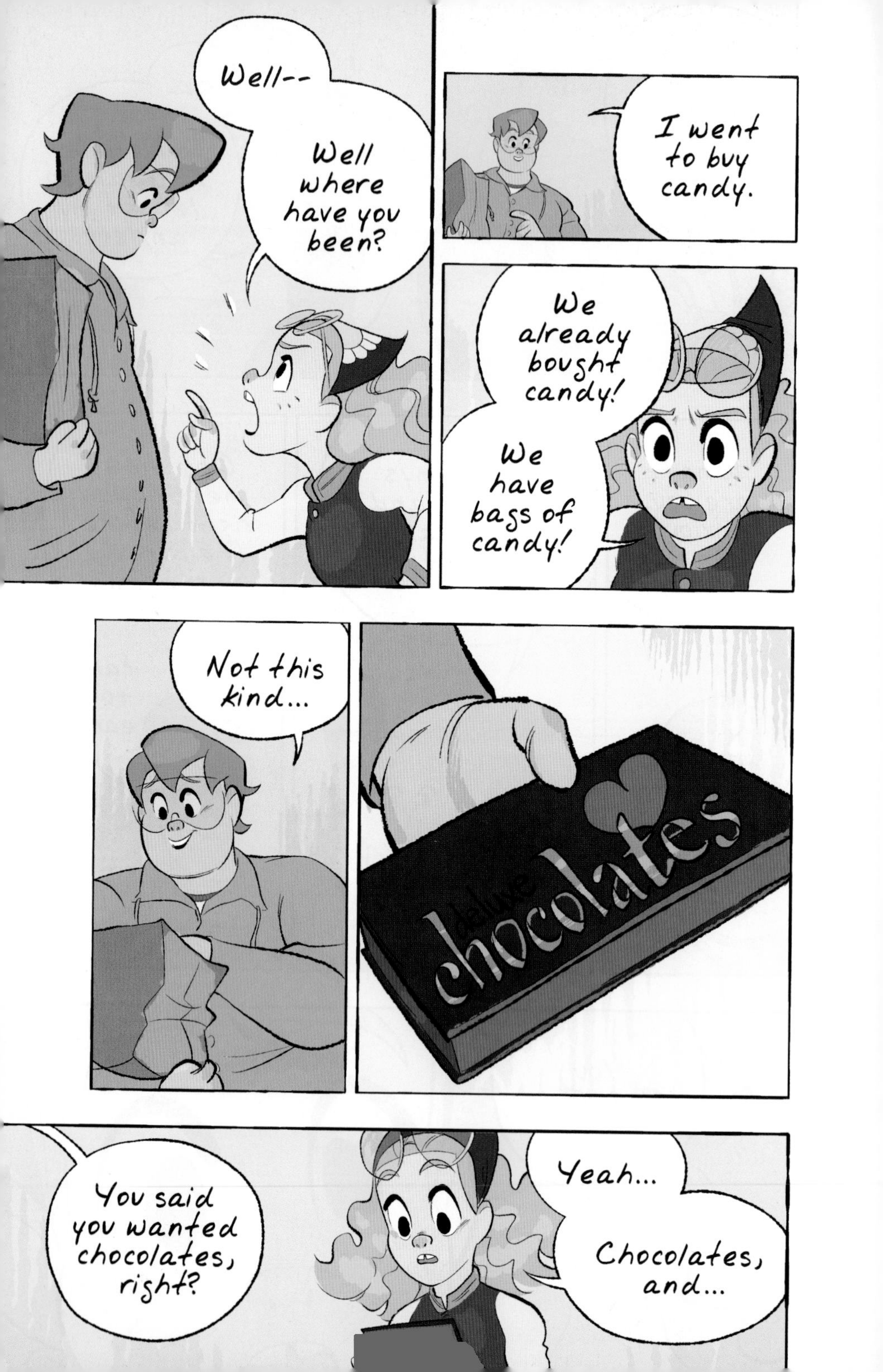
Well--
Well where have you been?
I went to buy candy.
We already bought candy!
We have bags of candy!
Not this kind...
deluxe chocolates
You said you wanted chocolates, right?
Yeah...
Chocolates, and...

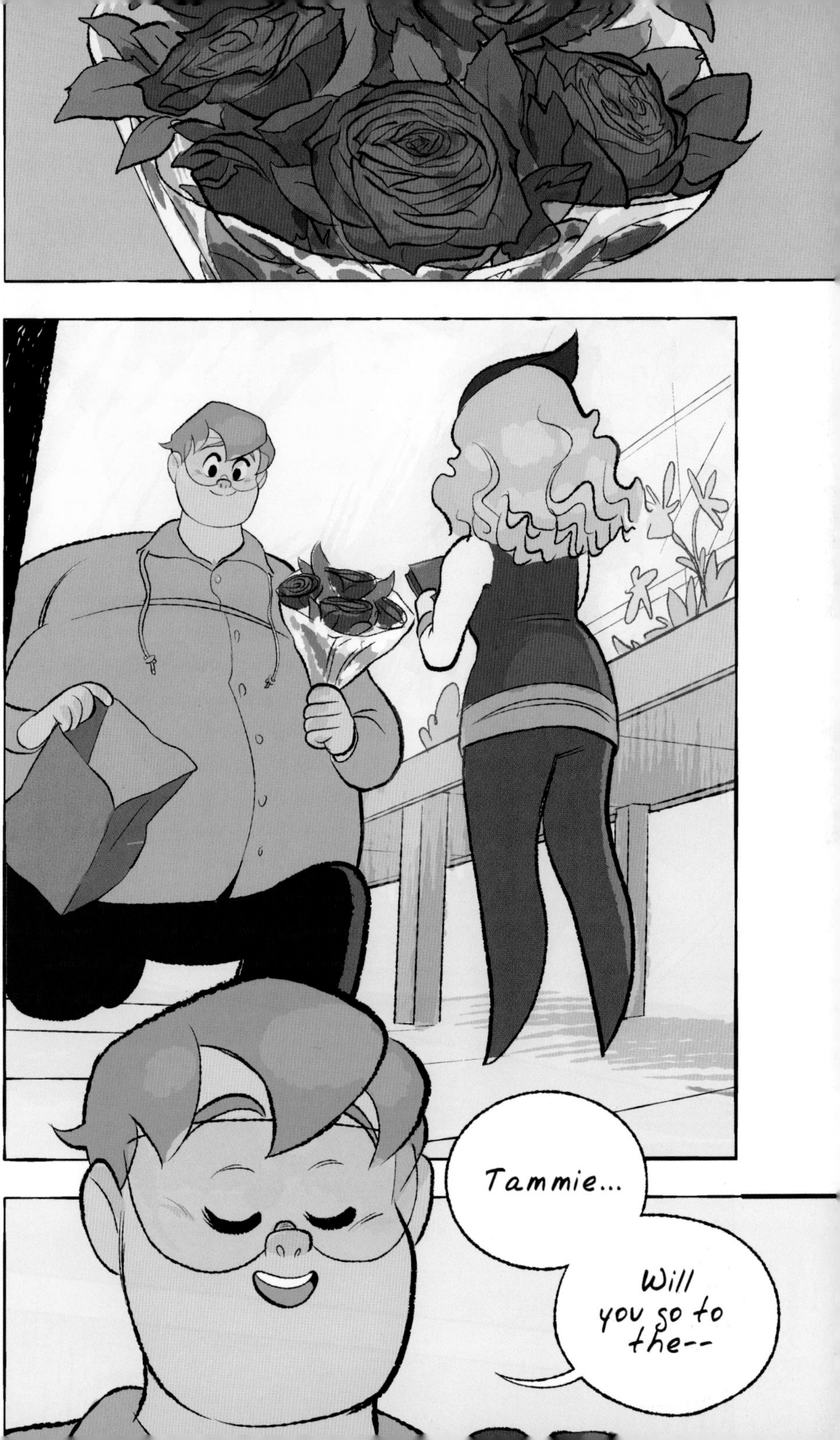
Tammie...
Will you go to the--

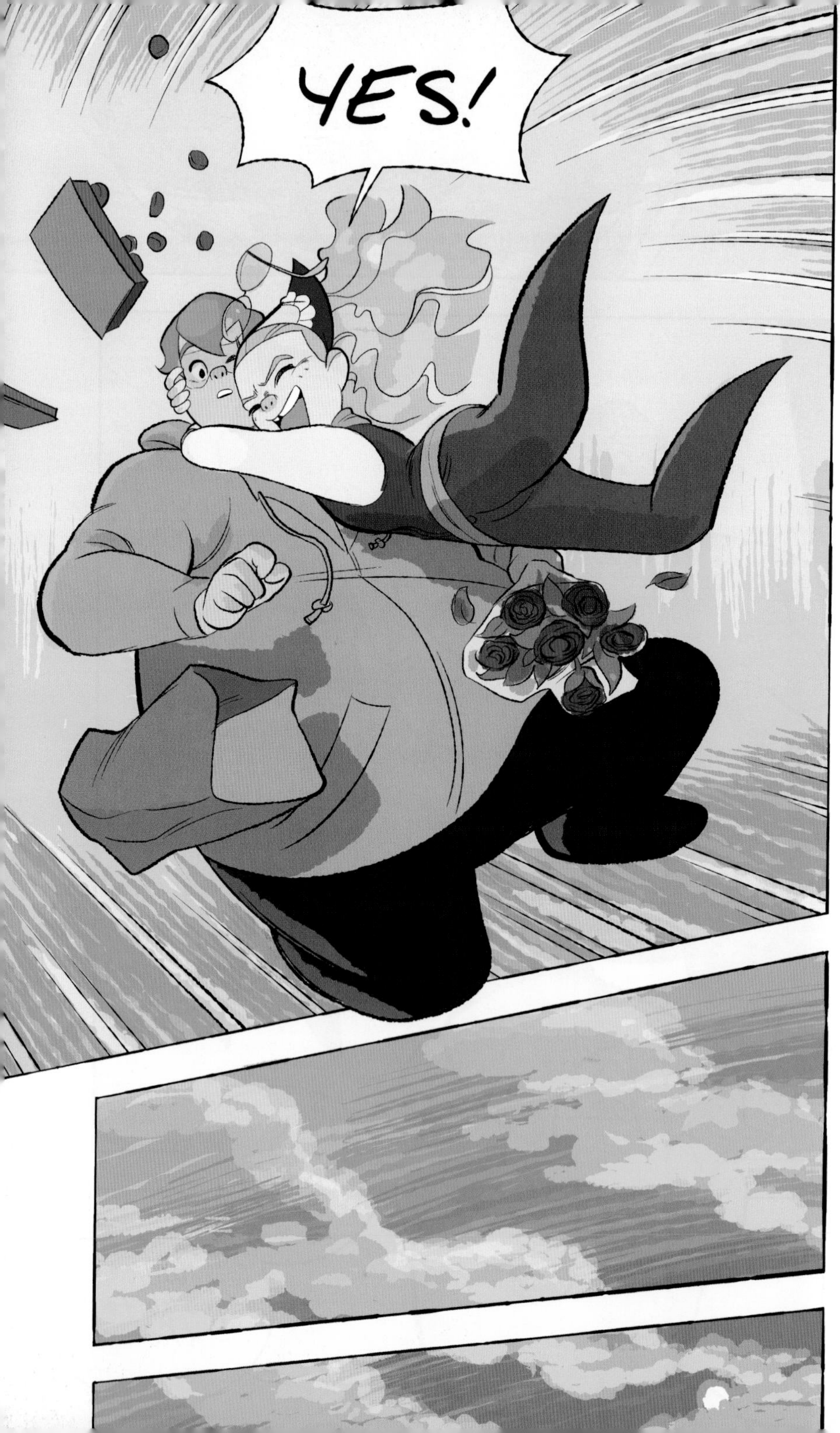
YES!

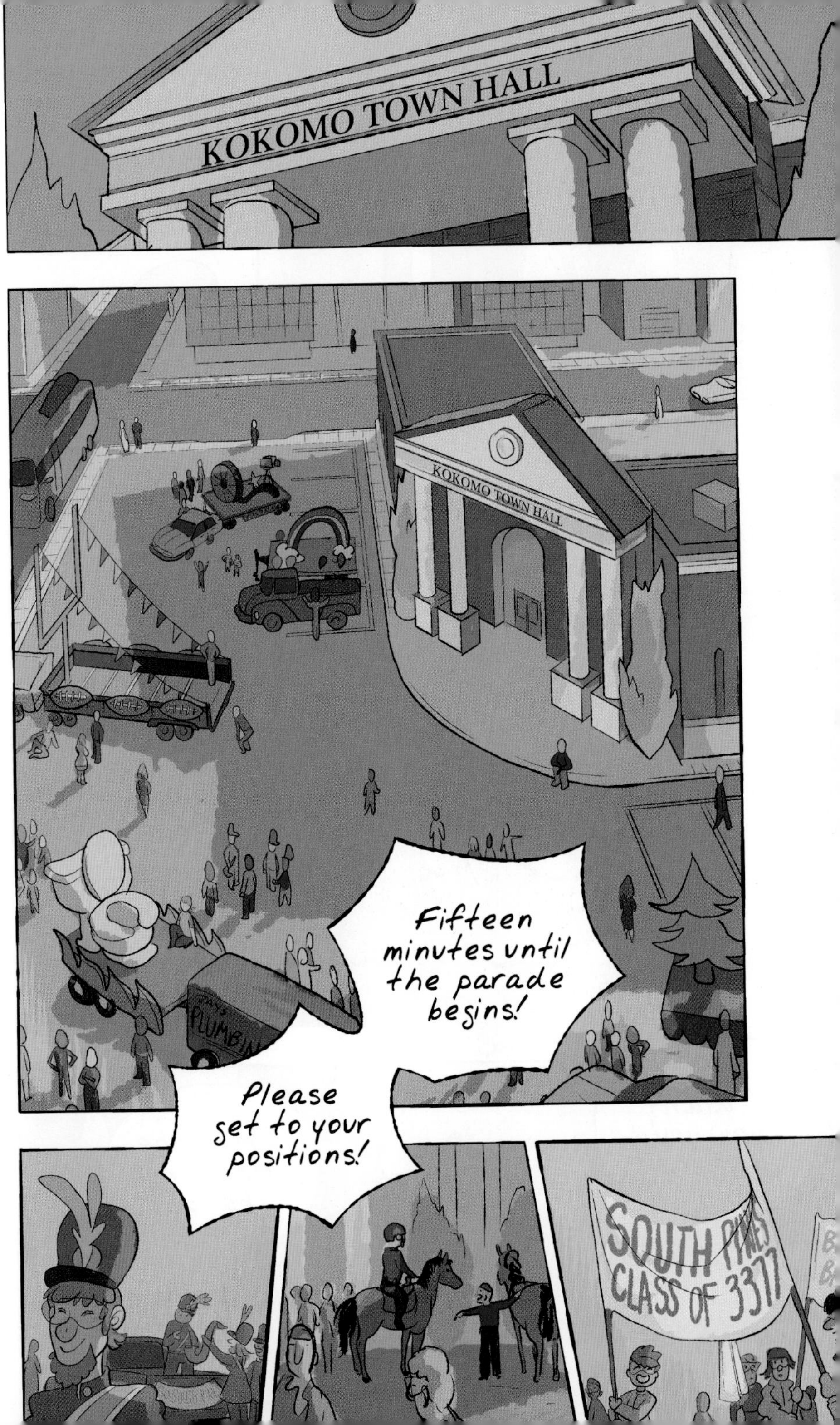
KOKOMO TOWN HALL
KOKOMO TOWN HALL
JAY'S PLUMBIN
Fifteen minutes until the parade begins!
Please get to your positions!
SOUTH PINES CLASS OF 3377

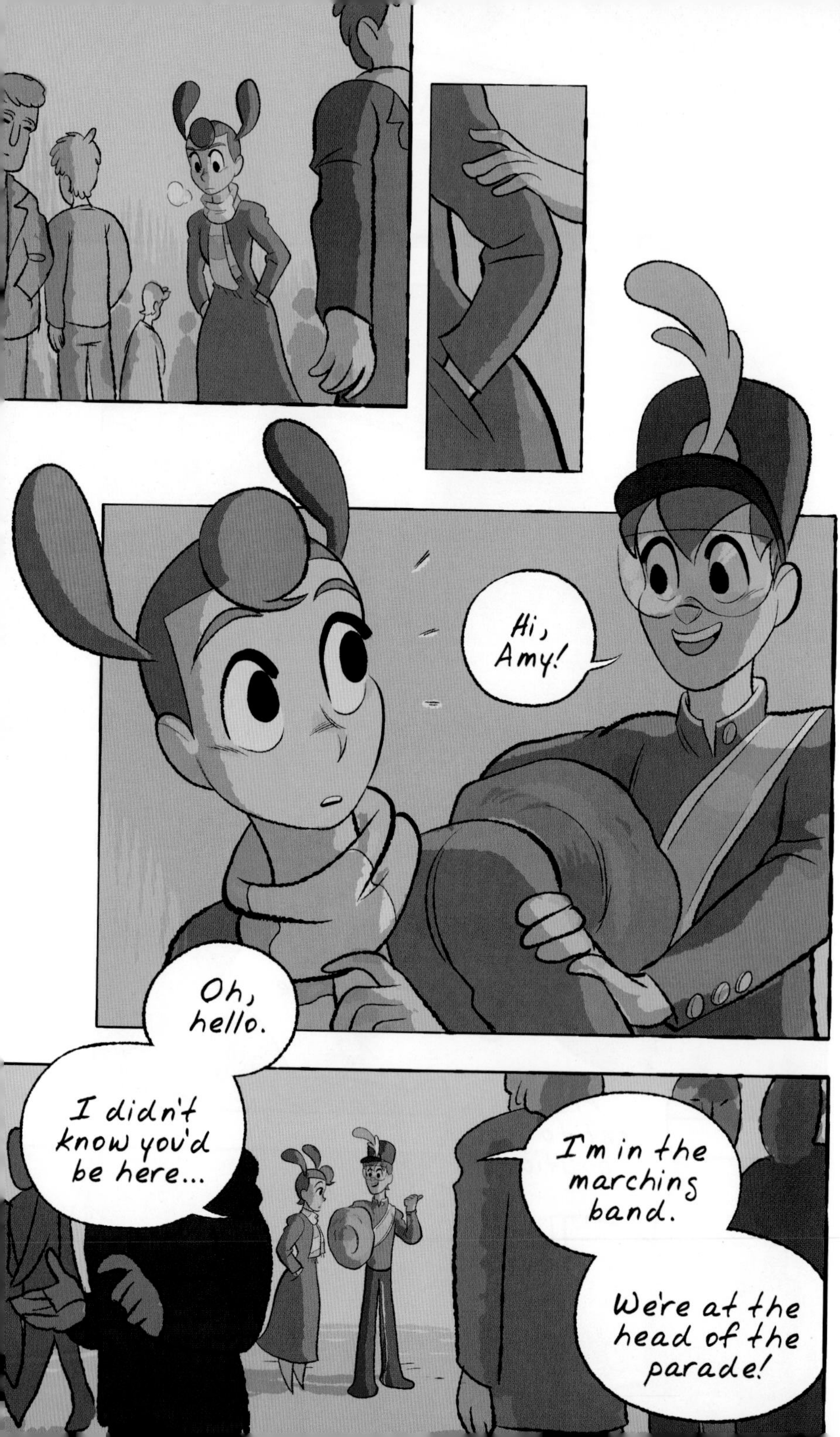
Hi, Amy!
Oh, hello.
I didn't know you'd be here...
I'm in the marching band.
We're at the head of the parade!

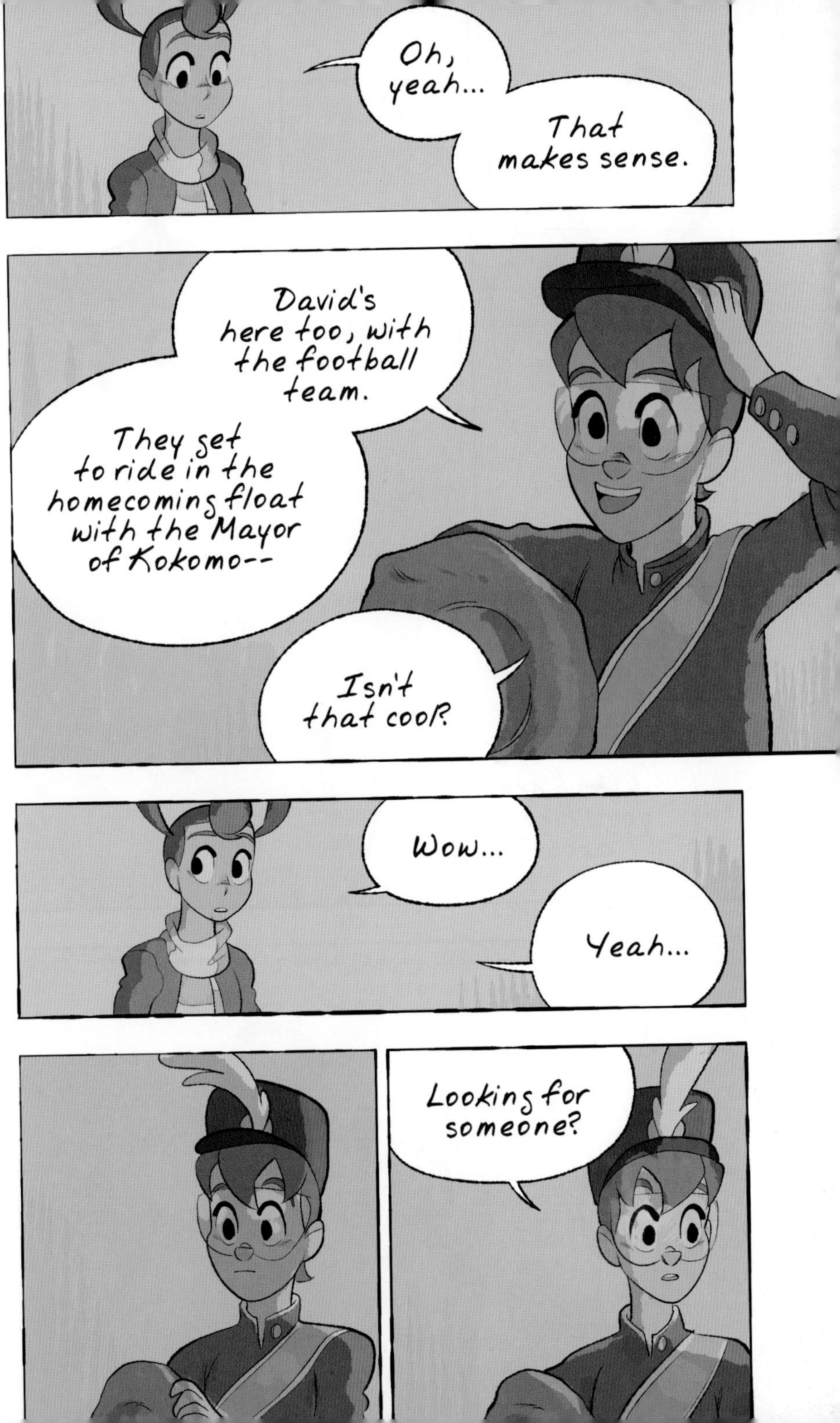
Oh, yeah...
That makes sense.
David's here too, with the football team.
They set to ride in the homecoming float with the Mayor of Kokomo--
Isn't that cool?
Wow...
Yeah...
Looking for someone?

Sorry--

What?

Something on your mind, Amy?

What are you thinking about?

I'm...

I'm trying to figure out what to do.

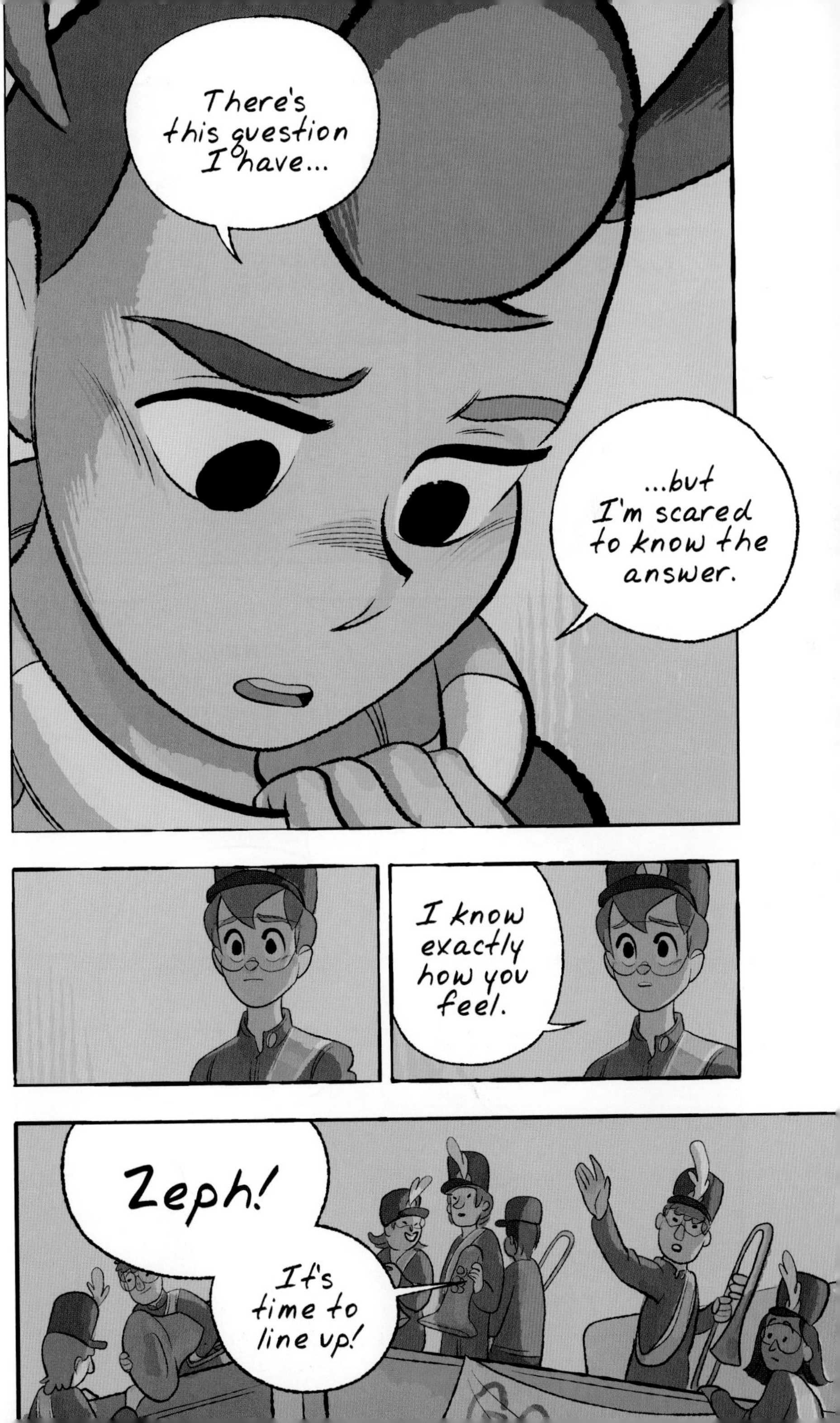
There's this question I have...
...but I'm scared to know the answer.
I know exactly how you feel.
Zeph!
It's time to line up!

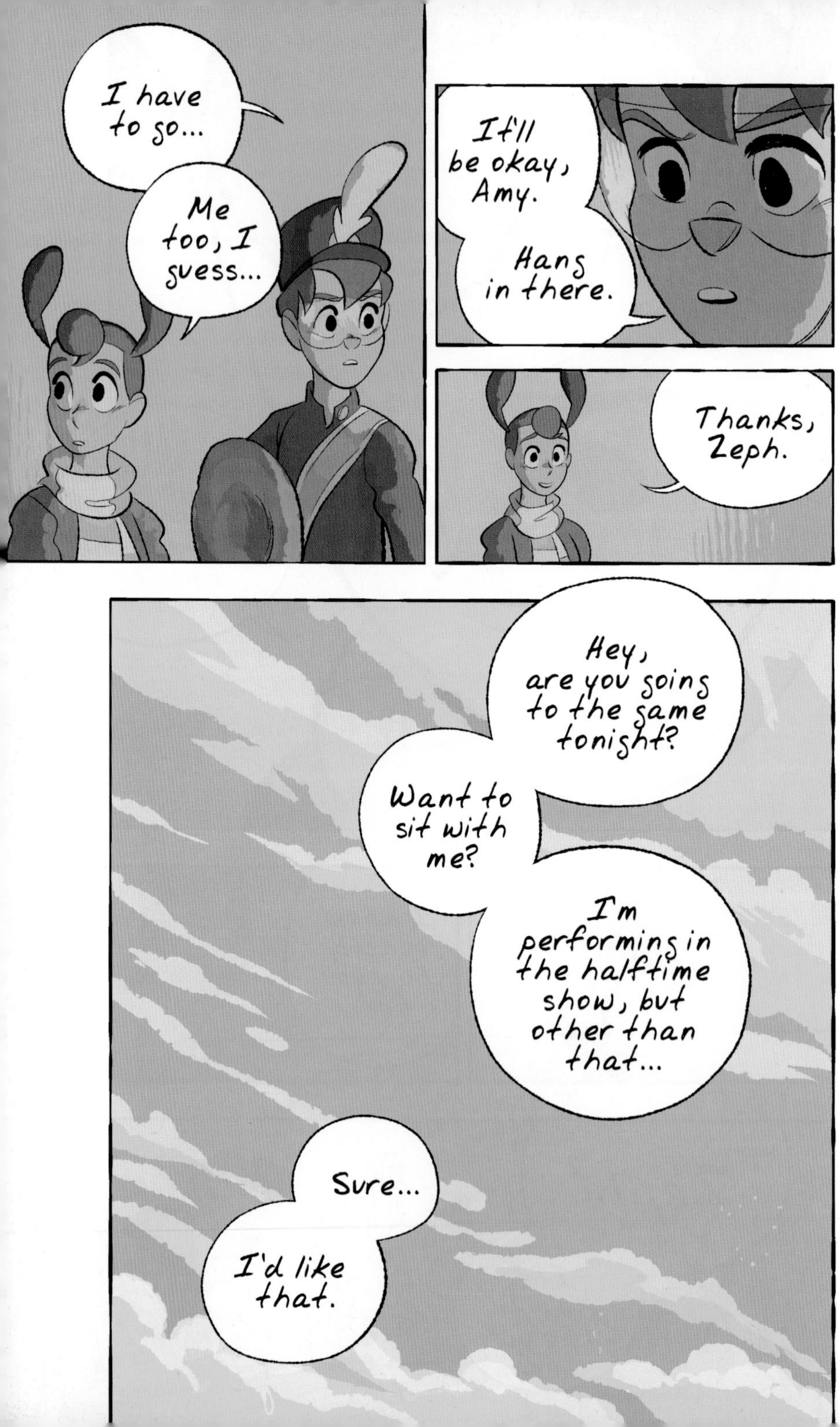

I have to go...
Me too, I guess...
It'll be okay, Amy.
Hang in there.
Thanks, Zeph.
Hey, are you going to the game tonight?
Want to sit with me?
I'm performing in the halftime show, but other than that...
Sure...
I'd like that.

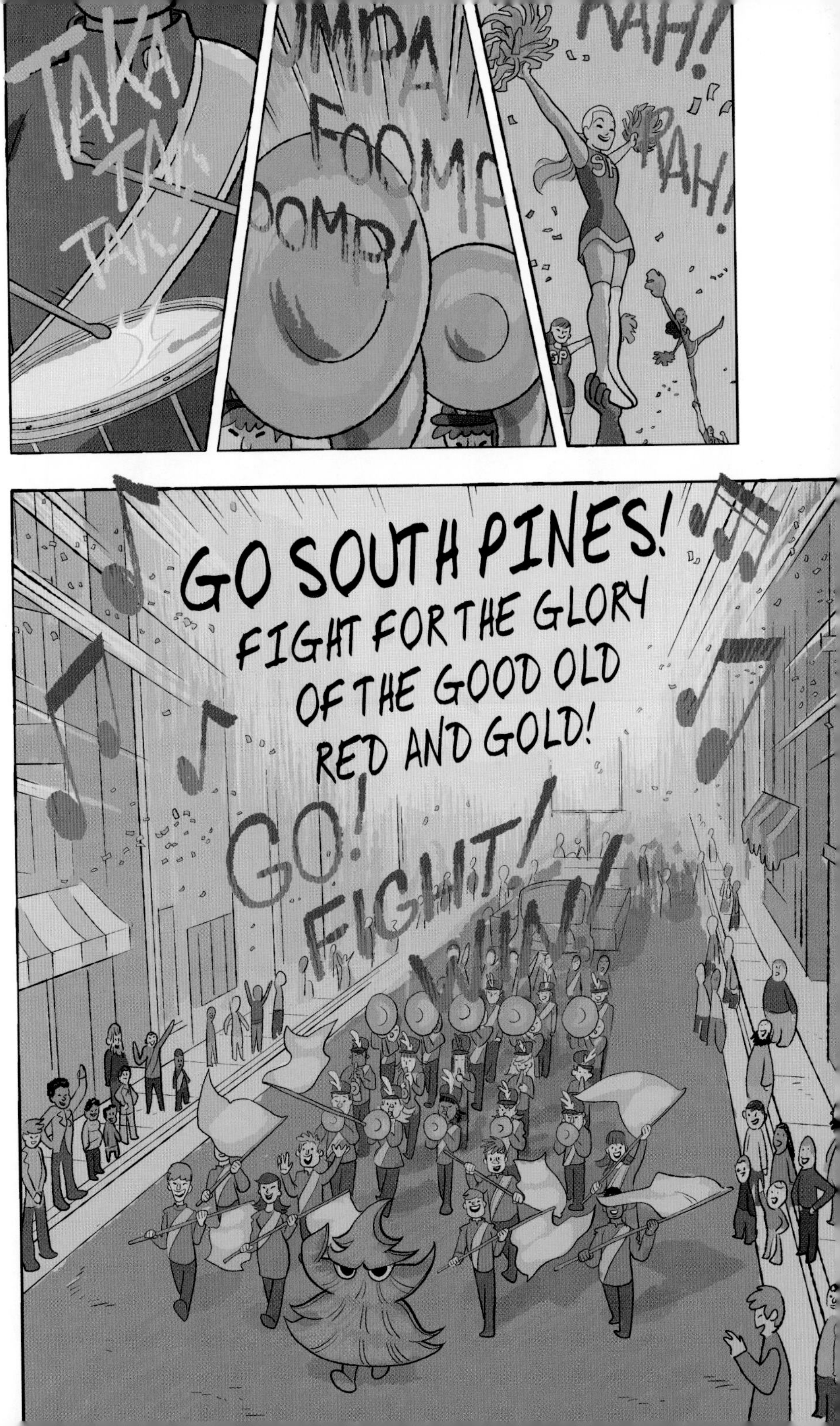
TAKA
TA!
TA!
FOOMP
RAH!
GO SOUTH PINES!
FIGHT FOR THE GLORY
OF THE GOOD OLD
RED AND GOLD!
GO!
FIGHT!
WIN!

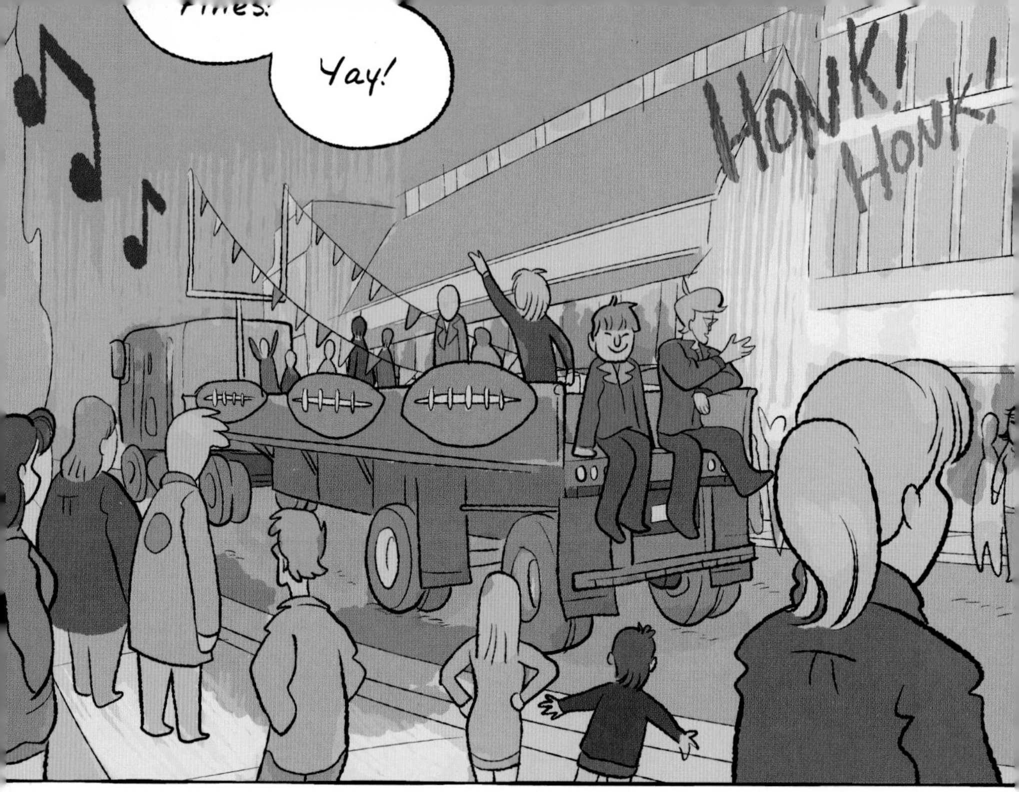
Yay!
HONK!
HONK!

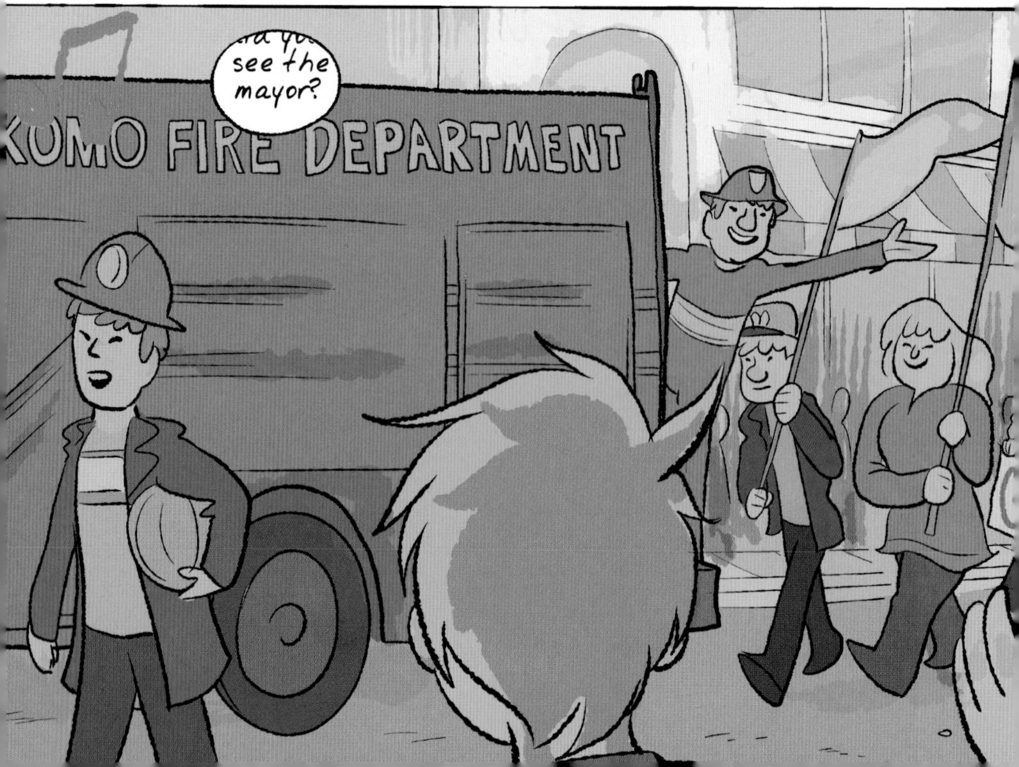
see the mayor?
FIRE DEPARTMENT

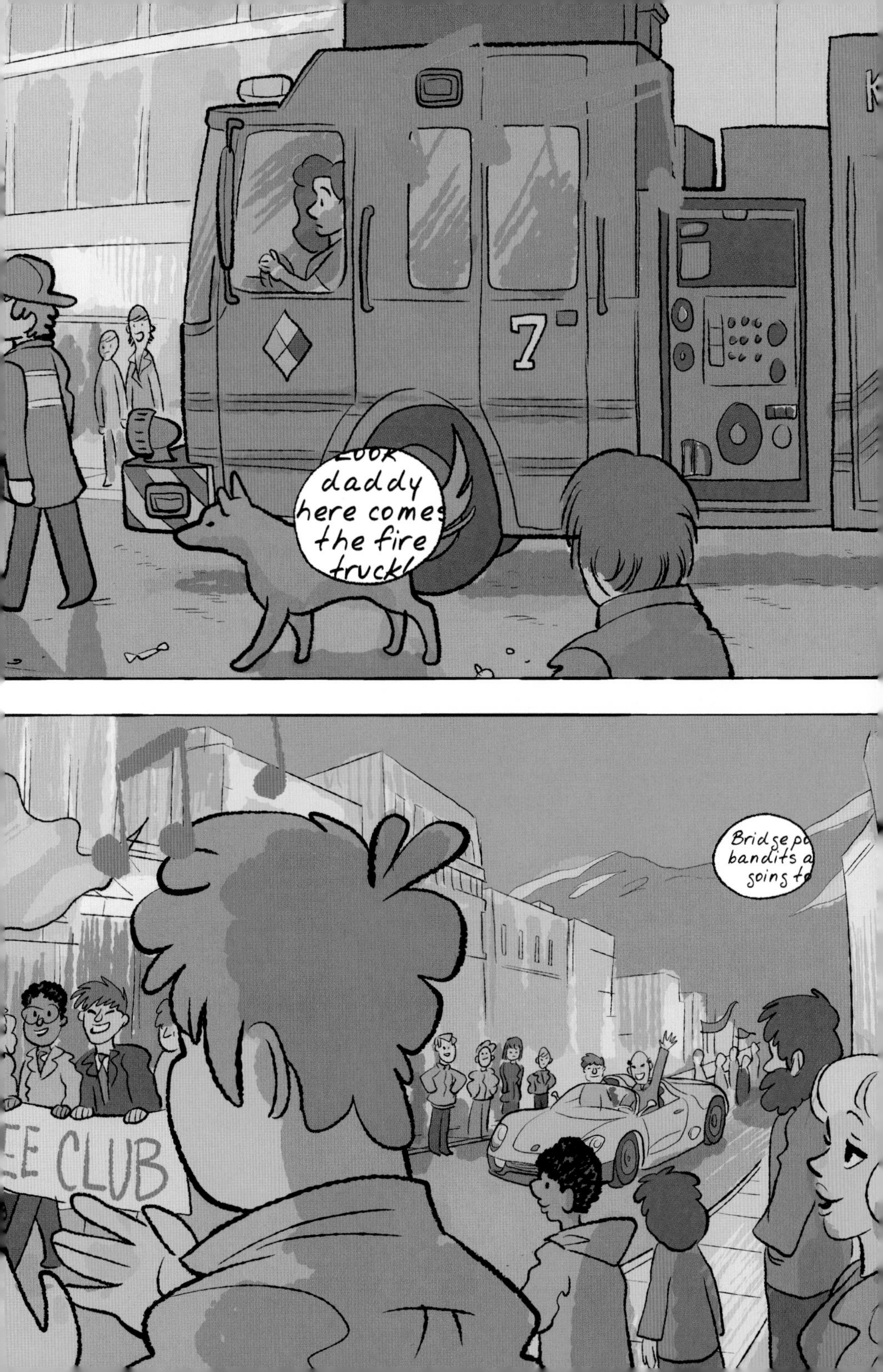
daddy here comes the fire
7
bandits
CLUB

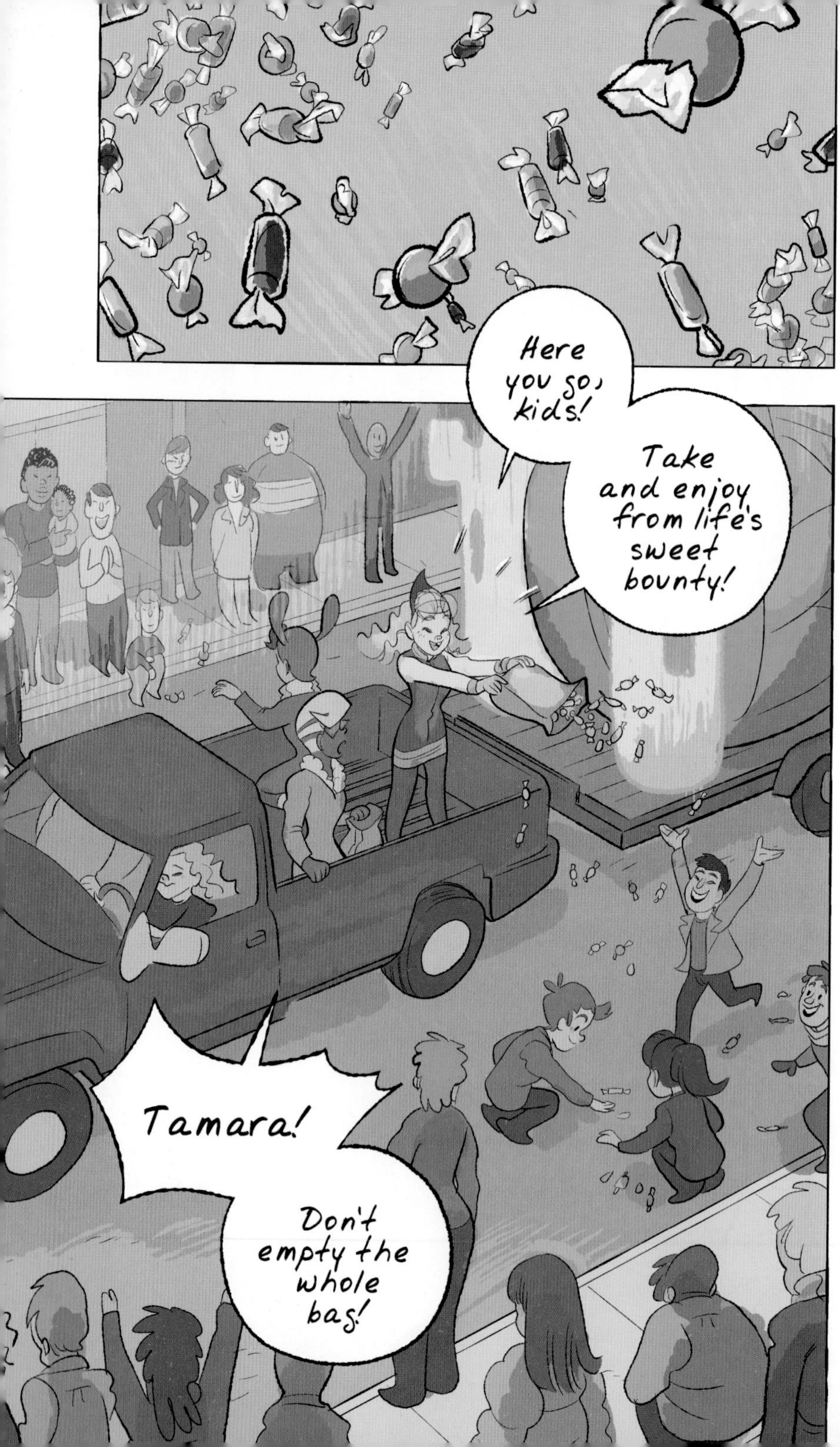
Here you go, kids!
Take and enjoy from life's sweet bounty!
Tamara!
Don't empty the whole bag!

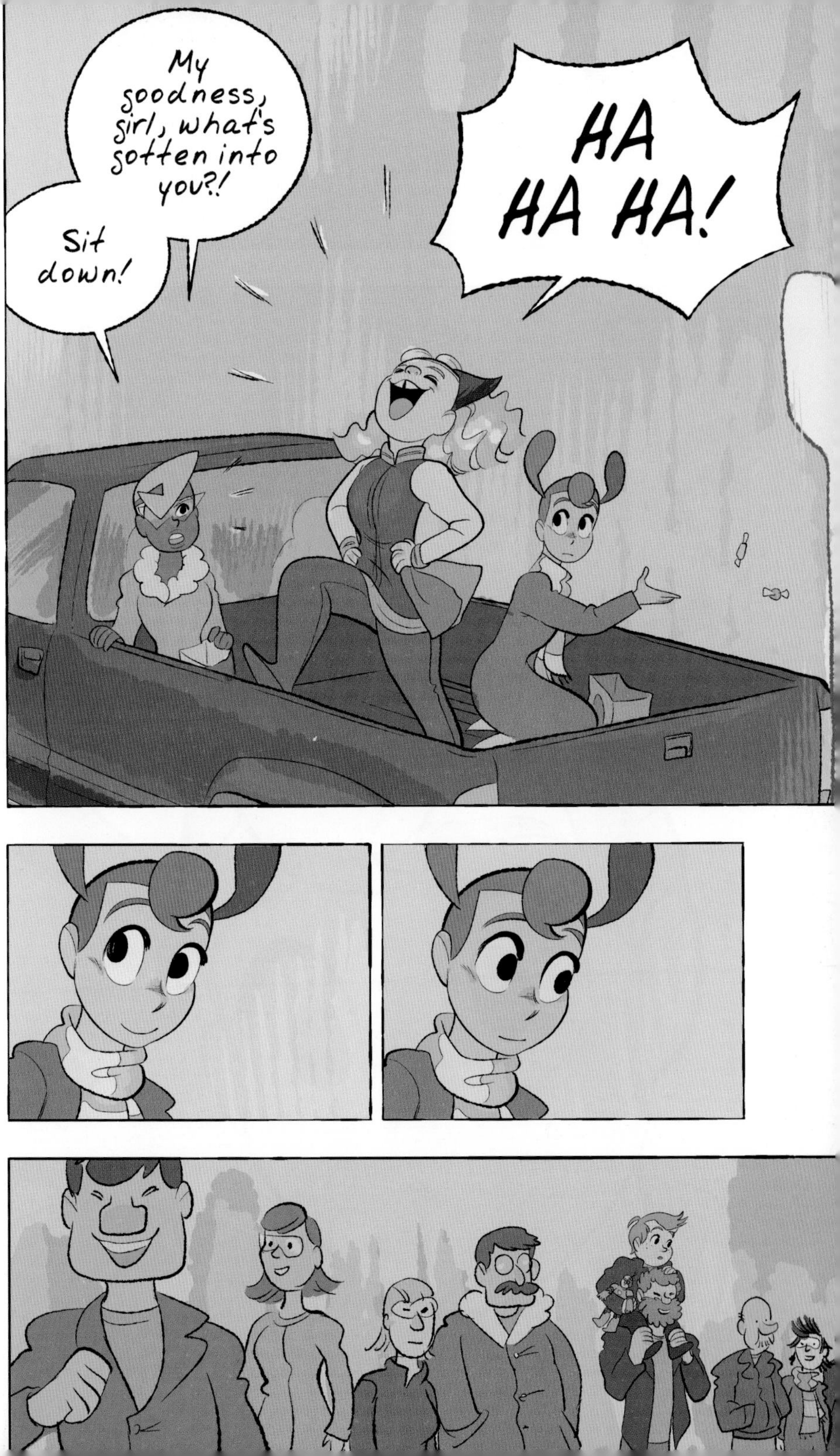
My goodness, girl, what's gotten into you?!
Sit down!
HA HA HA HA!

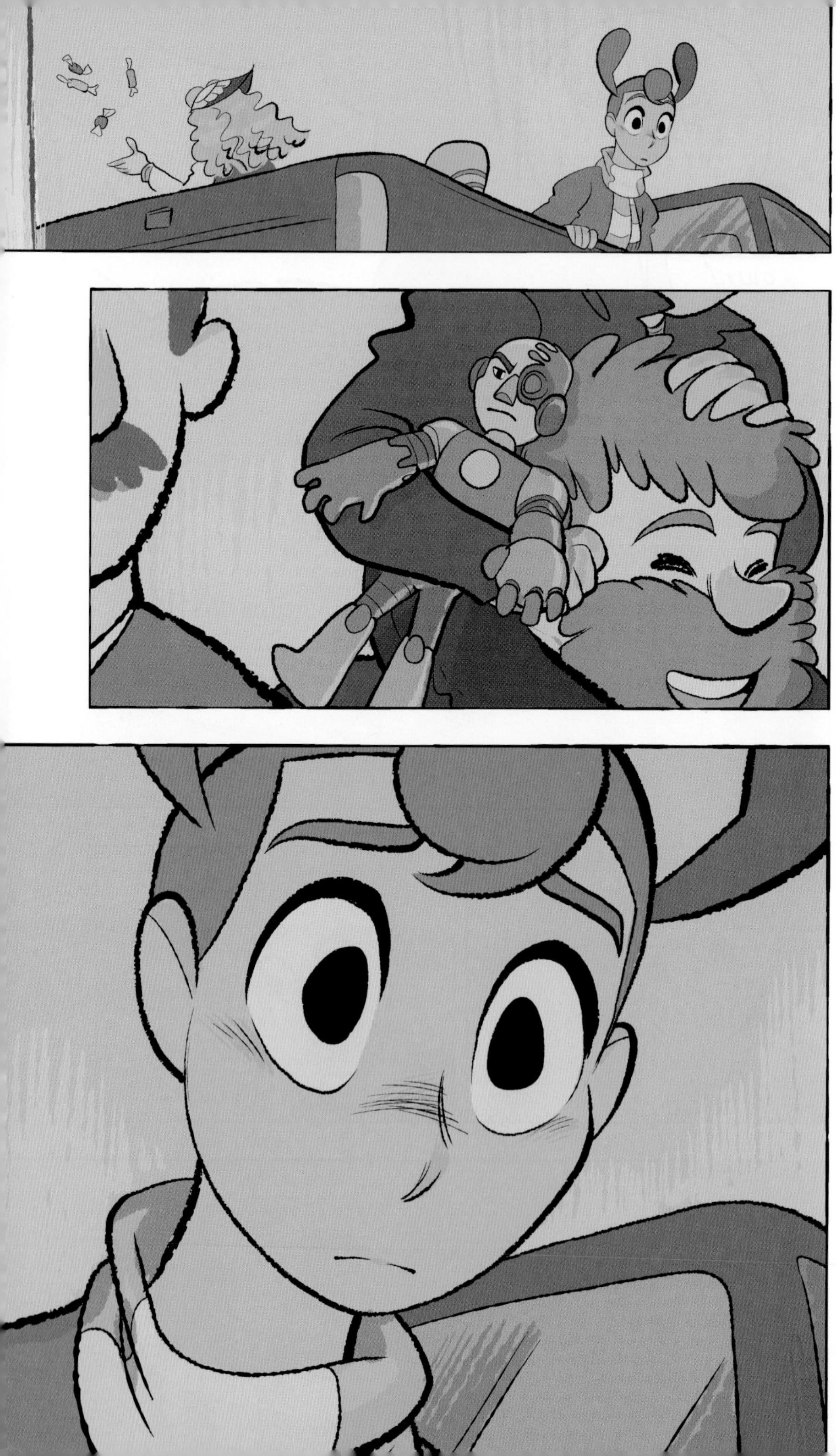

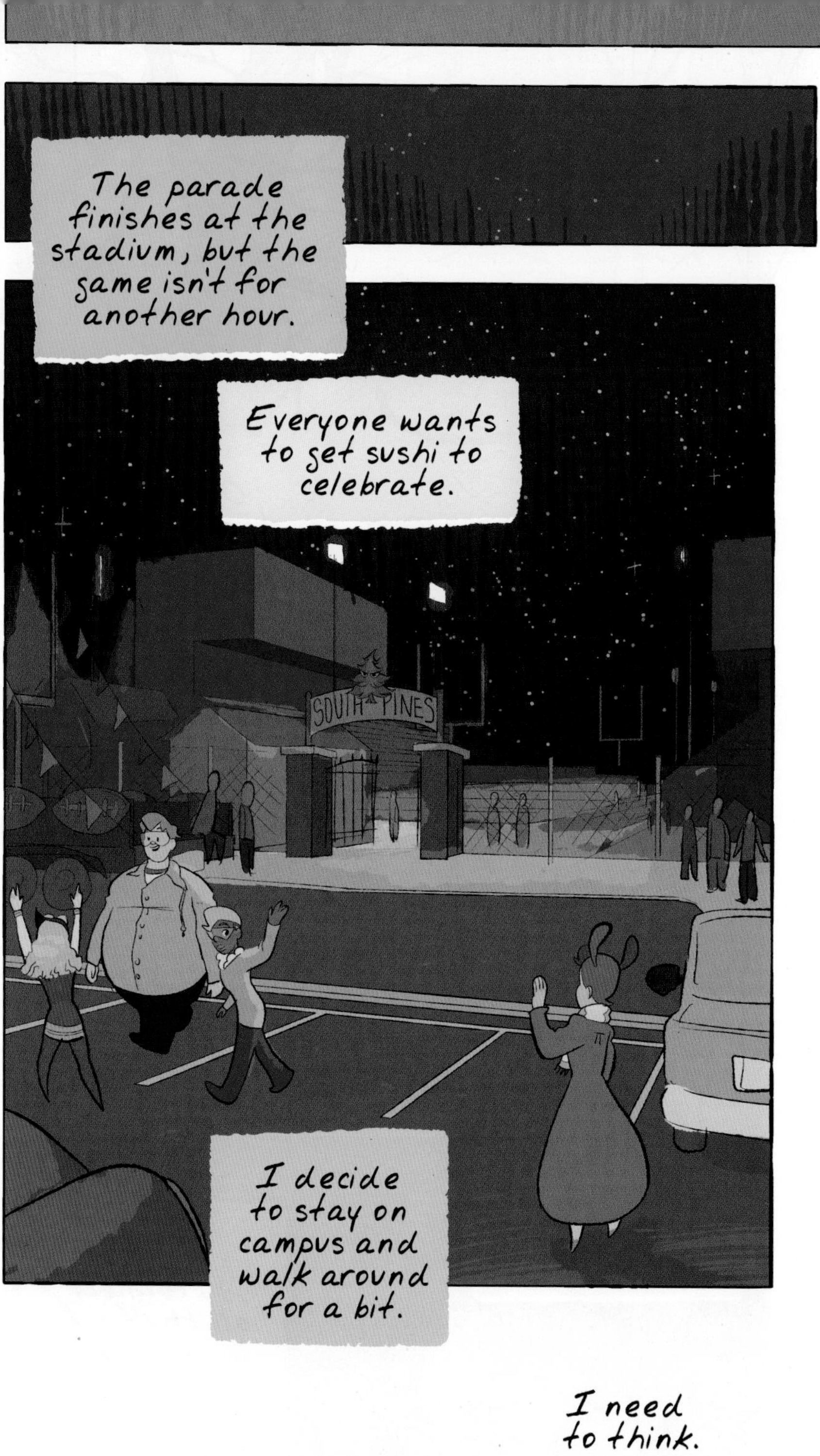
The parade finishes at the stadium, but the game isn't for another hour.
Everyone wants to get sushi to celebrate.
SOUTH PINES
I decide to stay on campus and walk around for a bit.

I need to think.

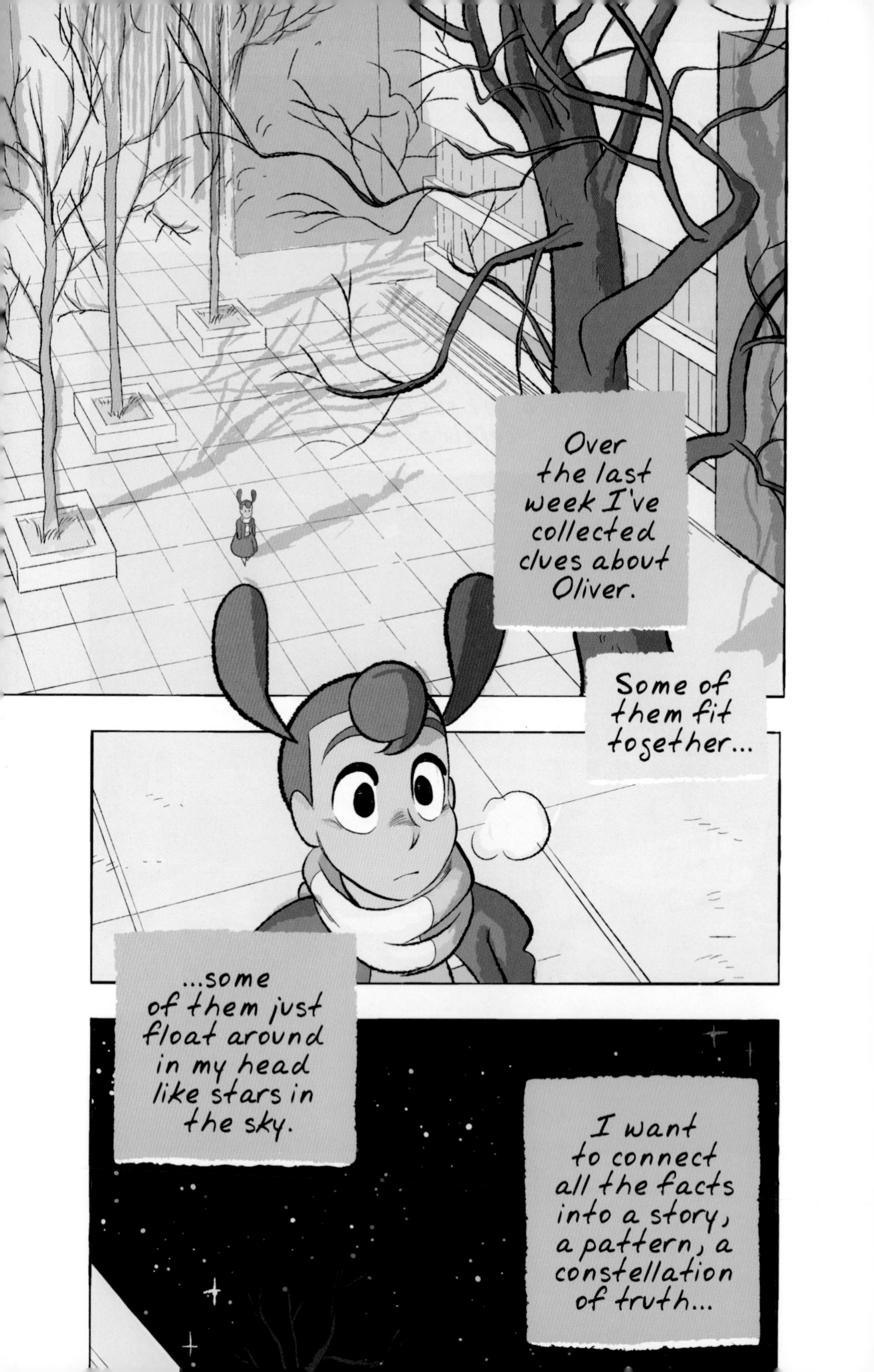
Over the last week I've collected clues about Oliver.
Some of them fit together...
...some of them just float around in my head like stars in the sky.
I want to connect all the facts into a story, a pattern, a constellation of truth...

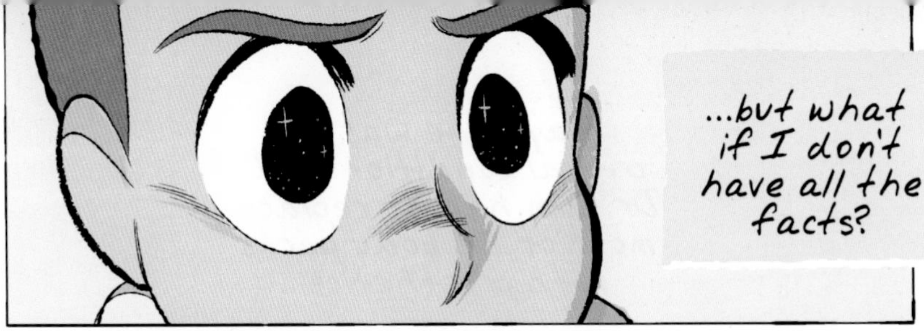
...but what if I don't have all the facts?

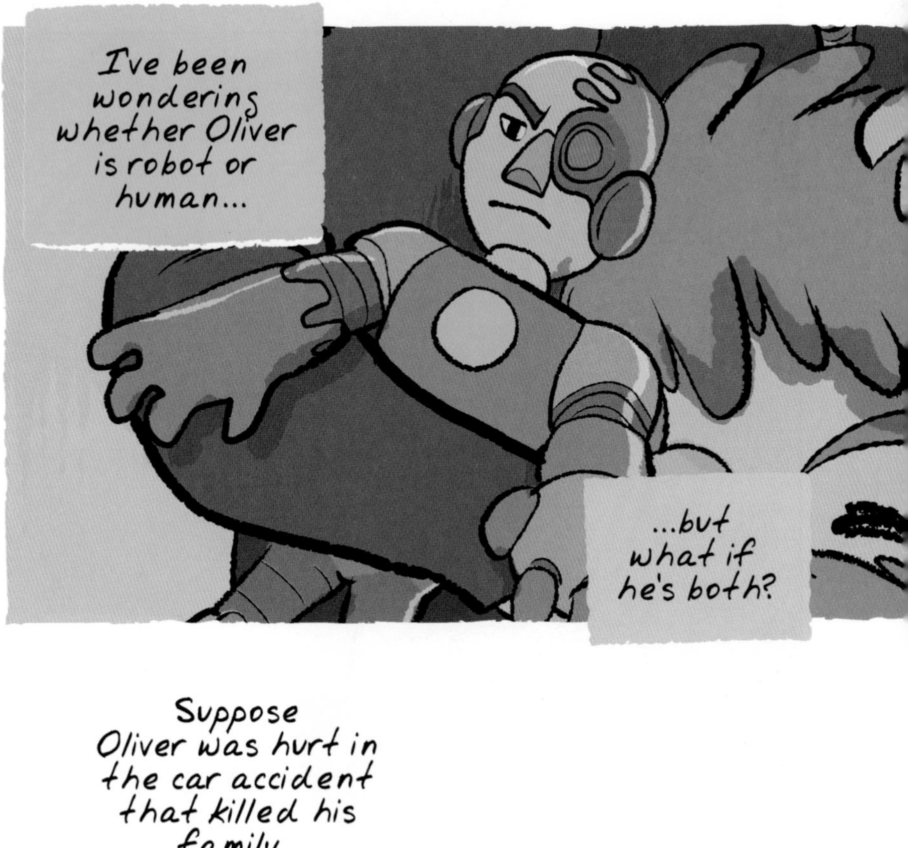
I've been wondering whether Oliver is robot or human...
...but what if he's both?

Suppose Oliver was hurt in the car accident that killed his family...

Perhaps he was taken to the hospital where Dr. Kim worked...

Maybe he was in critical condition and Dr. Kim had to replace most of his body parts with prosthetics...

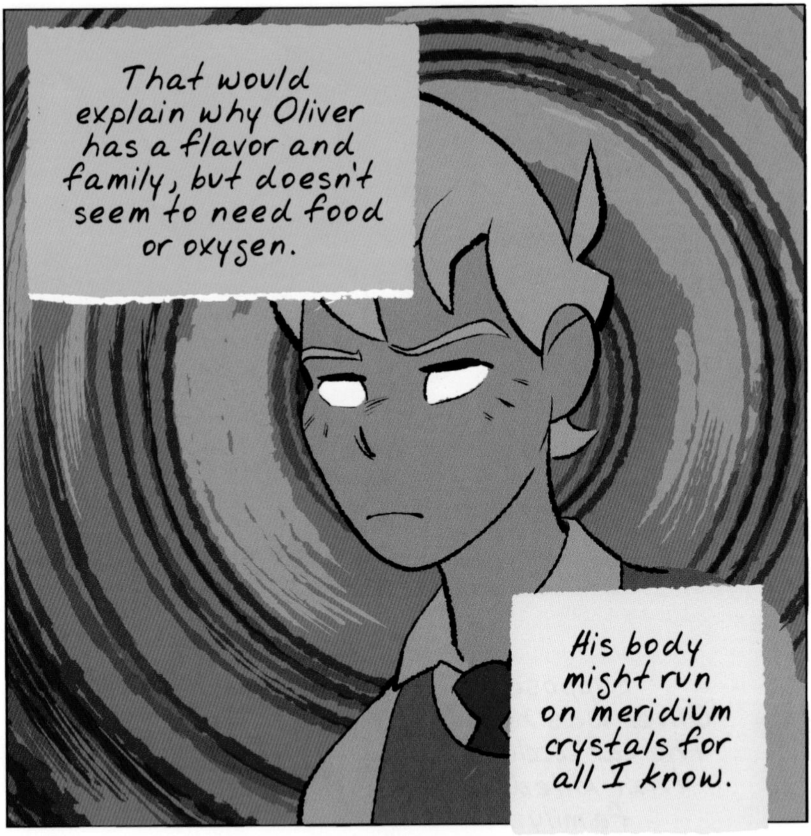
That would explain why Oliver has a flavor and family, but doesn't seem to need food or oxygen.
His body might run on meridium crystals for all I know.

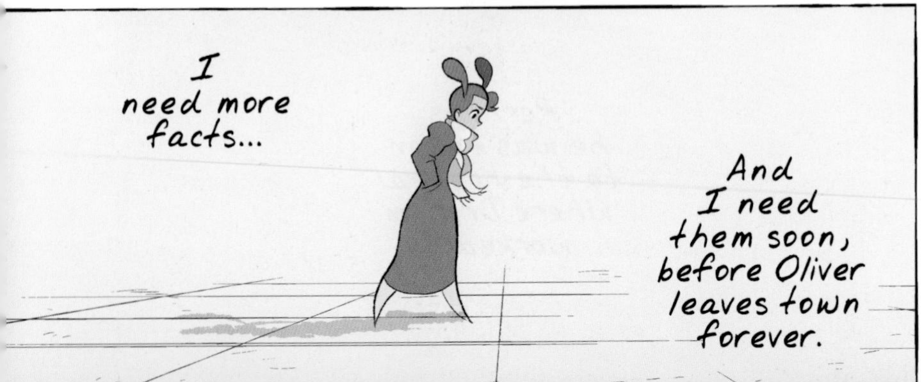
I need more facts...
And I need them soon, before Oliver leaves town forever.

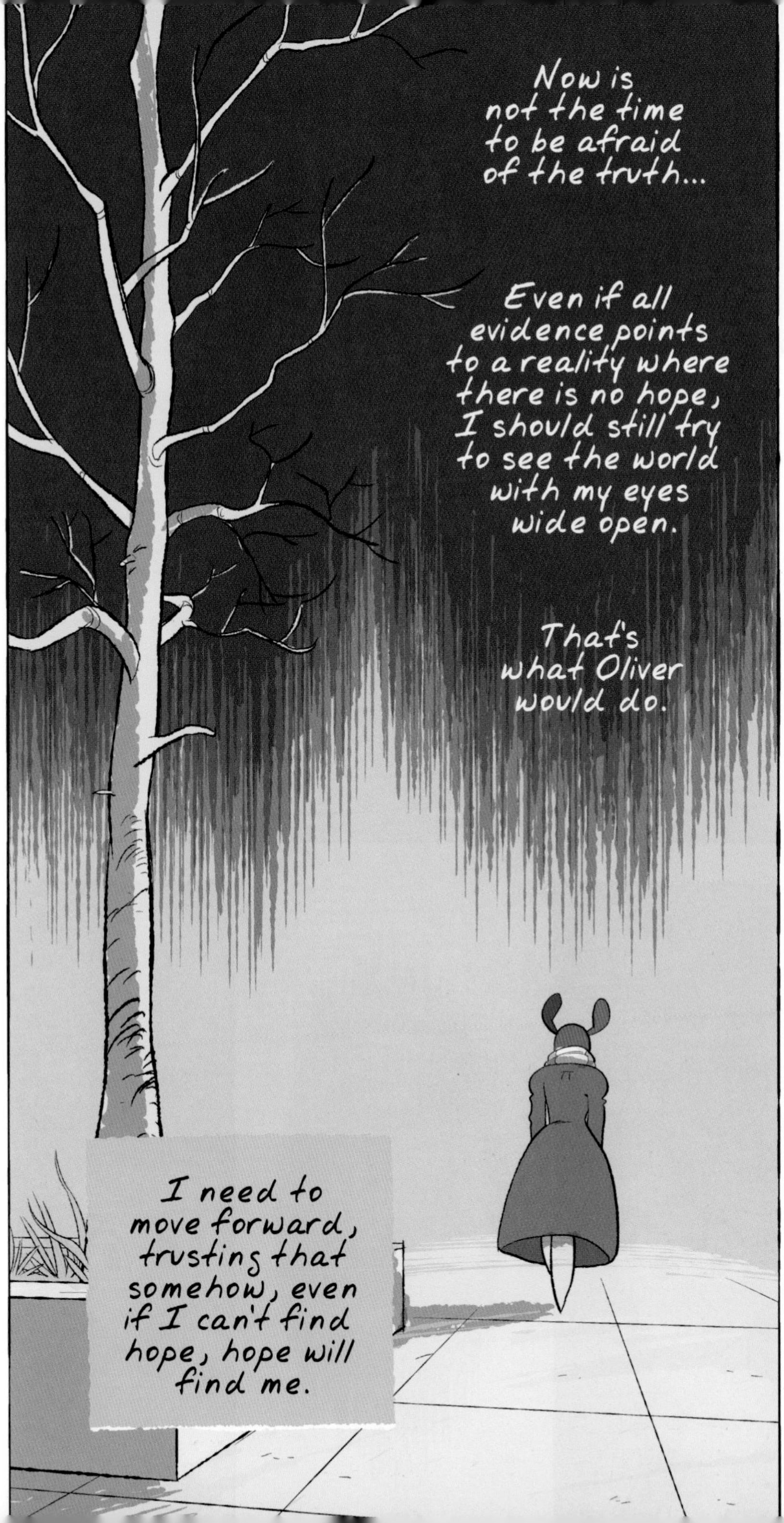
Now is not the time to be afraid of the truth...
Even if all evidence points to a reality where there is no hope, I should still try to see the world with my eyes wide open.
That's what Oliver would do.
I need to move forward, trusting that somehow, even if I can't find hope, hope will find me.

And besides, I made a promise.

I have to try.

So...

What's the next step?

Where do I go from here?

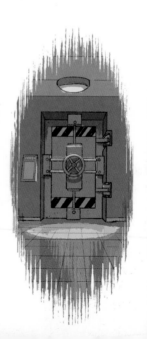

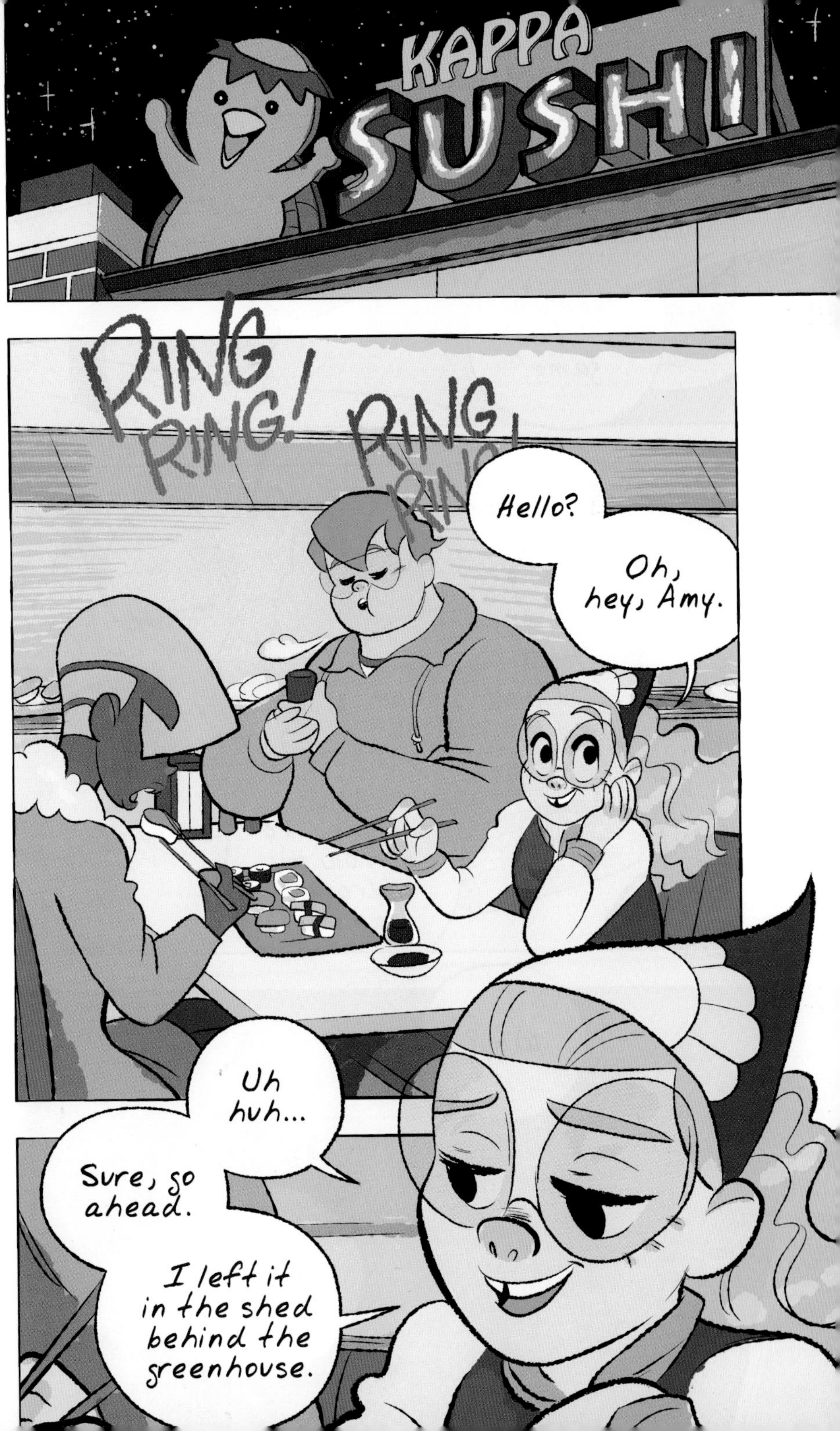
KAPPA SUSHI
RING RING!
RING RING!
Hello?
Oh, hey, Amy.
Uh huh...
Sure, go ahead.
I left it in the shed behind the greenhouse.

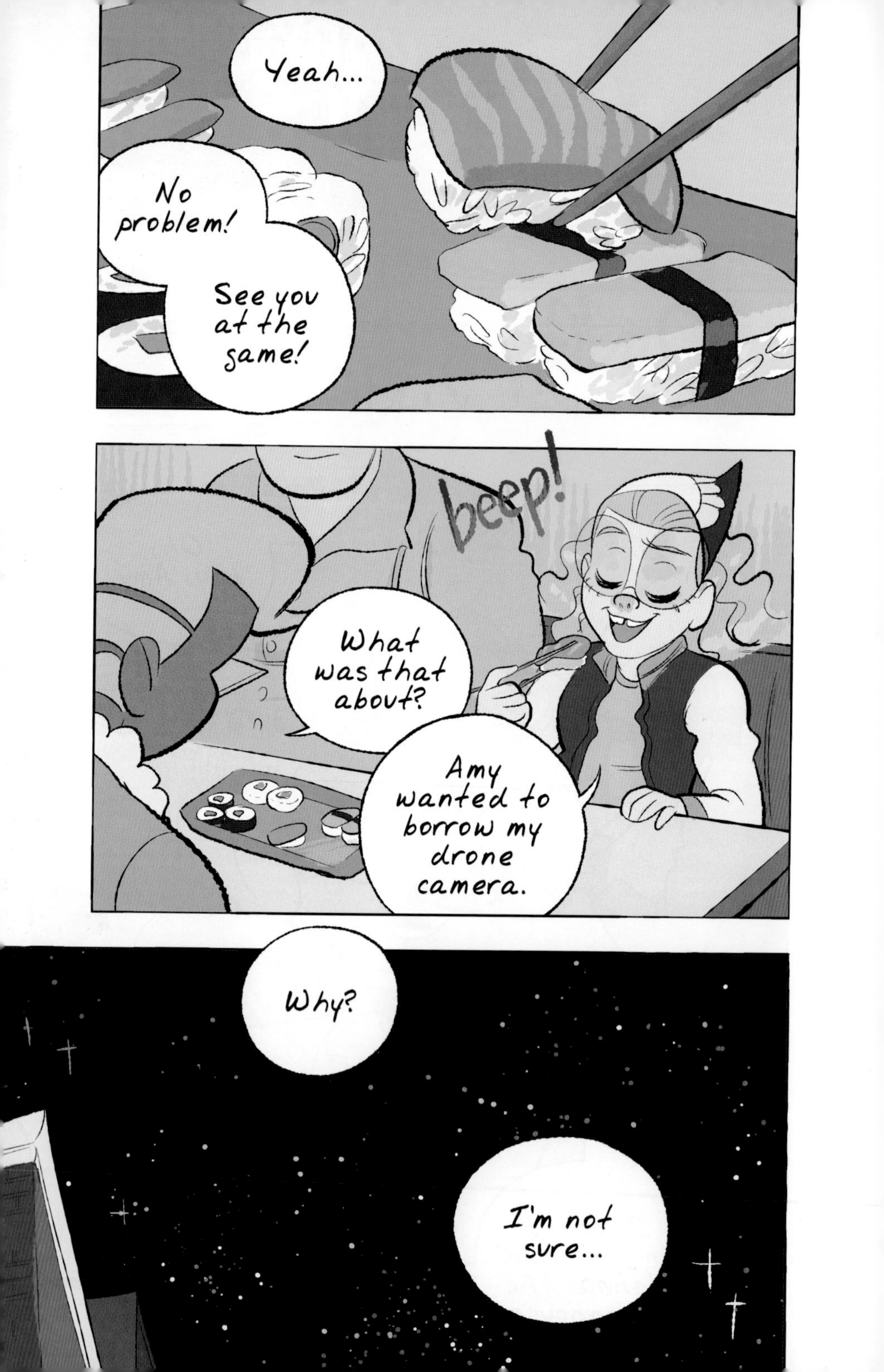
Yeah...
No problem!
See you at the game!
beep!
What was that about?
Amy wanted to borrow my drone camera.
Why?
I'm not sure...

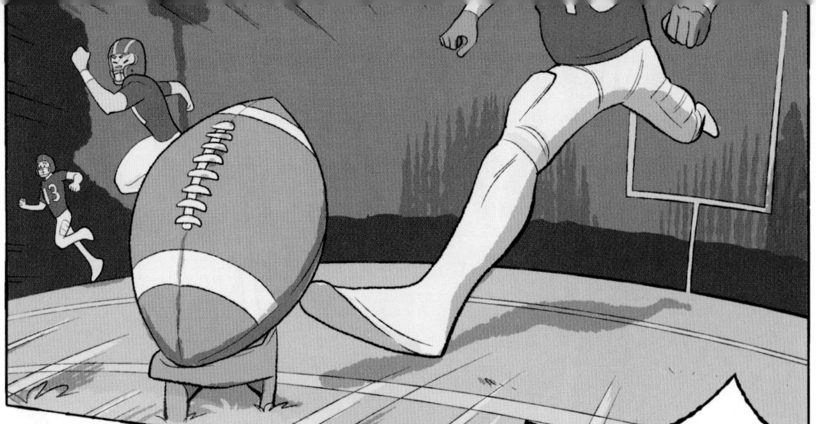

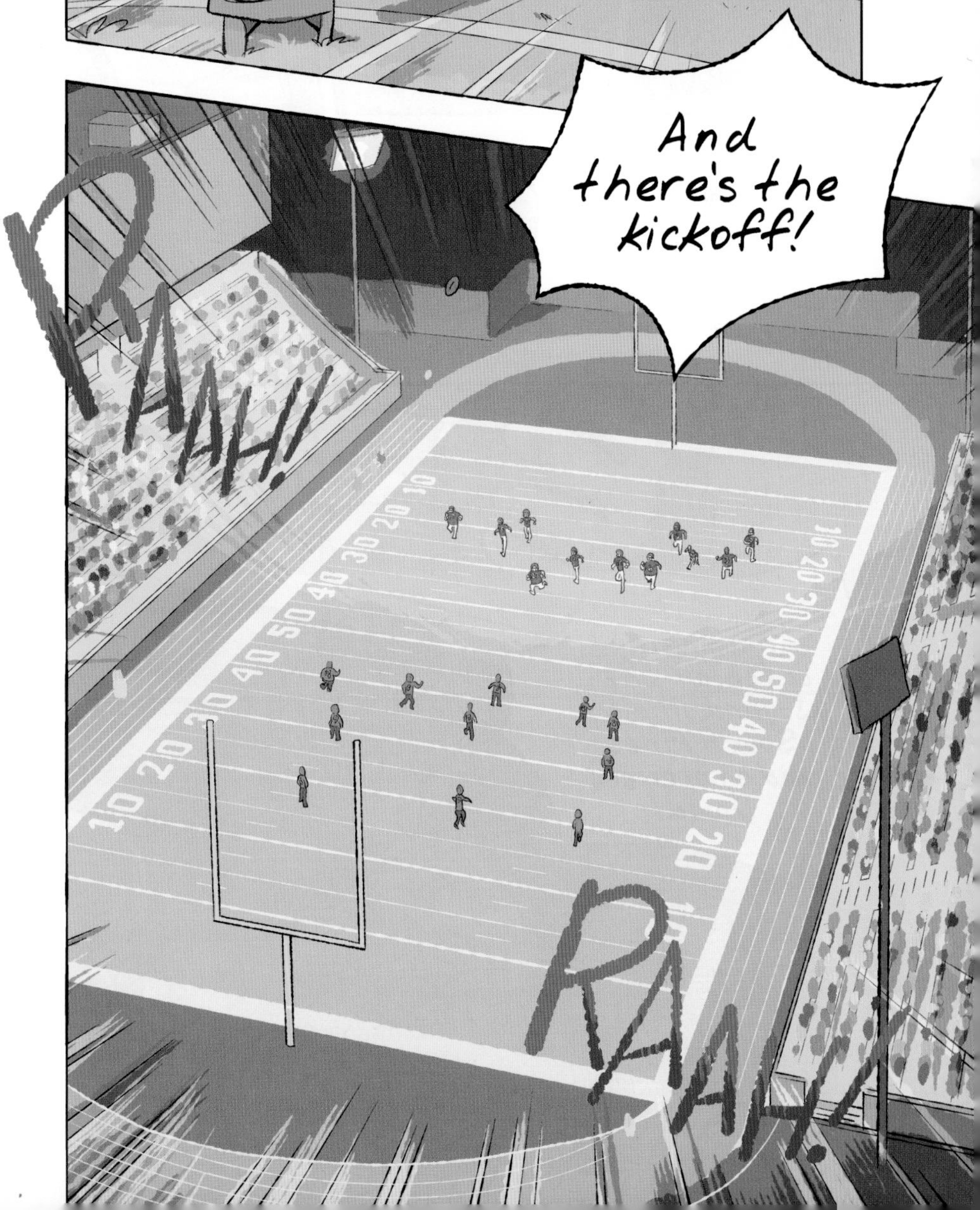
And there's the kickoff!
RAAH!
RAAH!

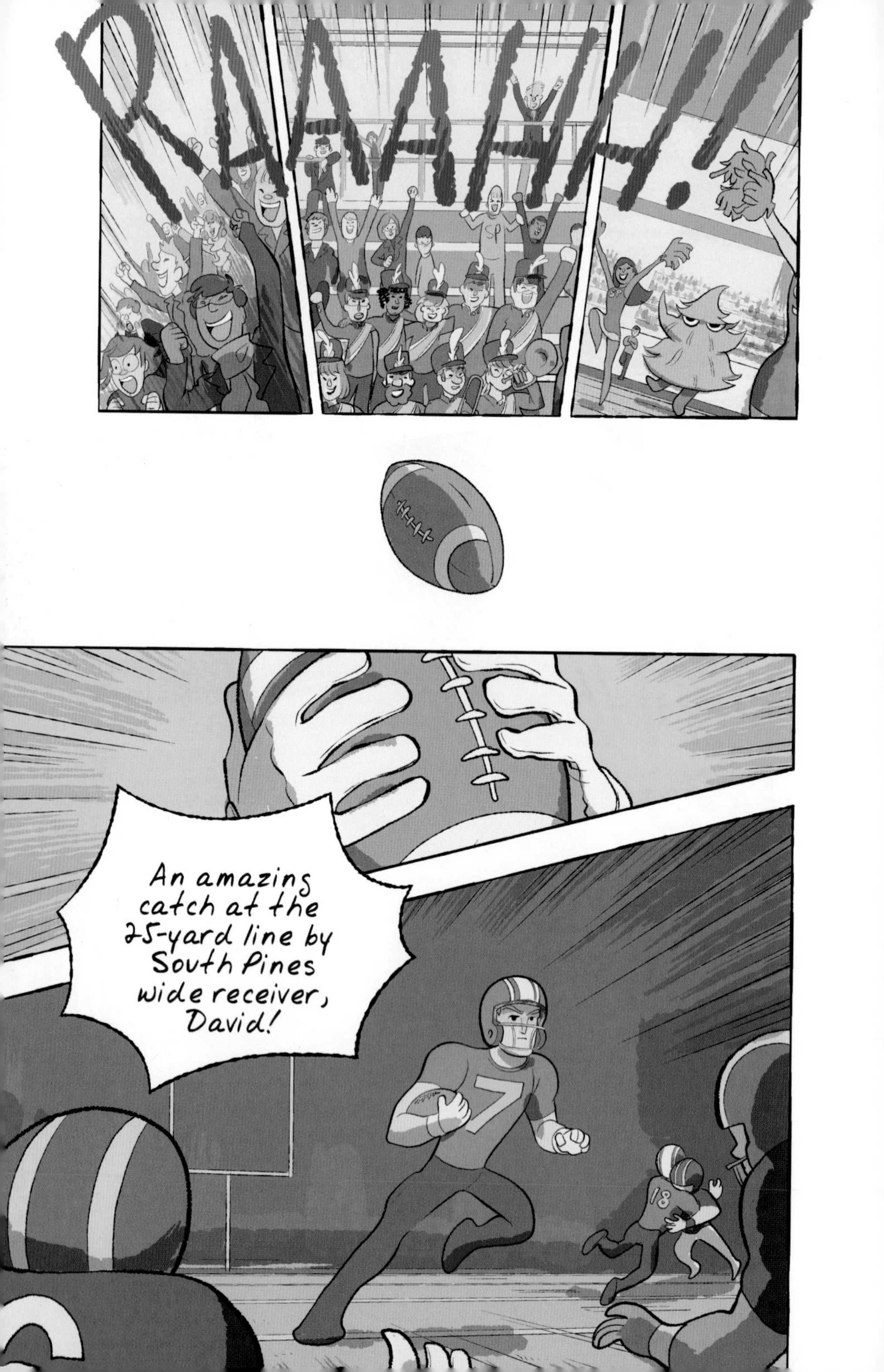
RAAAHH!!
An amazing catch at the 25-yard line by South Pines wide receiver, David!

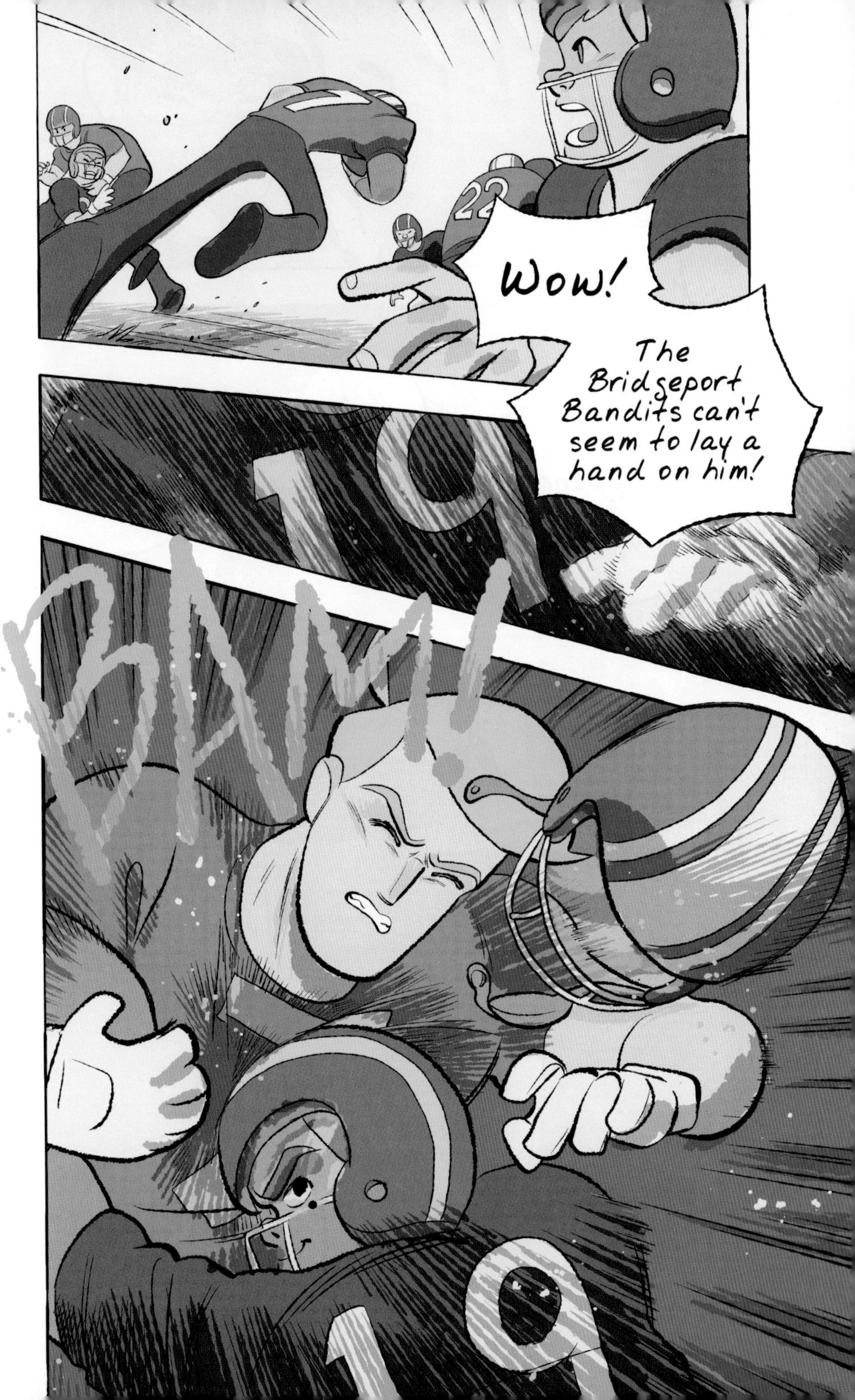
Wow!
The Bridgeport Bandits can't seem to lay a hand on him!
BAM!

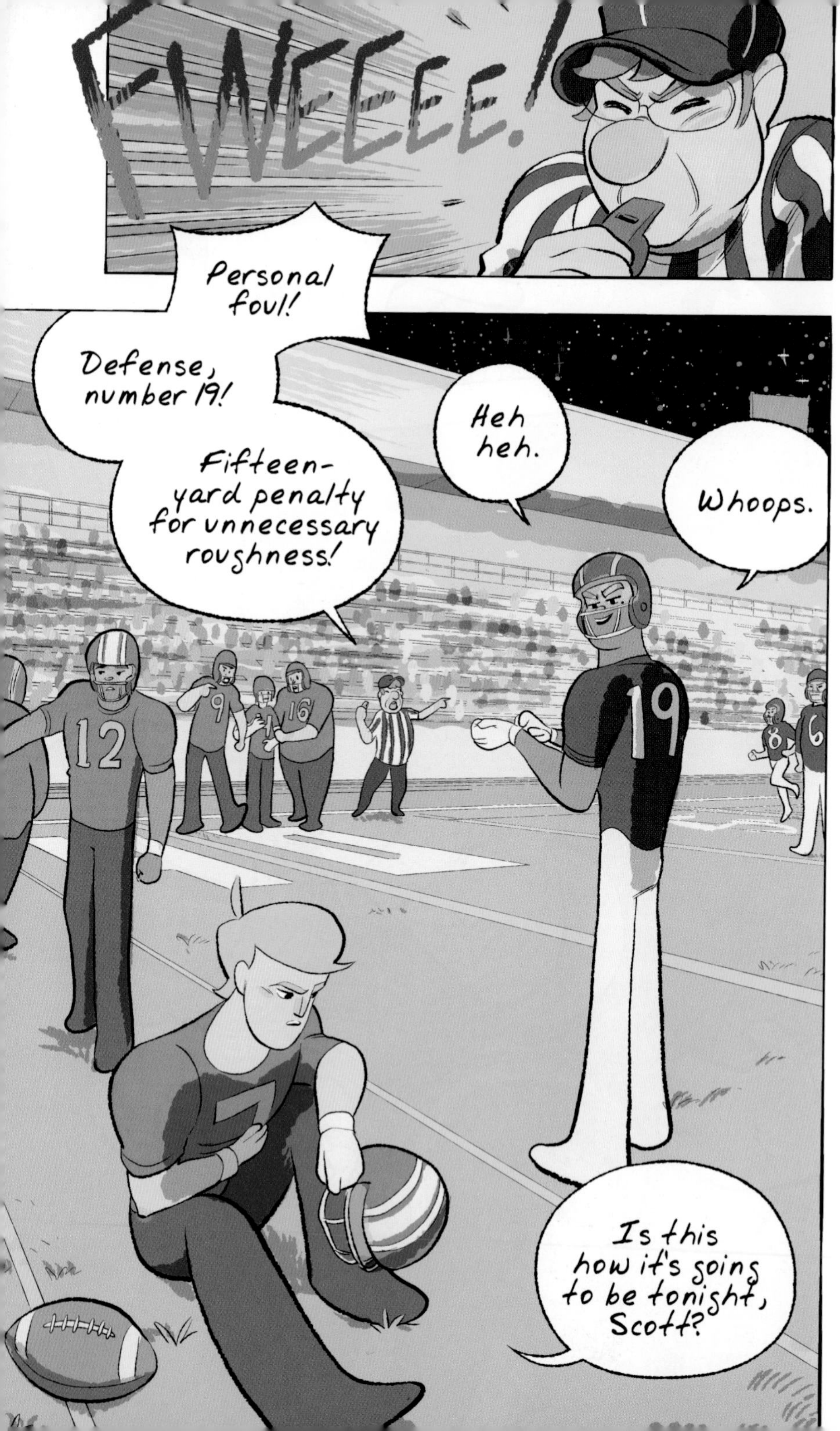
FWEEEE!
Personal foul!
Defense, number 19!
Fifteen-yard penalty for unnecessary roughness!
Heh heh.
Whoops.
Is this how it's going to be tonight, Scott?

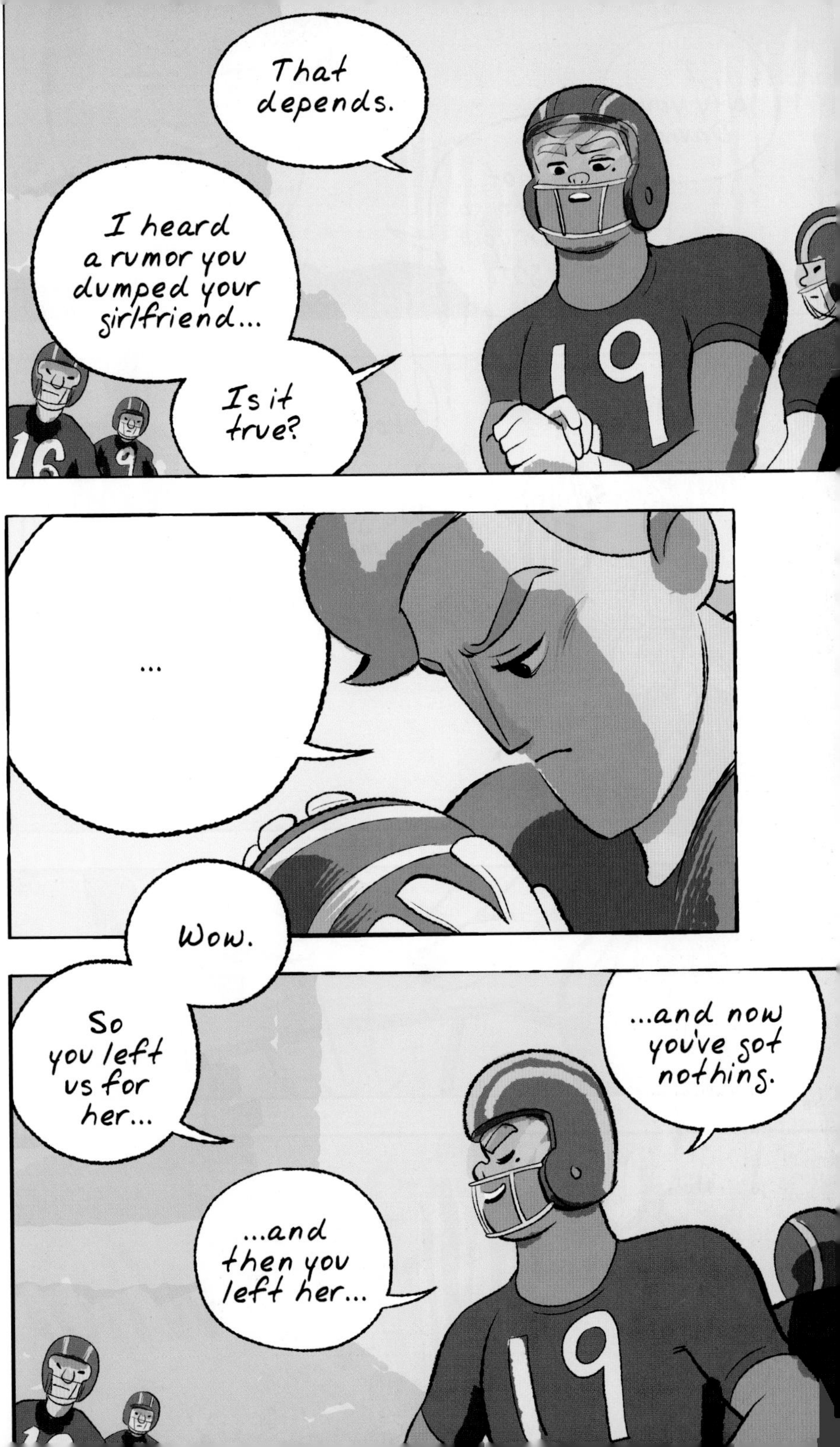
That depends.
I heard a rumor you dumped your girlfriend...
Is it true?
16
9
19
...
Wow.
So you left us for her...
...and now you've got nothing.
...and then you left her...
19

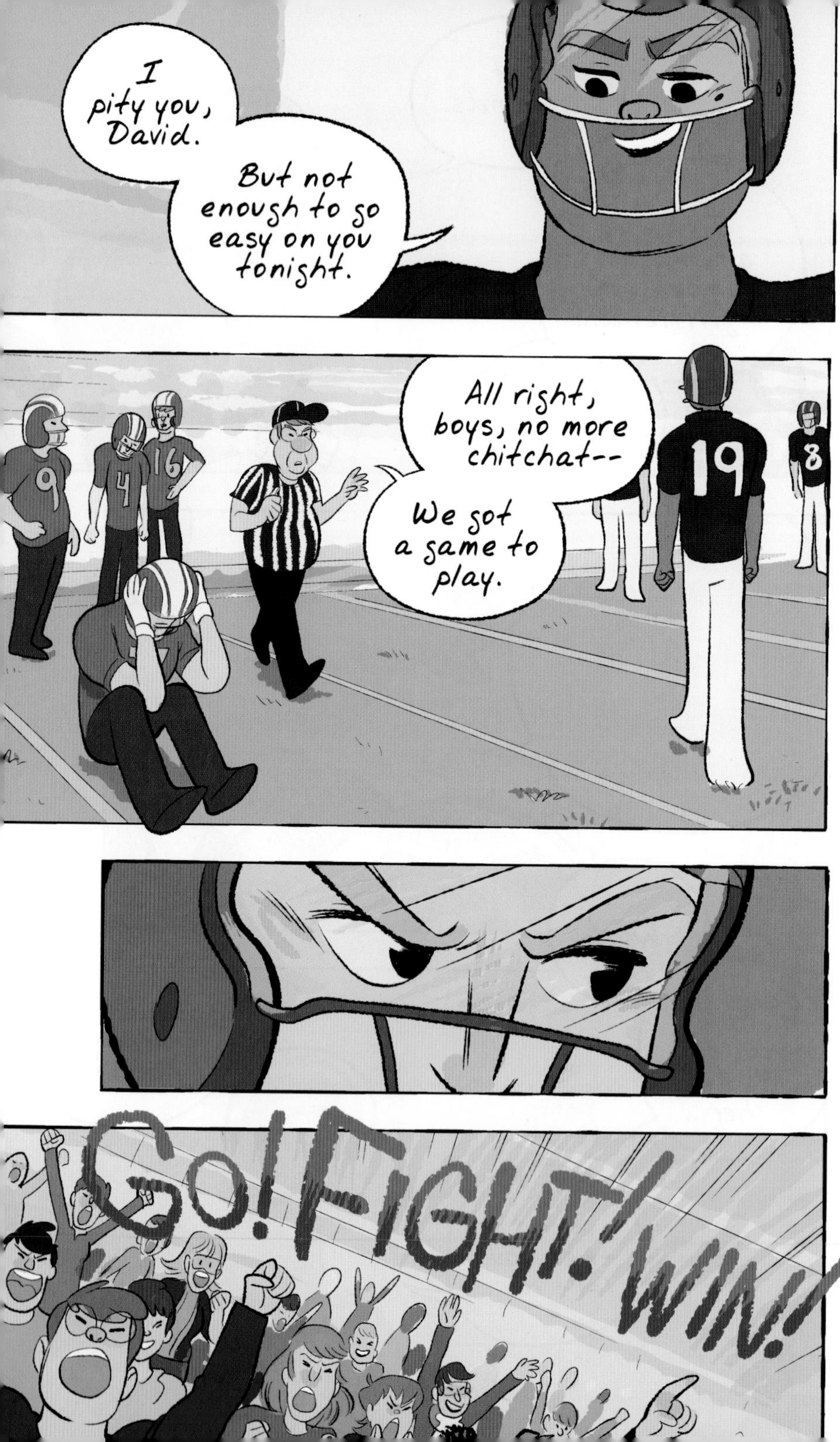
I pity you, David.
But not enough to go easy on you tonight.
All right, boys, no more chitchat--
We got a game to play.
GO! FIGHT! WIN!

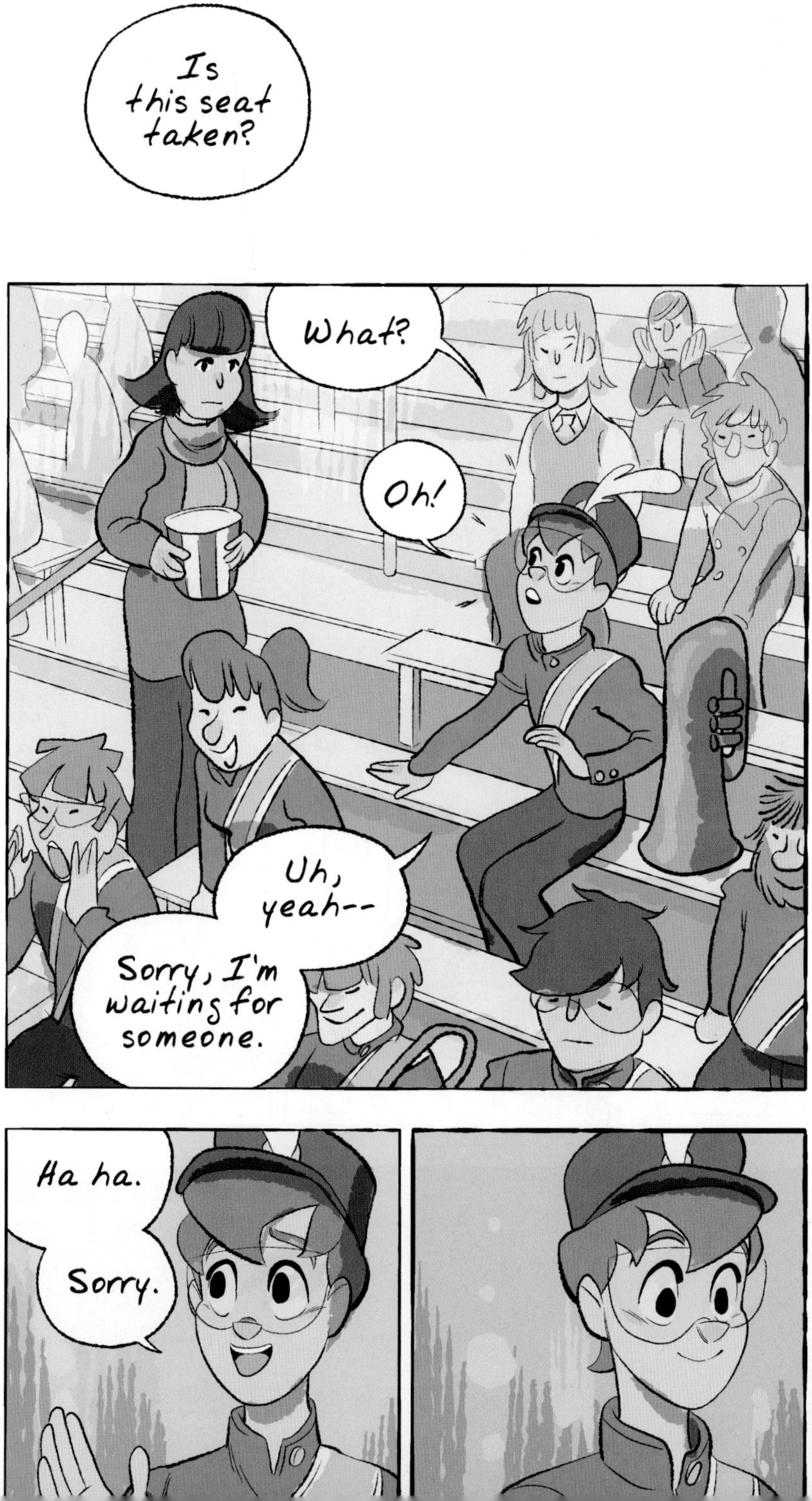
Is this seat taken?
What?
Oh!
Uh, yeah--
Sorry, I'm waiting for someone.
Ha ha.
Sorry.

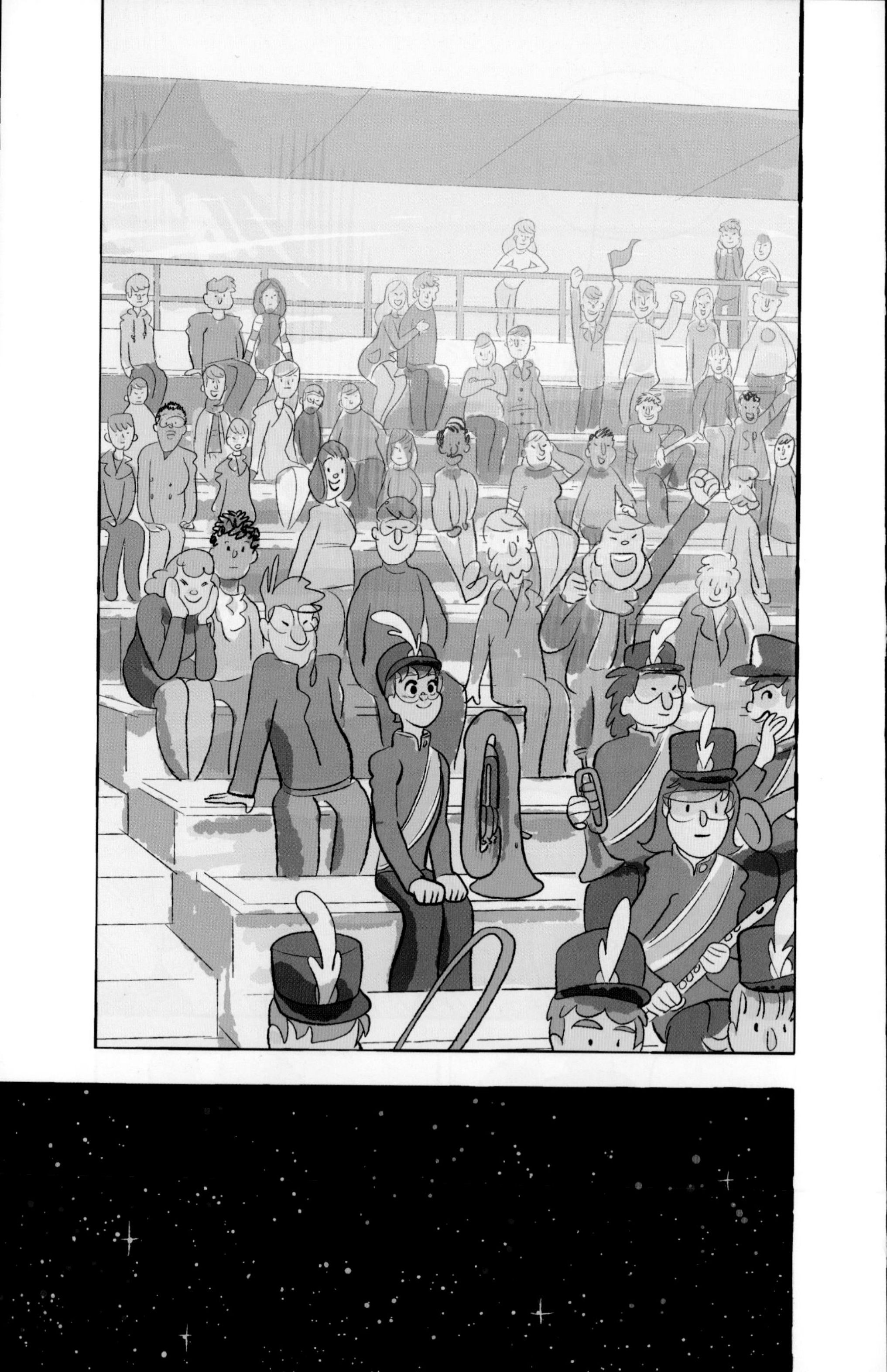

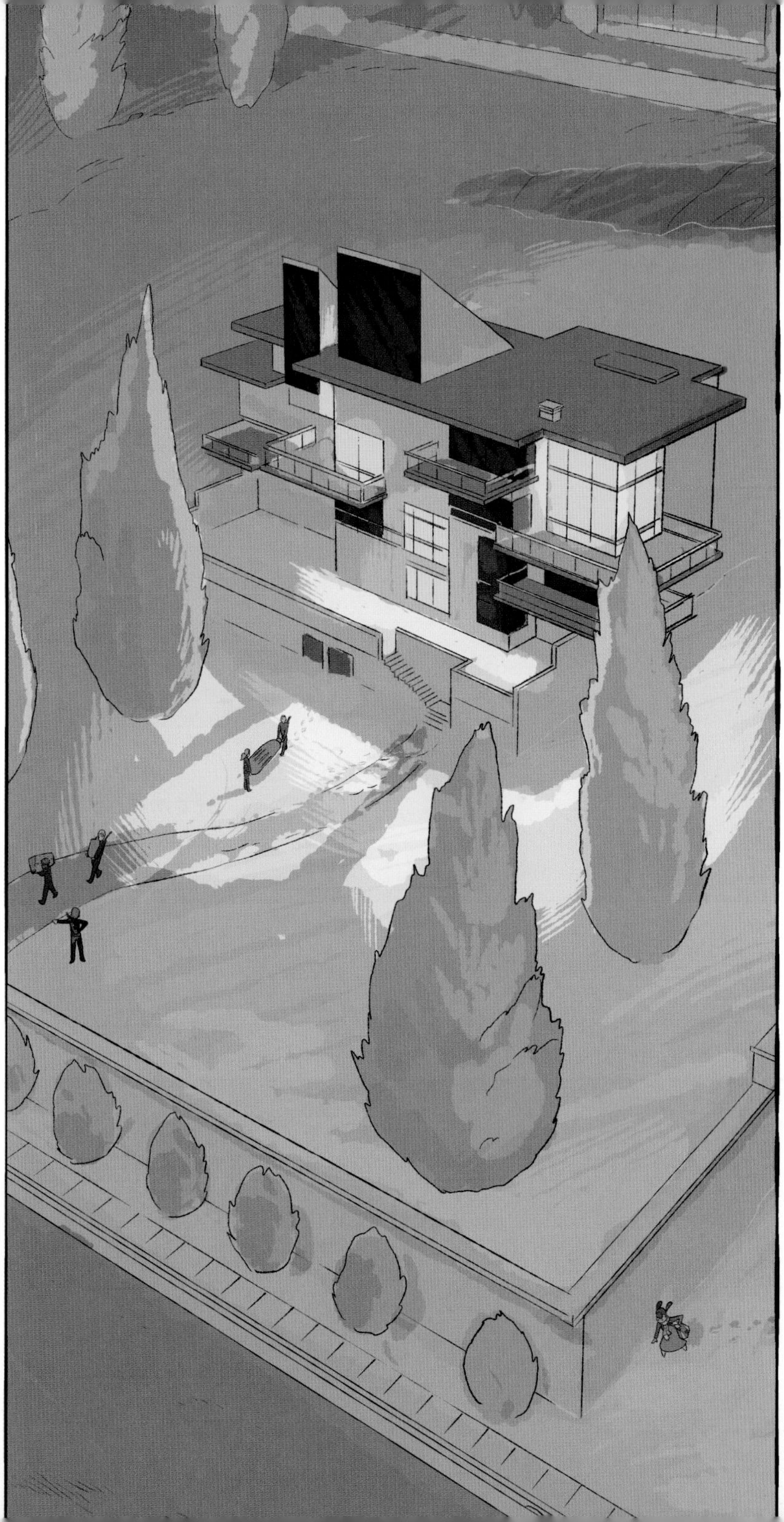

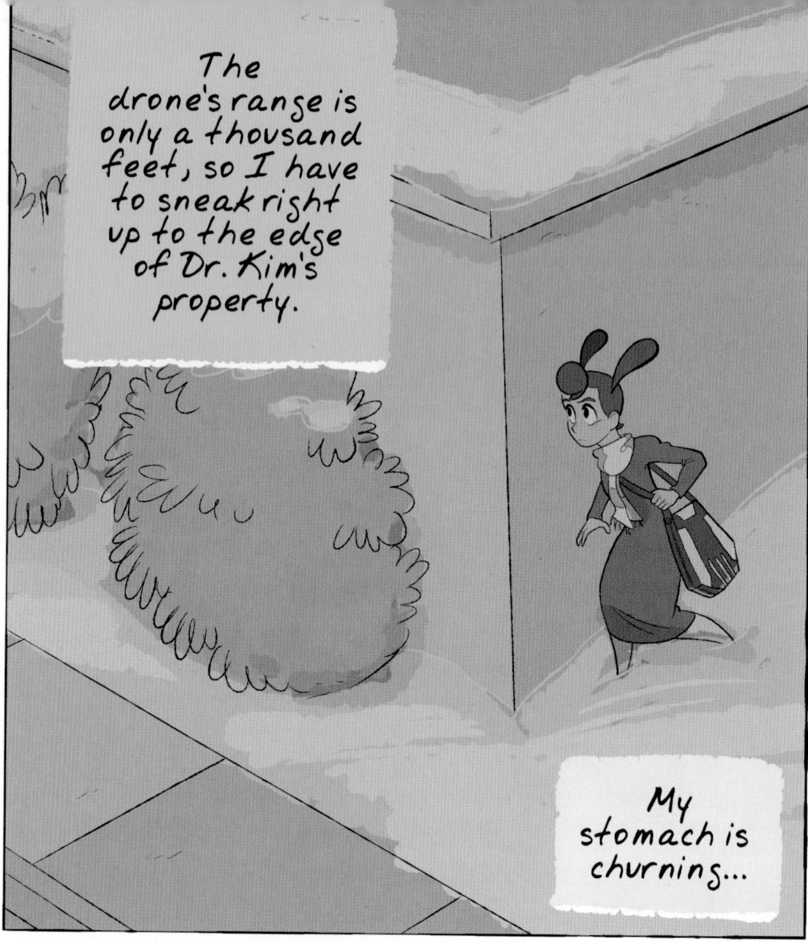
The drone's range is only a thousand feet, so I have to sneak right up to the edge of Dr. Kim's property.
My stomach is churning...

This is a crazy, stupid plan.

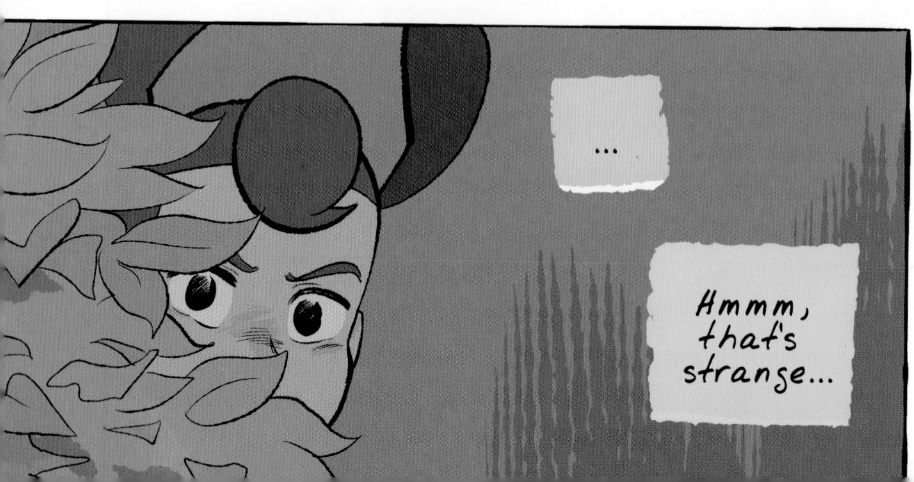
...
Hmmm, that's strange...

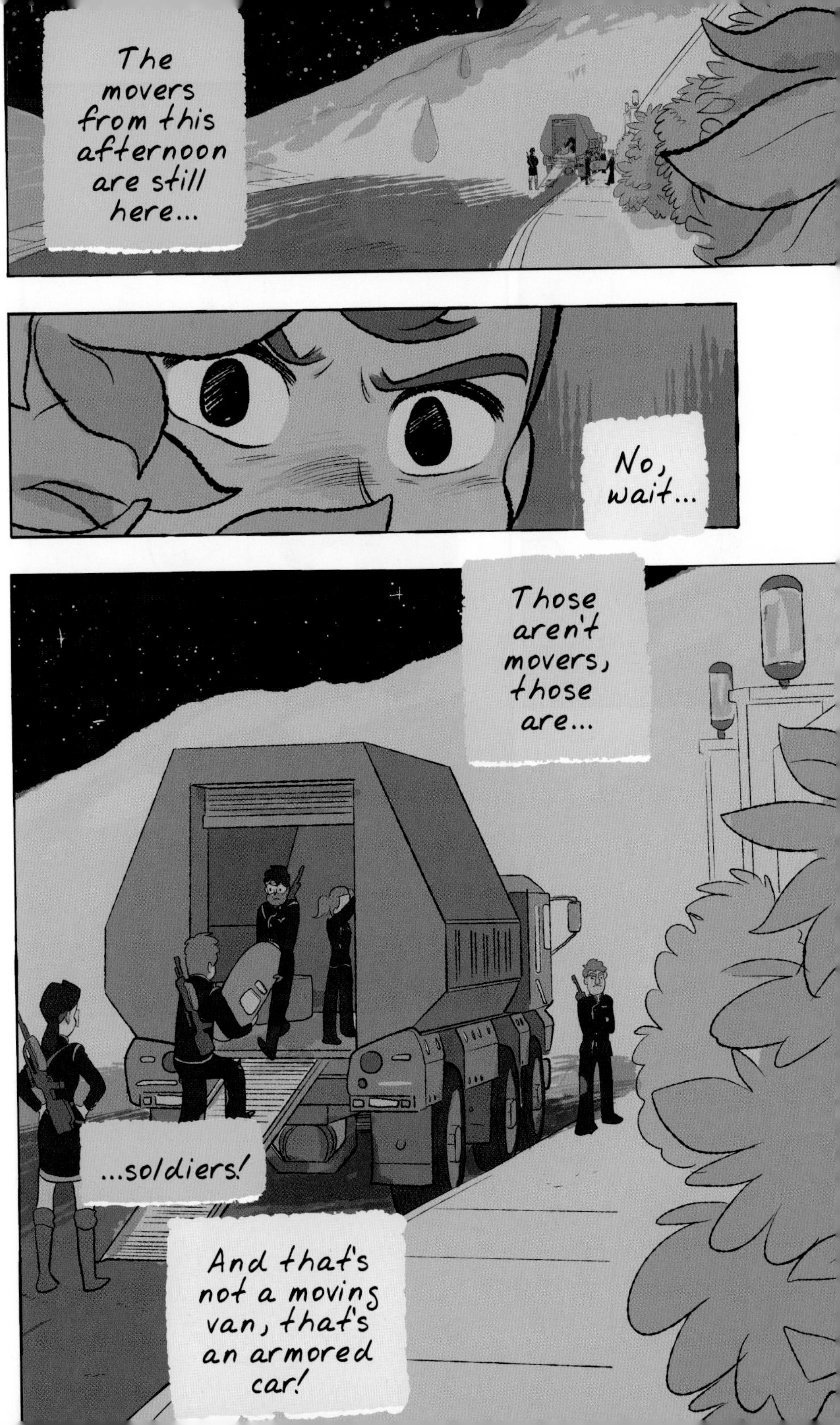
The movers from this afternoon are still here...
No, wait...
Those aren't movers, those are...
...soldiers!
And that's not a moving van, that's an armored car!

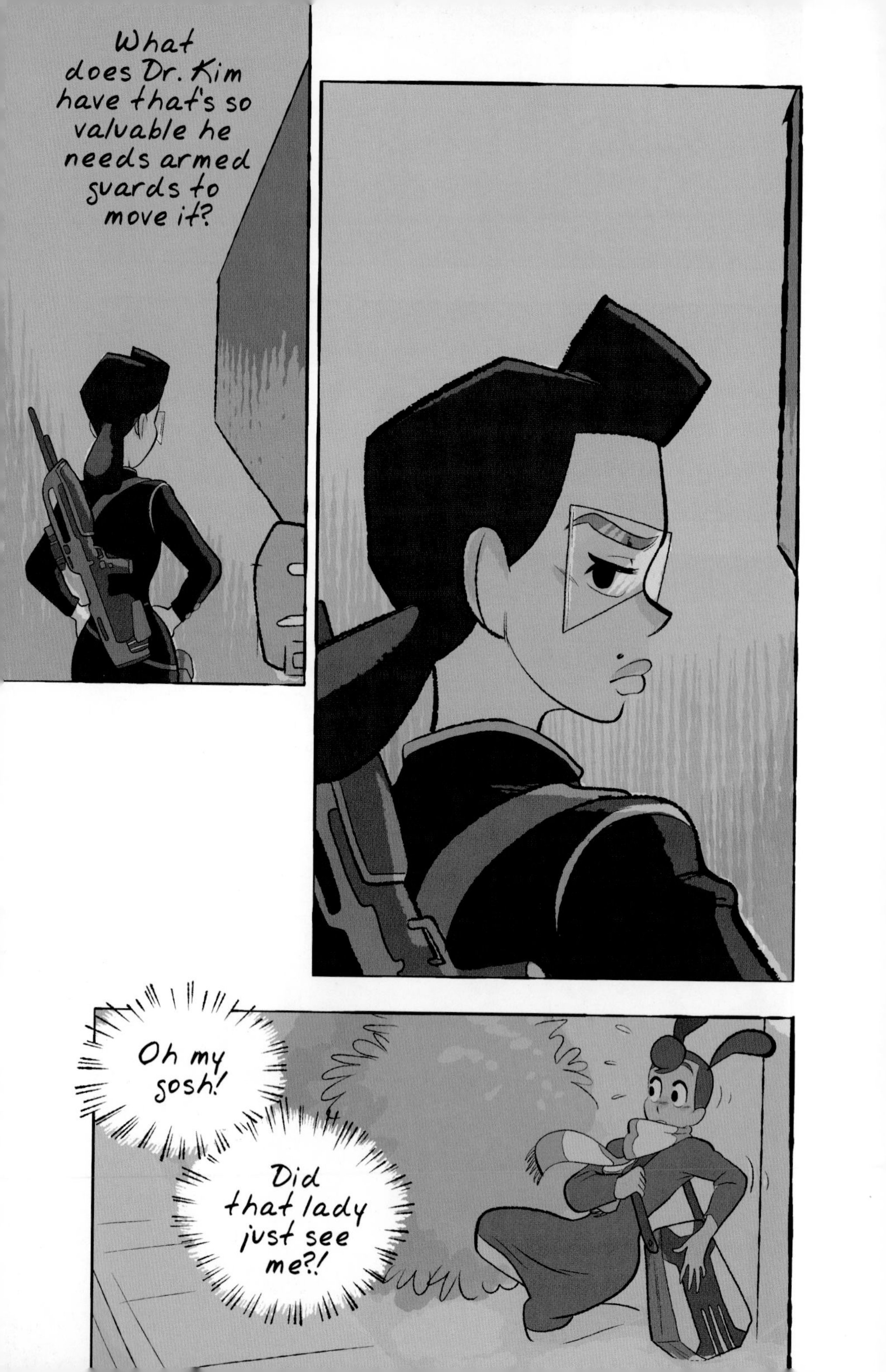
What does Dr. Kim have that's so valuable he needs armed guards to move it?
Oh my gosh!
Did that lady just see me?!

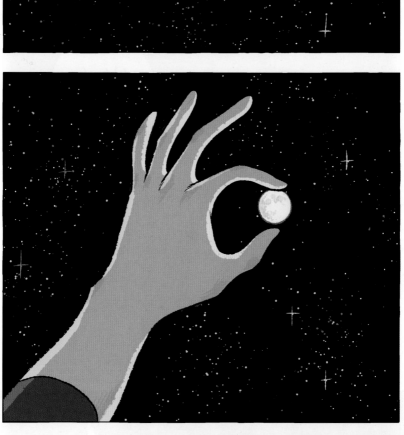

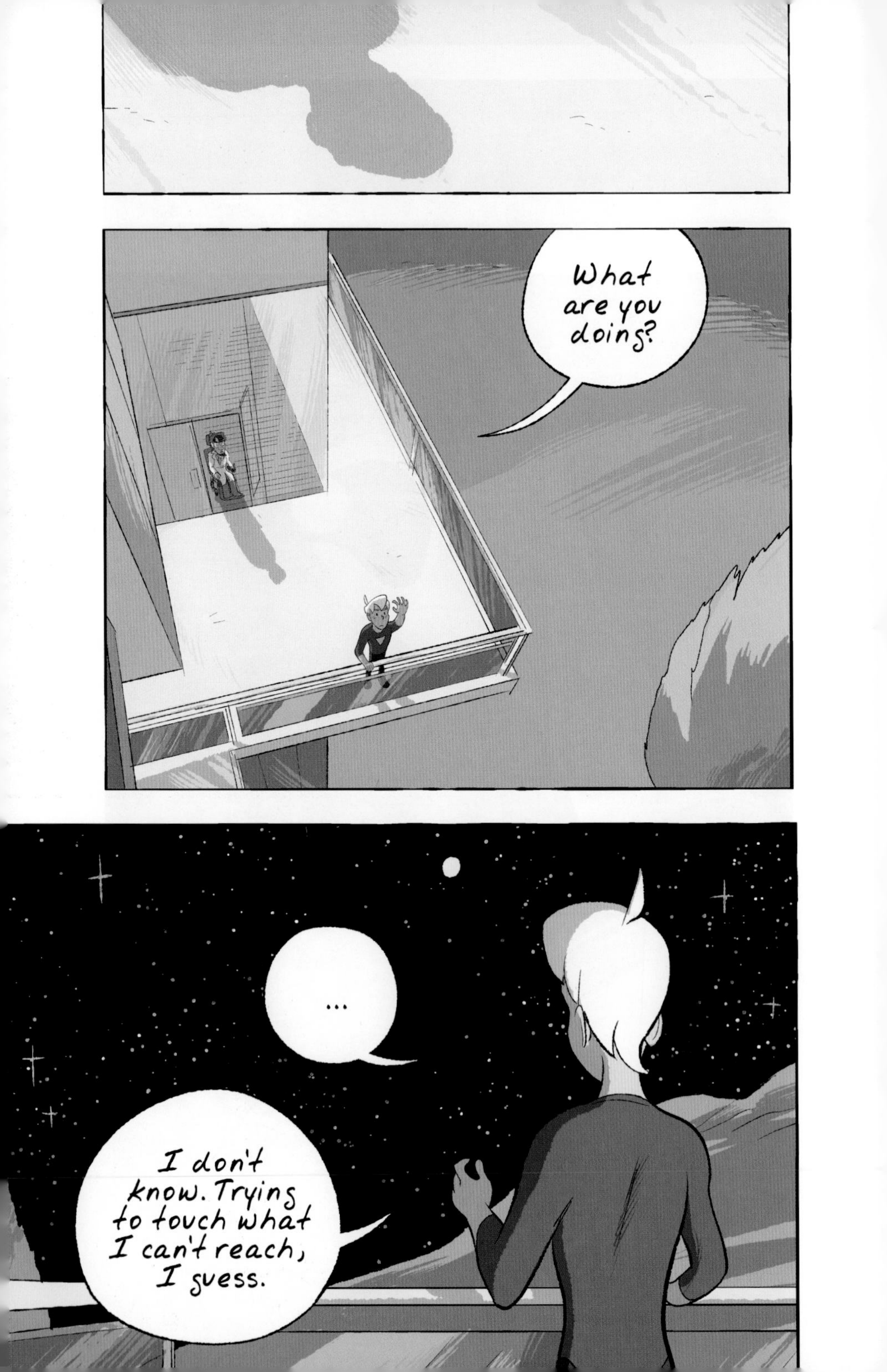
What are you doing?
...
I don't know. Trying to touch what I can't reach, I guess.

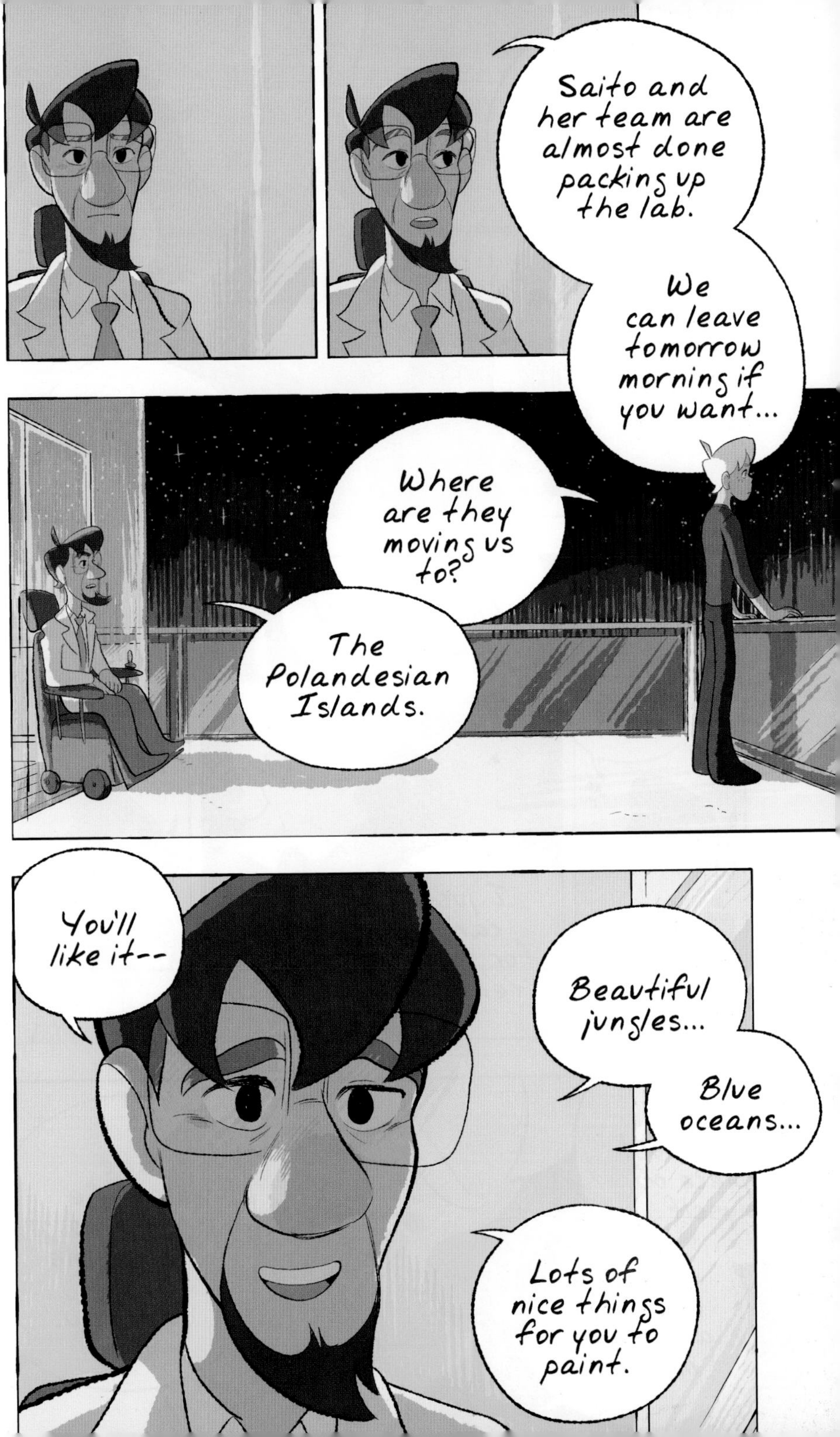
Saito and her team are almost done packing up the lab.
We can leave tomorrow morning if you want...
Where are they moving us to?
The Polandesian Islands.
You'll like it--
Beautiful jungles...
Blue oceans...
Lots of nice things for you to paint.

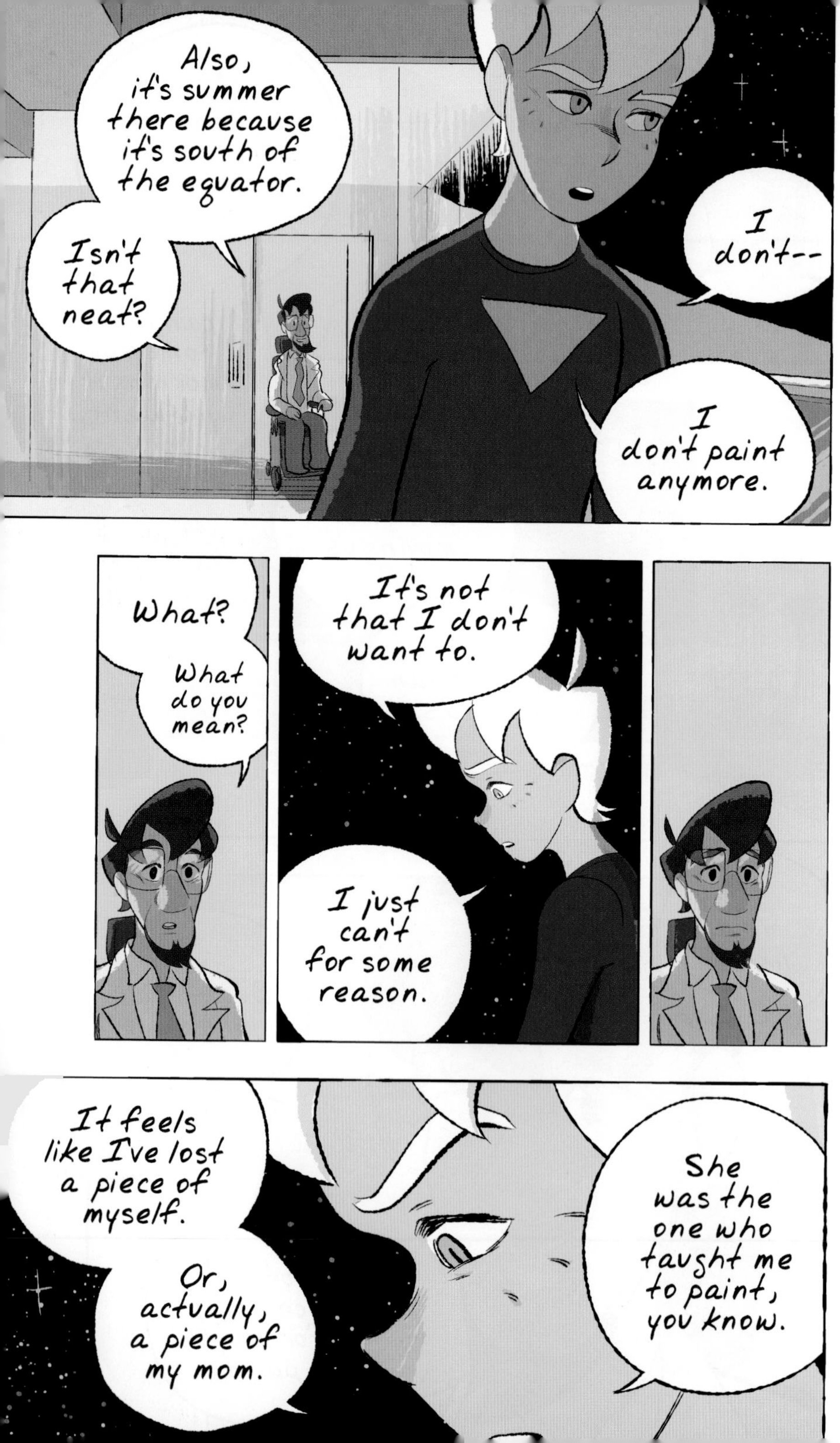

Also, it's summer there because it's south of the equator.
Isn't that neat?
I don't--
I don't paint anymore.
What?
What do you mean?
It's not that I don't want to.
I just can't for some reason.
It feels like I've lost a piece of myself.
Or, actually, a piece of my mom.
She was the one who taught me to paint, you know.

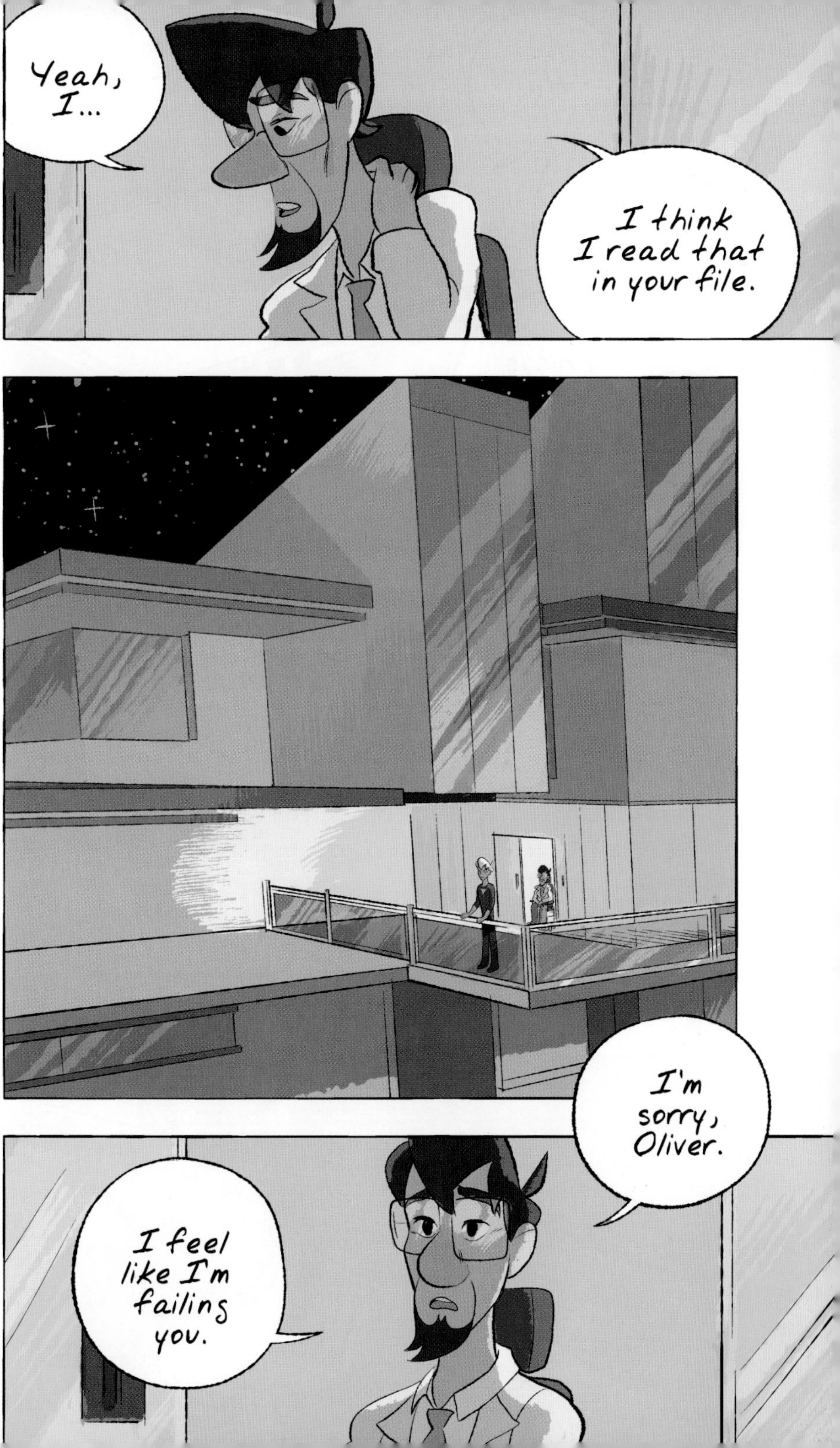
Yeah, I...
I think I read that in your file.
I'm sorry, Oliver.
I feel like I'm failing you.

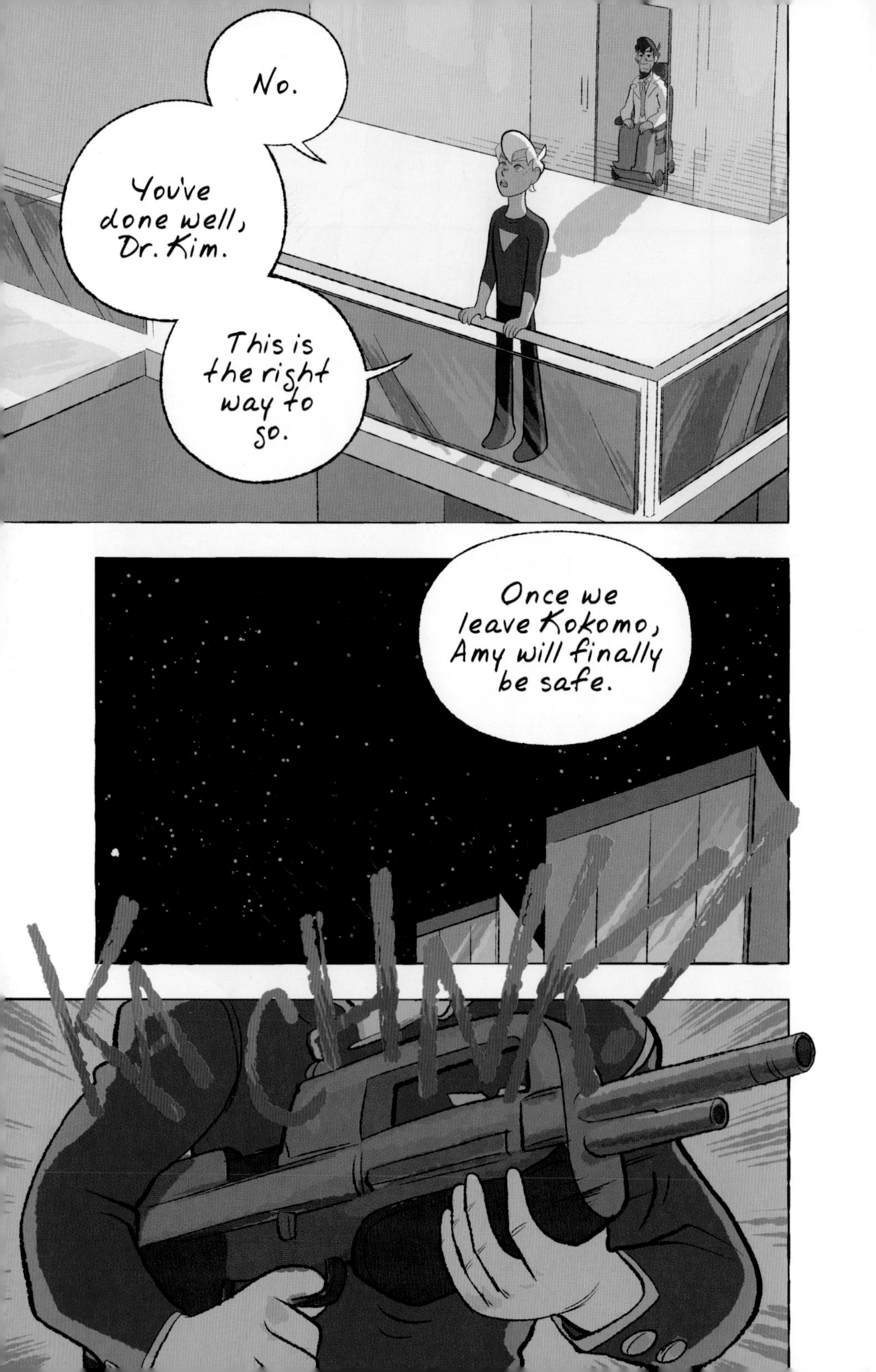
No.
You've done well, Dr. Kim.
This is the right way to go.
Once we leave Kokomo, Amy will finally be safe.
KACHAK

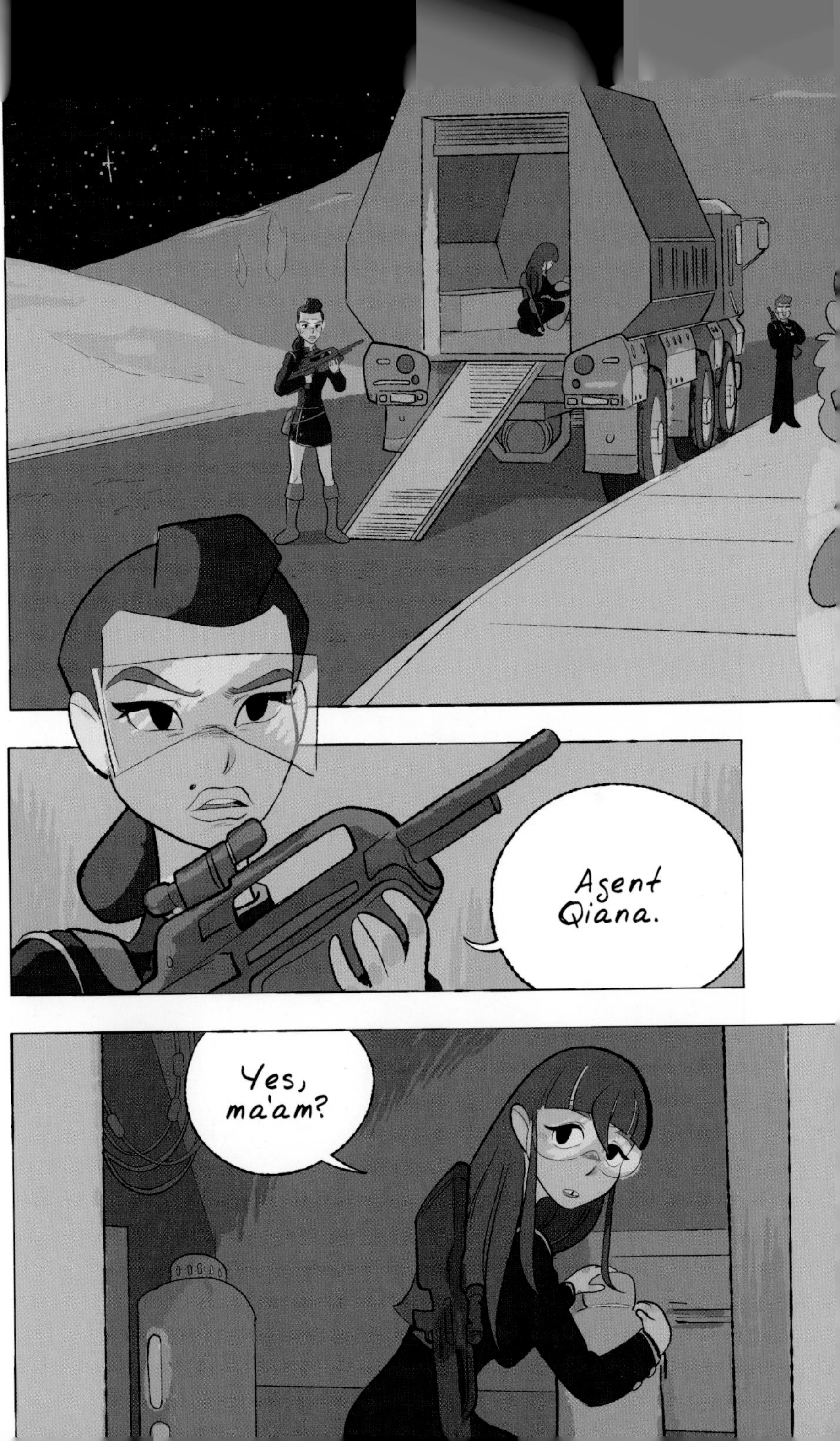
Agent Qiana.
Yes, ma'am?

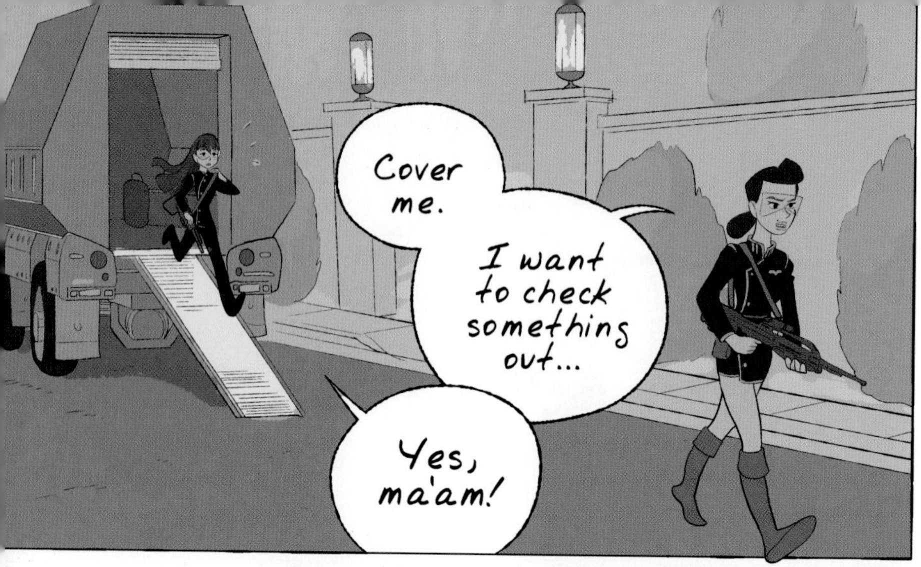
Cover me.
I want to check something out...
Yes, ma'am!
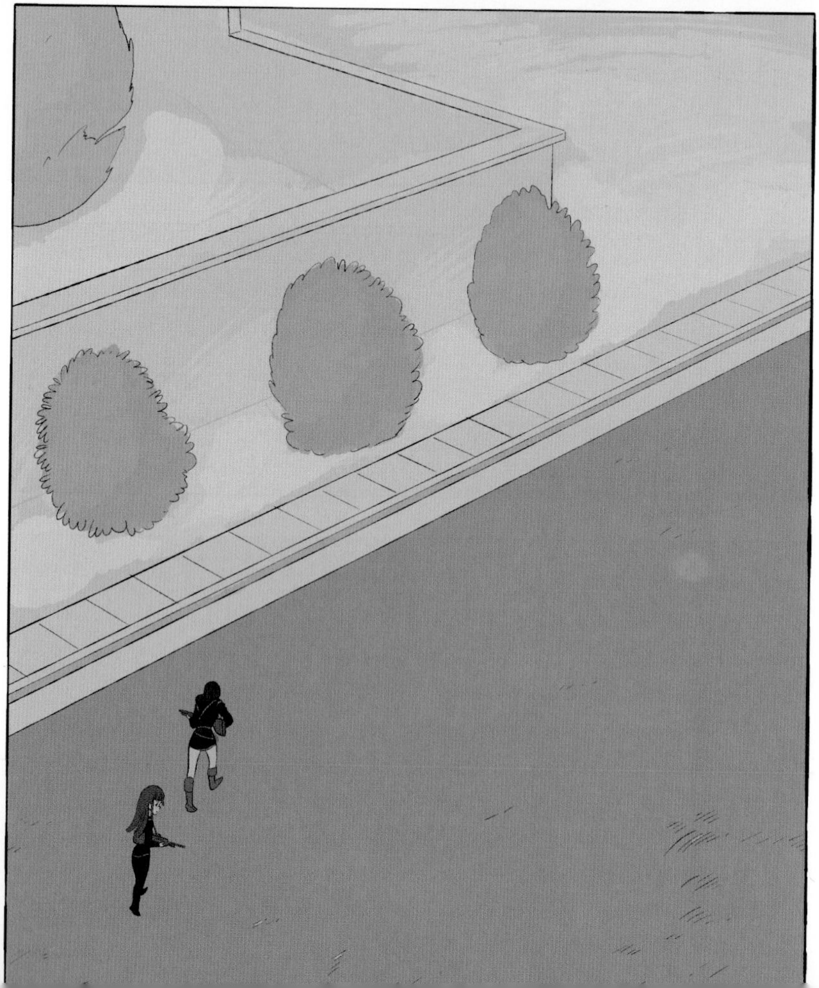

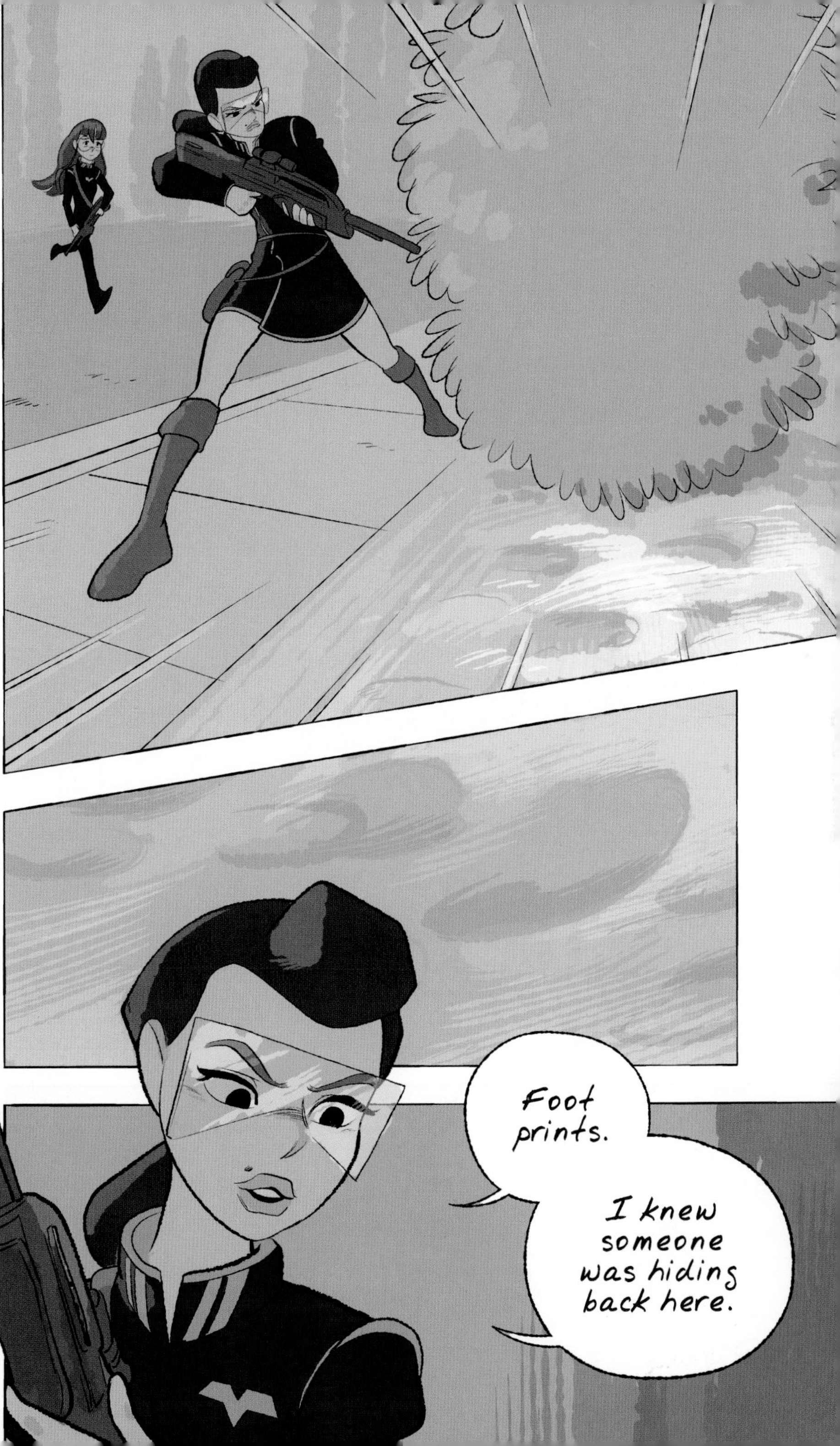
Foot prints.
I knew someone was hiding back here.

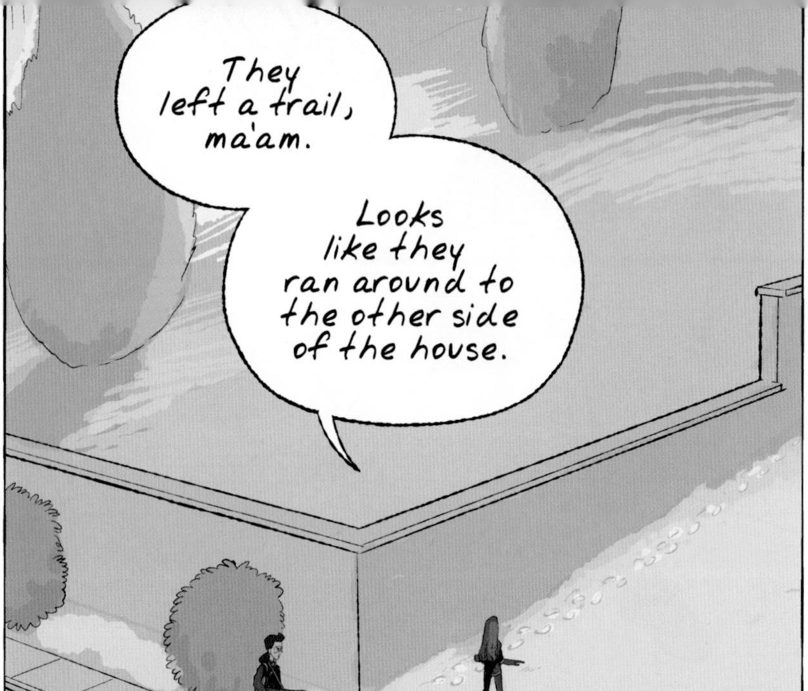
They left a trail, ma'am.
Looks like they ran around to the other side of the house.
Who could be spying on us?
The Cubanians? The Global Alliance?

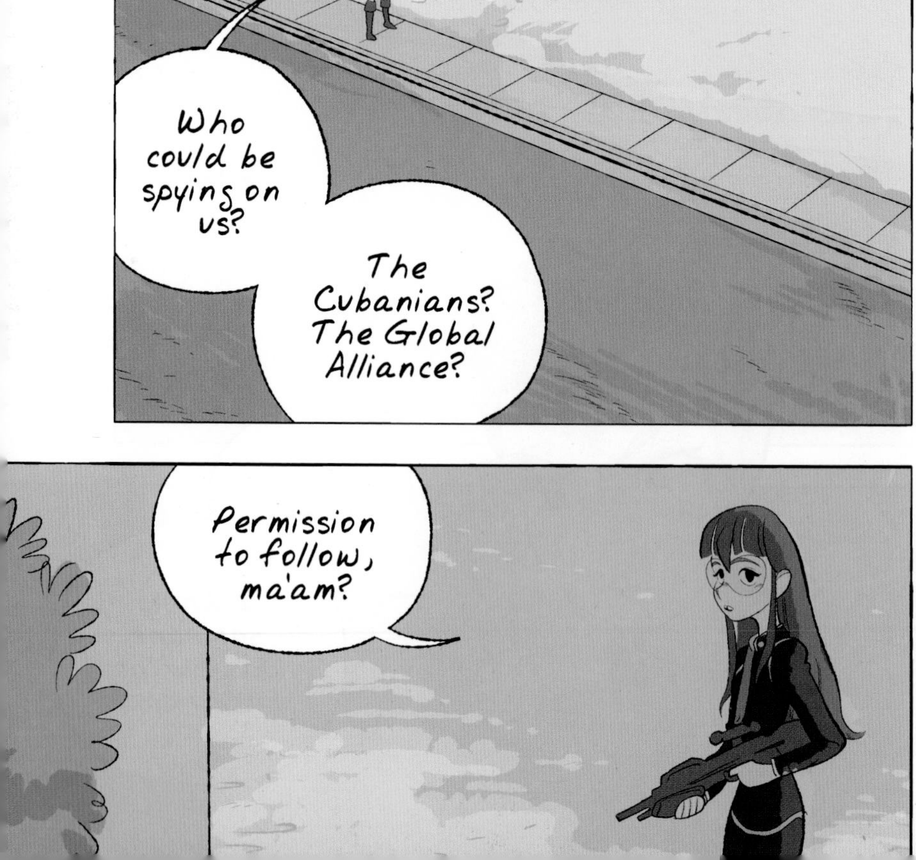
Permission to follow, ma'am?

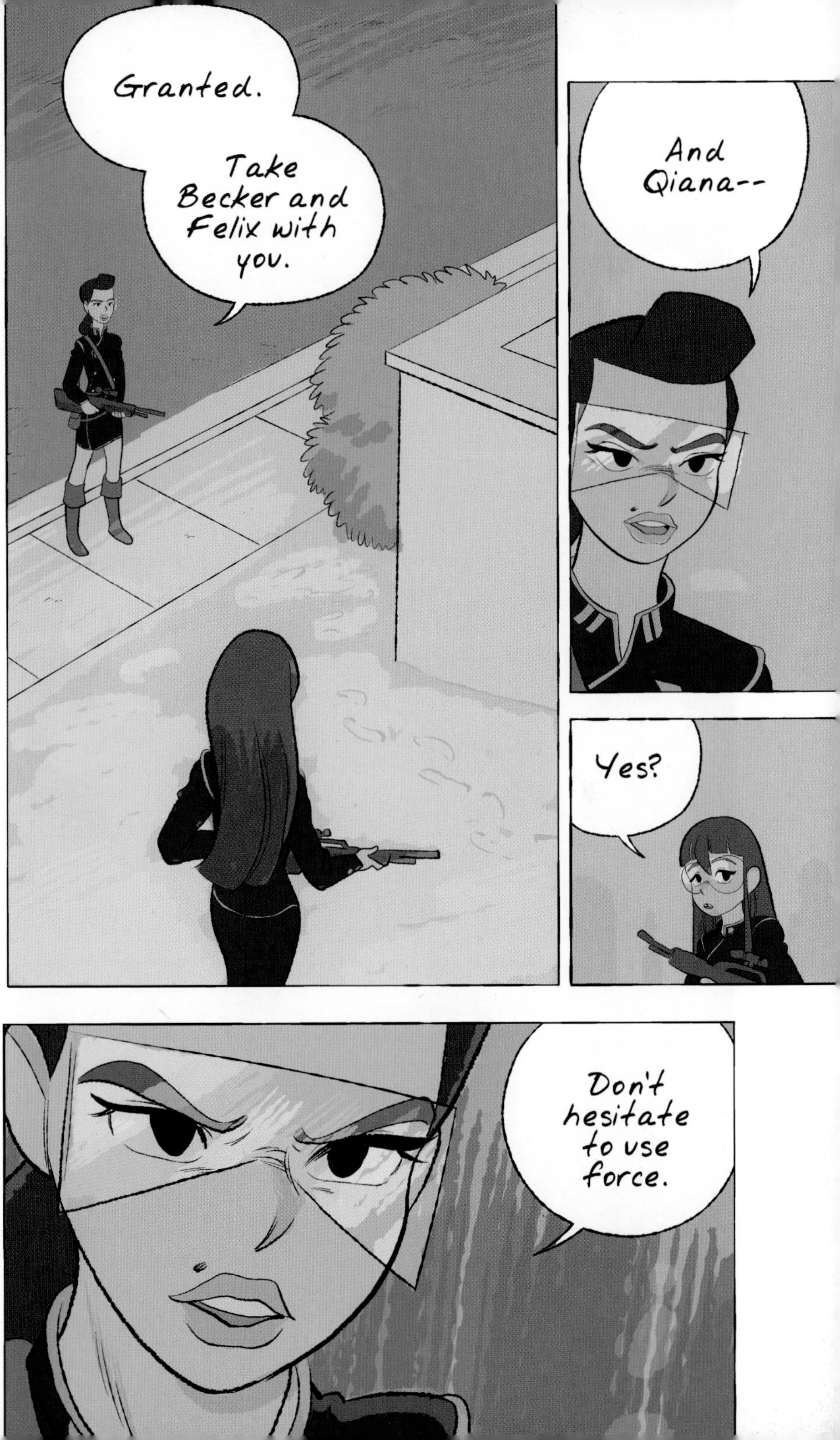
Granted.
Take Becker and Felix with you.
And Qiana--
Yes?
Don't hesitate to use force.

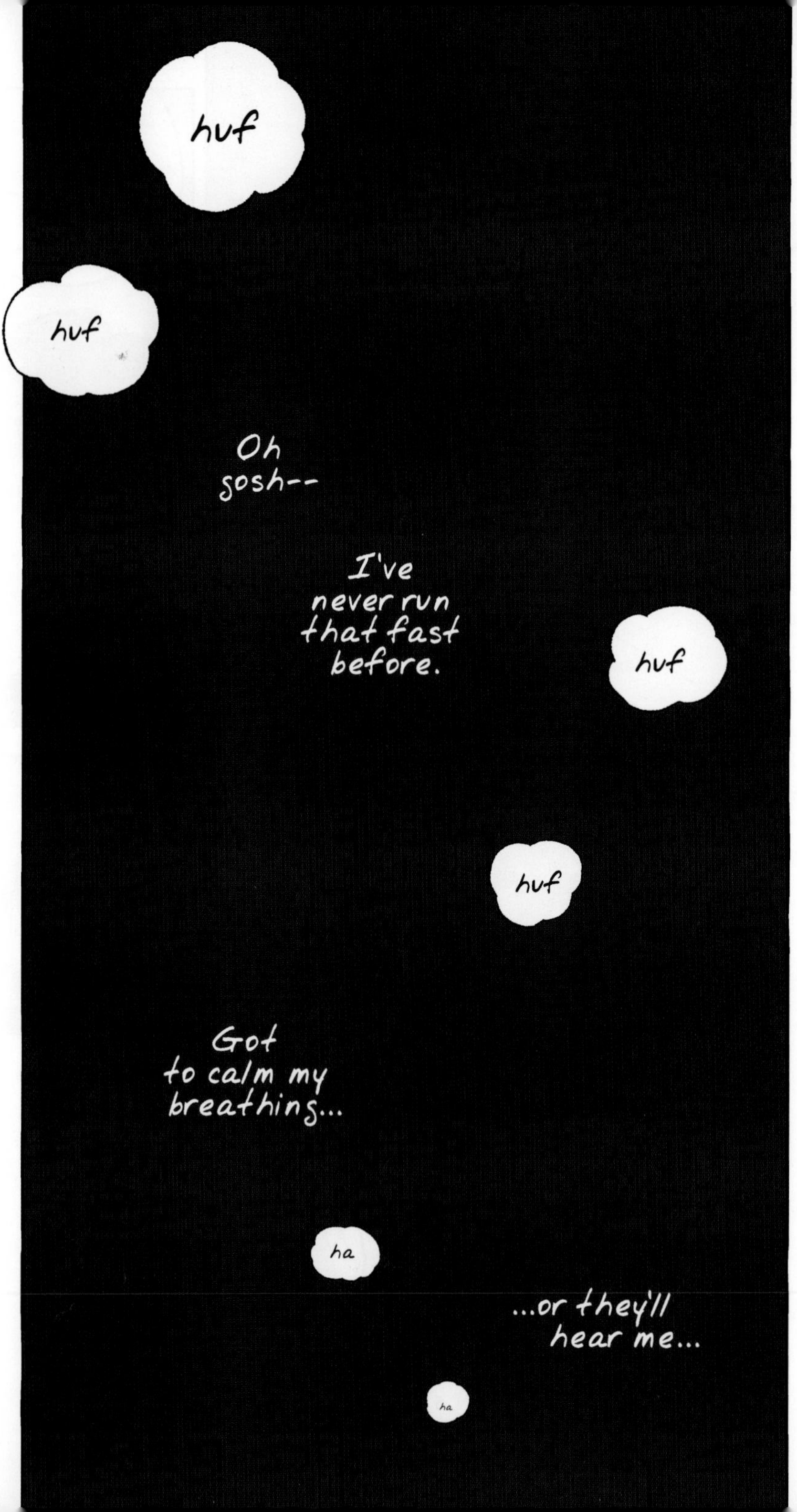
huf
huf
Oh gosh--
I've never run that fast before.
huf
huf
Got to calm my breathing...
ha
...or they'll hear me...
ha

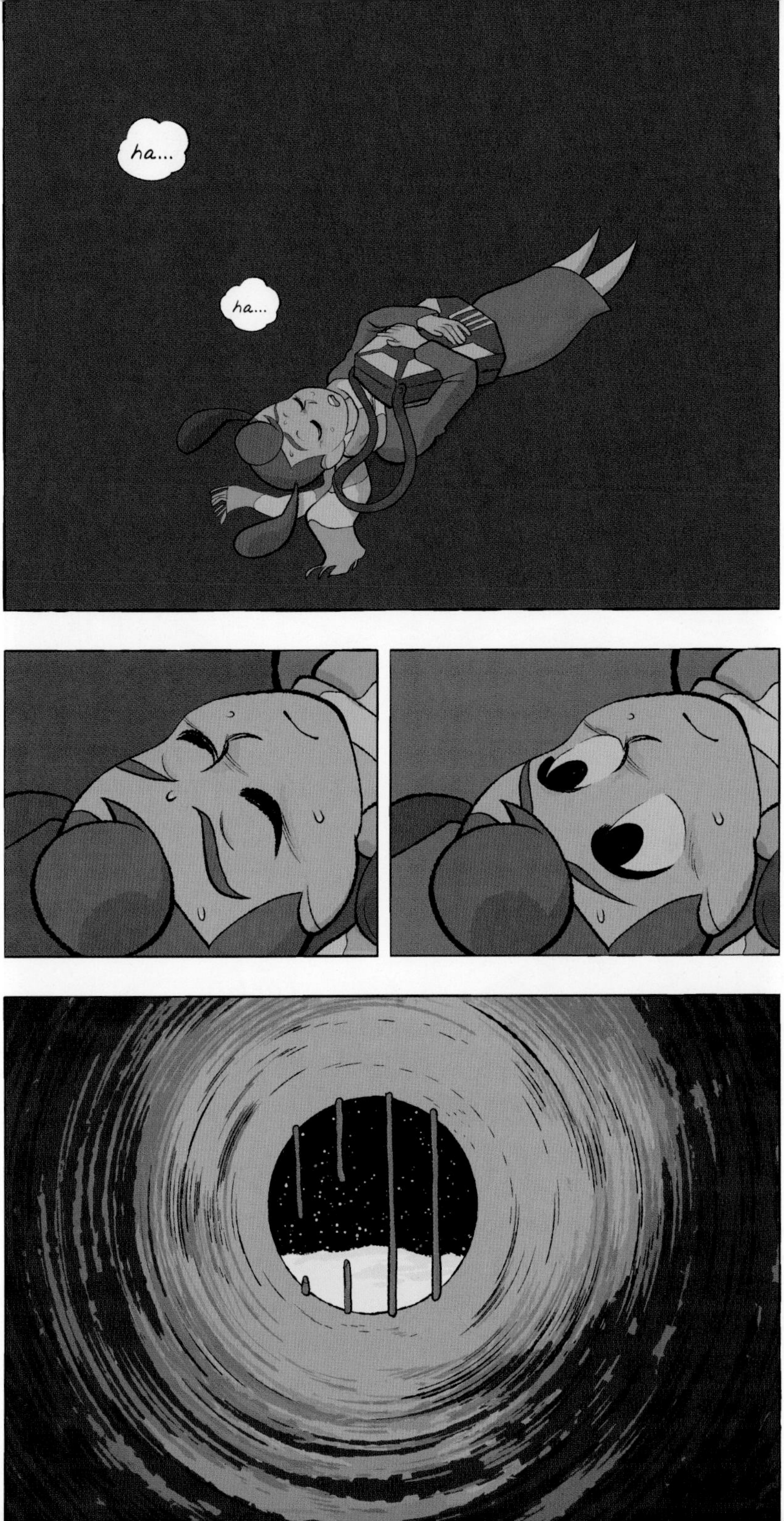

ha...
ha...

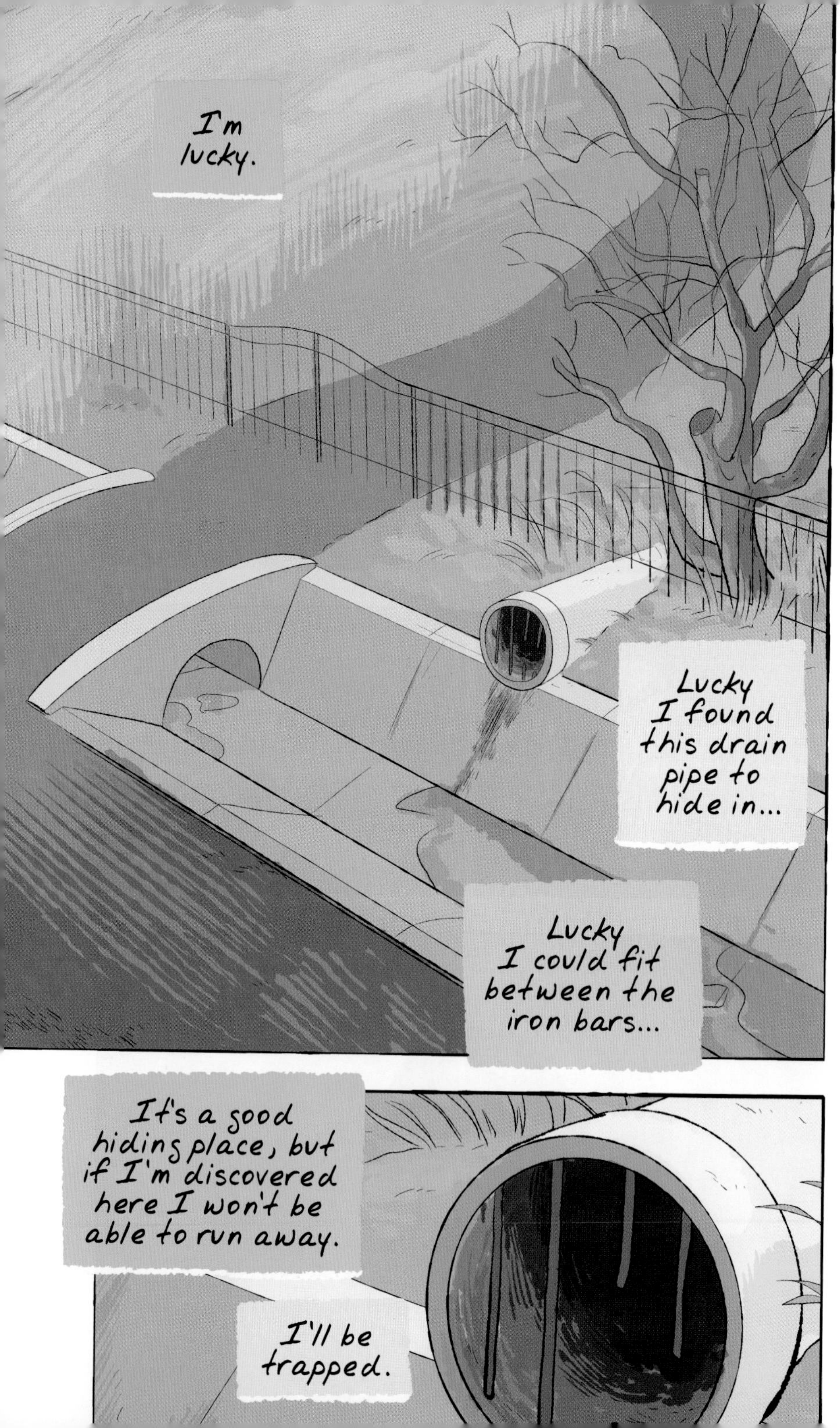
I'm lucky.
Lucky I found this drain pipe to hide in...
Lucky I could fit between the iron bars...
It's a good hiding place, but if I'm discovered here I won't be able to run away.
I'll be trapped.

I need to get out of here,
but I don't want to get shot.

Maybe that's my fear talking.
Soldiers don't shoot civilians, right?

That woman with the piercing gaze--
she would shoot someone if given the chance.
I could tell.

There was poison in her flavor.

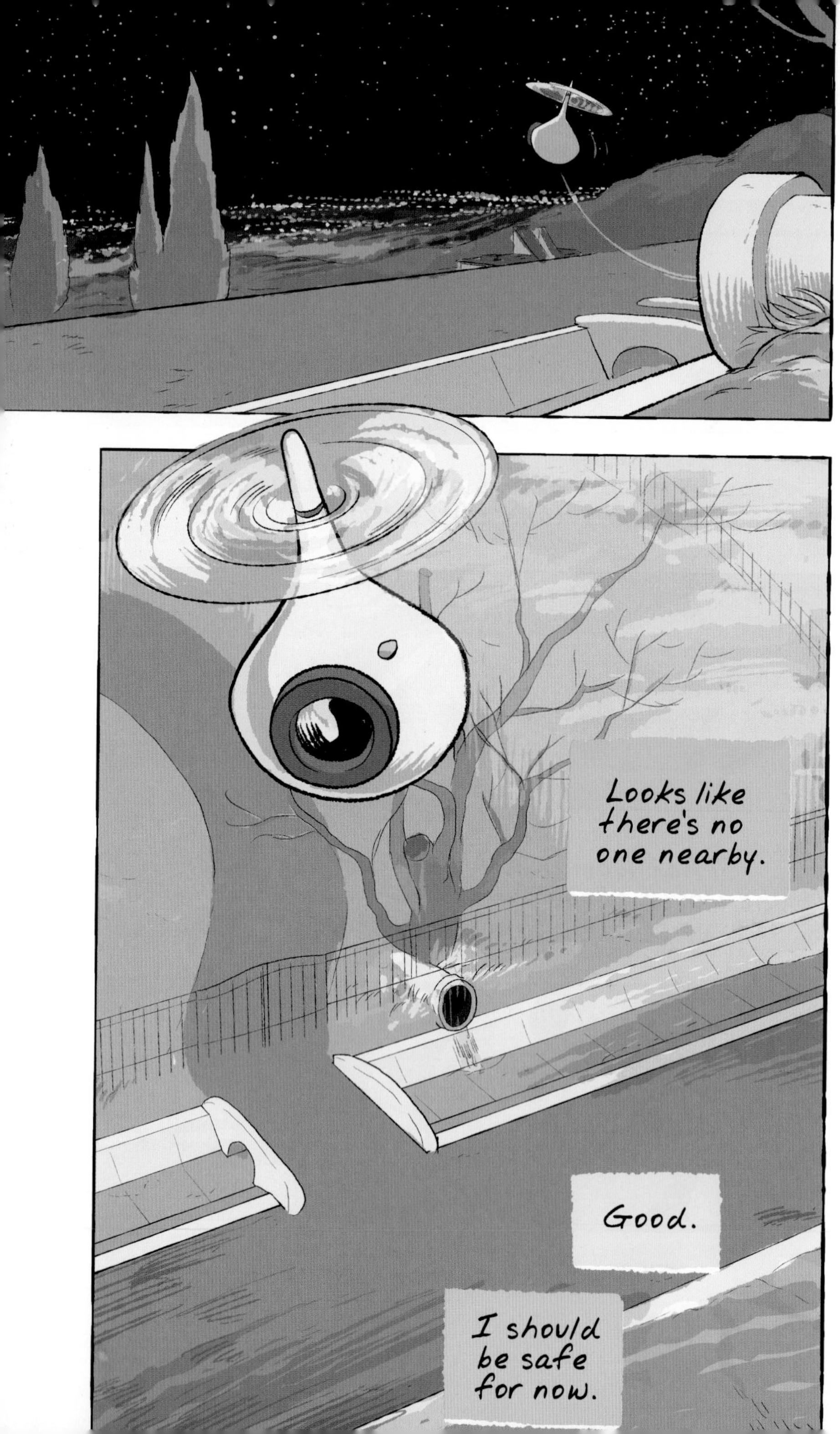
Looks like there's no one nearby.
Good.
I should be safe for now.

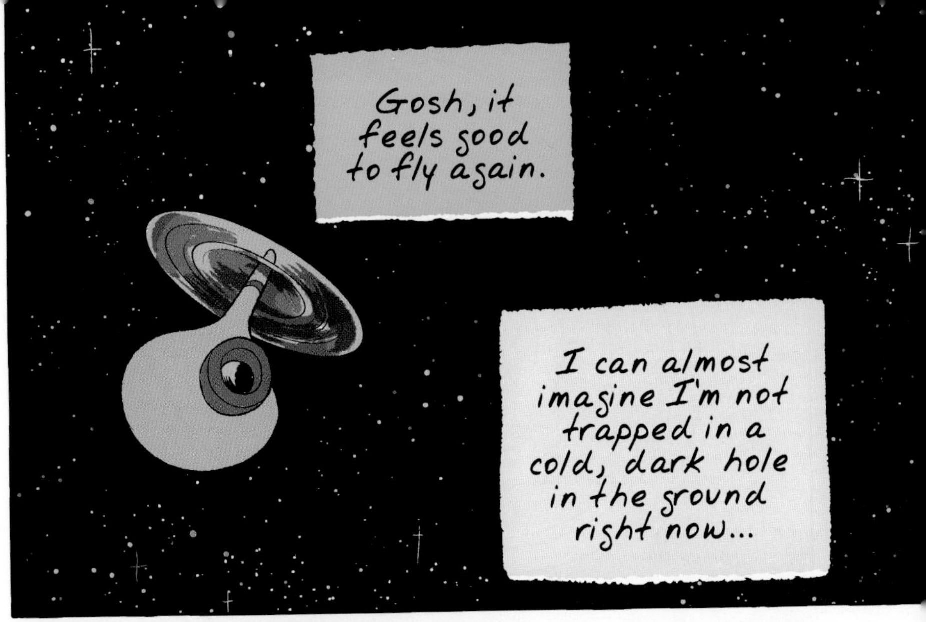
Gosh, it feels good to fly again.
I can almost imagine I'm not trapped in a cold, dark hole in the ground right now...

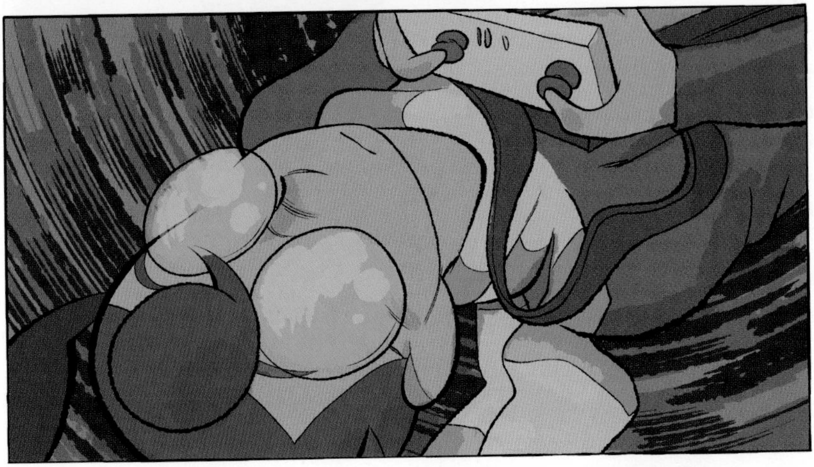

Almost.

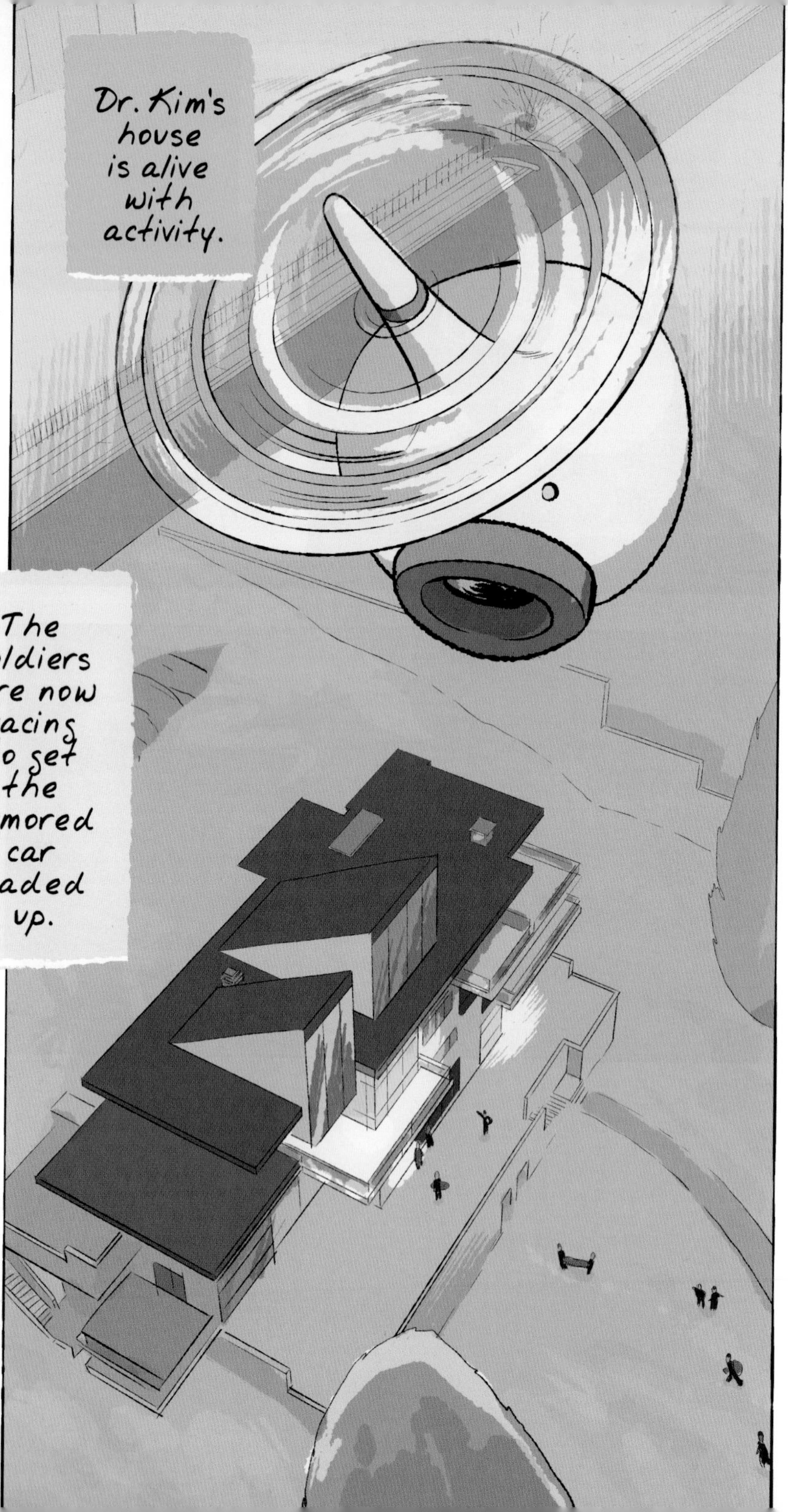
Dr. Kim's house is alive with activity.
The soldiers are now racing to get the armored car loaded up.

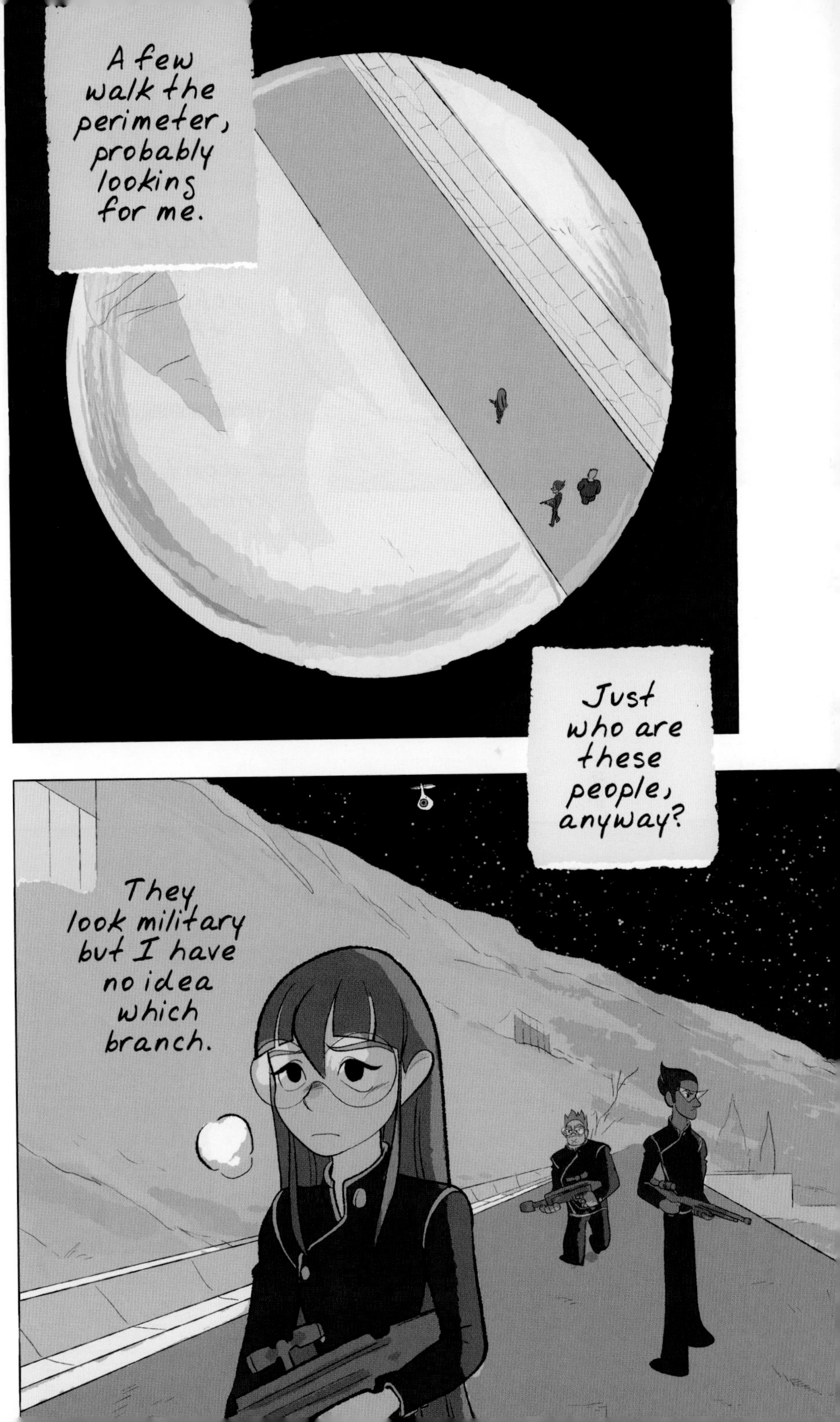
A few walk the perimeter, probably lookings for me.
Just who are these people, anyway?
They look military but I have no idea which branch.

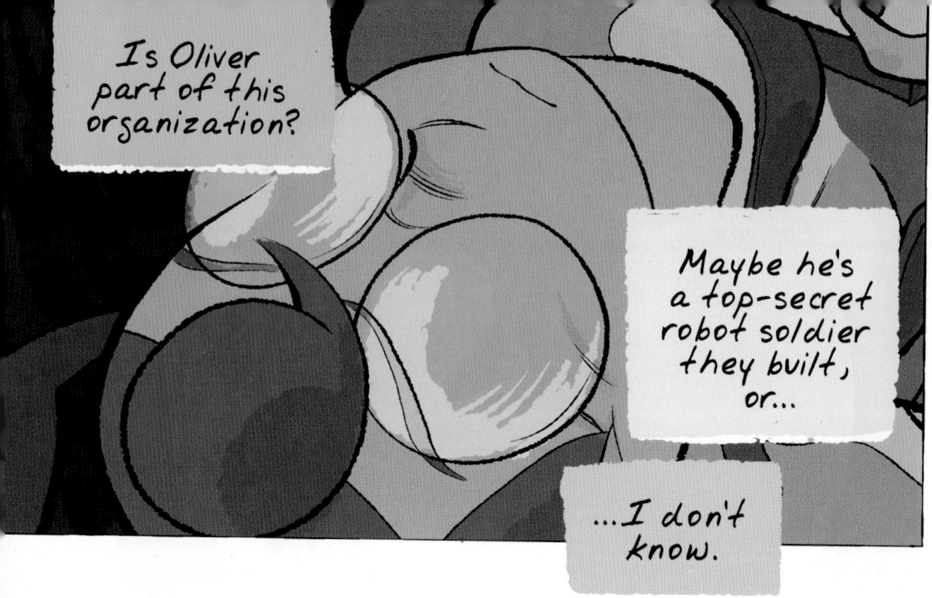
Is Oliver part of this organization?
Maybe he's a top-secret robot soldier they built, or...
...I don't know.

If I want to find out more, I need to follow through with my plan.

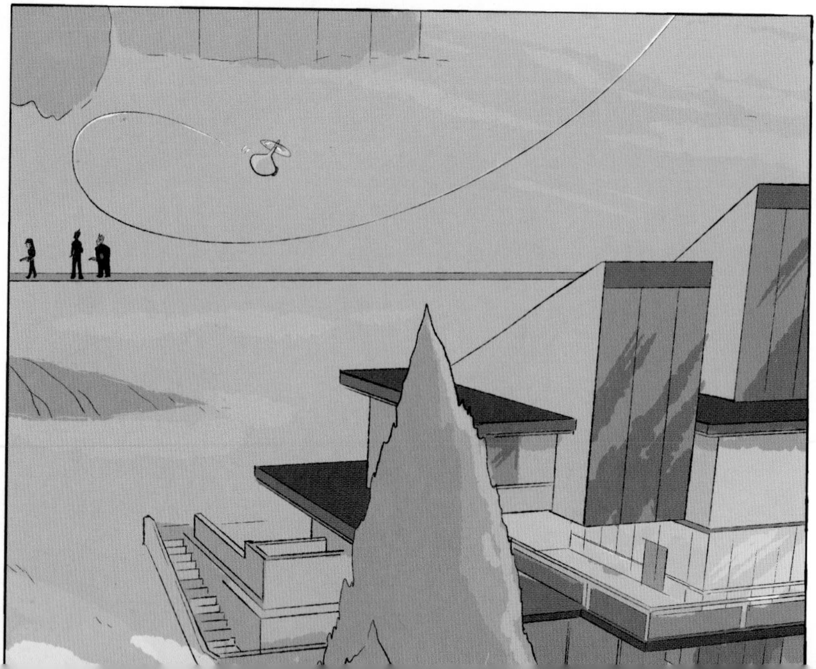

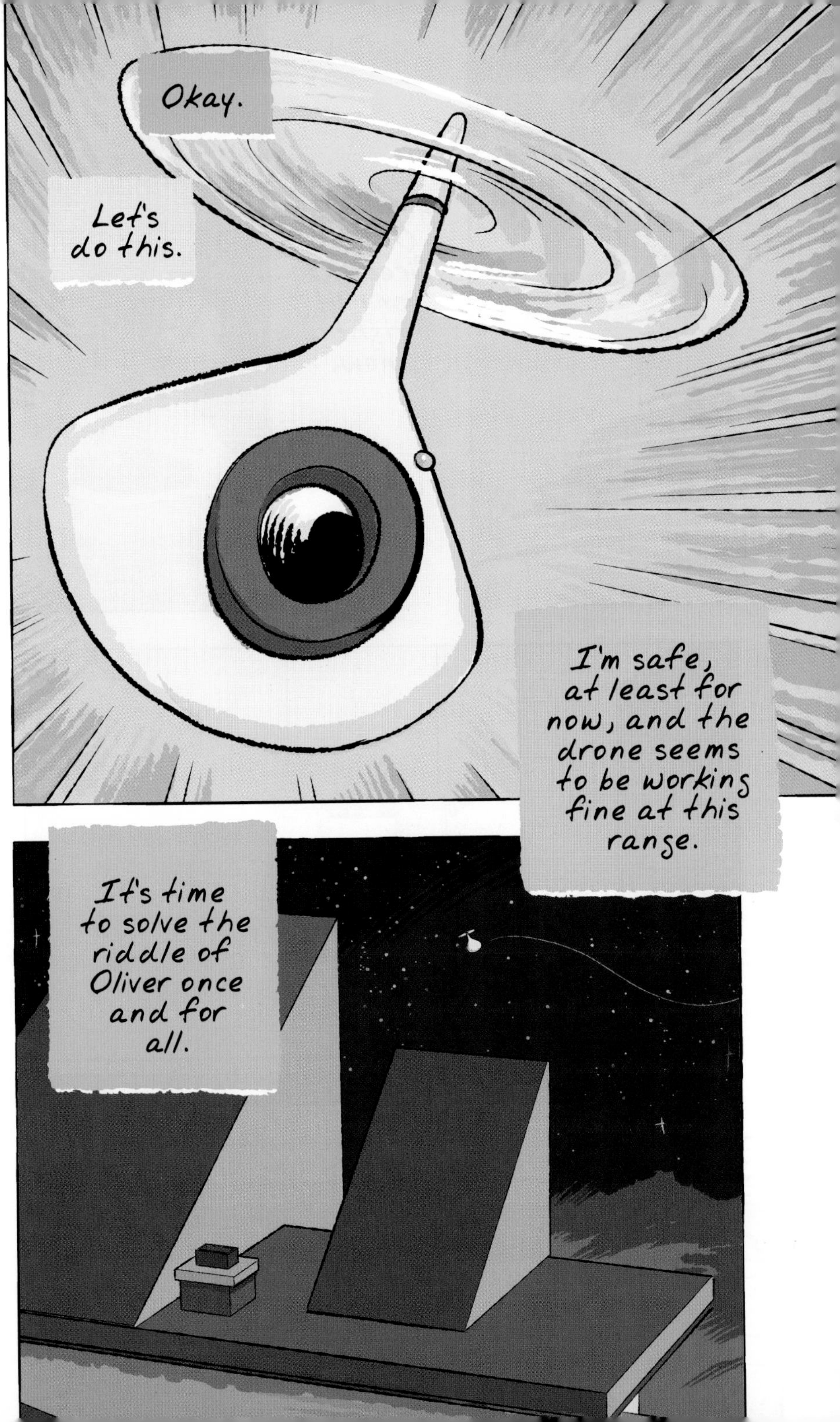
Okay.
Let's do this.
I'm safe, at least for now, and the drone seems to be working fine at this range.
It's time to solve the riddle of Oliver once and for all.

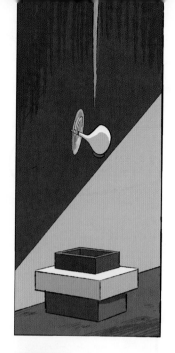

Hopefully Oliver's fireplace isn't lit right now.

FOOMP!

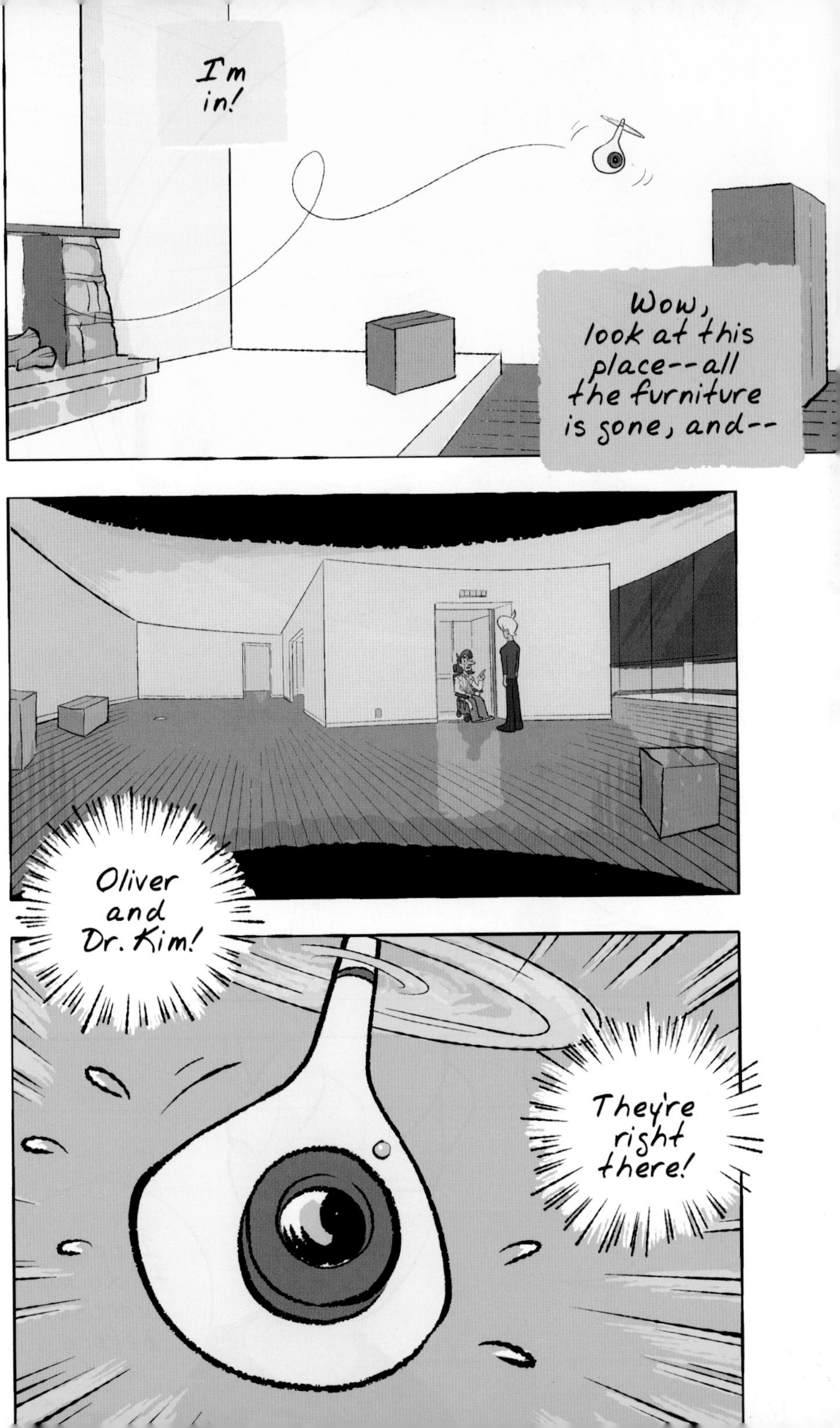
I'm in!
Wow, look at this place--all the furniture is gone, and--
Oliver and Dr. Kim!
They're right there!

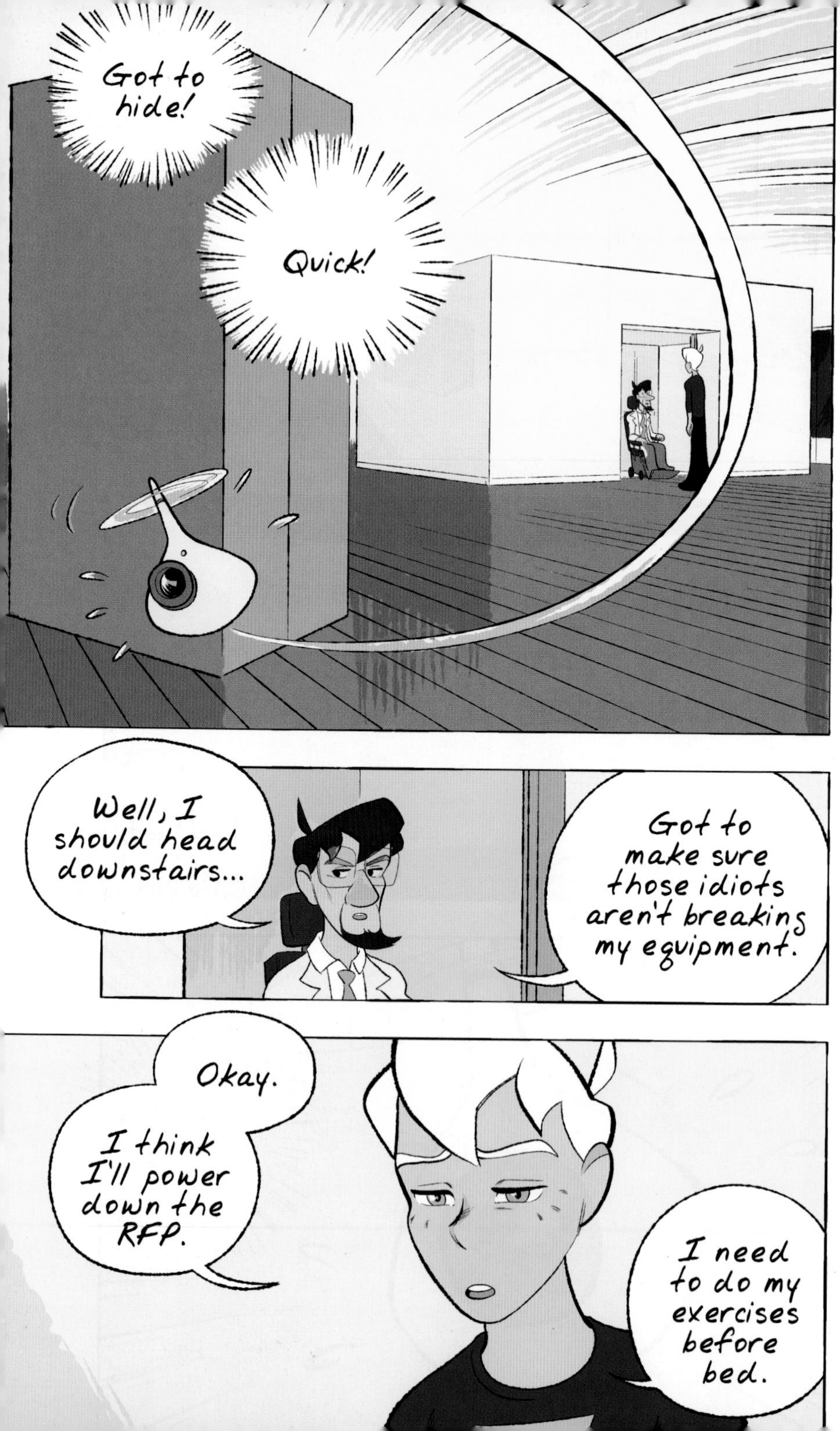
Got to hide!
Quick!
Well, I should head downstairs...
Got to make sure those idiots aren't breaking my equipment.
Okay.
I think I'll power down the RFP.
I need to do my exercises before bed.

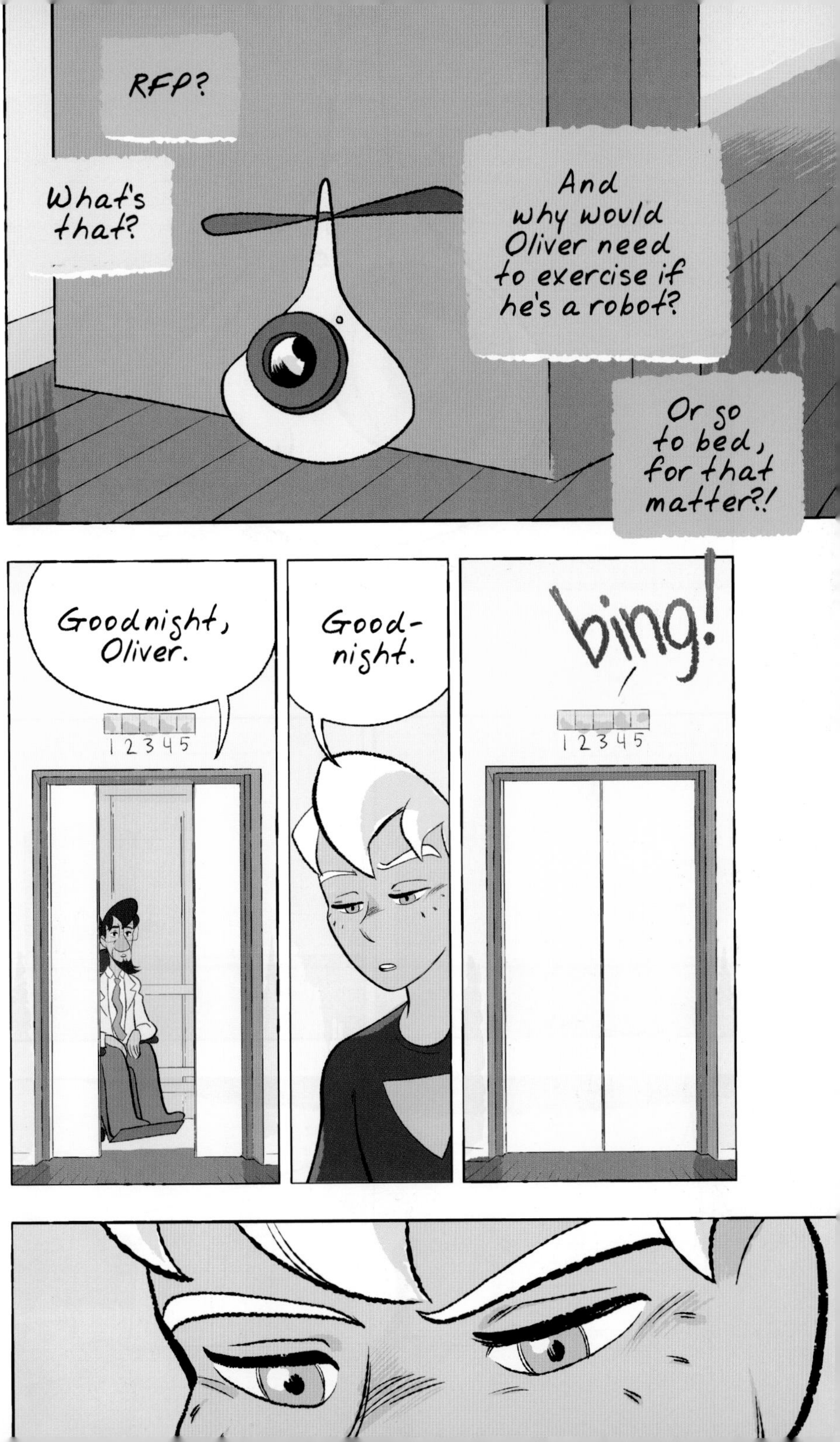
RFP?
What's that?
And why would Oliver need to exercise if he's a robot?
Or so to bed, for that matter?!
Goodnight, Oliver.
Good-night.
bing!
1 2 3 4 5
1 2 3 4 5

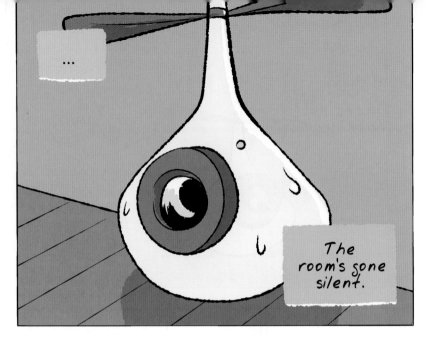

...

The room's gone silent.

Is it safe to come out?

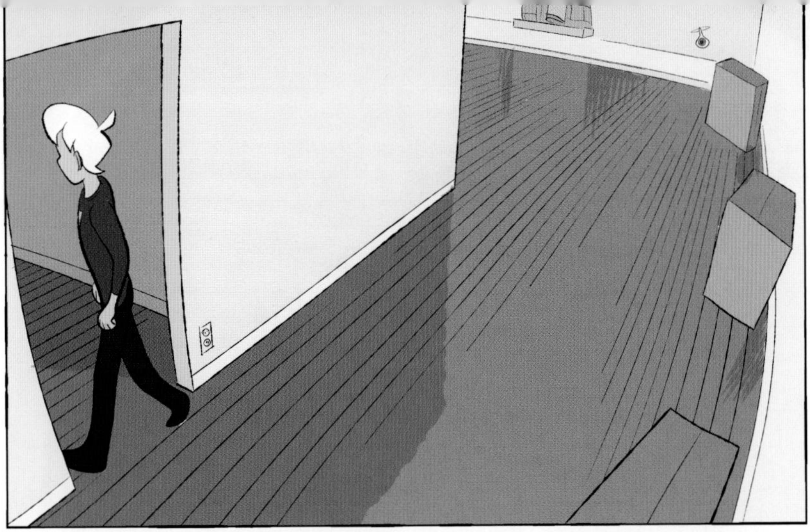
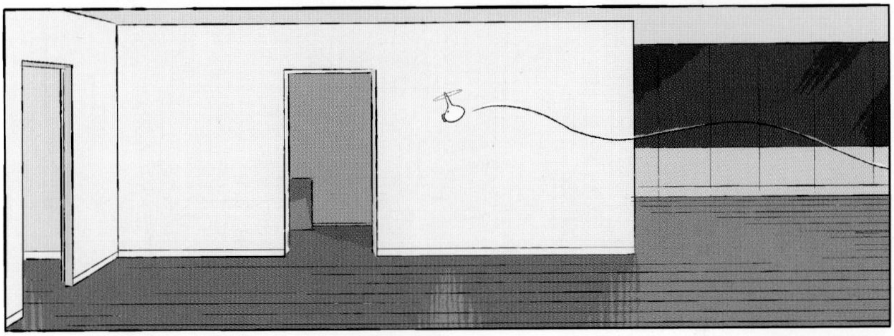
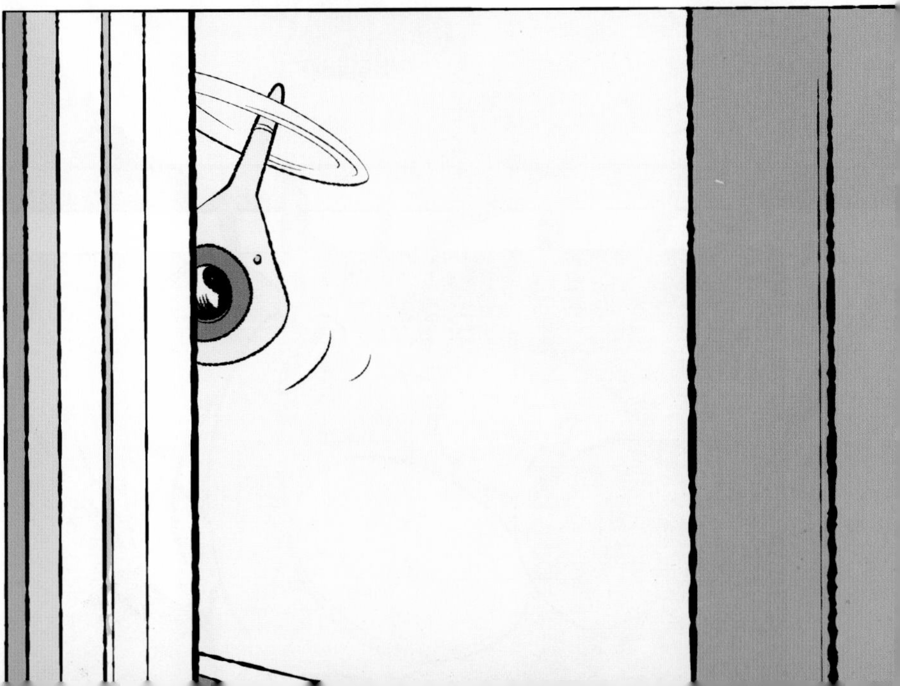

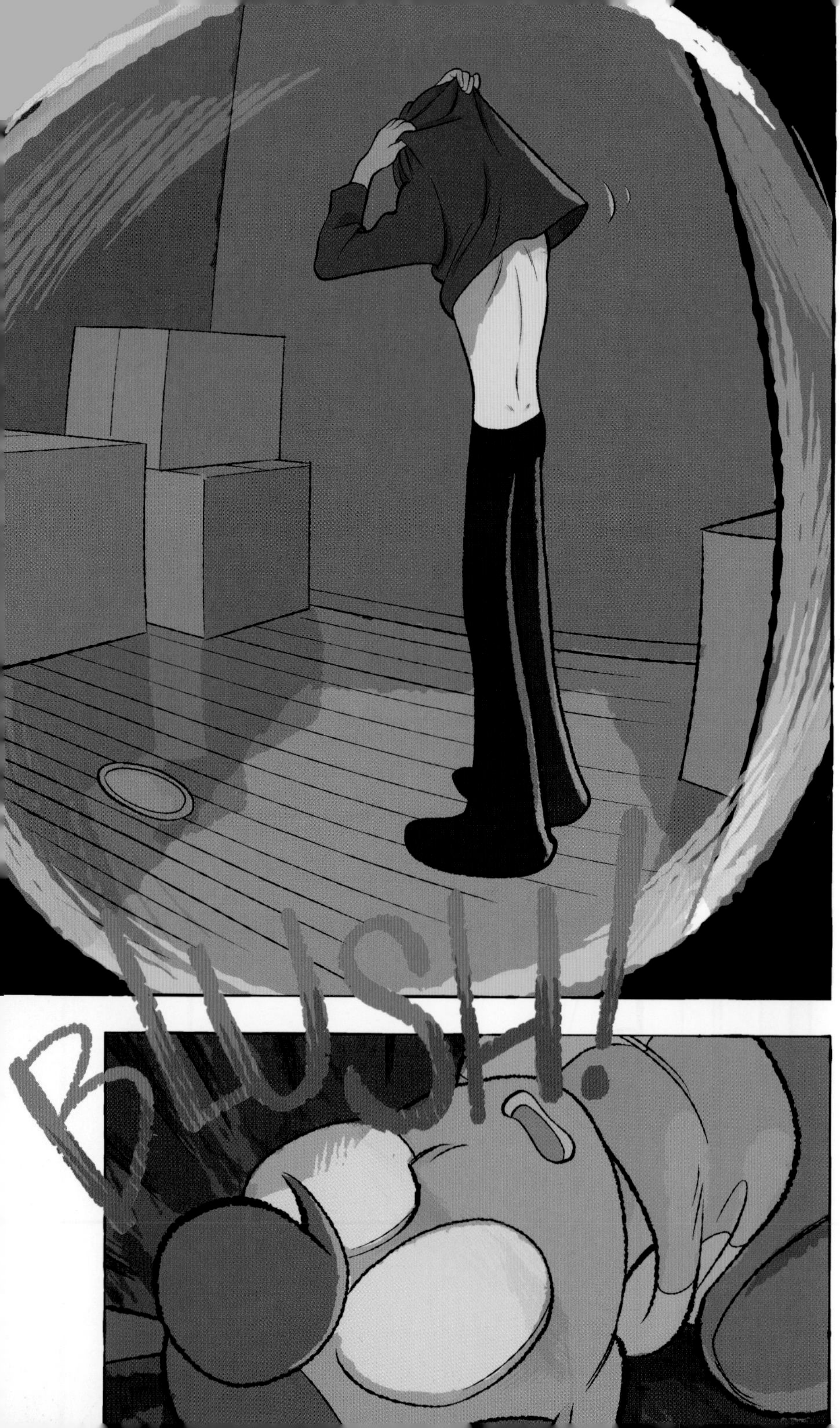
BLUSH!

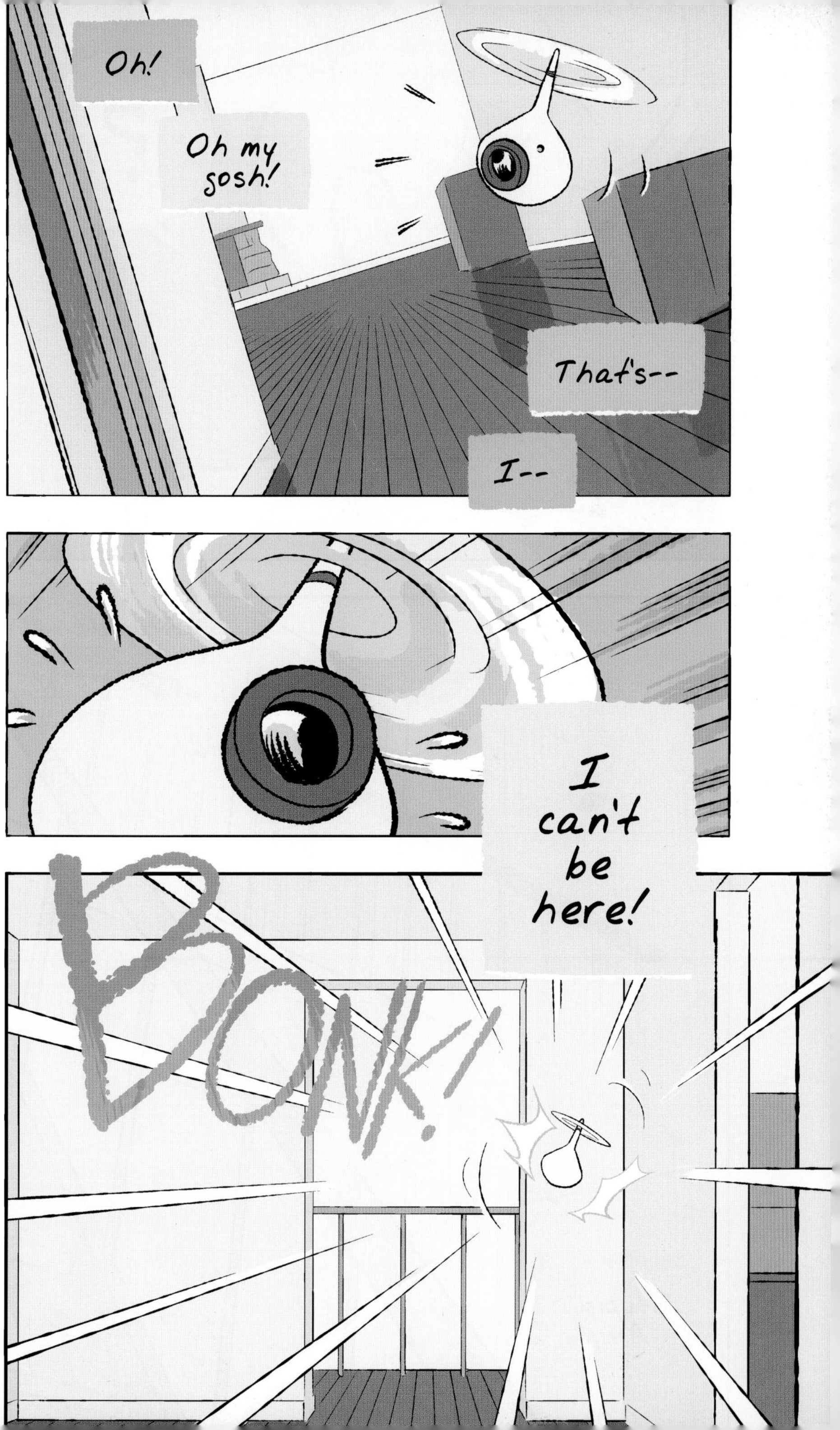
Oh!
Oh my gosh!
That's--
I--
I can't be here!
BONK!

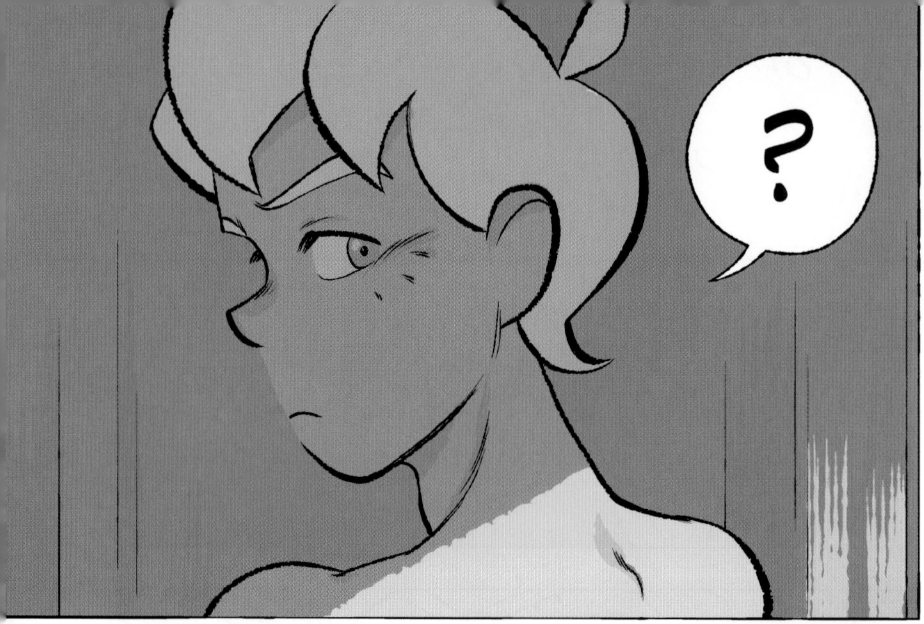
?

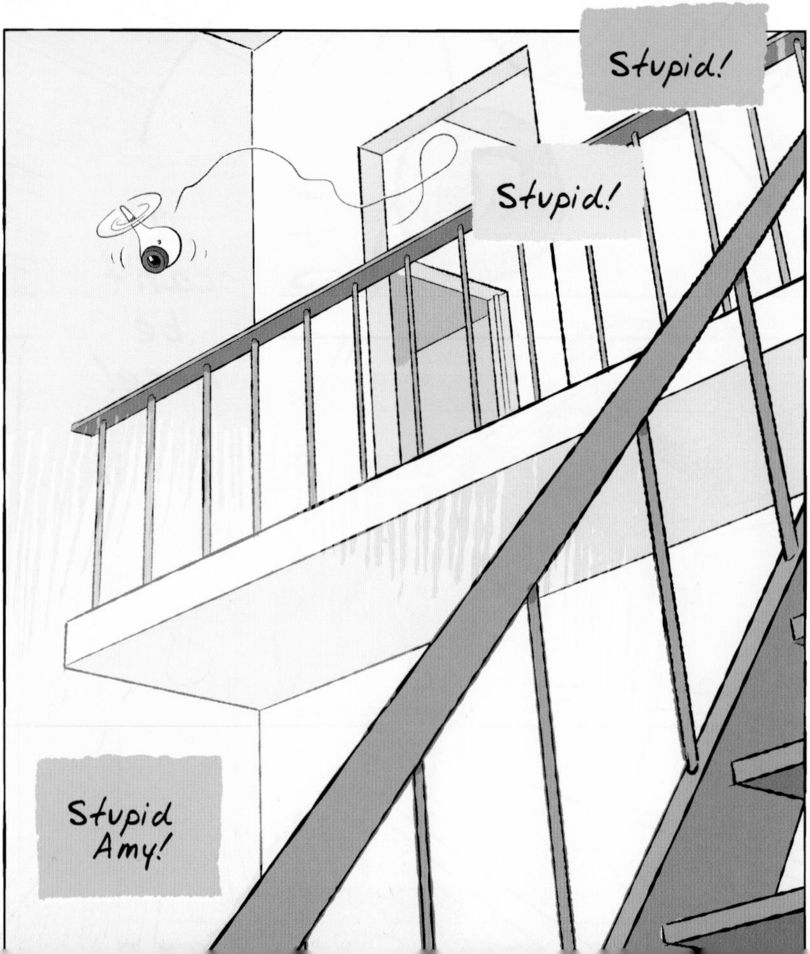
Stupid!
Stupid!
Stupid Amy!

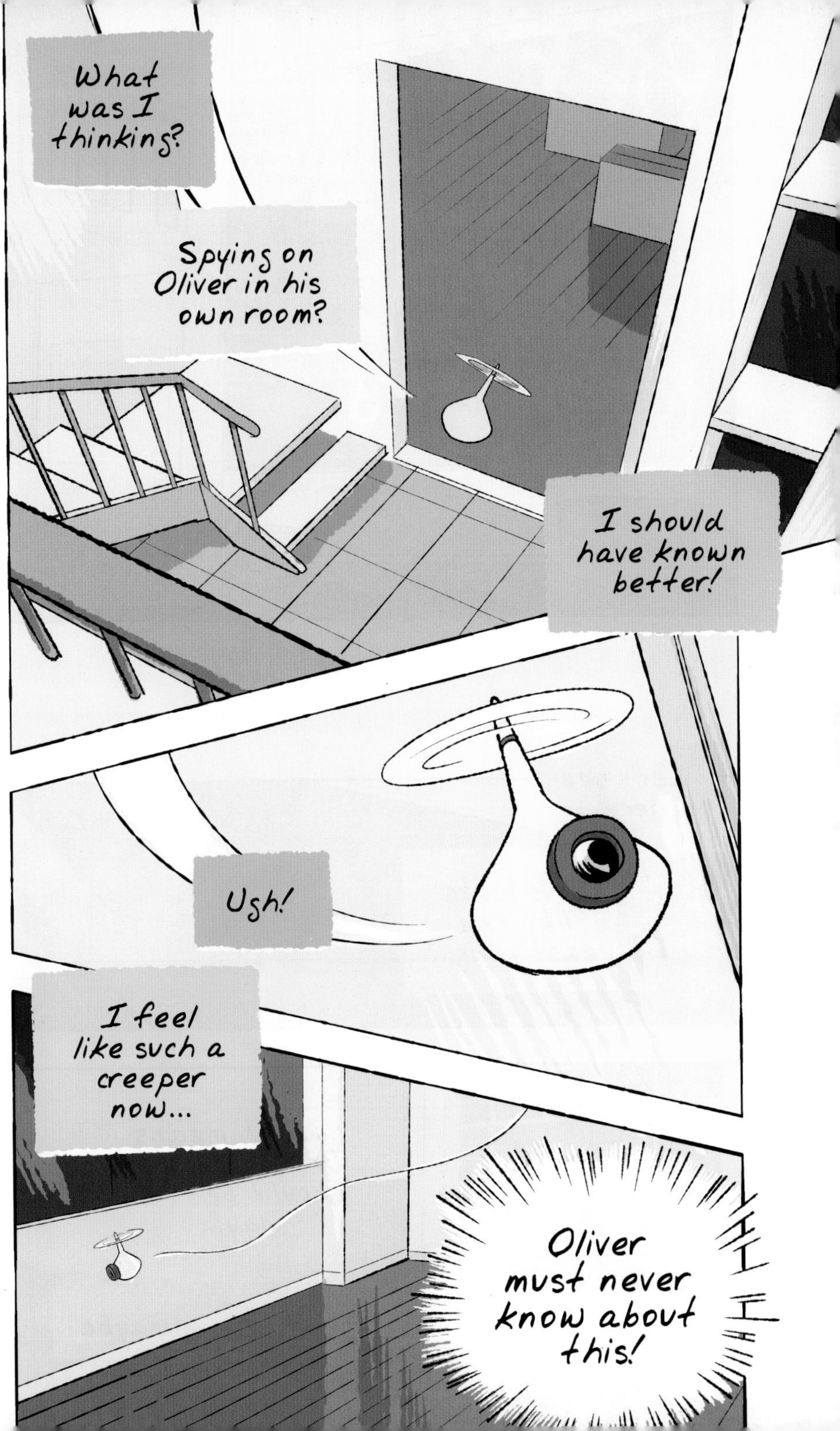
What was I thinking?
Spying on Oliver in his own room?
I should have known better!
Ugh!
I feel like such a creeper now...
Oliver must never know about this!

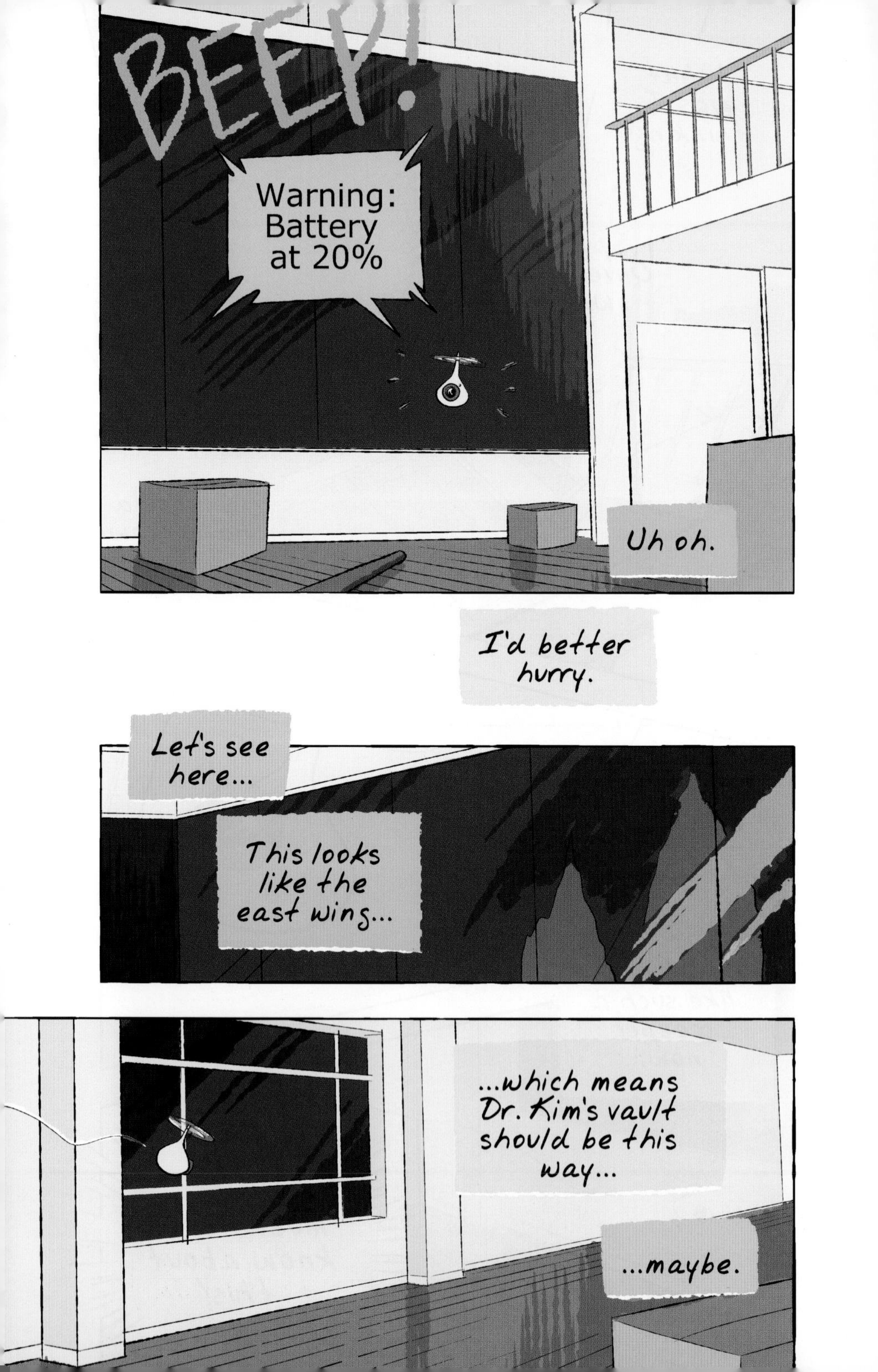
BEEP!
Warning: Battery at 20%
Uh oh.
I'd better hurry.
Let's see here...
This looks like the east wing...
...which means Dr. Kim's vault should be this way...
...maybe.

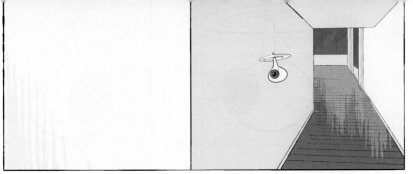

KLANG!

Careful, dude!

Whoops, ha ha.

Dr. Kim will skin us alive if there's even a scratch on this machine!

Whatever.

I'm not afraid of that old cripple...

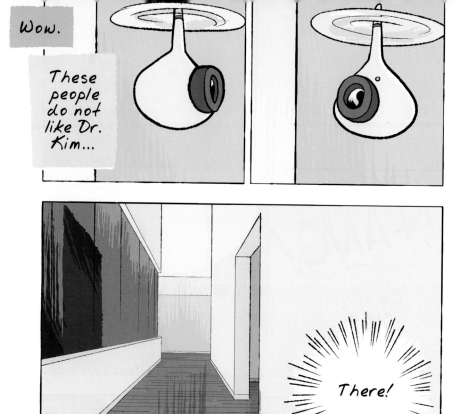

Wow.

These people do not like Dr. Kim...

There!

There it is!

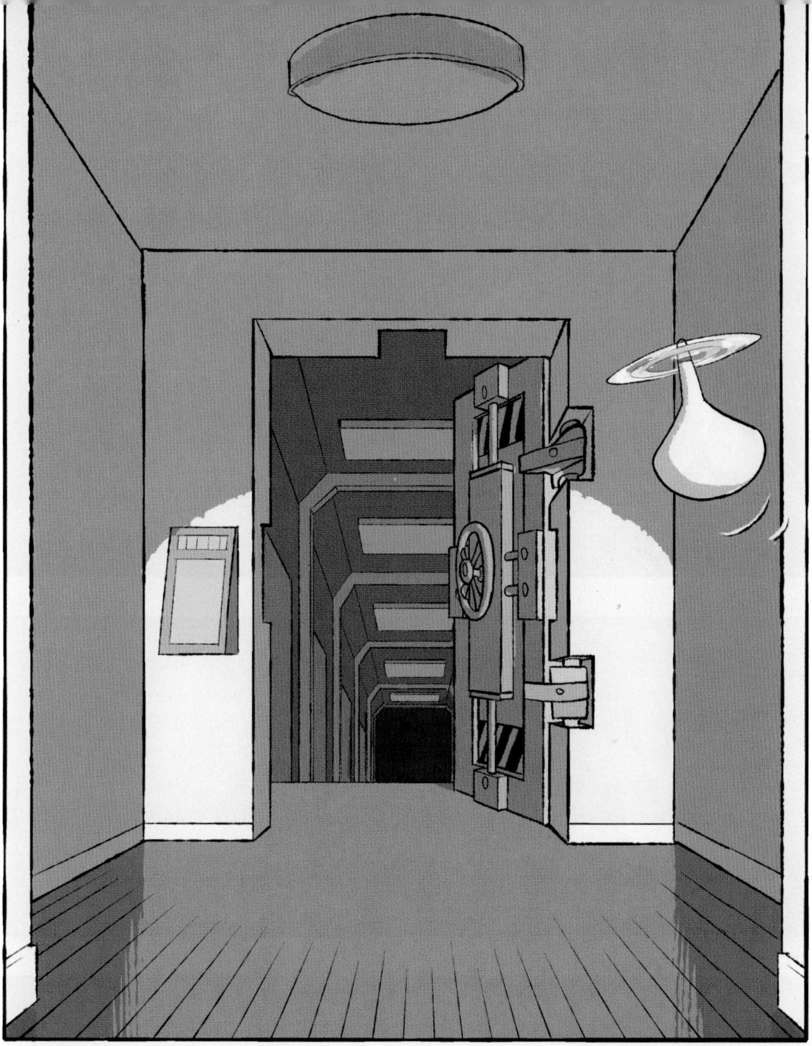

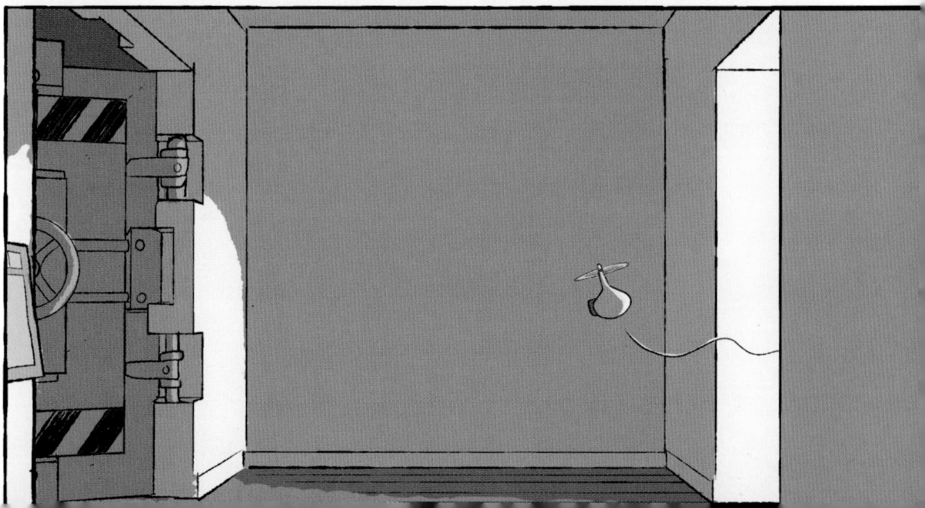

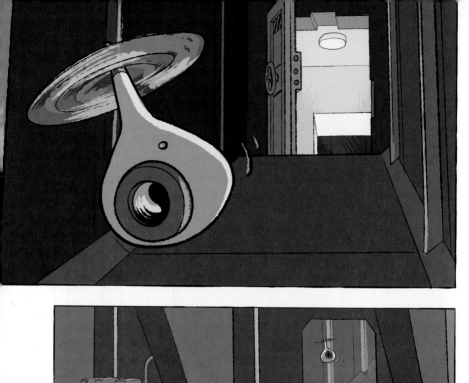

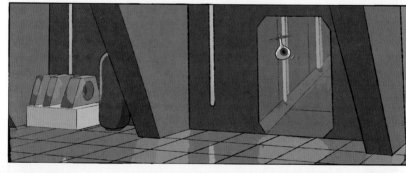

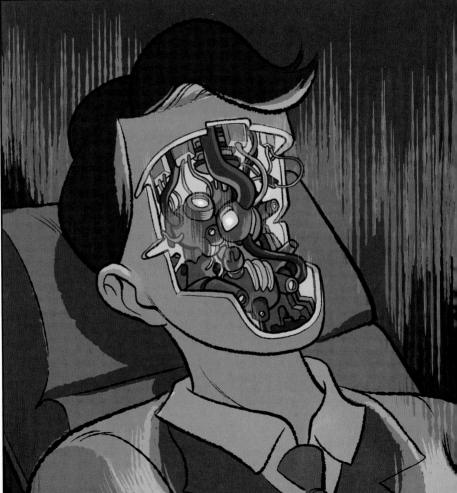

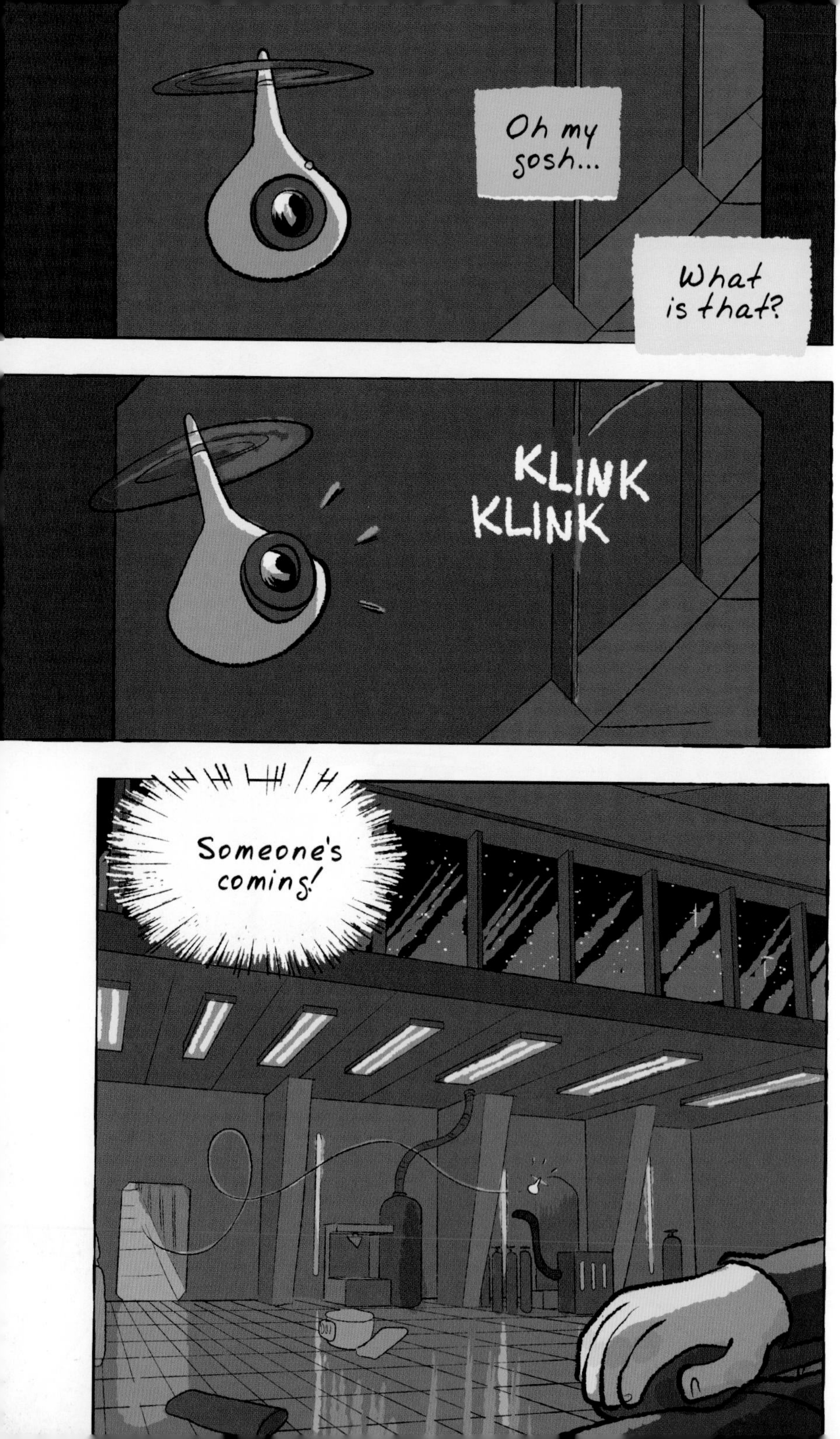
Oh my gosh...
What is that?
KLINK
KLINK
Someone's coming!

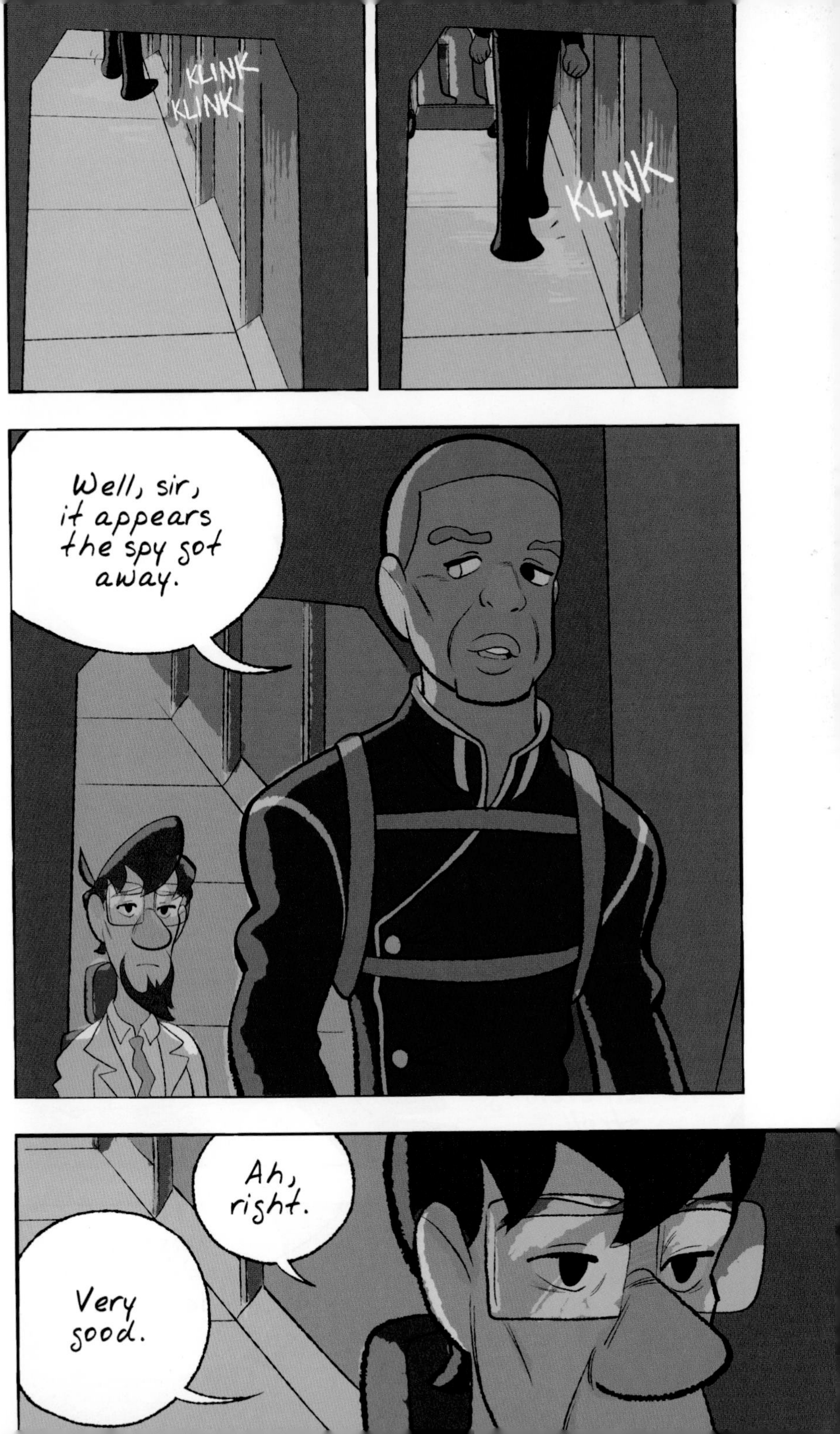
KLINK
KLINK
KLINK
Well, sir, it appears the spy got away.
Ah, right.
Very good.

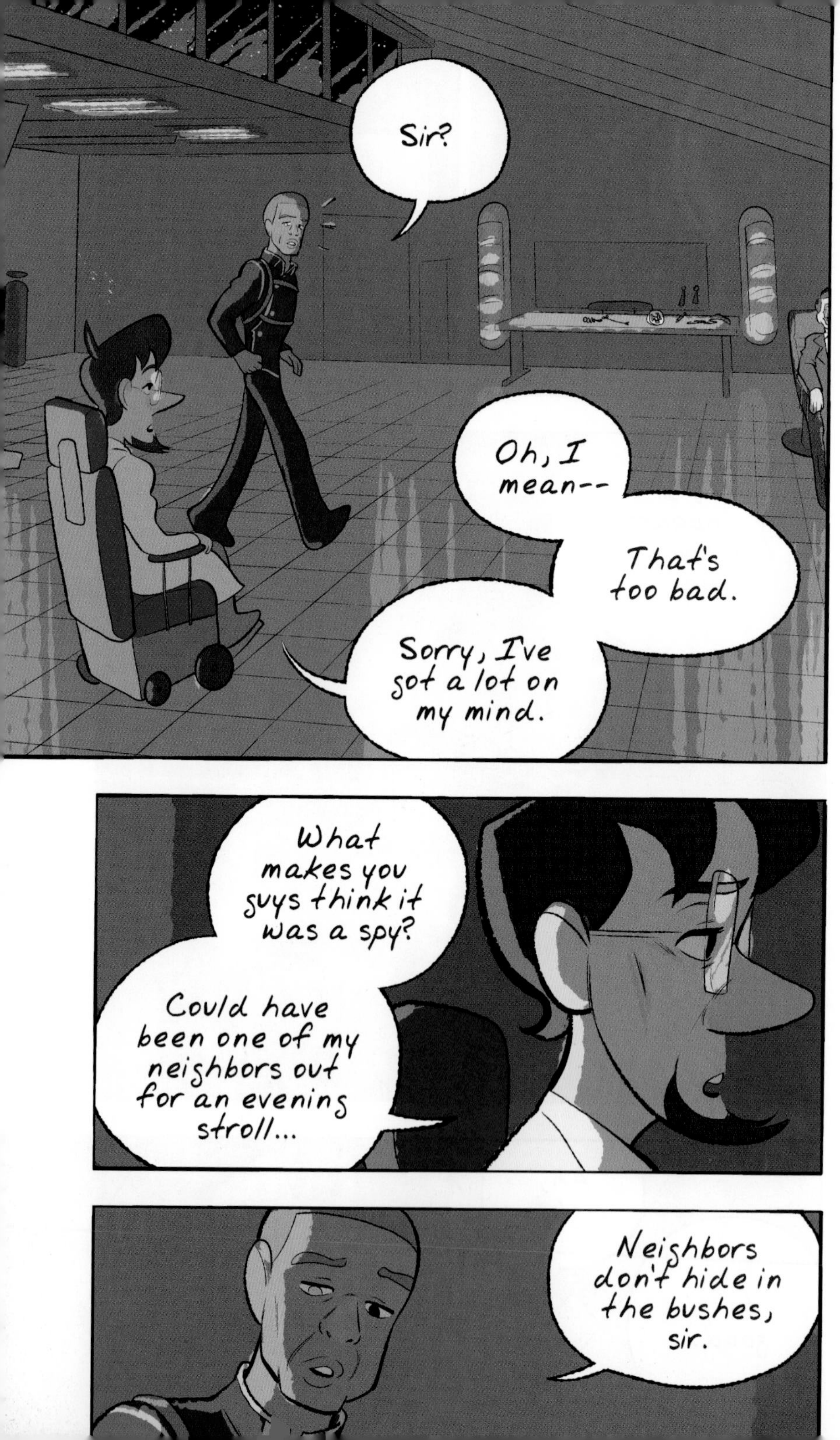
Sir?
Oh, I mean--
That's too bad.
Sorry, I've got a lot on my mind.
What makes you guys think it was a spy?
Could have been one of my neighbors out for an evening stroll...
Neighbors don't hide in the bushes, sir.

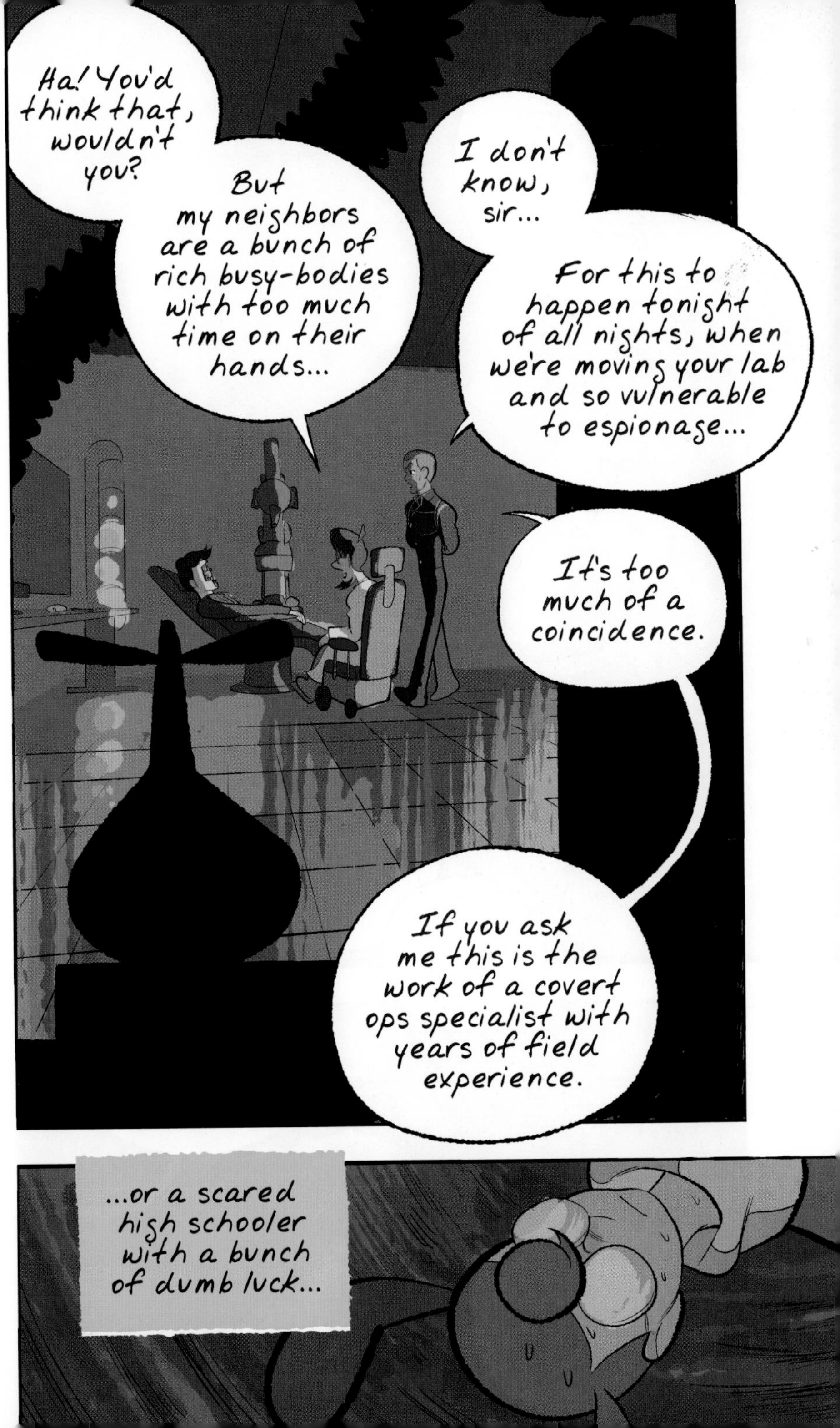
Ha! You'd think that, wouldn't you?
But my neighbors are a bunch of rich busy-bodies with too much time on their hands...
I don't know, sir...
For this to happen tonight of all nights, when we're moving your lab and so vulnerable to espionage...
It's too much of a coincidence.
If you ask me this is the work of a covert ops specialist with years of field experience.
...or a scared high schooler with a bunch of dumb luck...

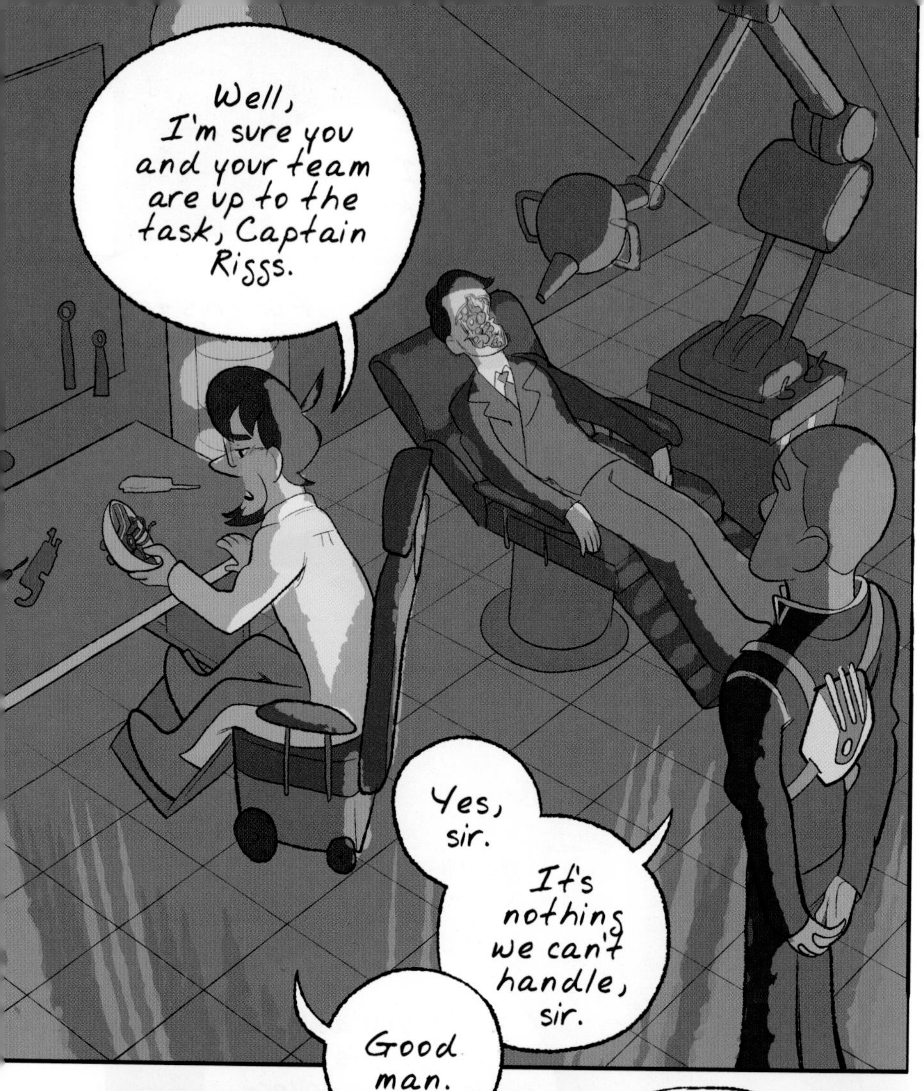
Well, I'm sure you and your team are up to the task, Captain Rissss.
Yes, sir.
It's nothing we can't handle, sir.
Good man.

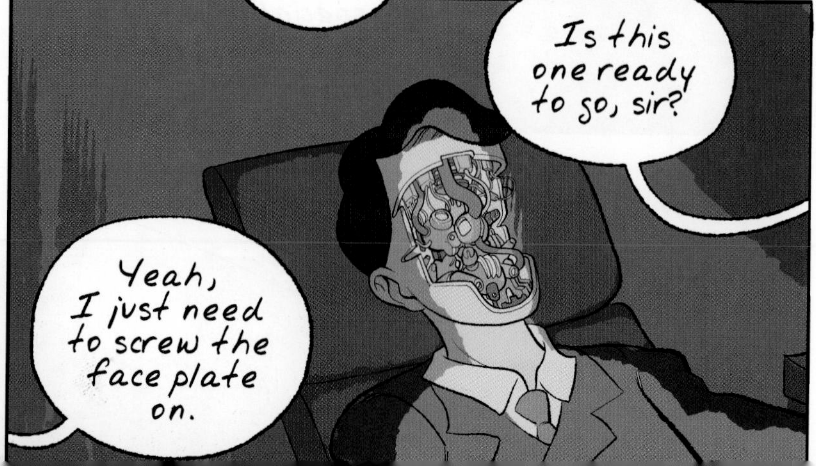
Is this one ready to go, sir?
Yeah, I just need to screw the face plate on.

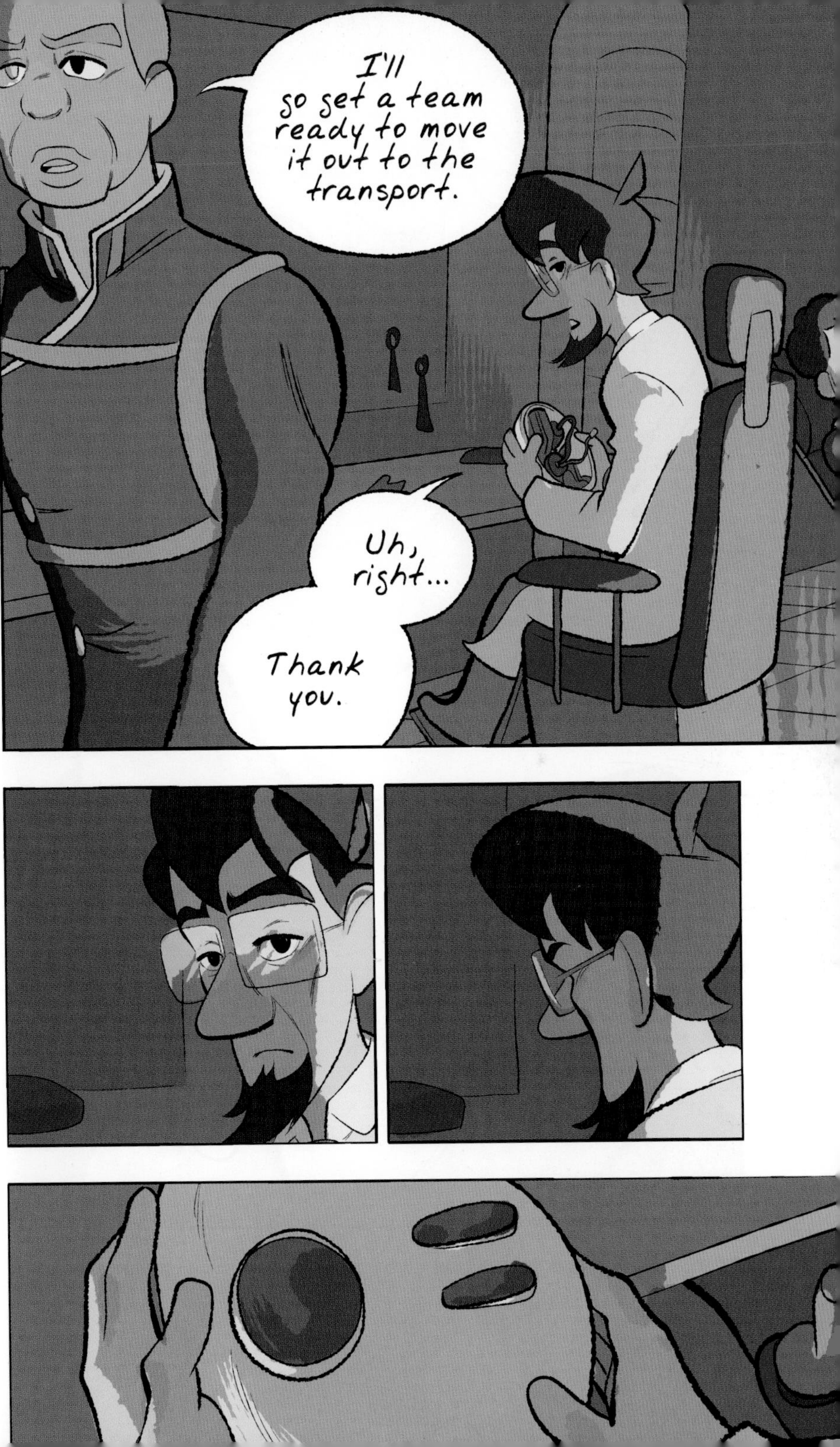
I'll go get a team ready to move it out to the transport.
Uh, right...
Thank you.

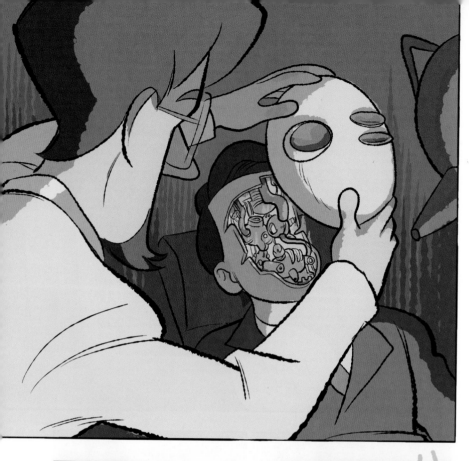

click!

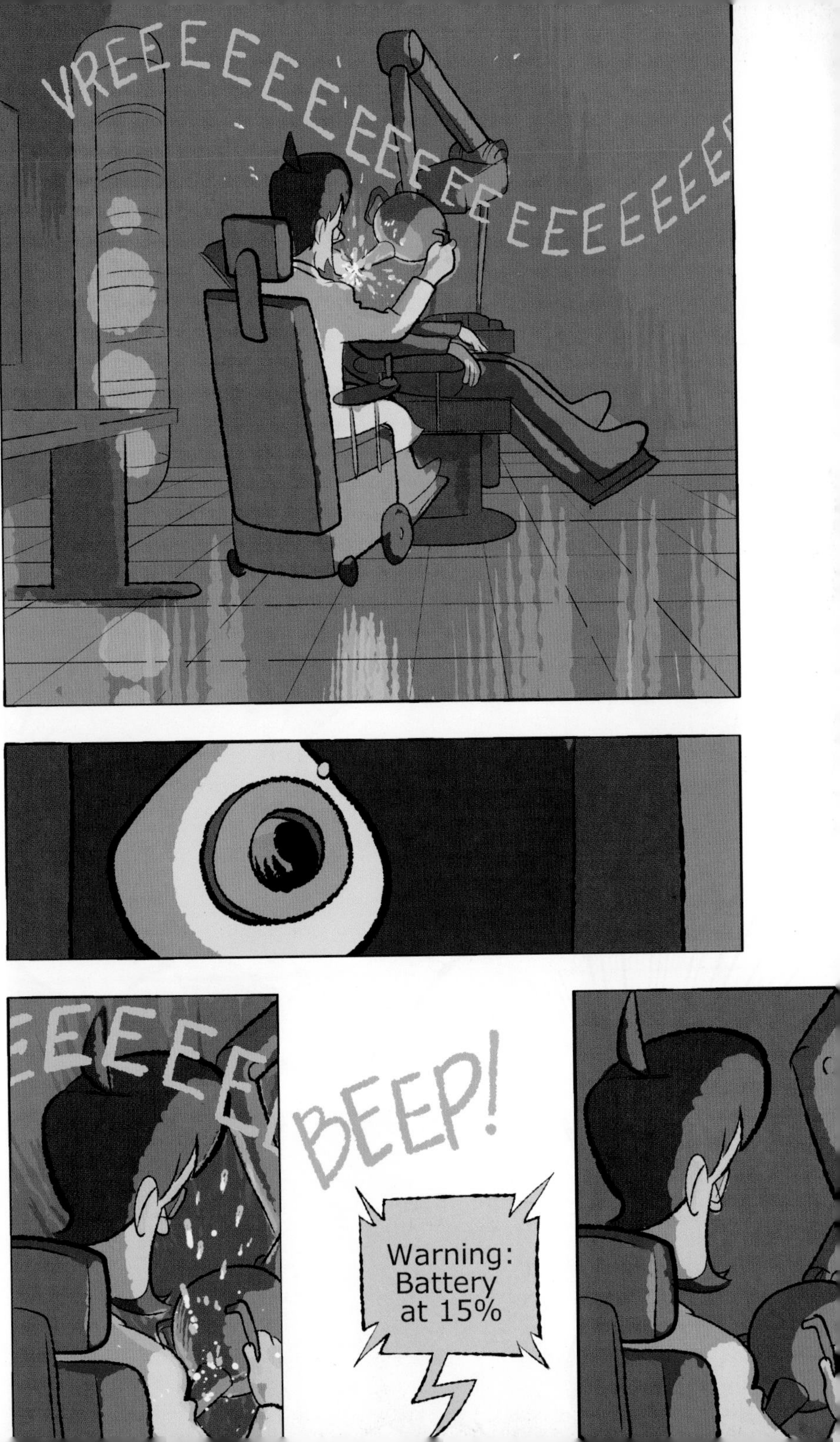
VREEEEEEEEEEEEEEEEEEE
EEEEEE
BEEP!
Warning: Battery at 15%

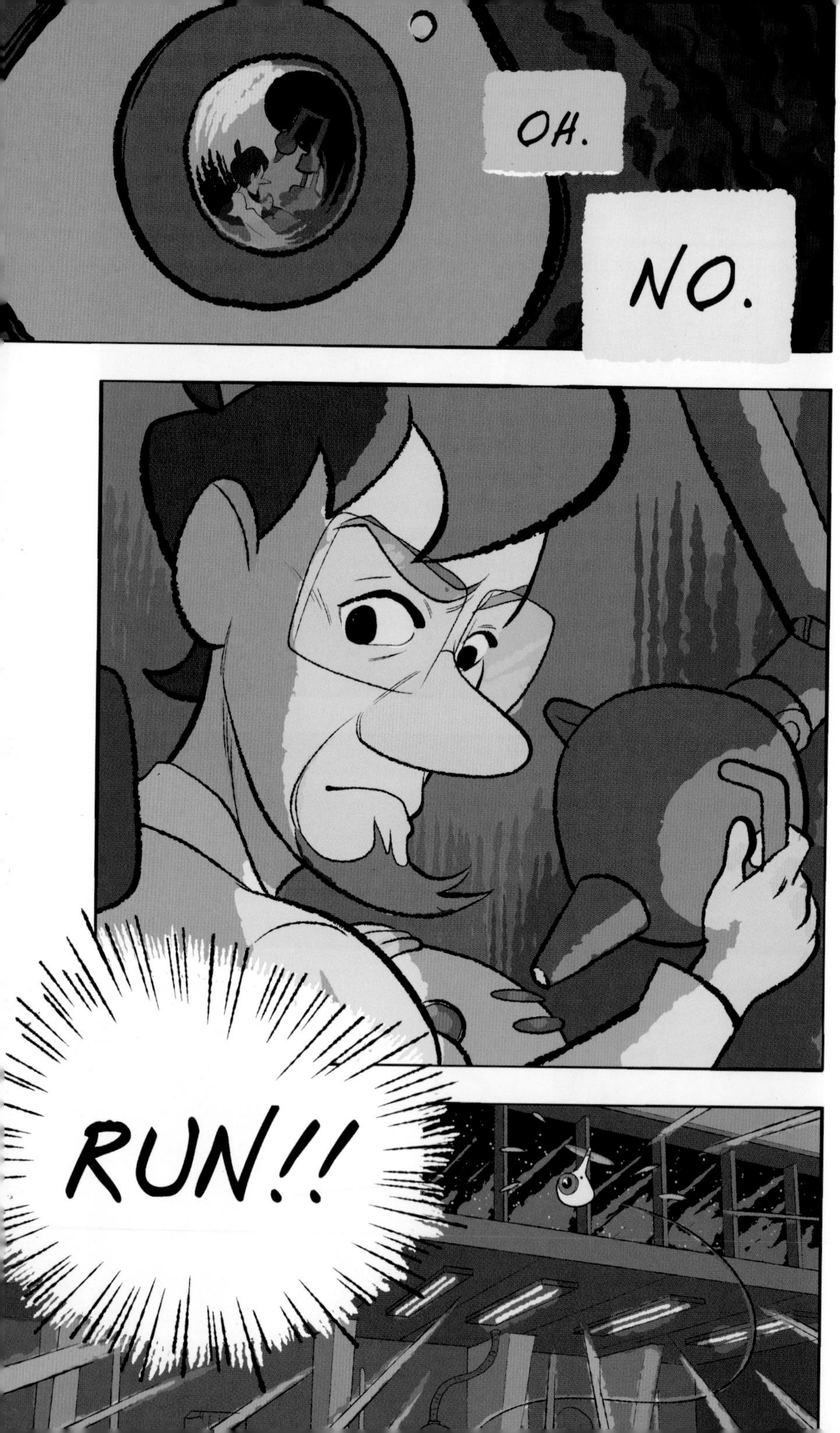
OH.
NO.
RUN!!

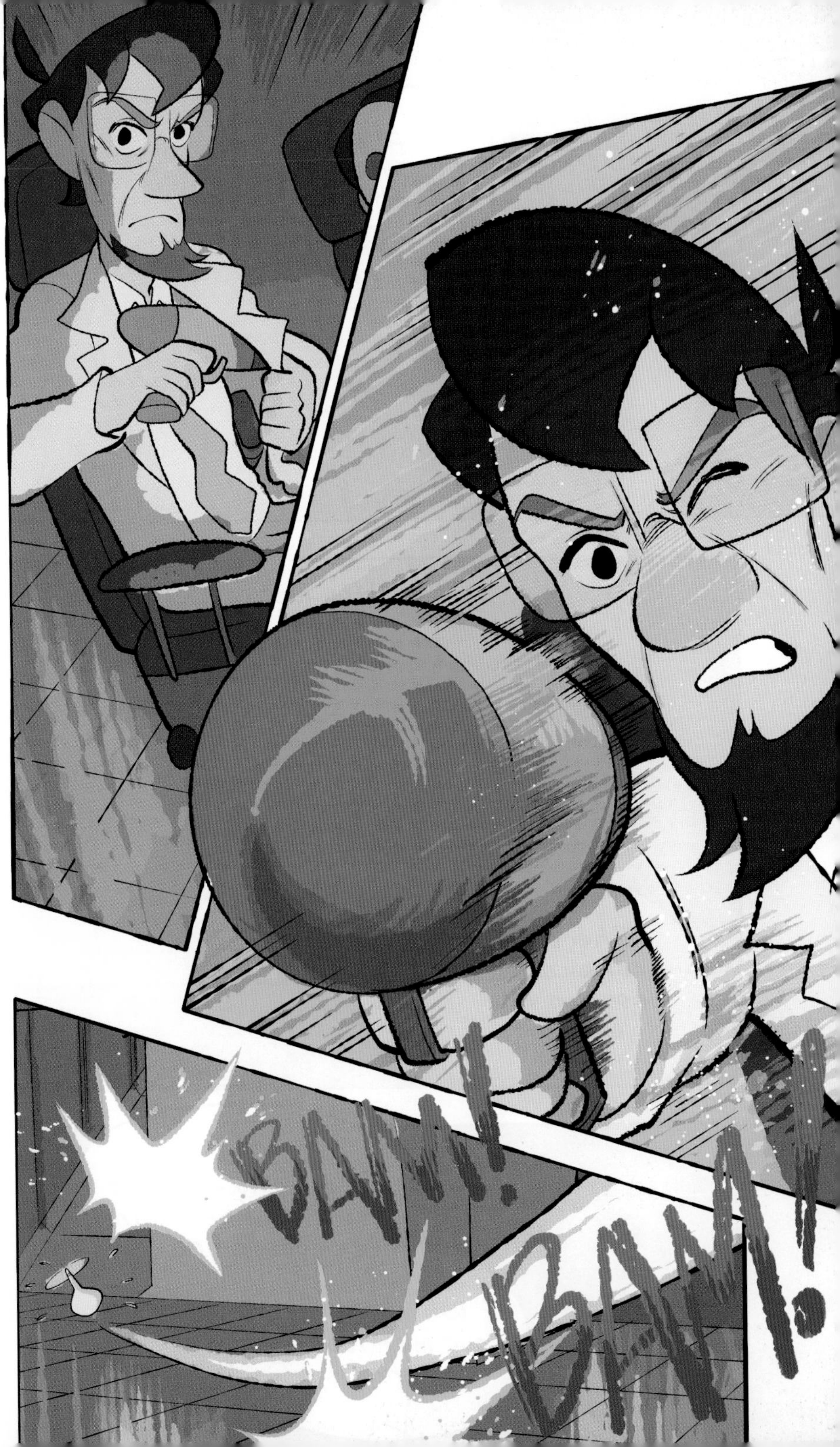
BAM!
BAM!

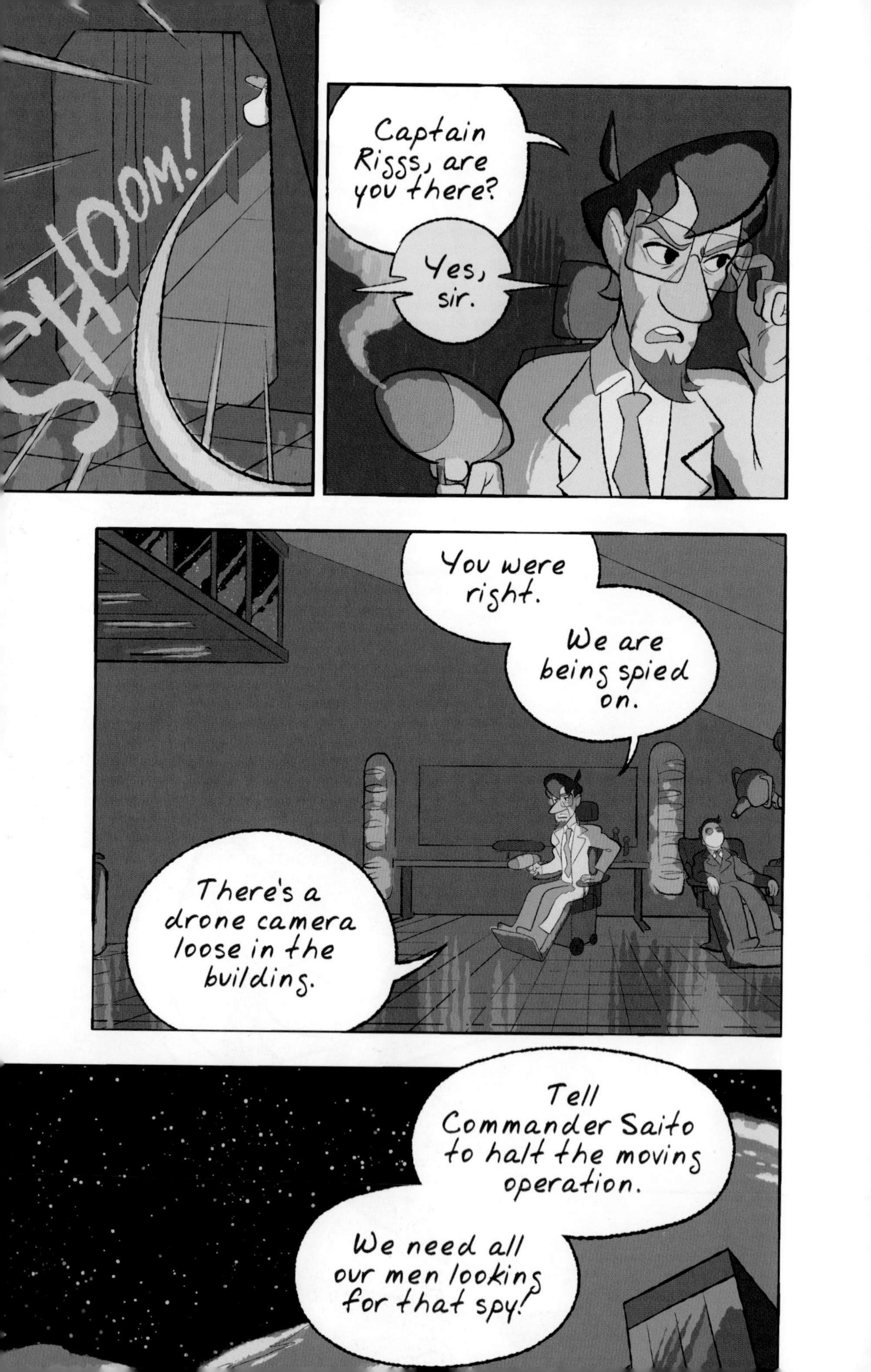
SHOOM!
Captain Risss, are you there?
Yes, sir.
You were right.
We are beins spied on.
There's a drone camera loose in the buildins.
Tell Commander Saito to halt the movins operation.
We need all our men lookins for that spy!

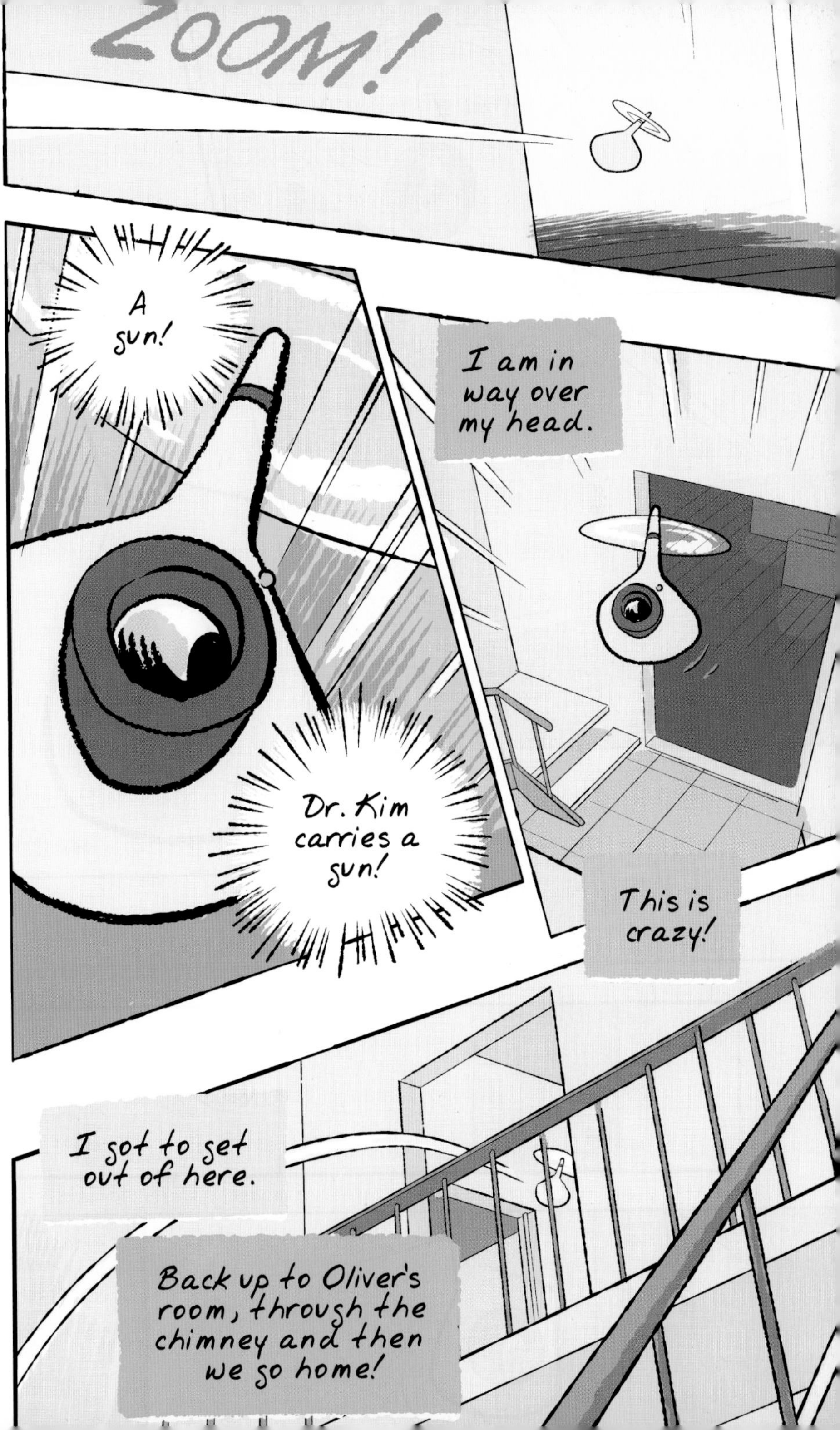
ZOOM!
A gun!
Dr. Kim carries a gun!
I am in way over my head.
This is crazy!
I got to get out of here.
Back up to Oliver's room, through the chimney and then we go home!

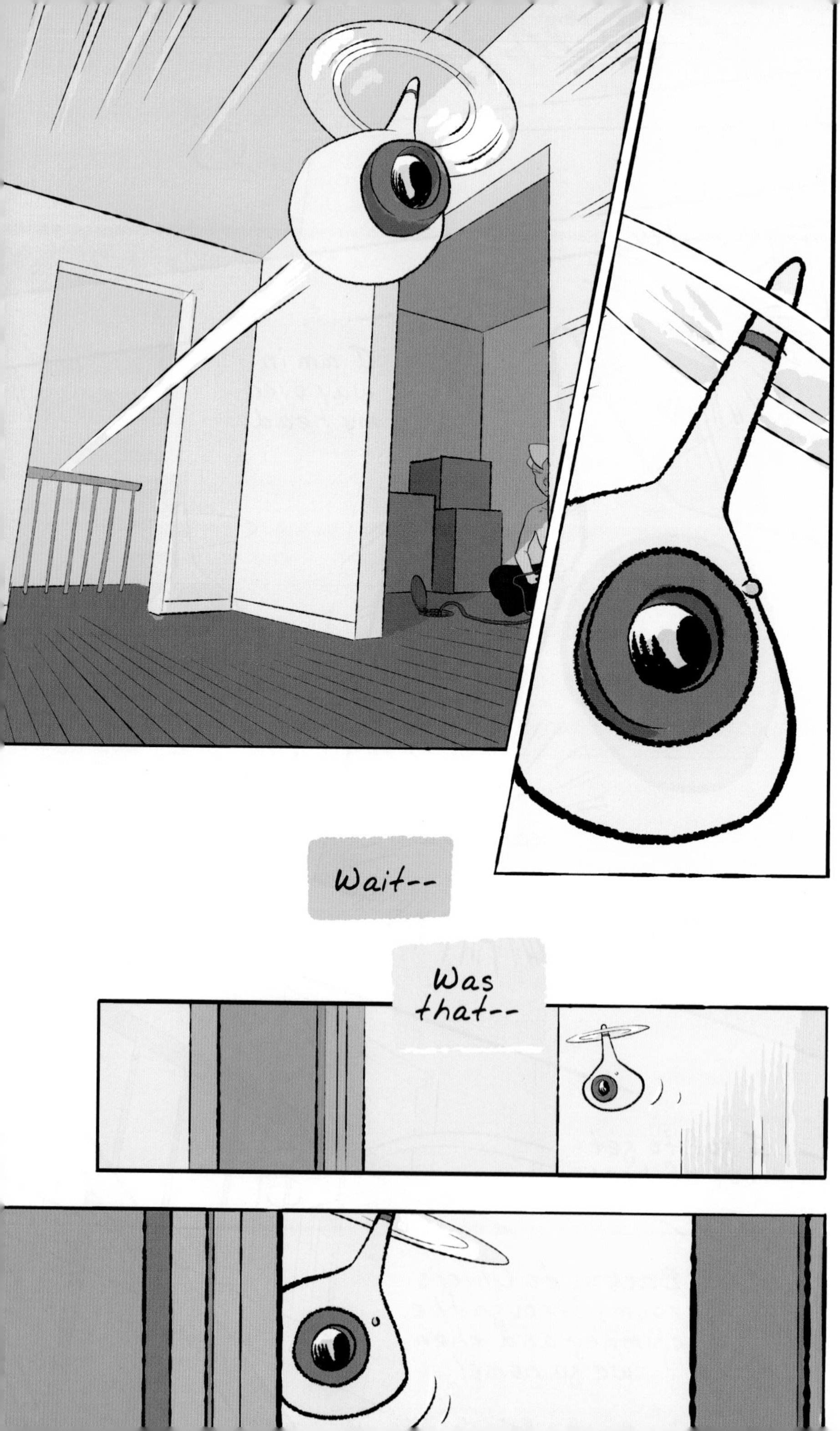
Wait--
Was that--

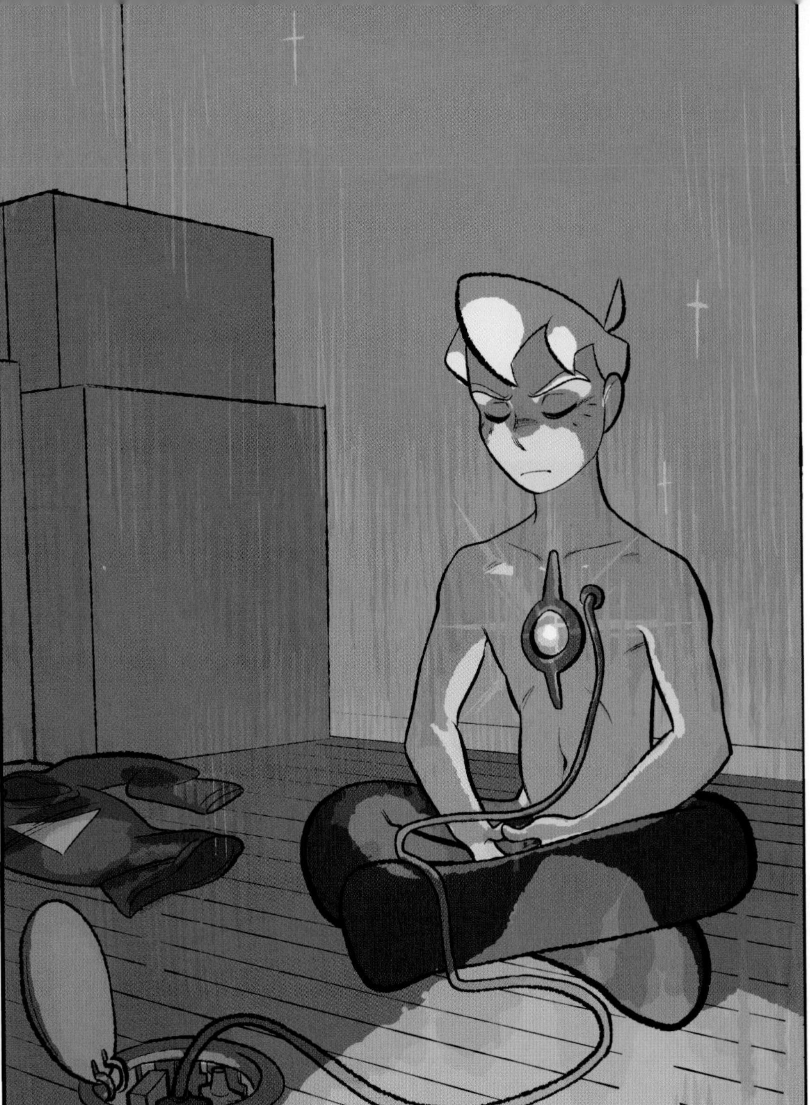

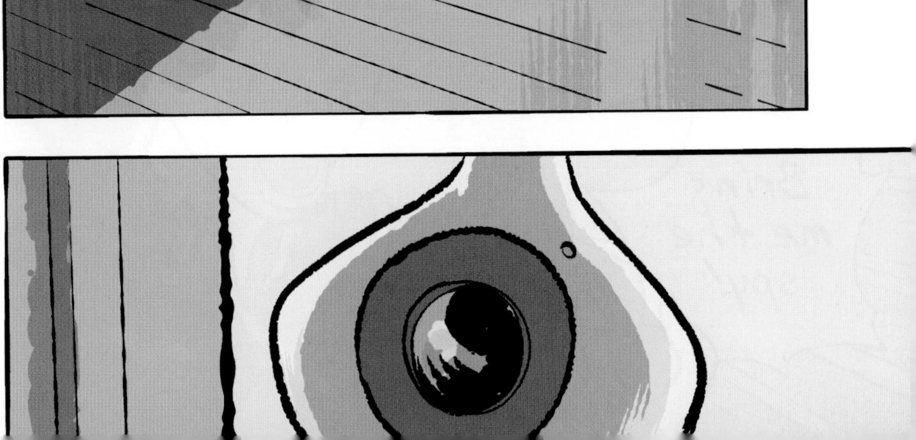

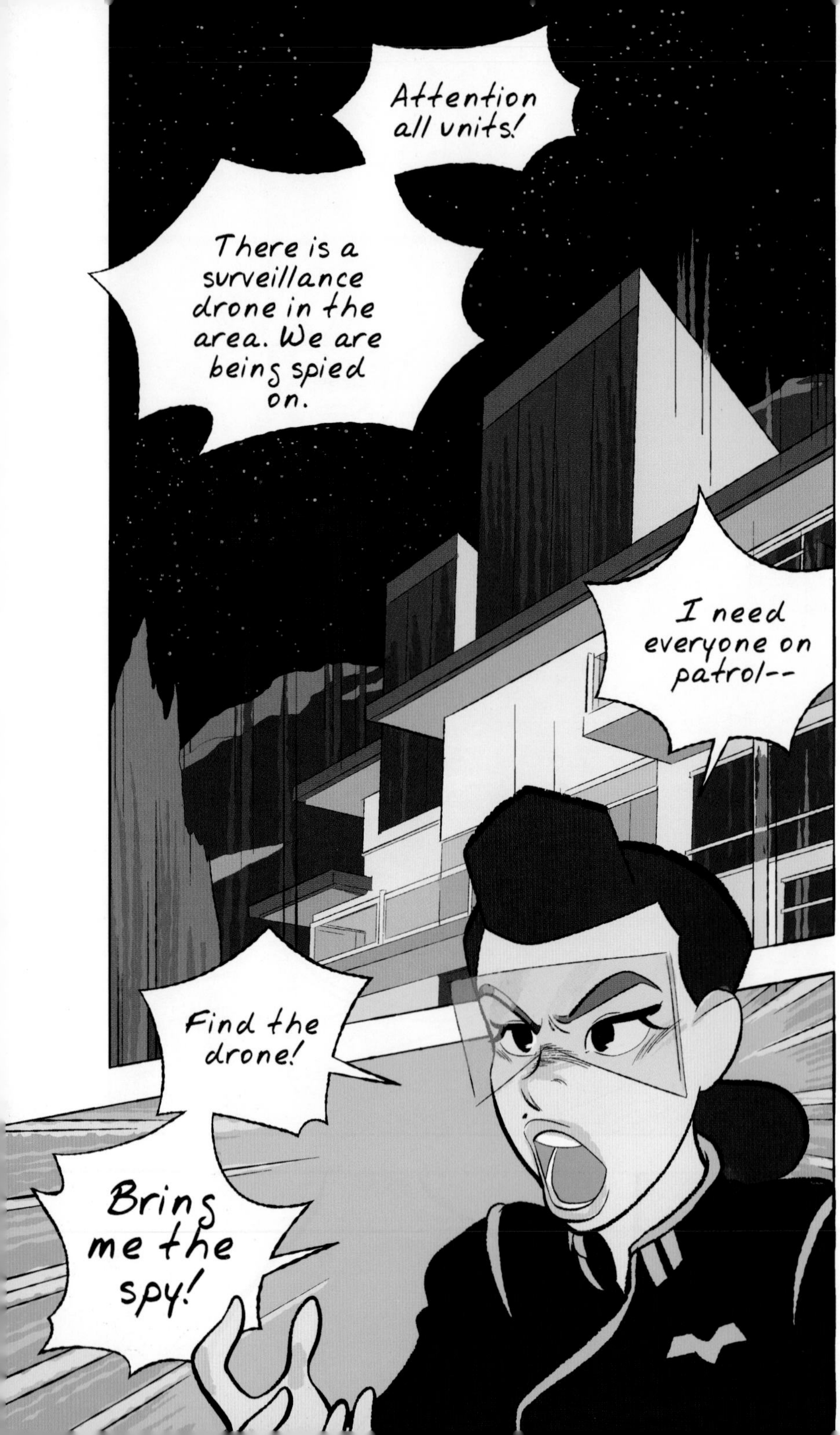
Attention all units!
There is a surveillance drone in the area. We are being spied on.
I need everyone on patrol--
Find the drone!
Bring me the spy!

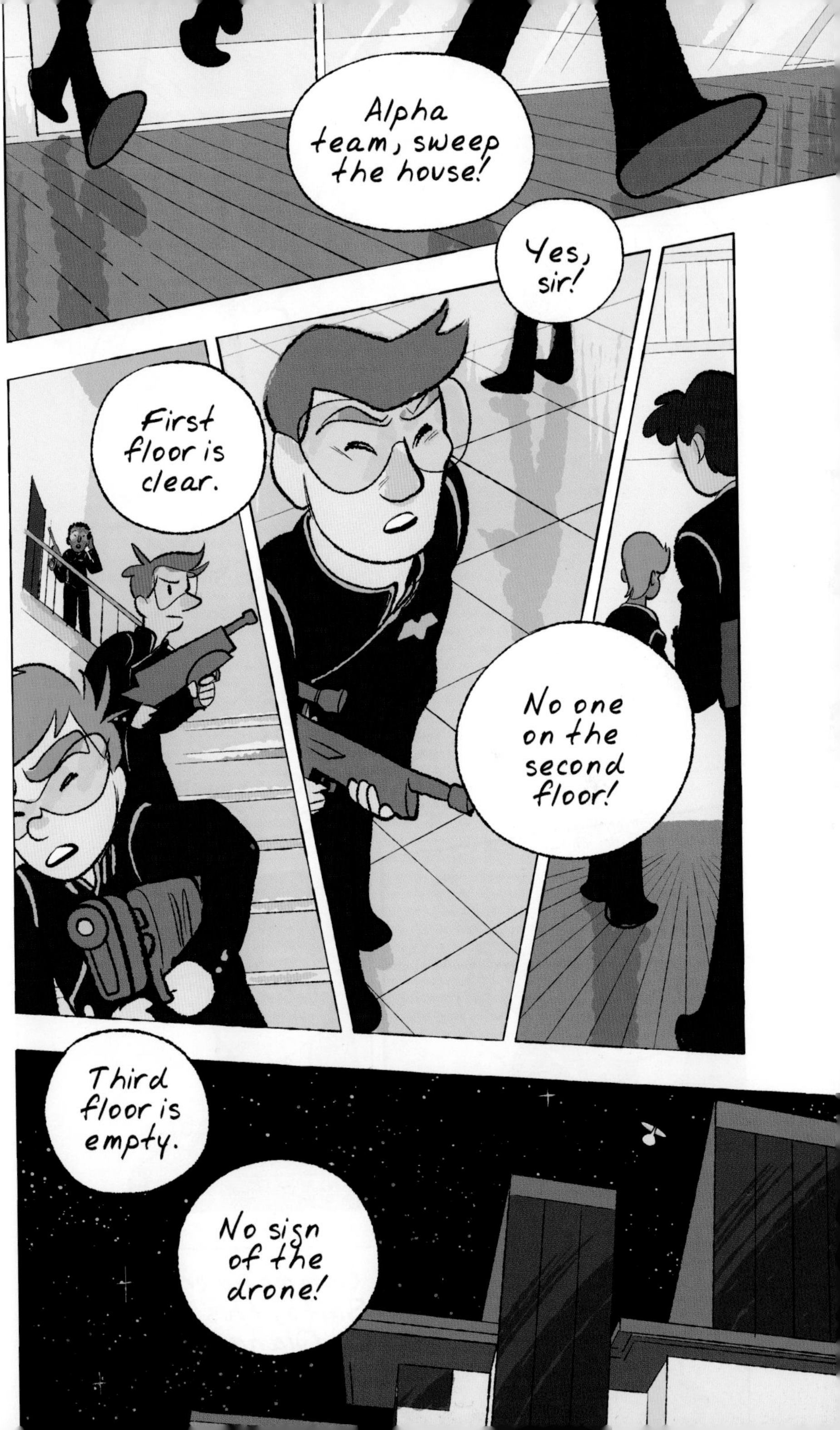
Alpha team, sweep the house!
Yes, sir!
First floor is clear.
No one on the second floor!
Third floor is empty.
No sign of the drone!

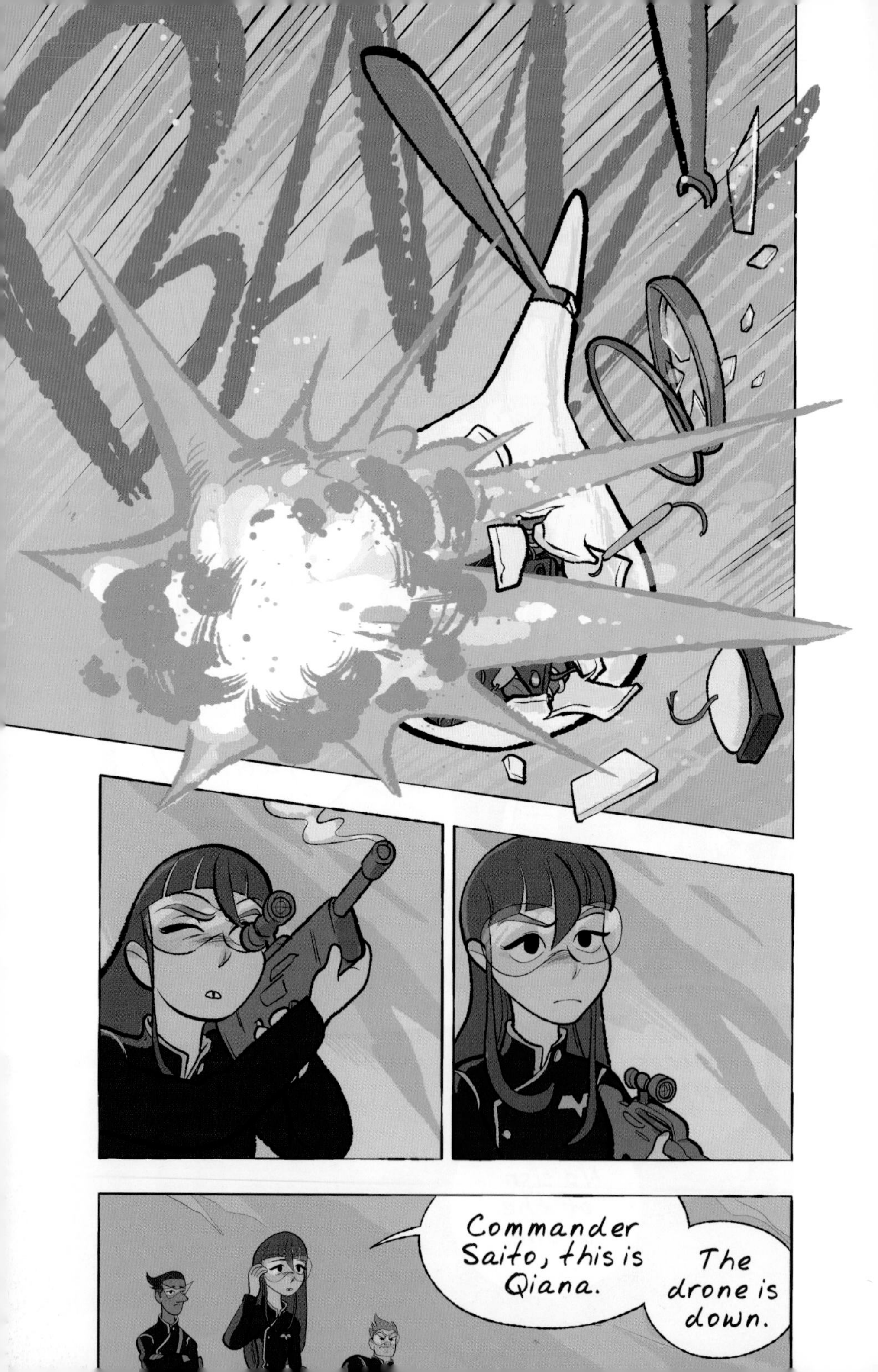
Commander Saito, this is Qiana.
The drone is down.

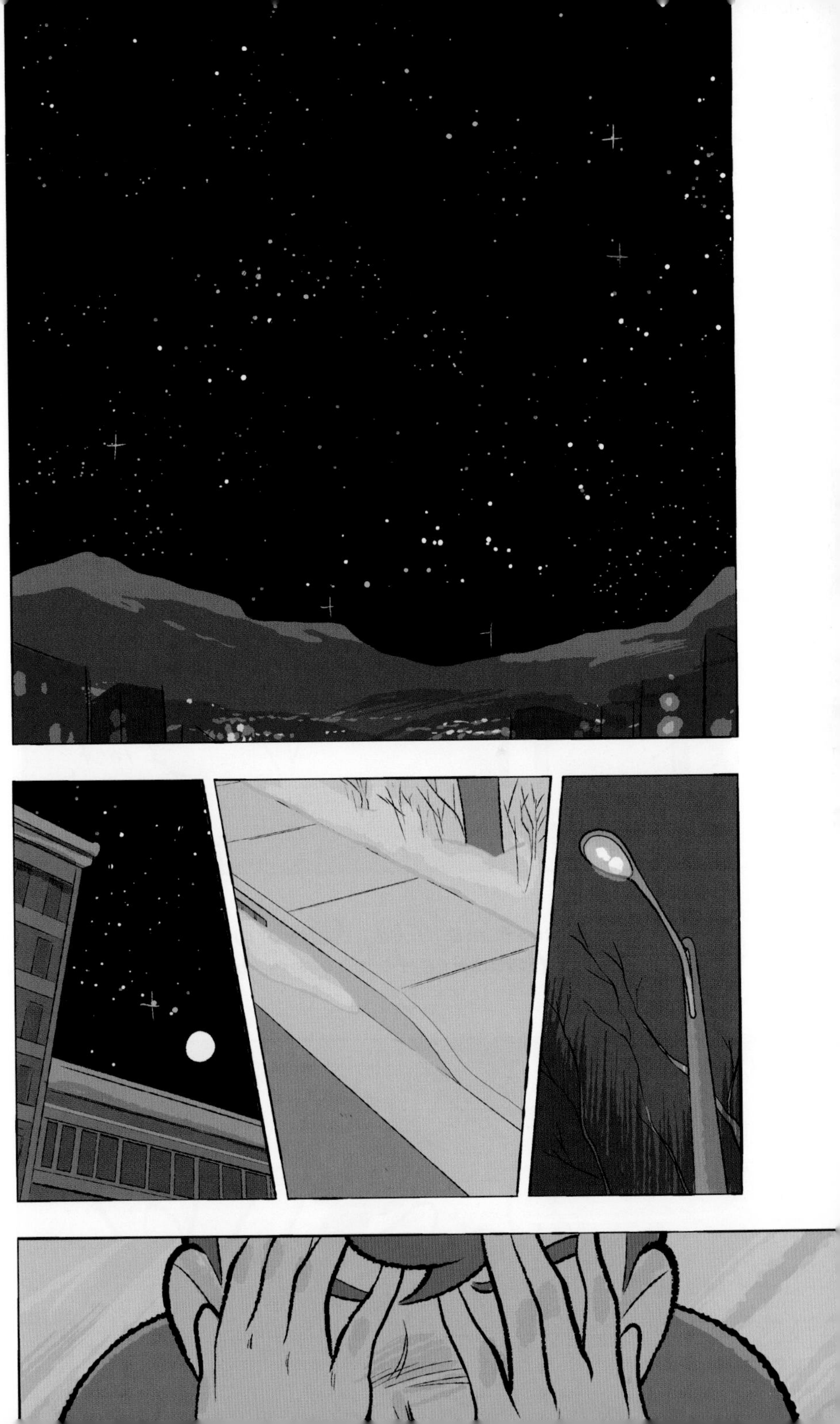

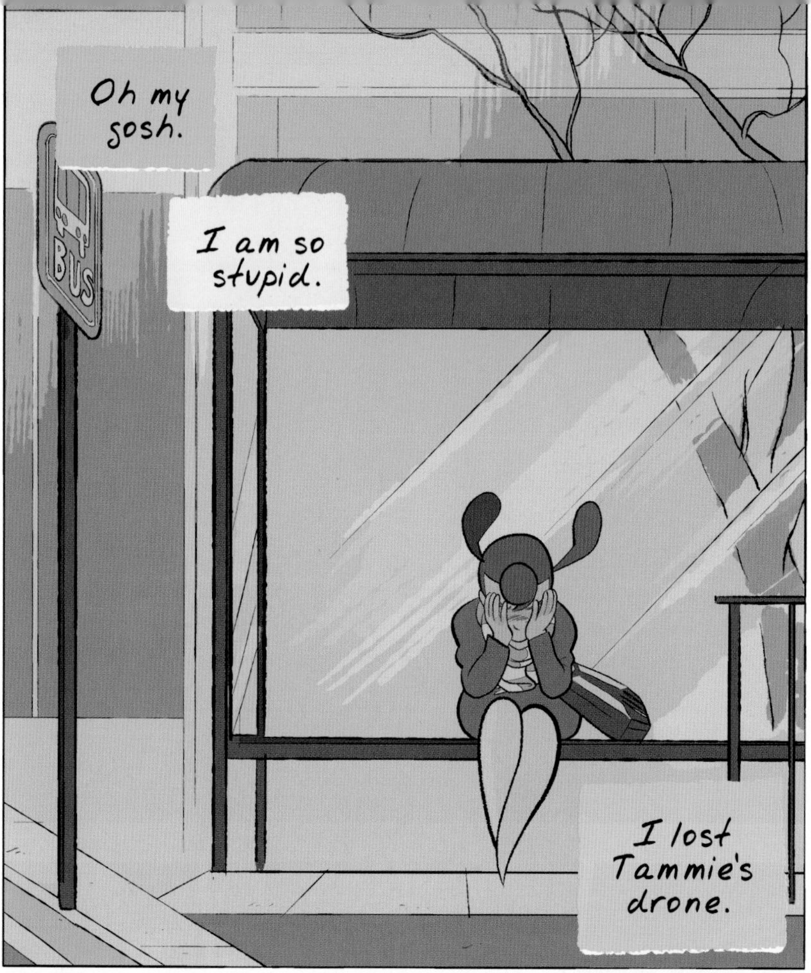
Oh my gosh.
I am so stupid.
BUS
I lost Tammie's drone.

*It'll cost me, like, thirty weeks of allowance to pay her back.*

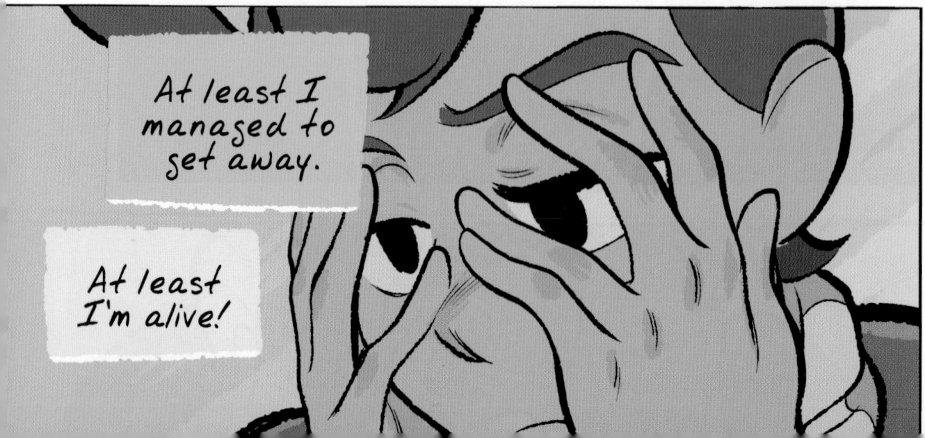
At least I managed to get away.
At least I'm alive!

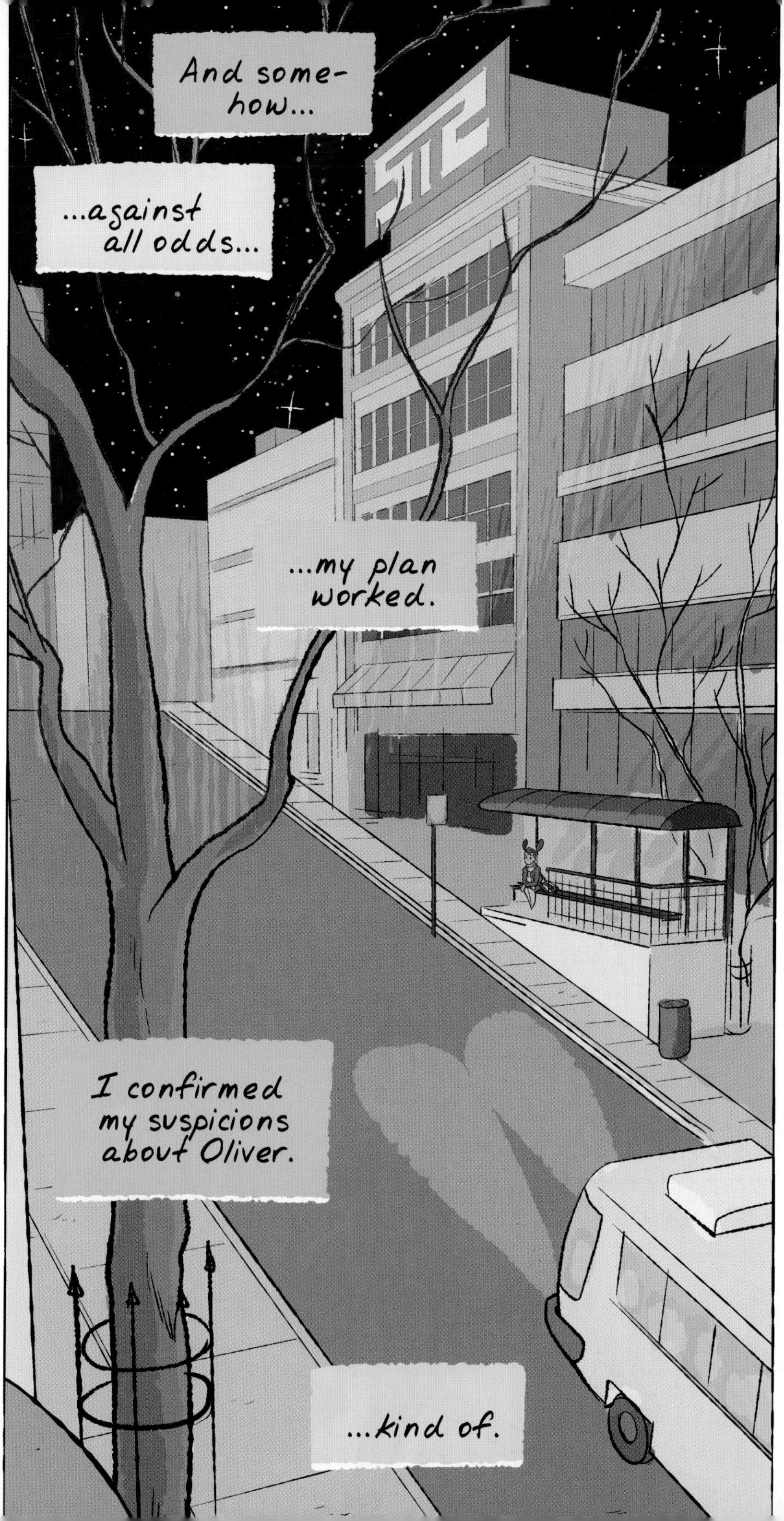
And some-how...
...against all odds...
...my plan worked.
I confirmed my suspicions about Oliver.
...kind of.

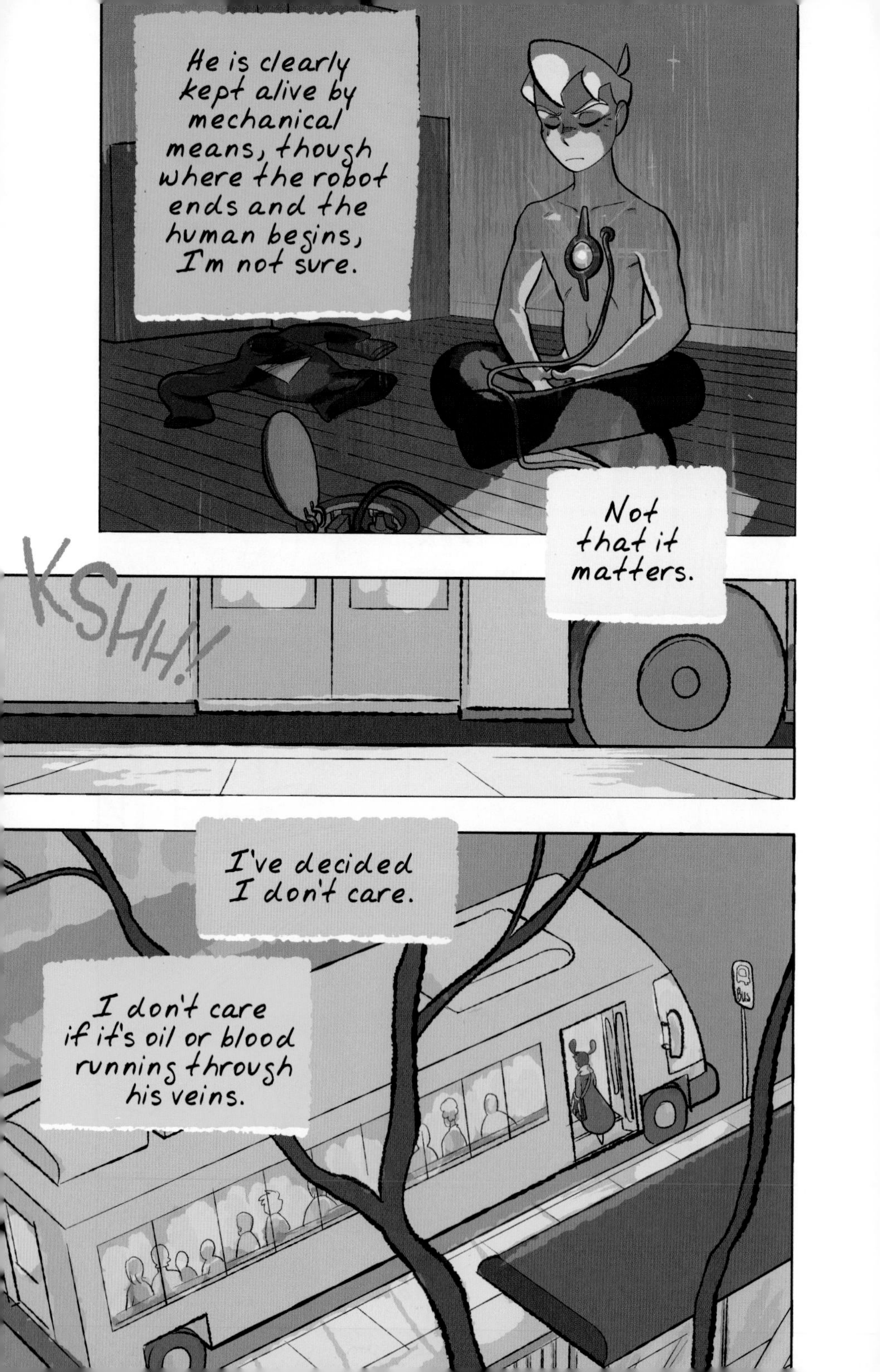
He is clearly kept alive by mechanical means, though where the robot ends and the human begins, I'm not sure.
Not that it matters.
KSHH!!
I've decided I don't care.
I don't care if it's oil or blood running through his veins.
BUS

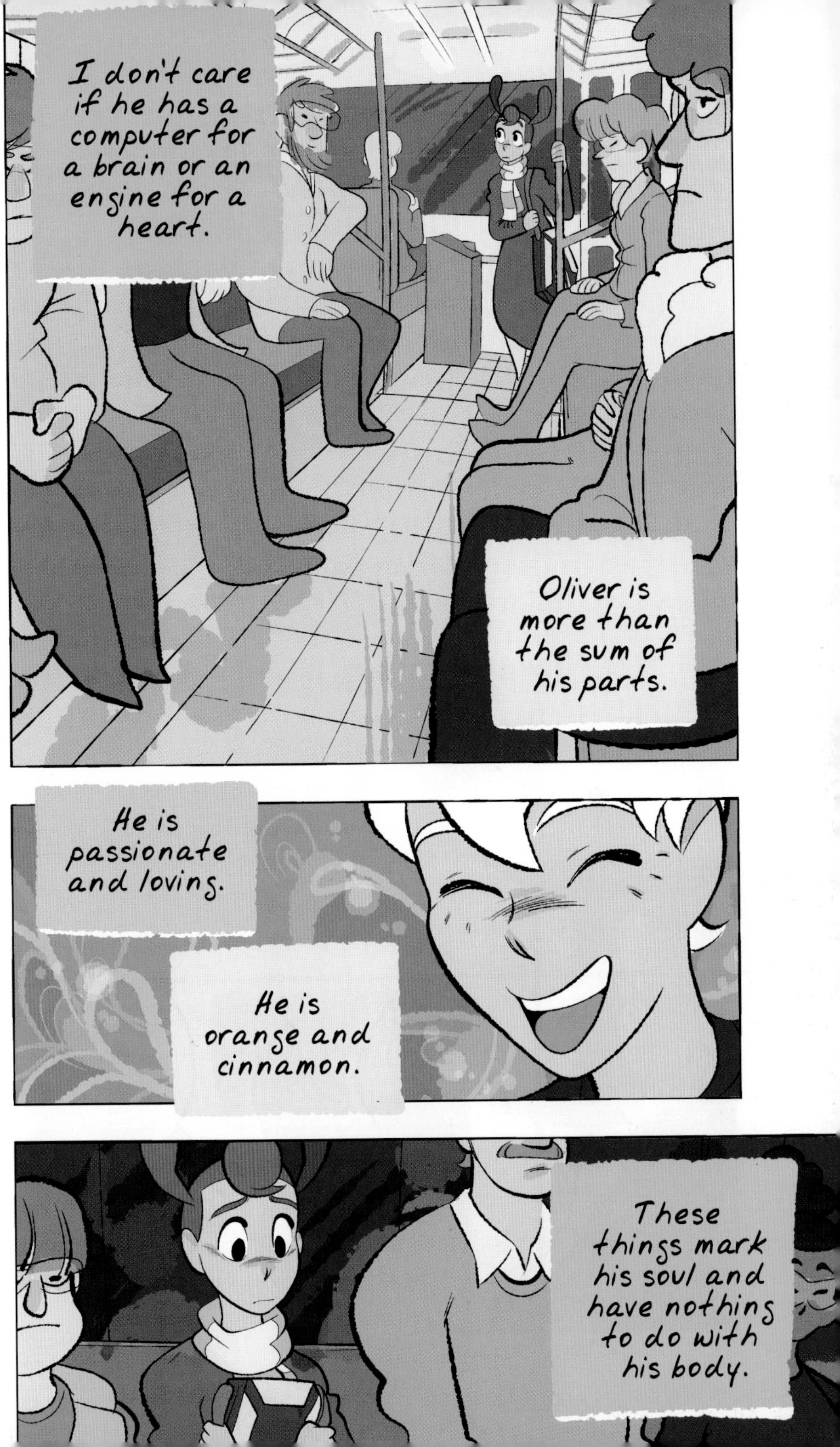
I don't care if he has a computer for a brain or an engine for a heart.
Oliver is more than the sum of his parts.
He is passionate and loving.
He is orange and cinnamon.
These things mark his soul and have nothing to do with his body.

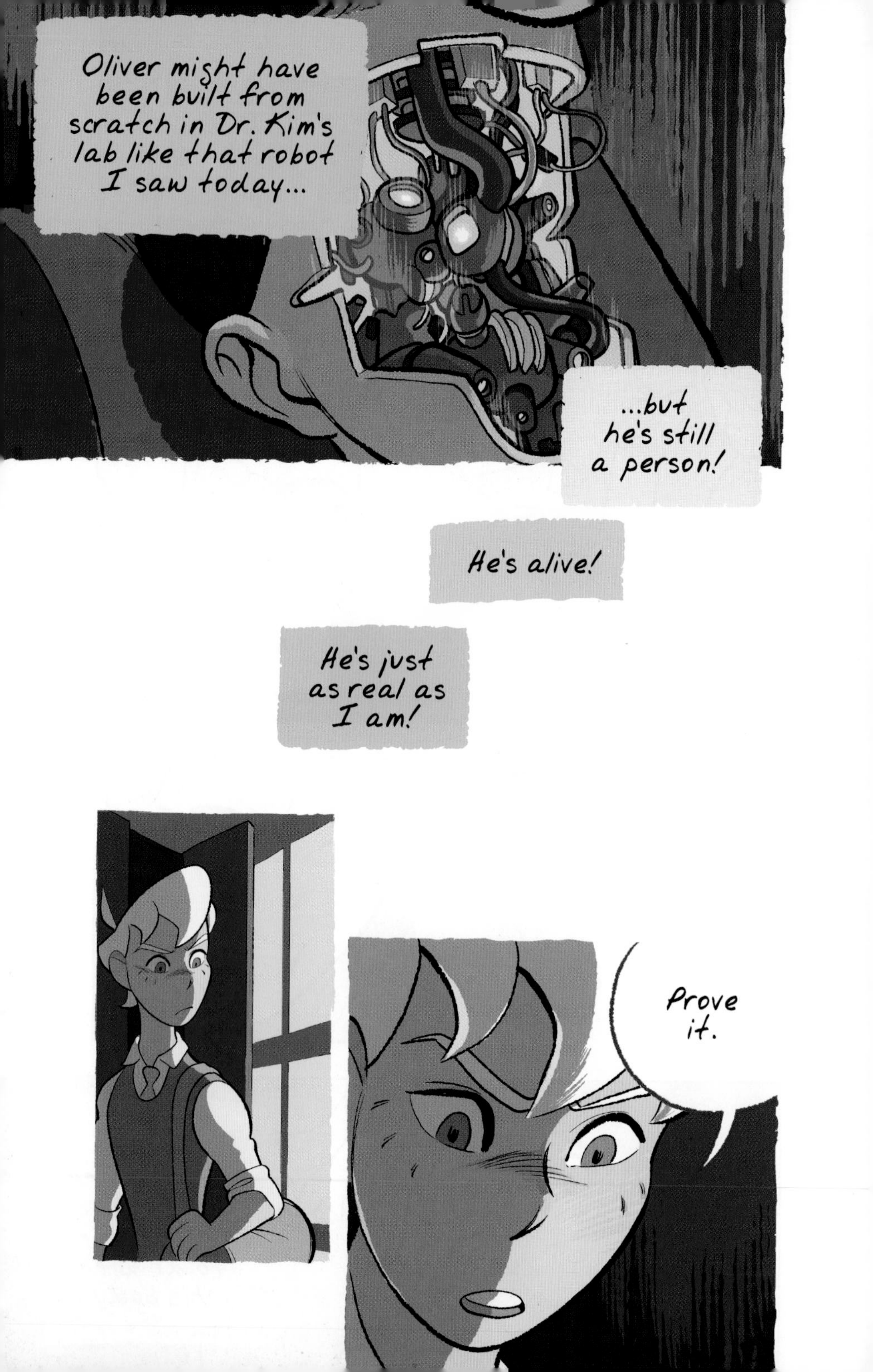
Oliver might have been built from scratch in Dr. Kim's lab like that robot I saw today...
...but he's still a person!
He's alive!
He's just as real as I am!
Prove it.

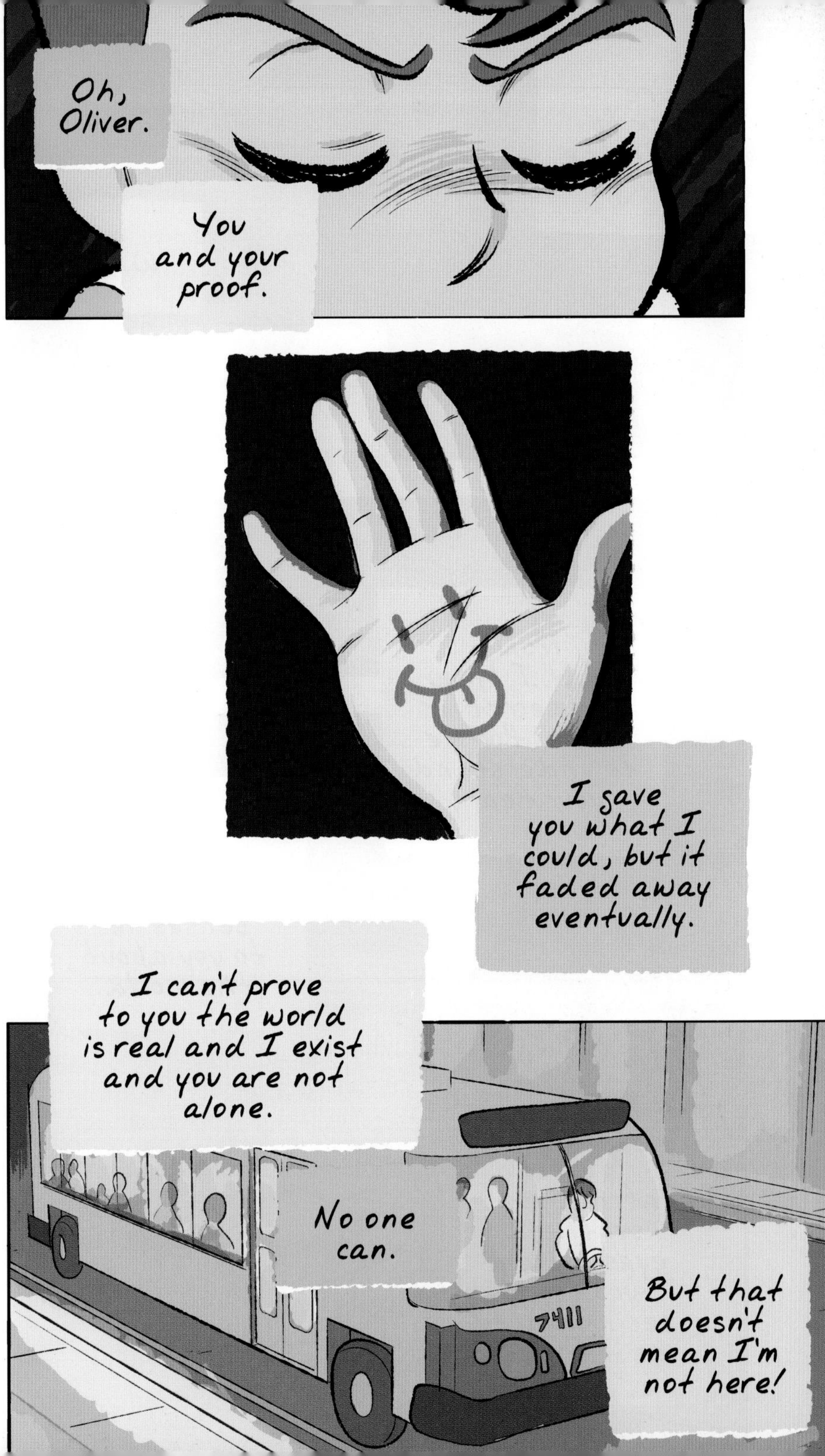
Oh, Oliver.
You and your proof.
I gave you what I could, but it faded away eventually.
I can't prove to you the world is real and I exist and you are not alone.
No one can.
But that doesn't mean I'm not here!

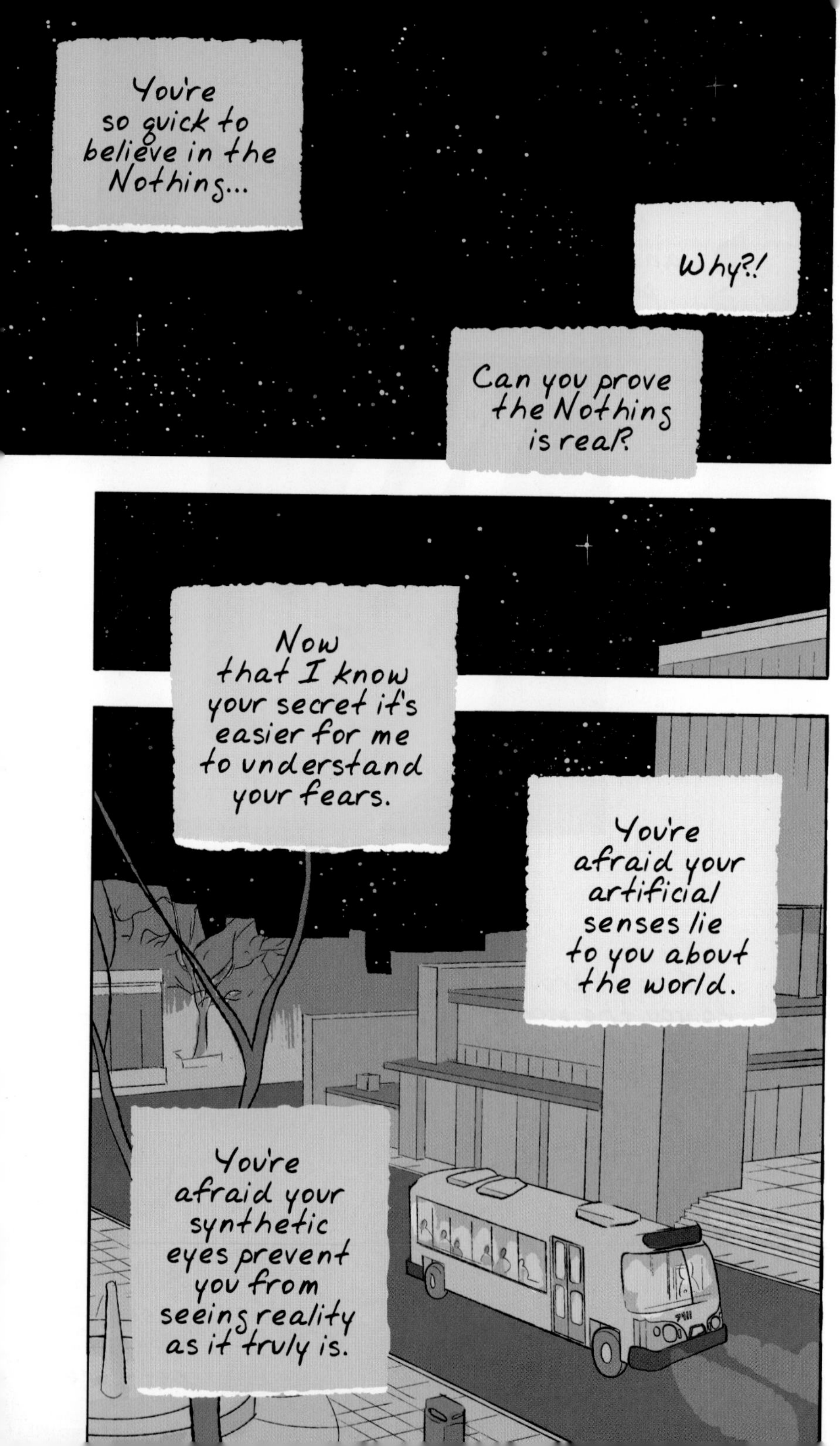
You're so quick to believe in the Nothing...
Why?!
Can you prove the Nothing is real?
Now that I know your secret it's easier for me to understand your fears.
You're afraid your artificial senses lie to you about the world.
You're afraid your synthetic eyes prevent you from seeing reality as it truly is.

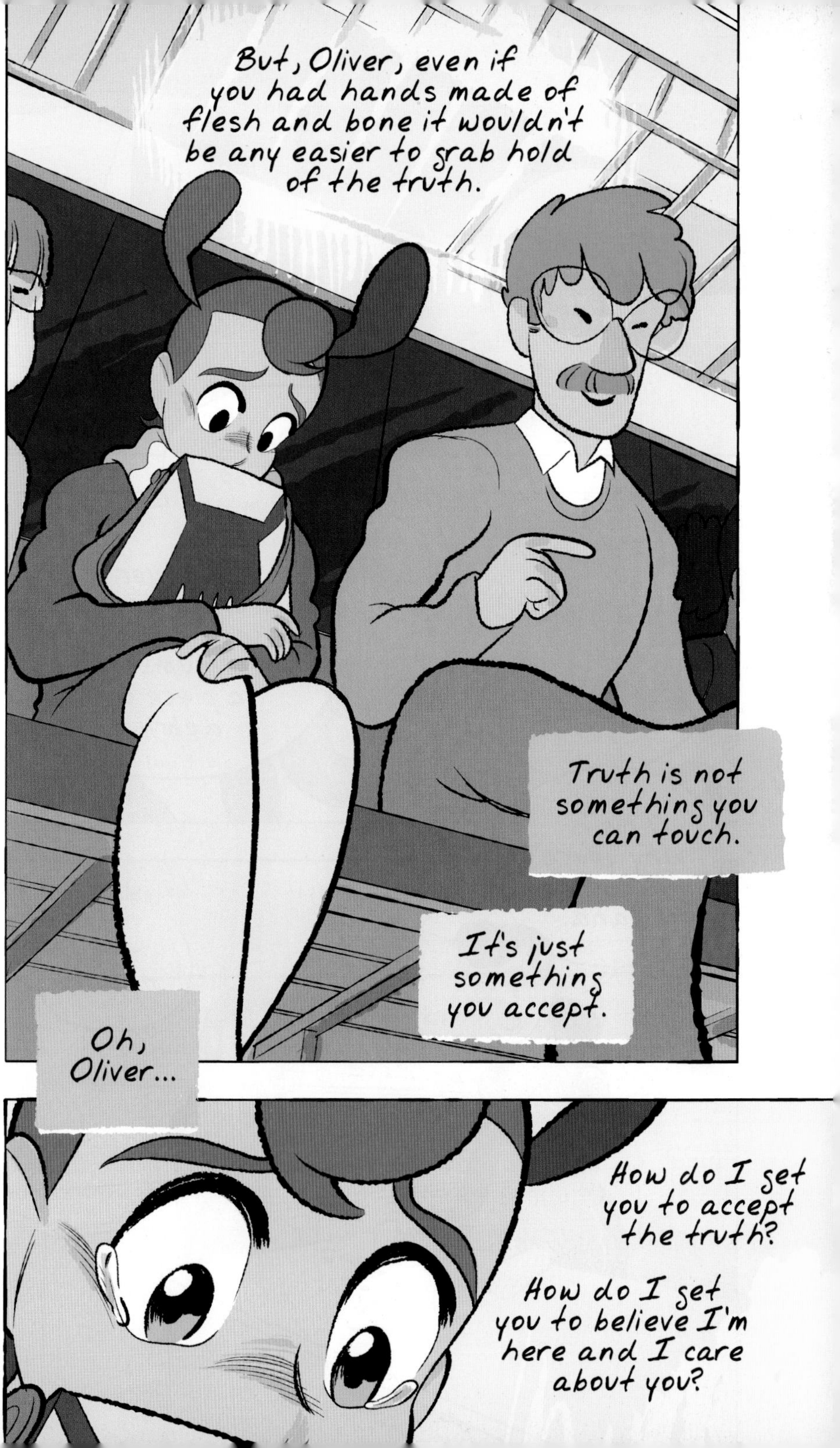
But, Oliver, even if you had hands made of flesh and bone it wouldn't be any easier to grab hold of the truth.
Truth is not something you can touch.
It's just something you accept.
Oh, Oliver...
How do I get you to accept the truth?
How do I get you to believe I'm here and I care about you?

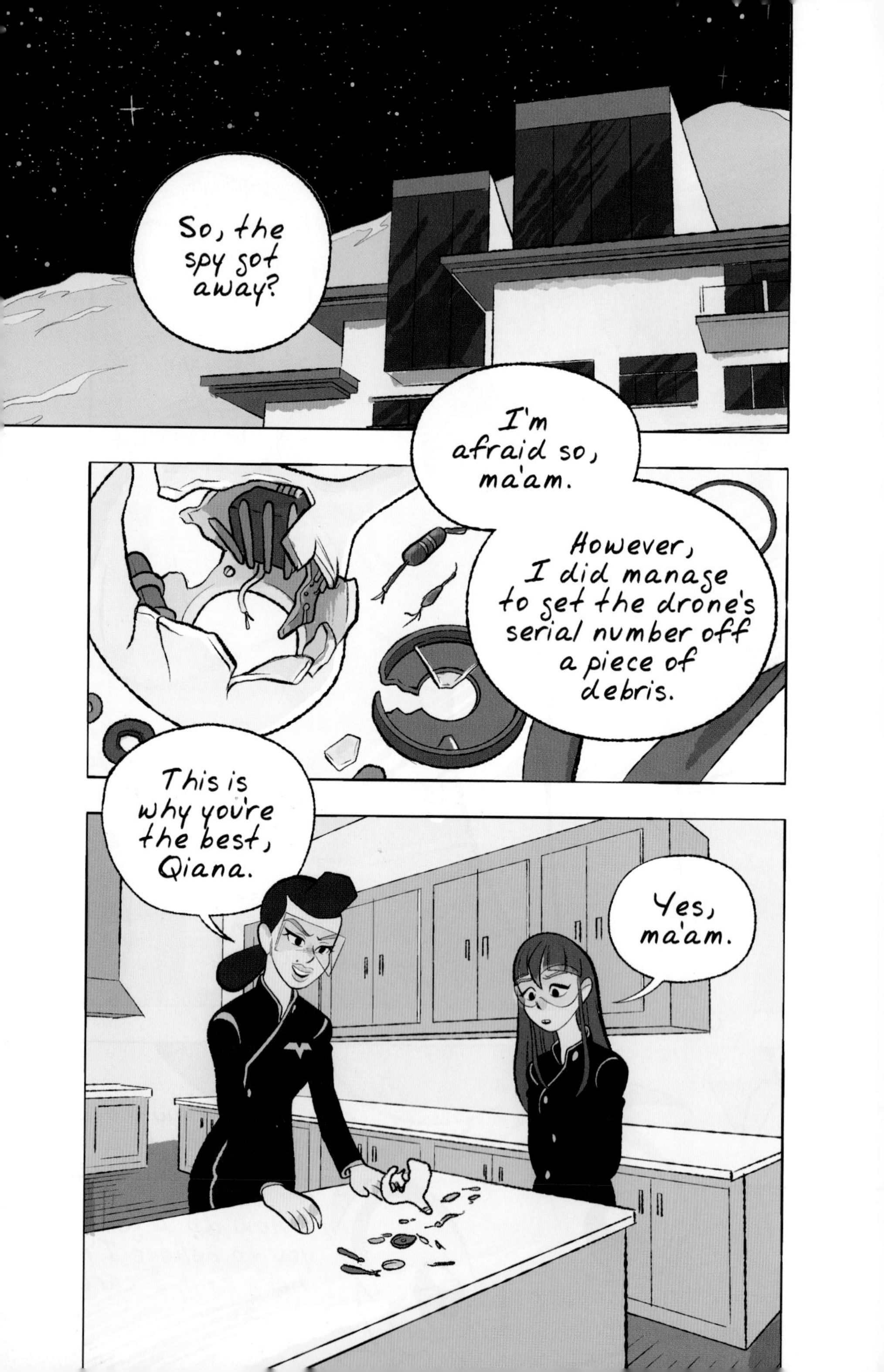
So, the spy got away?
I'm afraid so, ma'am.
However, I did manage to get the drone's serial number off a piece of debris.
This is why you're the best, Qiana.
Yes, ma'am.

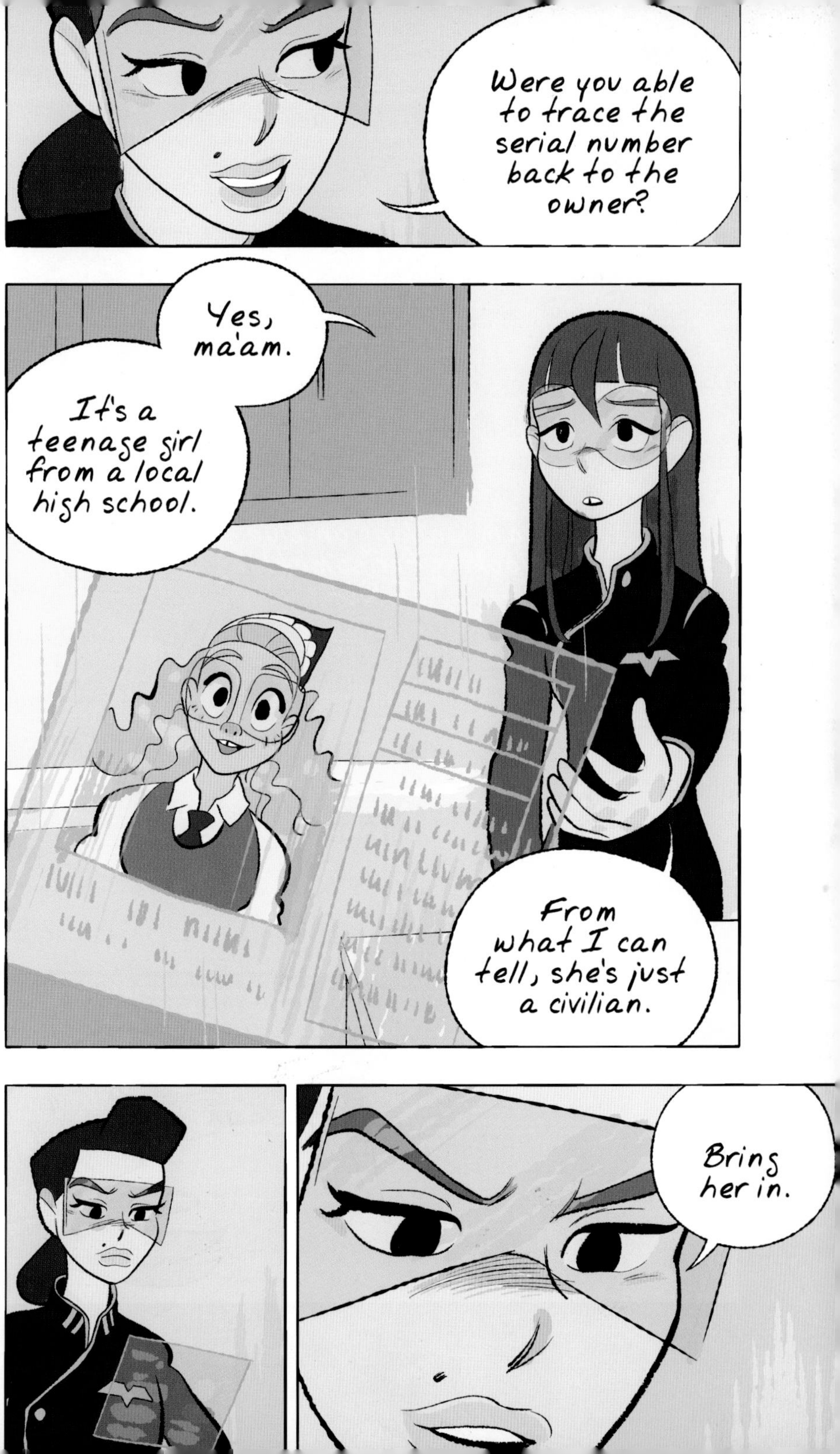
Were you able to trace the serial number back to the owner?
Yes, ma'am.
It's a teenage girl from a local high school.
From what I can tell, she's just a civilian.
Bring her in.

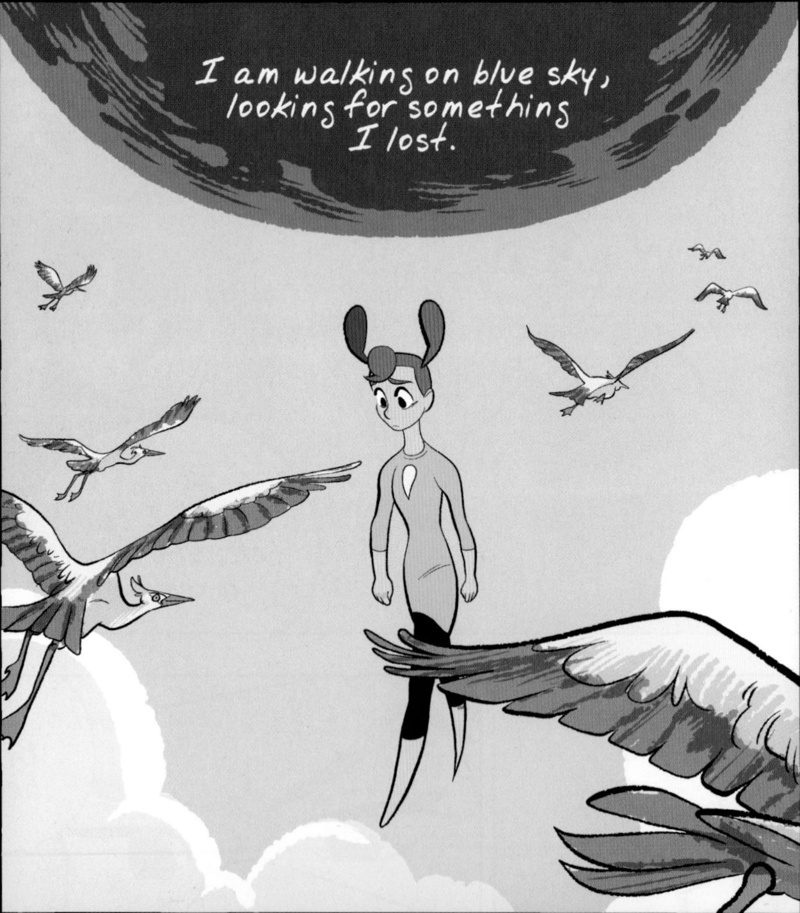
I am walking on blue sky, looking for something I lost.

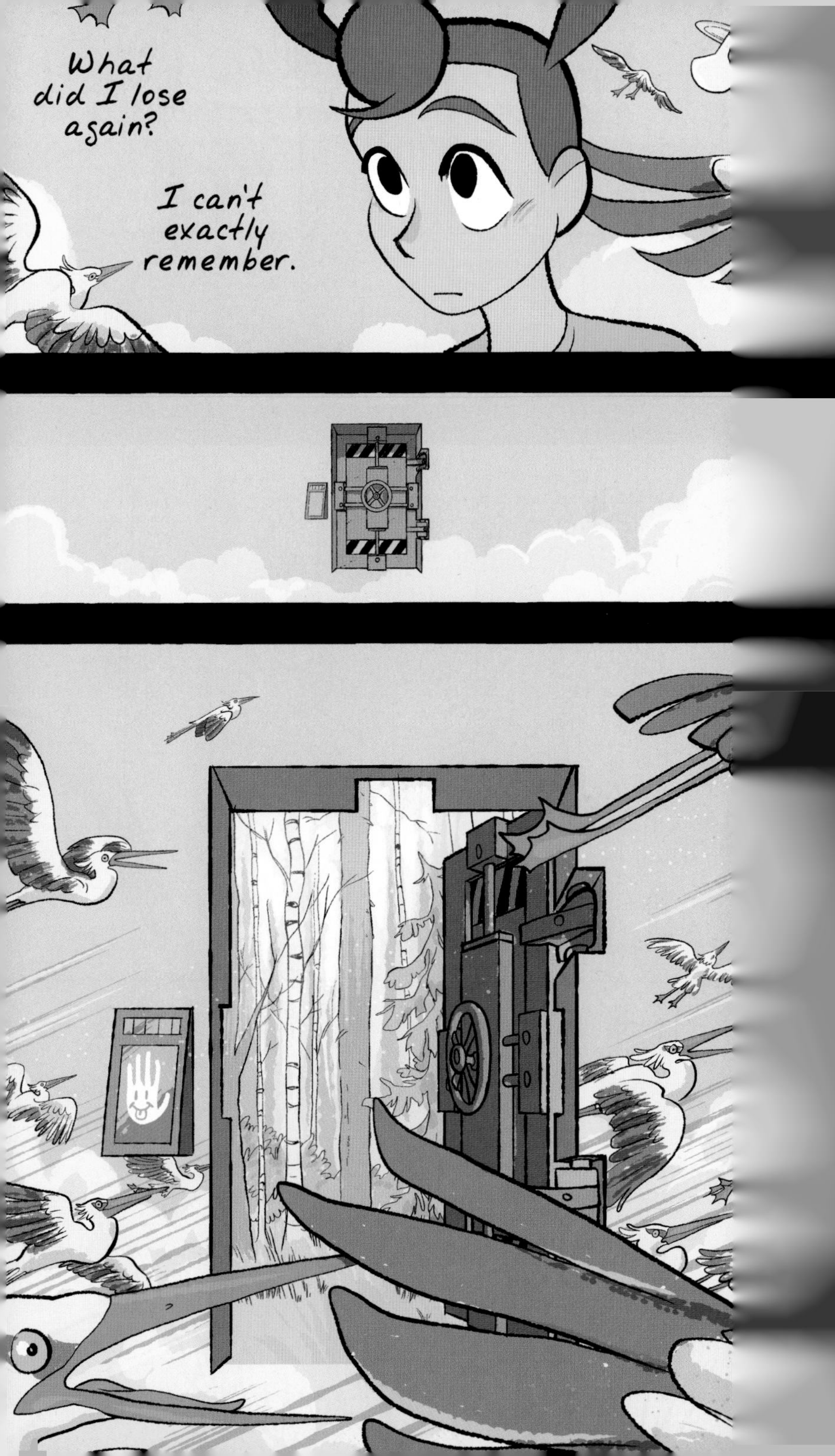
What did I lose again?
I can't exactly remember.

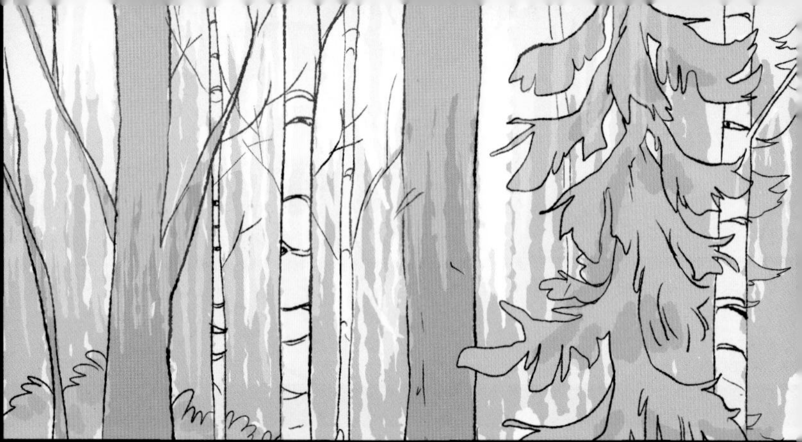
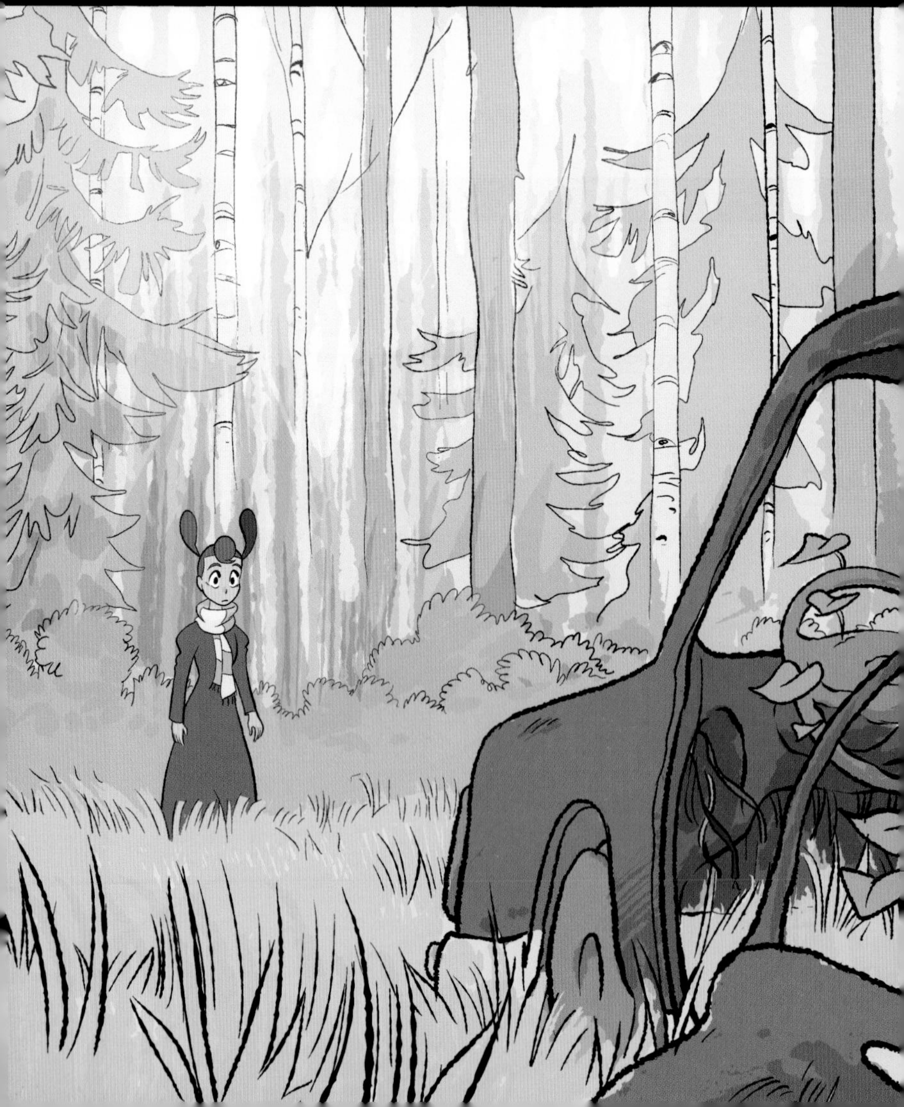

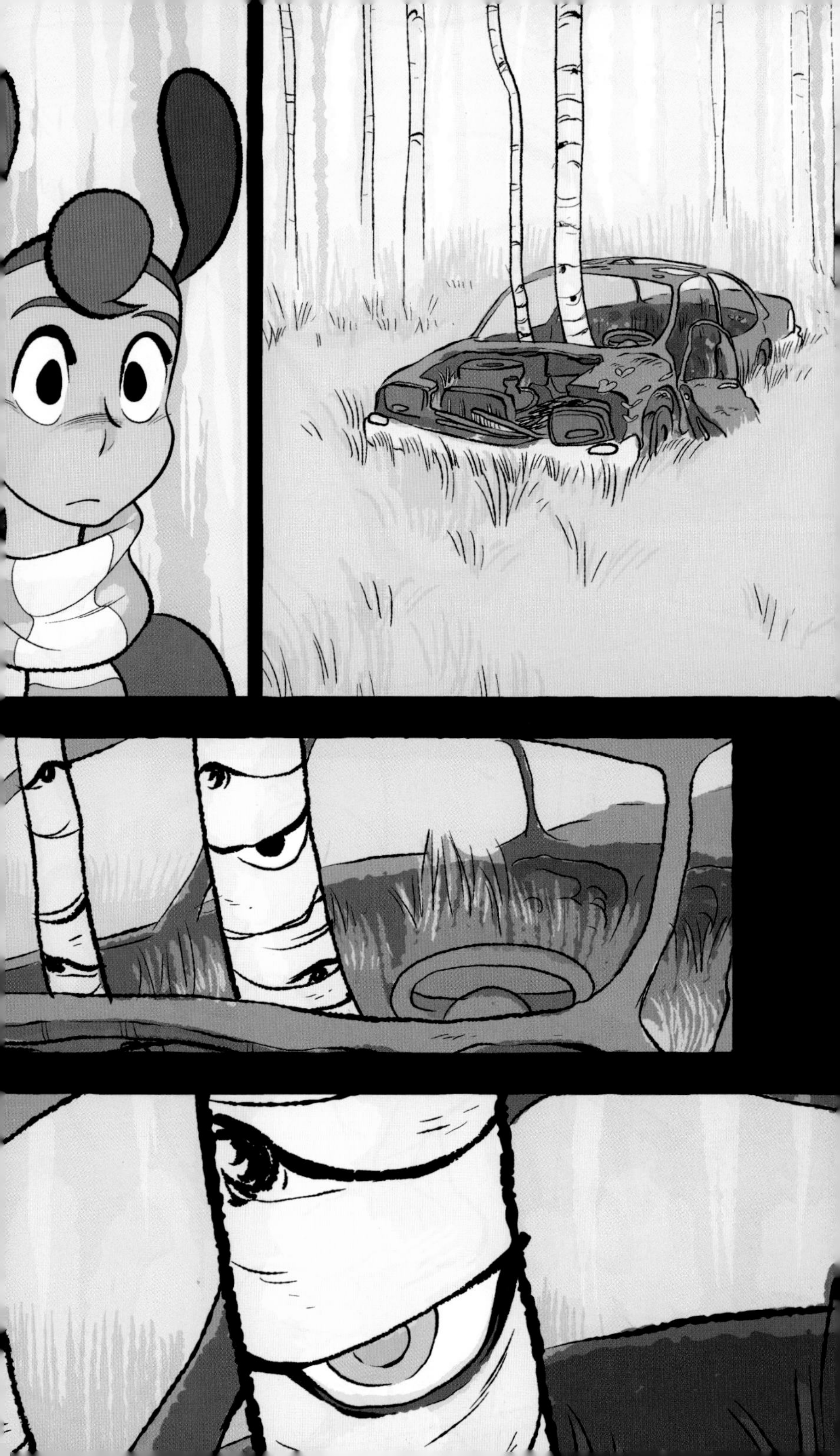

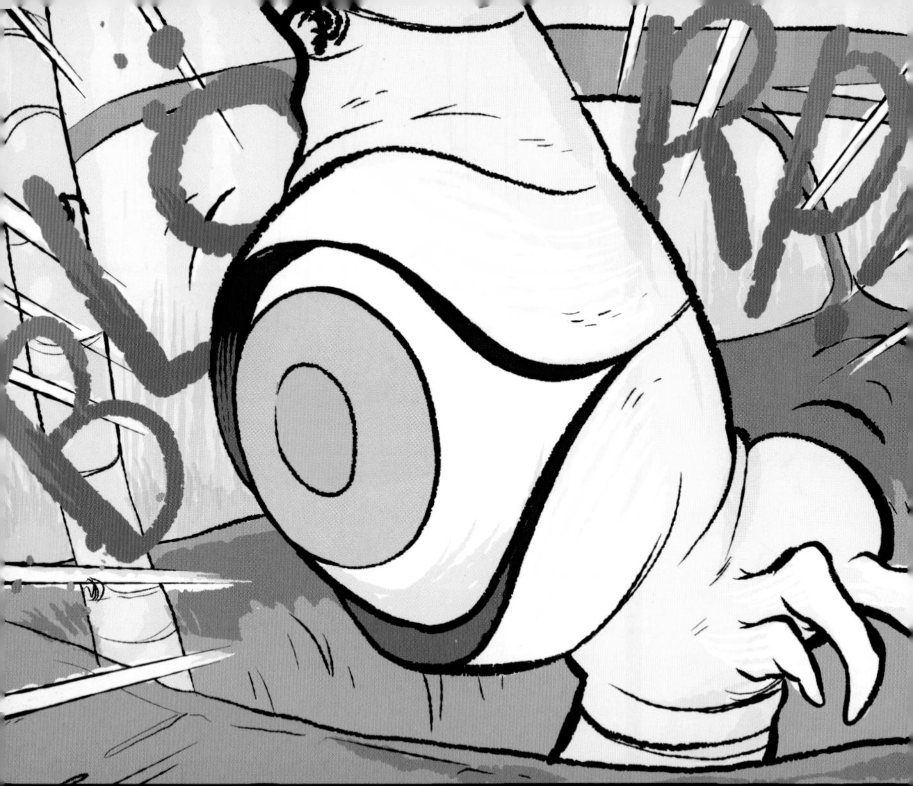
BLORP

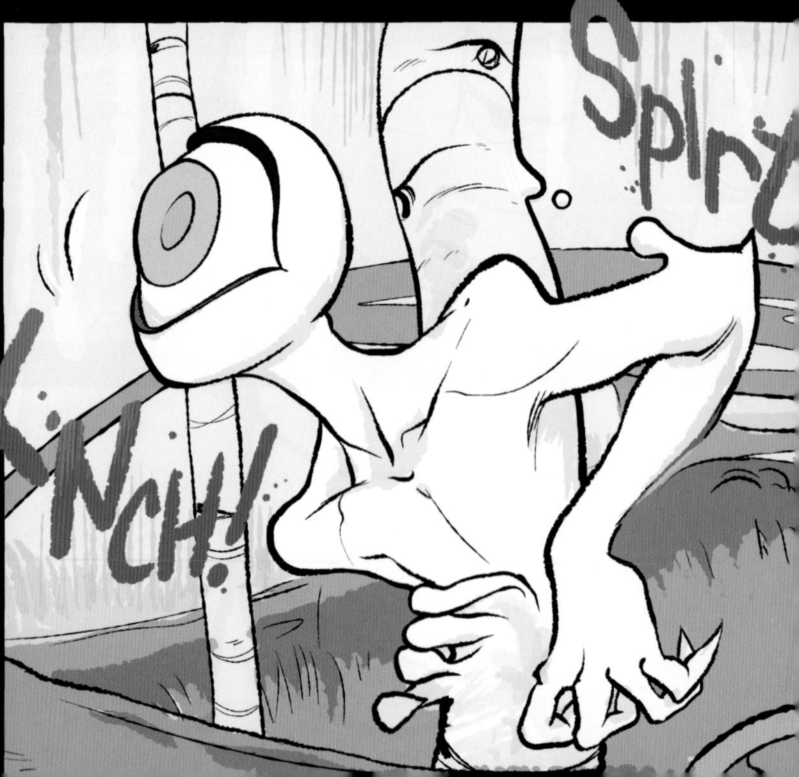
Splr
KNCH!

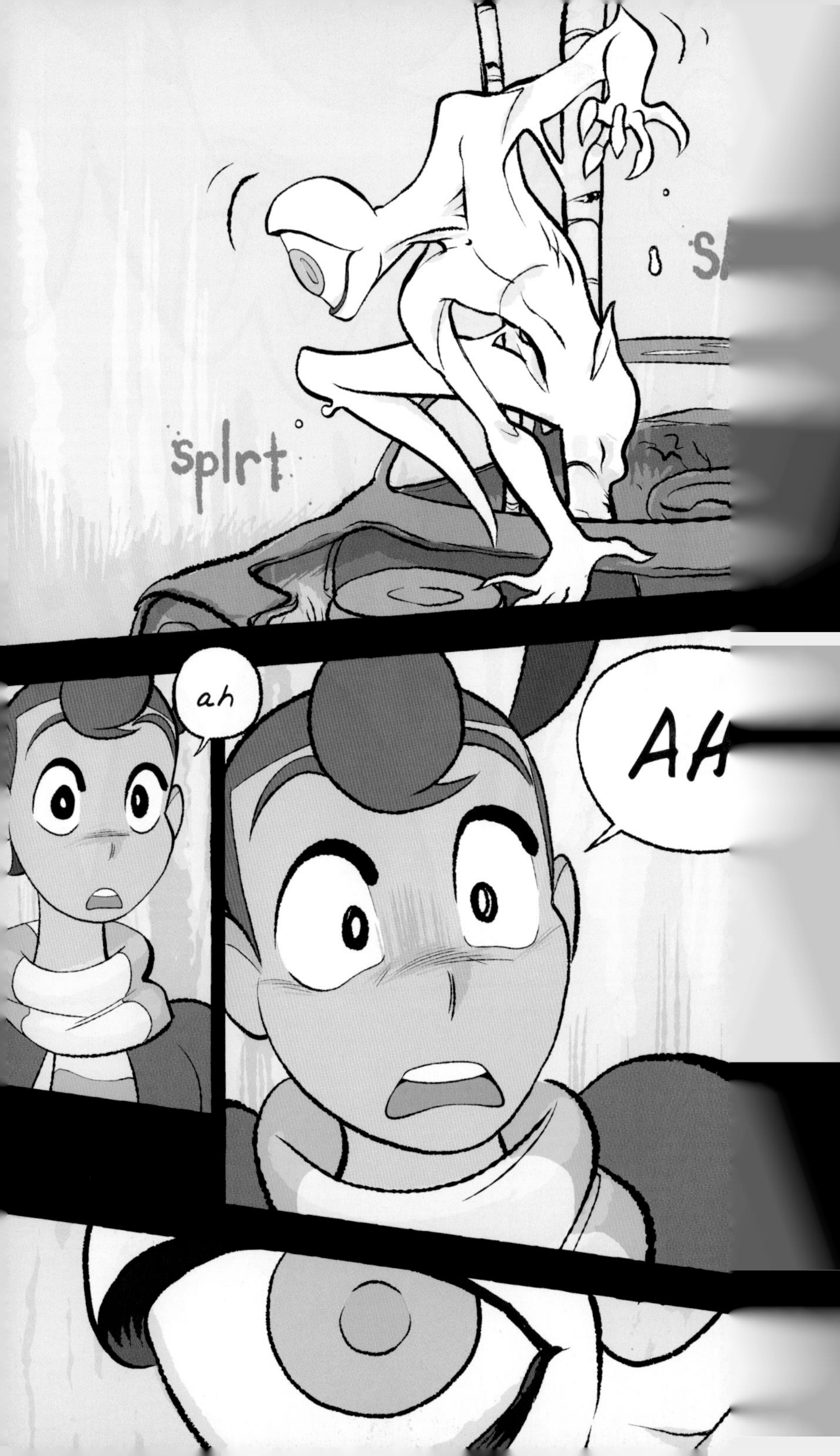
splrt
ah
AH

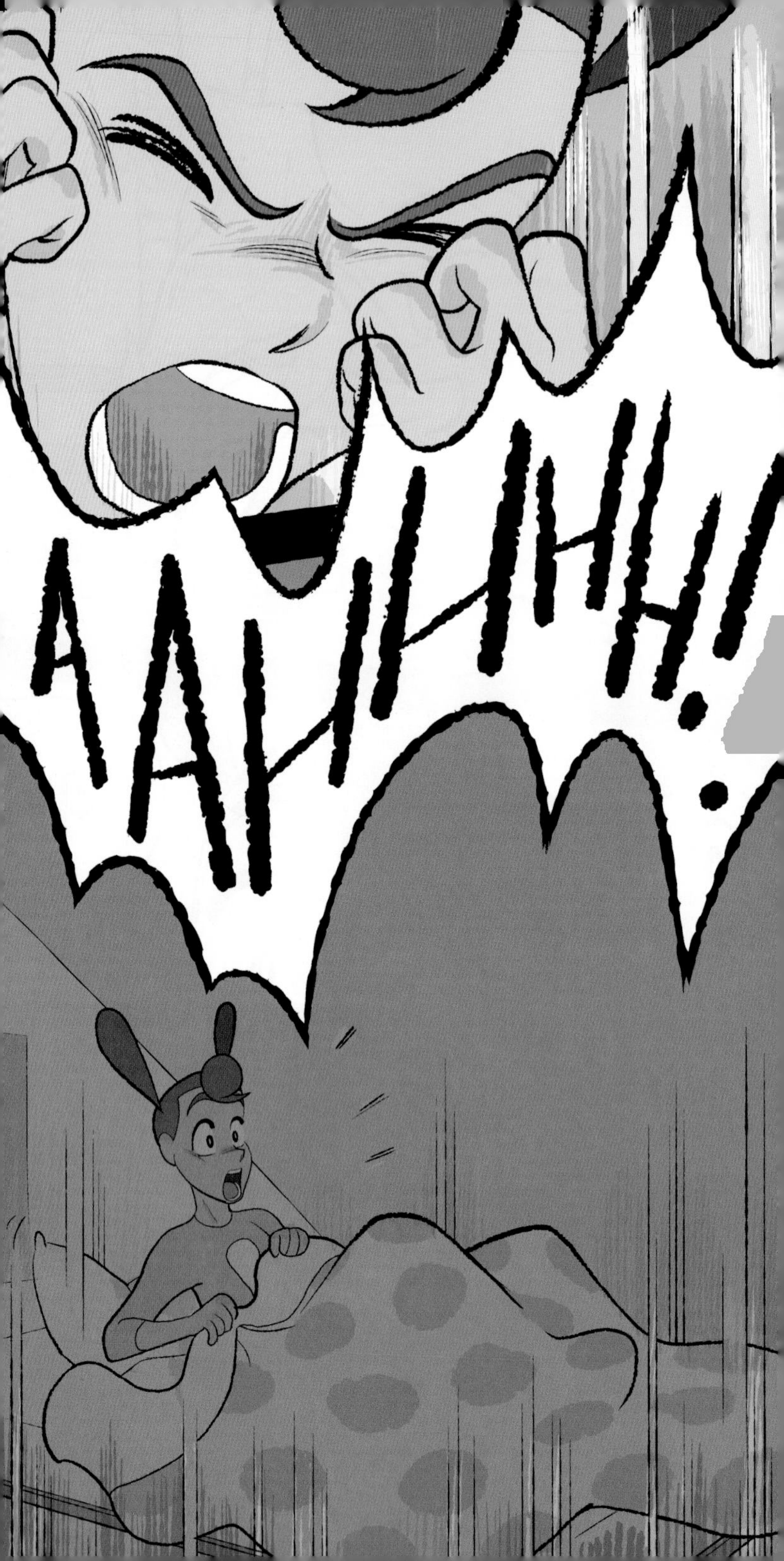
AAHHHH!!

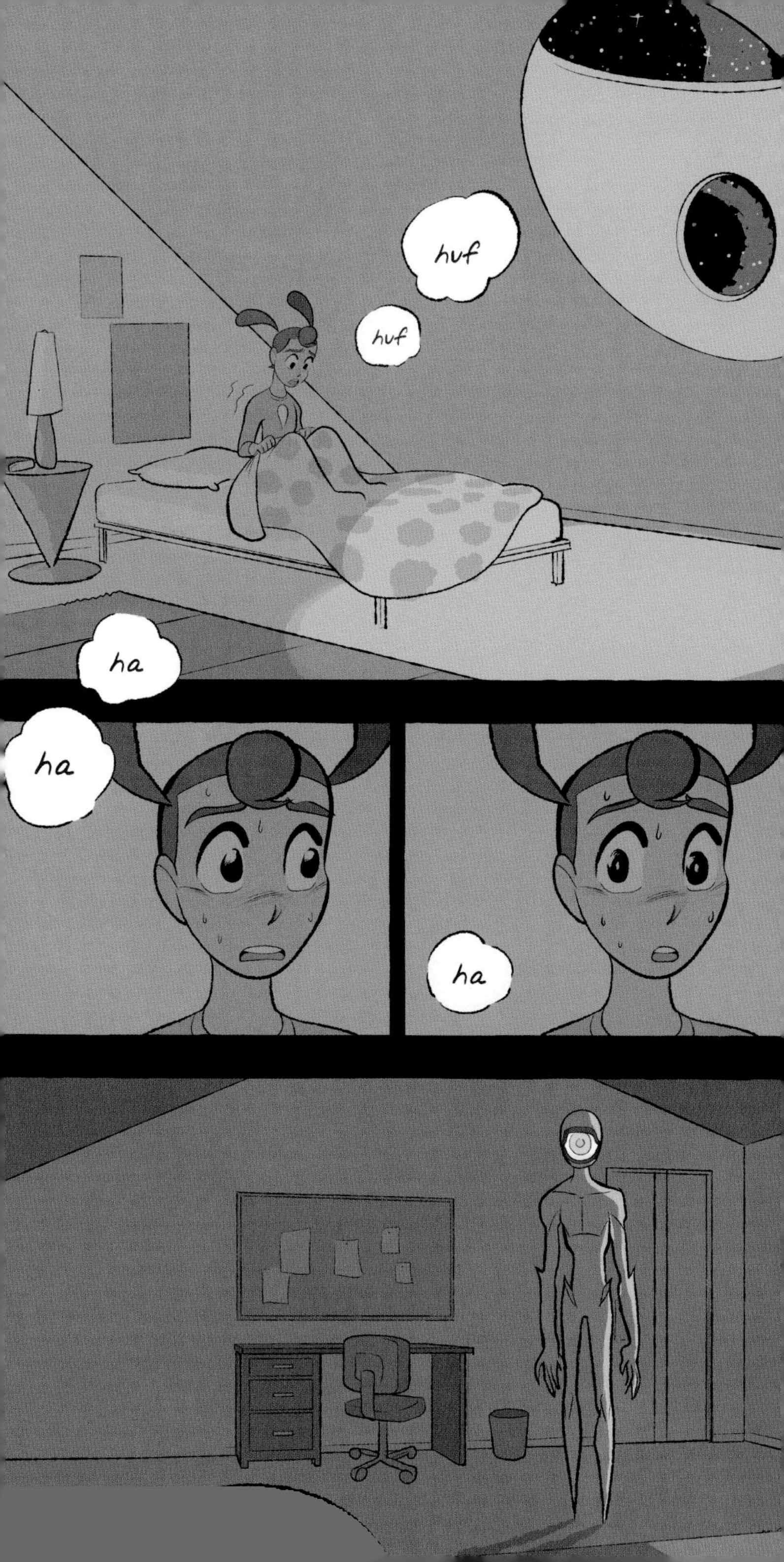
huf
huf
ha
ha
ha

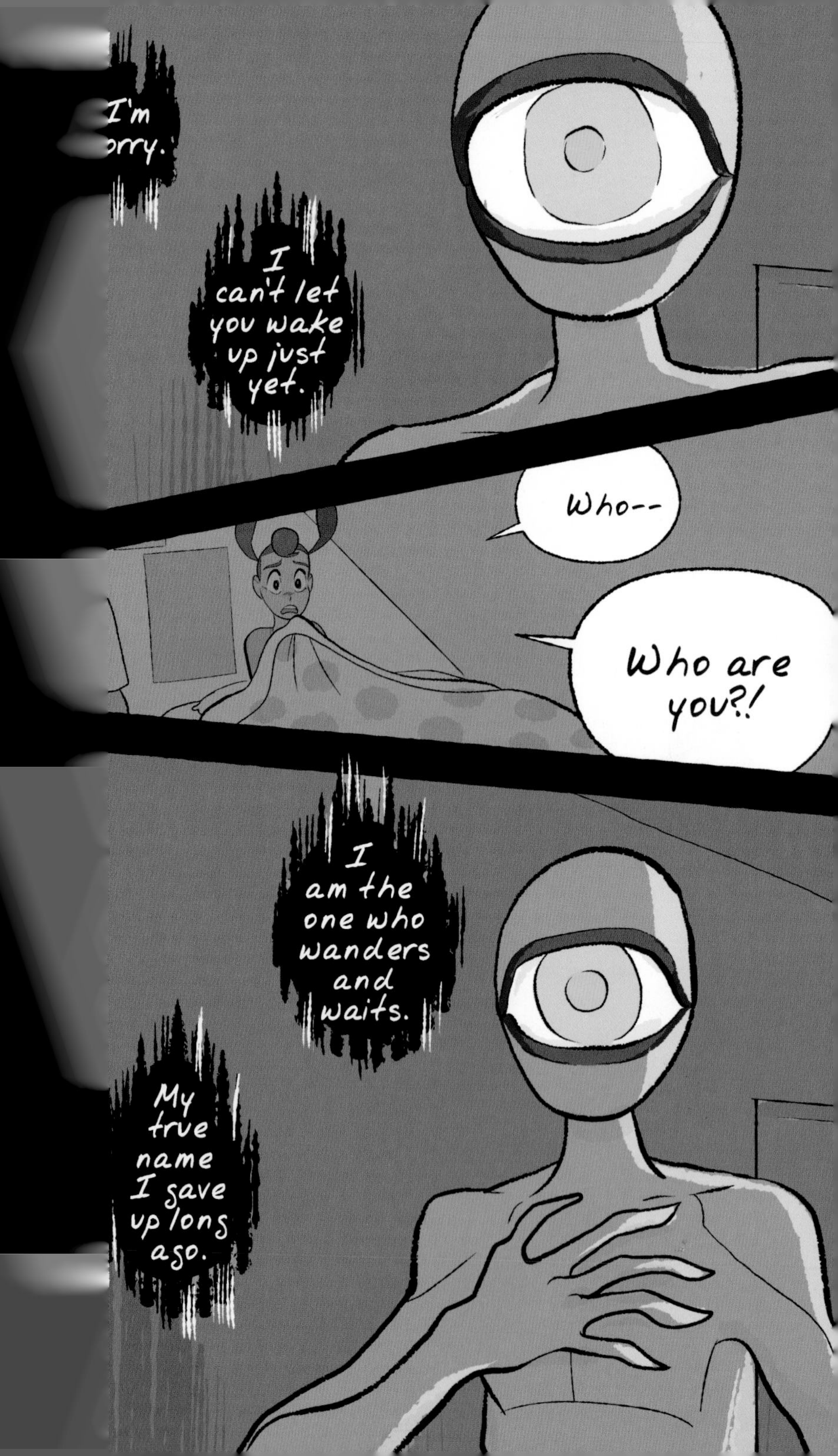
I'm
orry.
I can't let you wake up just yet.
Who--
Who are you?!
I am the one who wanders and waits.
My true name I gave up long ago.

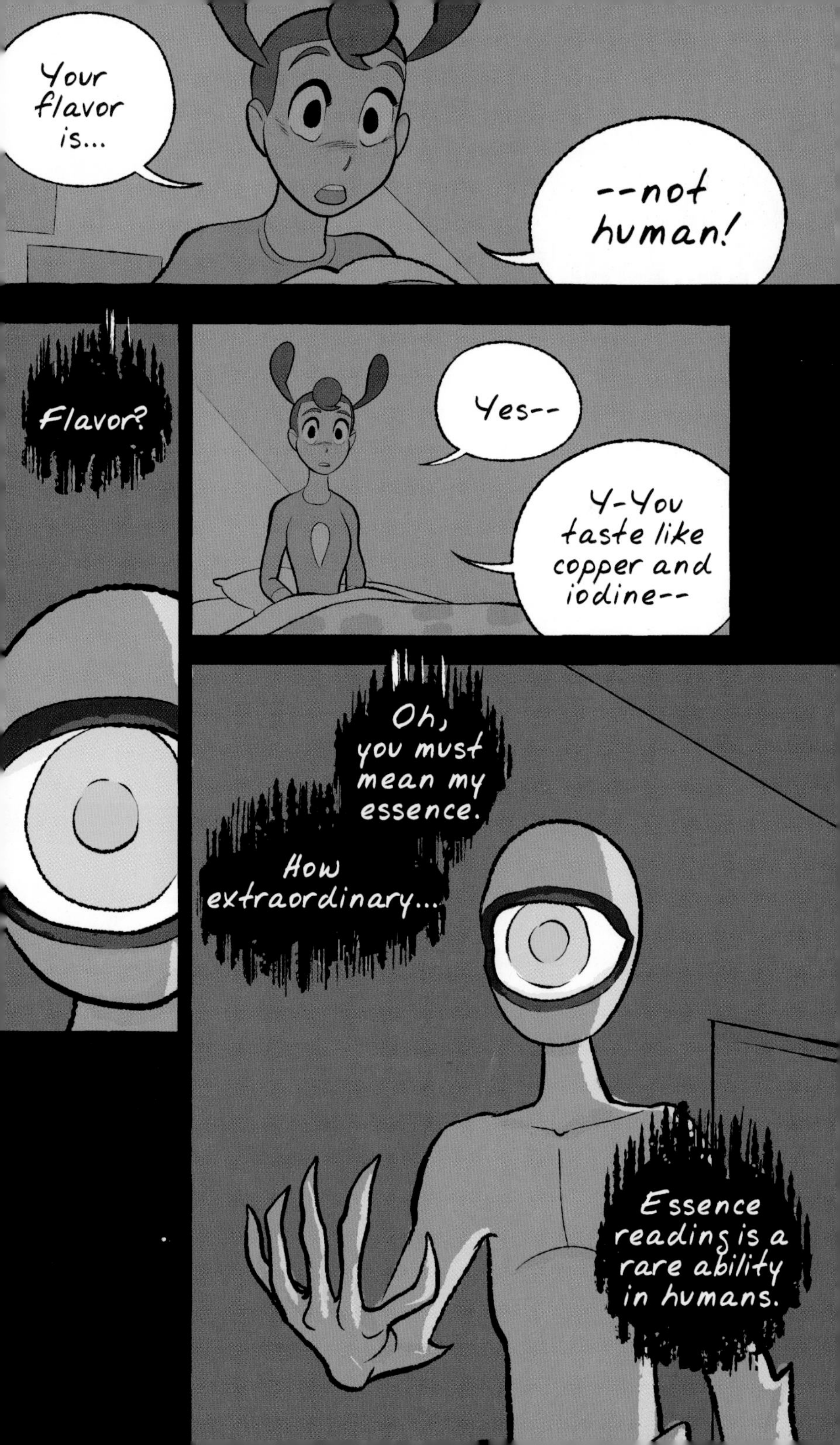
Your flavor is...
--not human!
Flavor?
Yes--
Y-You taste like copper and iodine--
Oh, you must mean my essence.
How extraordinary...
Essence reading is a rare ability in humans.

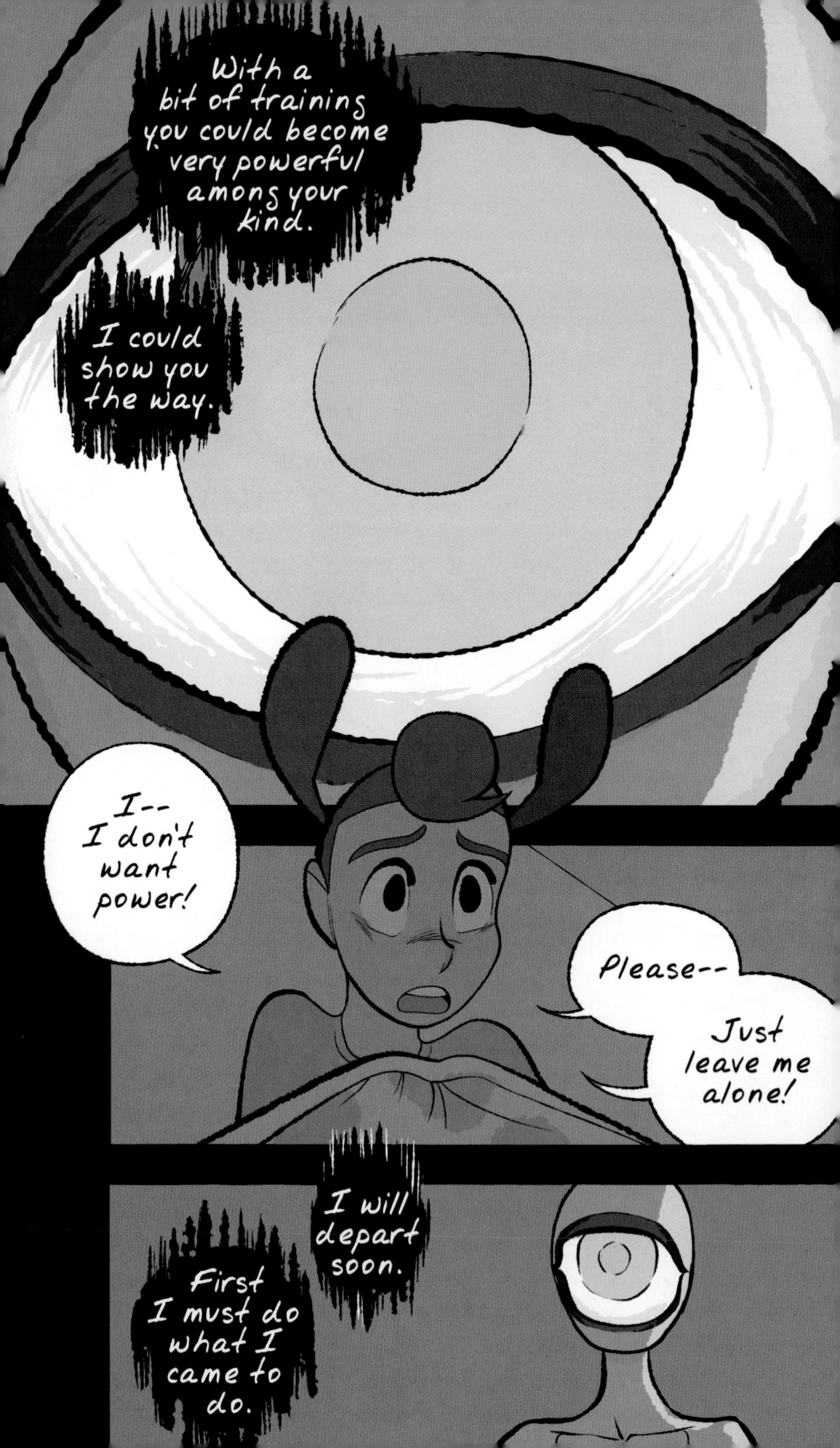
With a bit of training you could become very powerful among your kind.
I could show you the way.
I-- I don't want power!
Please--
Just leave me alone!
I will depart soon.
First I must do what I came to do.

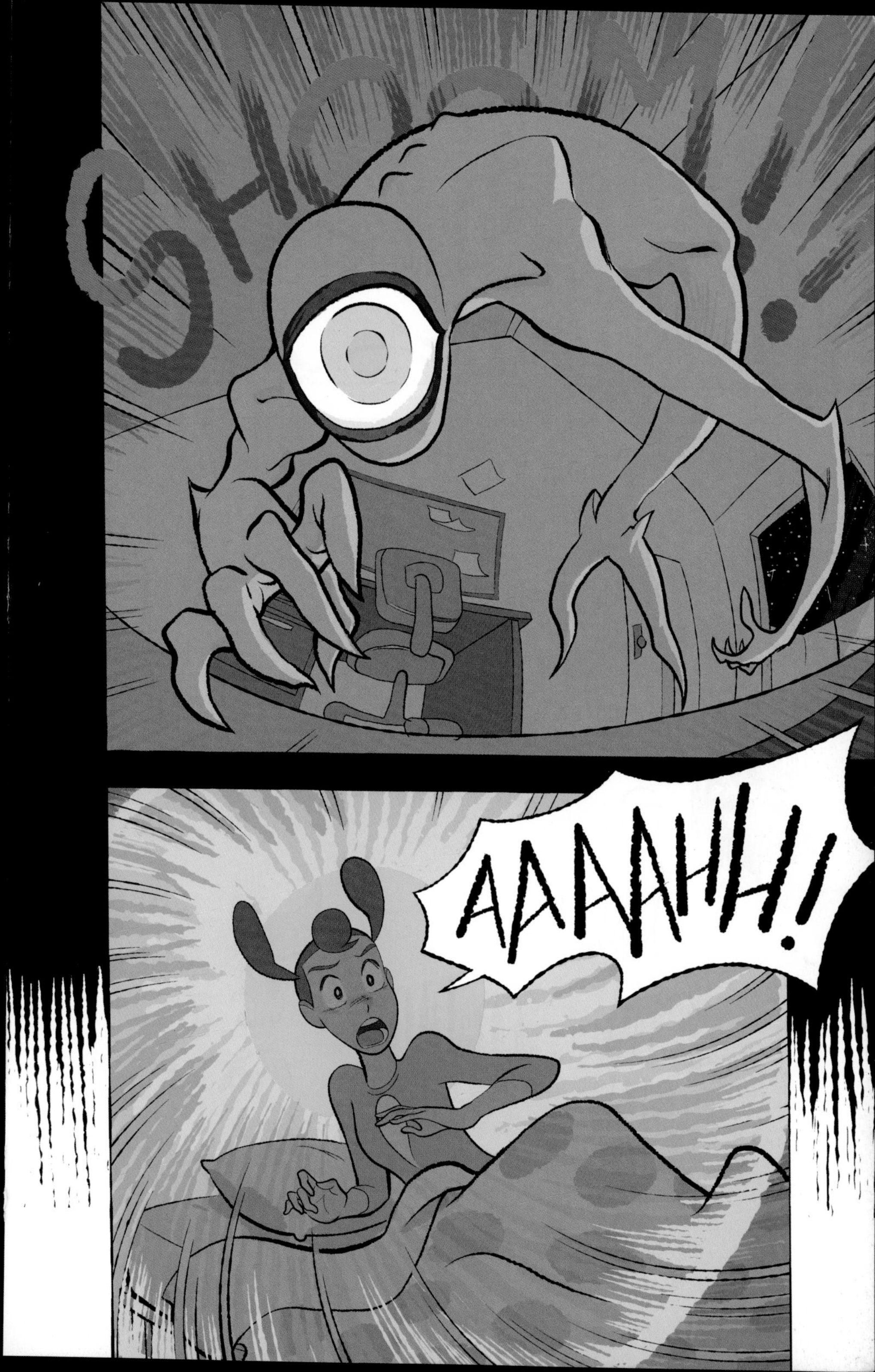
SHOOM!!
AAAAHH!

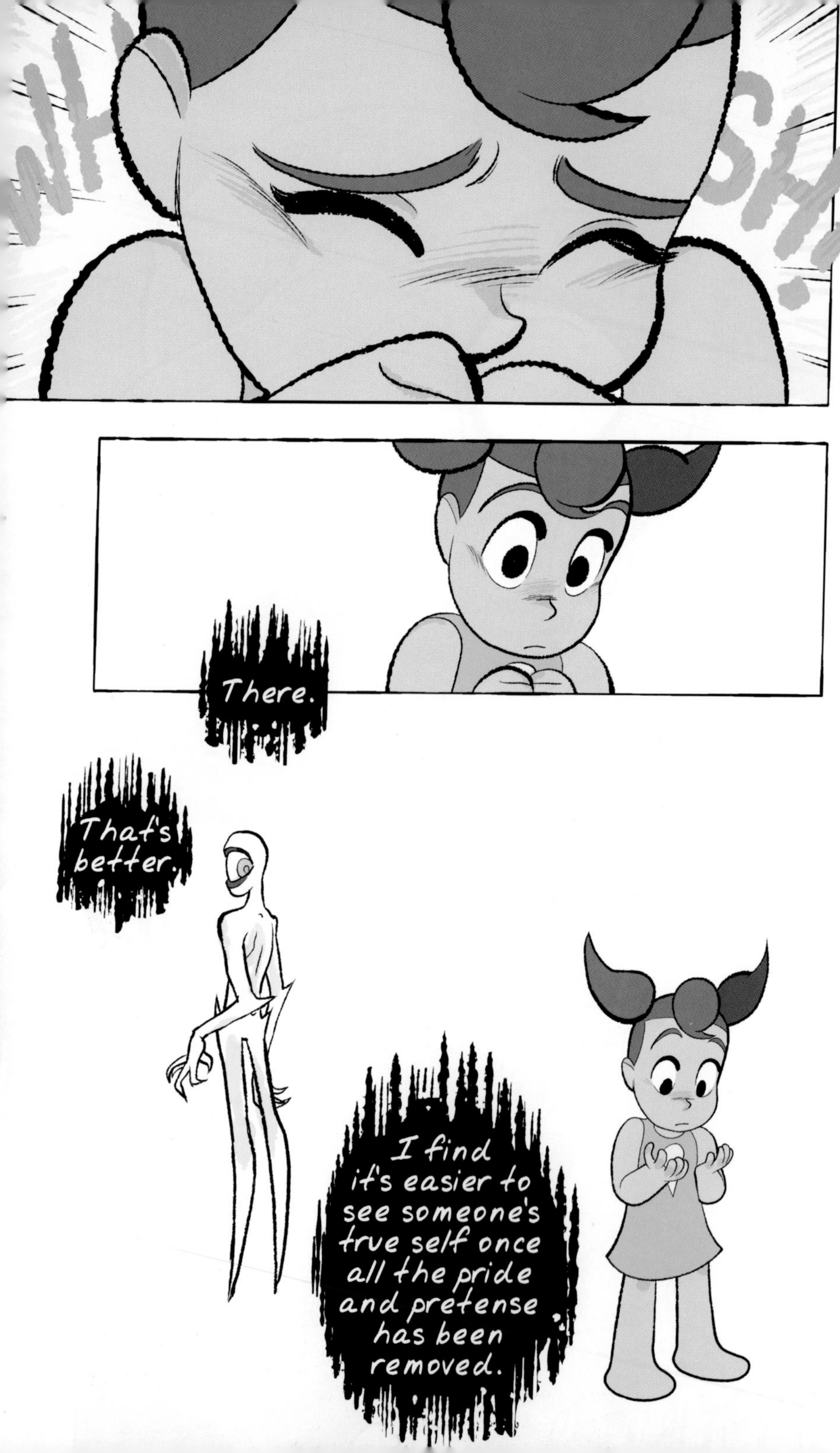
WH
SH!
There.
That's better.
I find it's easier to see someone's true self once all the pride and pretense has been removed.

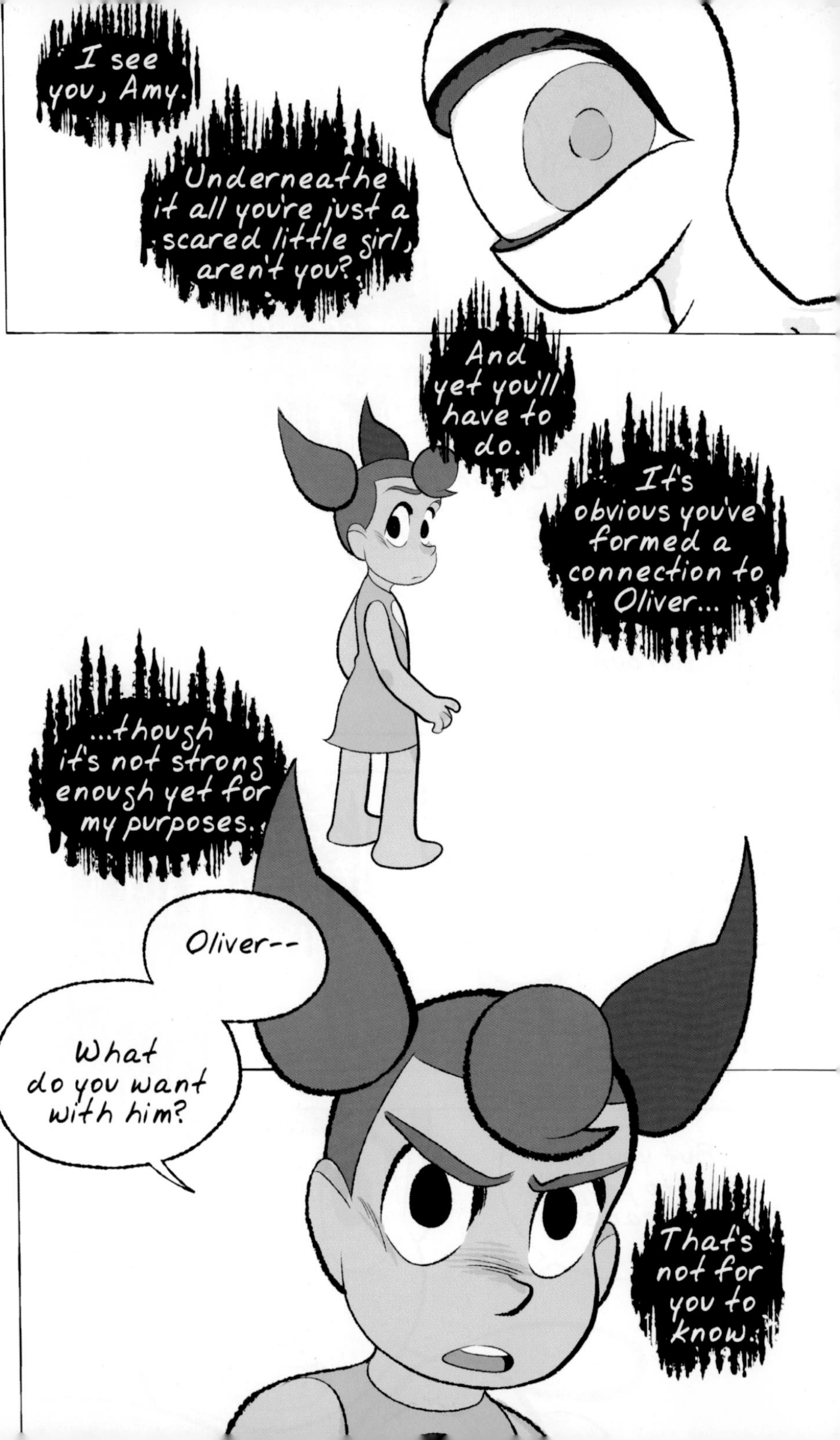
I see you, Amy.
Underneathe it all you're just a scared little girl, aren't you?
And yet you'll have to do.
It's obvious you've formed a connection to Oliver...
...though it's not strong enough yet for my purposes.
Oliver--
What do you want with him?
That's not for you to know.

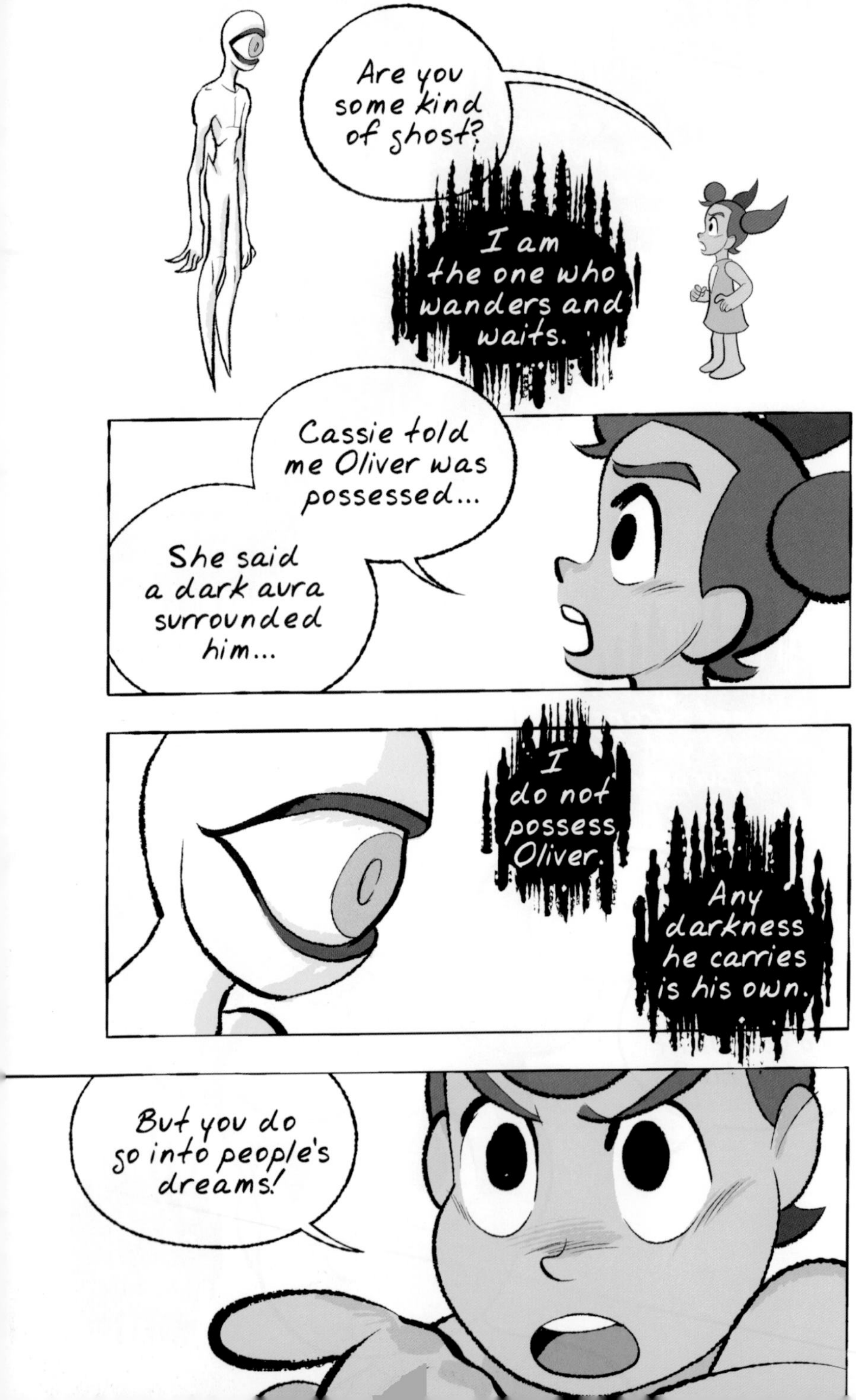
Are you some kind of ghost?
I am the one who wanders and waits.
Cassie told me Oliver was possessed...
She said a dark aura surrounded him...
I do not possess Oliver.
Any darkness he carries is his own.
But you do go into people's dreams!

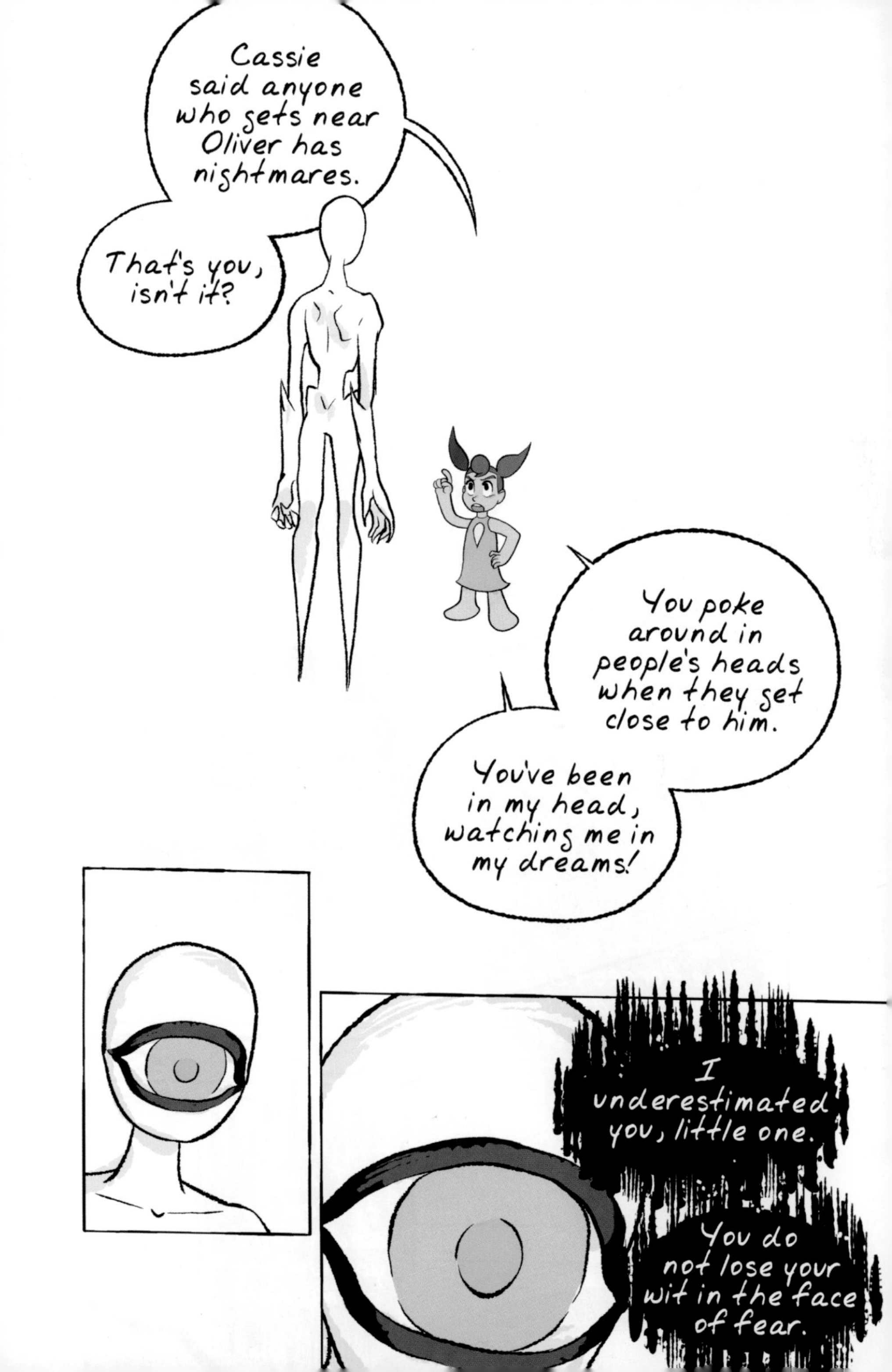
Cassie said anyone who gets near Oliver has nightmares.
That's you, isn't it?
You poke around in people's heads when they get close to him.
You've been in my head, watching me in my dreams!
I underestimated you, little one.
You do not lose your wit in the face of fear.

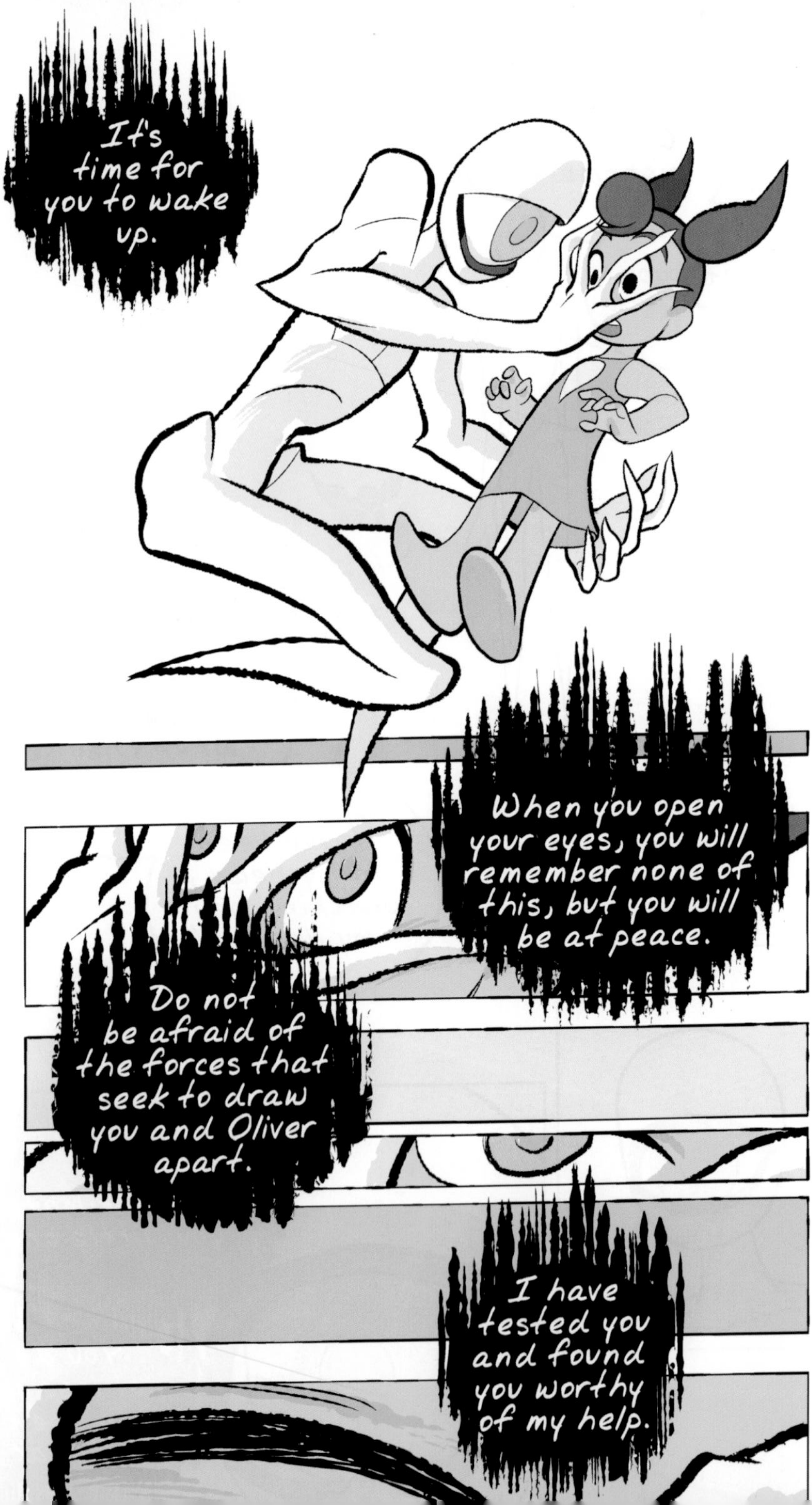
It's time for you to wake up.
When you open your eyes, you will remember none of this, but you will be at peace.
Do not be afraid of the forces that seek to draw you and Oliver apart.
I have tested you and found you worthy of my help.

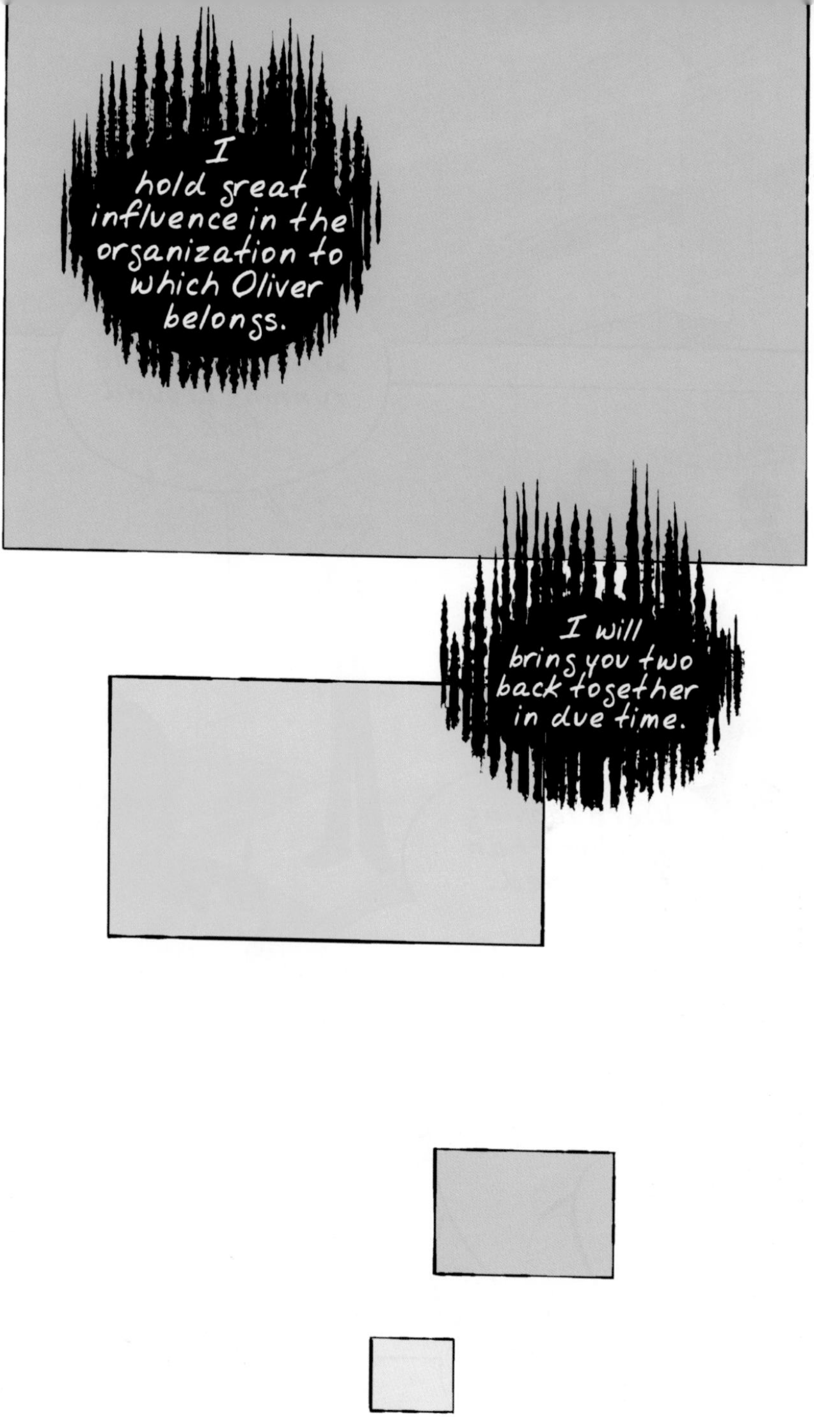
I hold great influence in the organization to which Oliver belongs.
I will bring you two back together in due time.

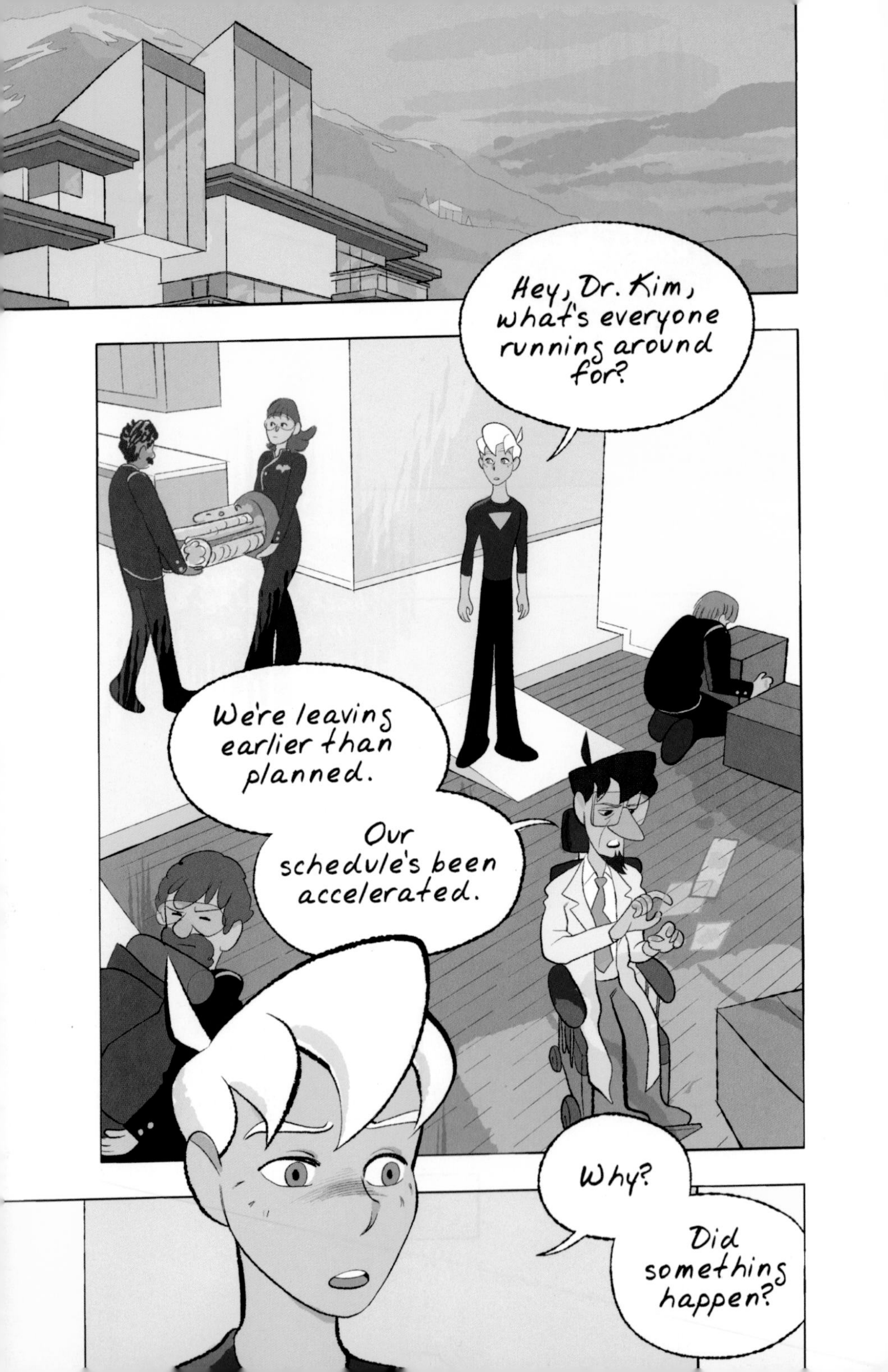
Hey, Dr. Kim, what's everyone running around for?
We're leaving earlier than planned.
Our schedule's been accelerated.
Why?
Did something happen?

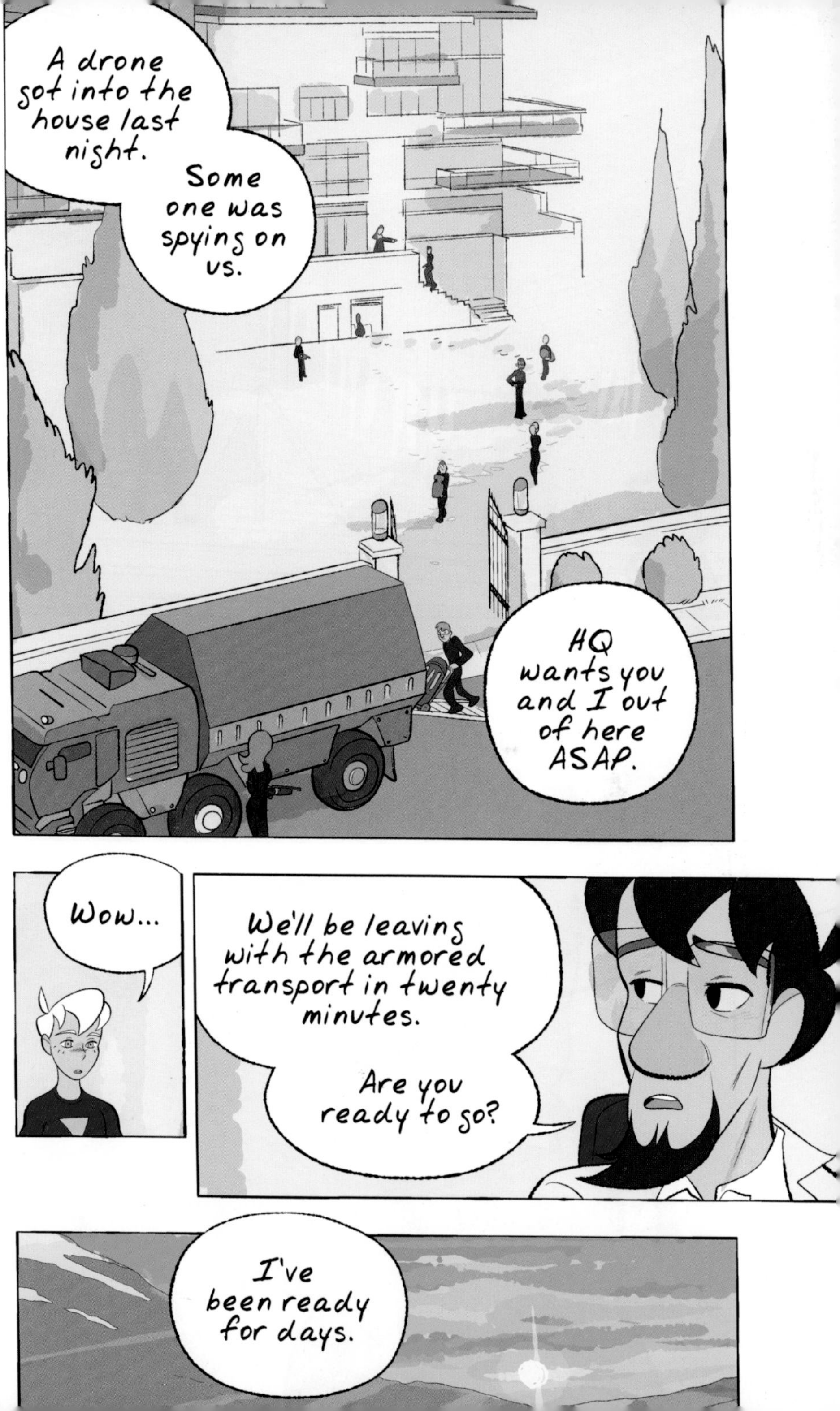
A drone got into the house last night.
Some one was spying on us.
HQ wants you and I out of here ASAP.
Wow...
We'll be leaving with the armored transport in twenty minutes.
Are you ready to go?
I've been ready for days.

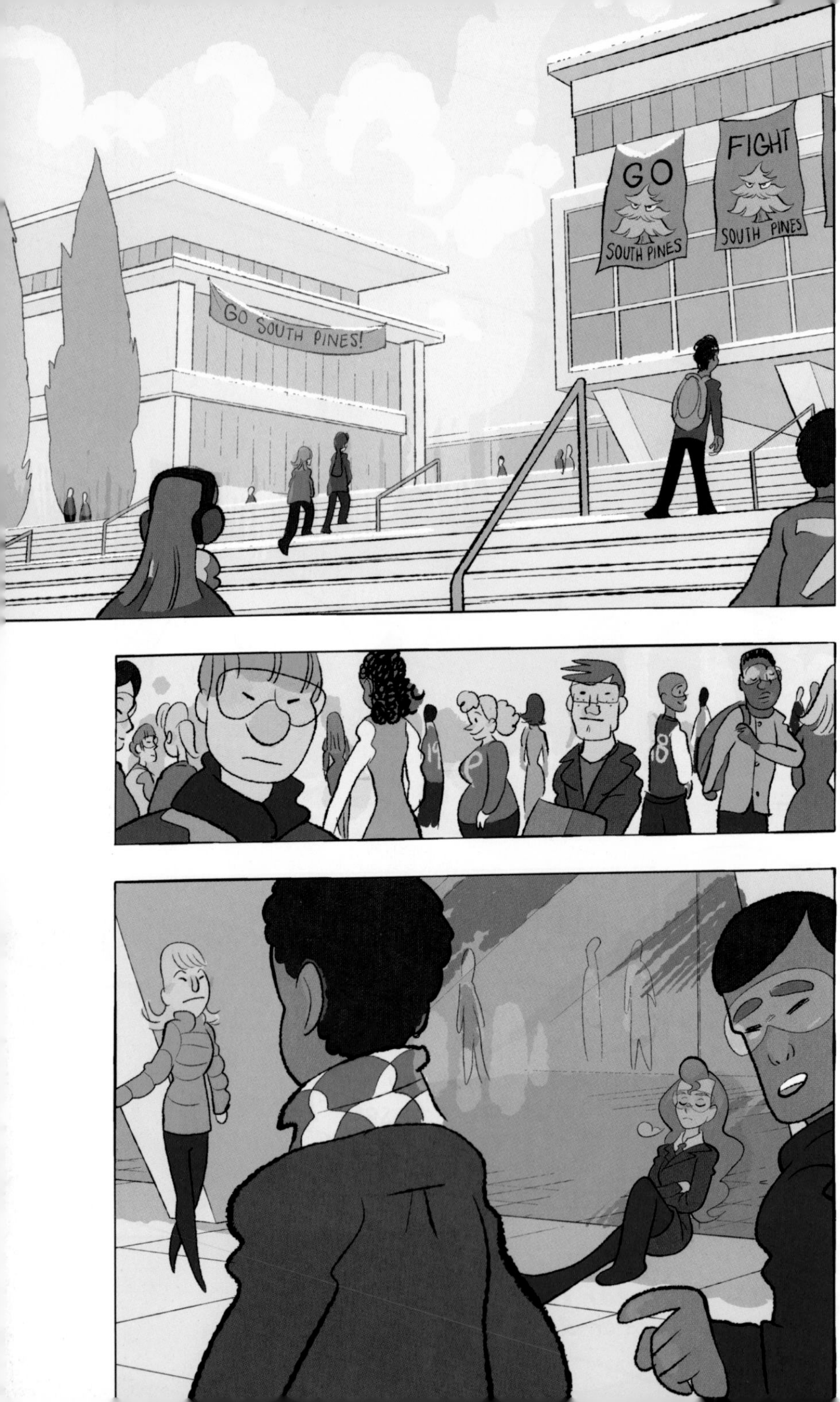
GO
SOUTH PINES
FIGHT
SOUTH PINES
GO SOUTH PINES!

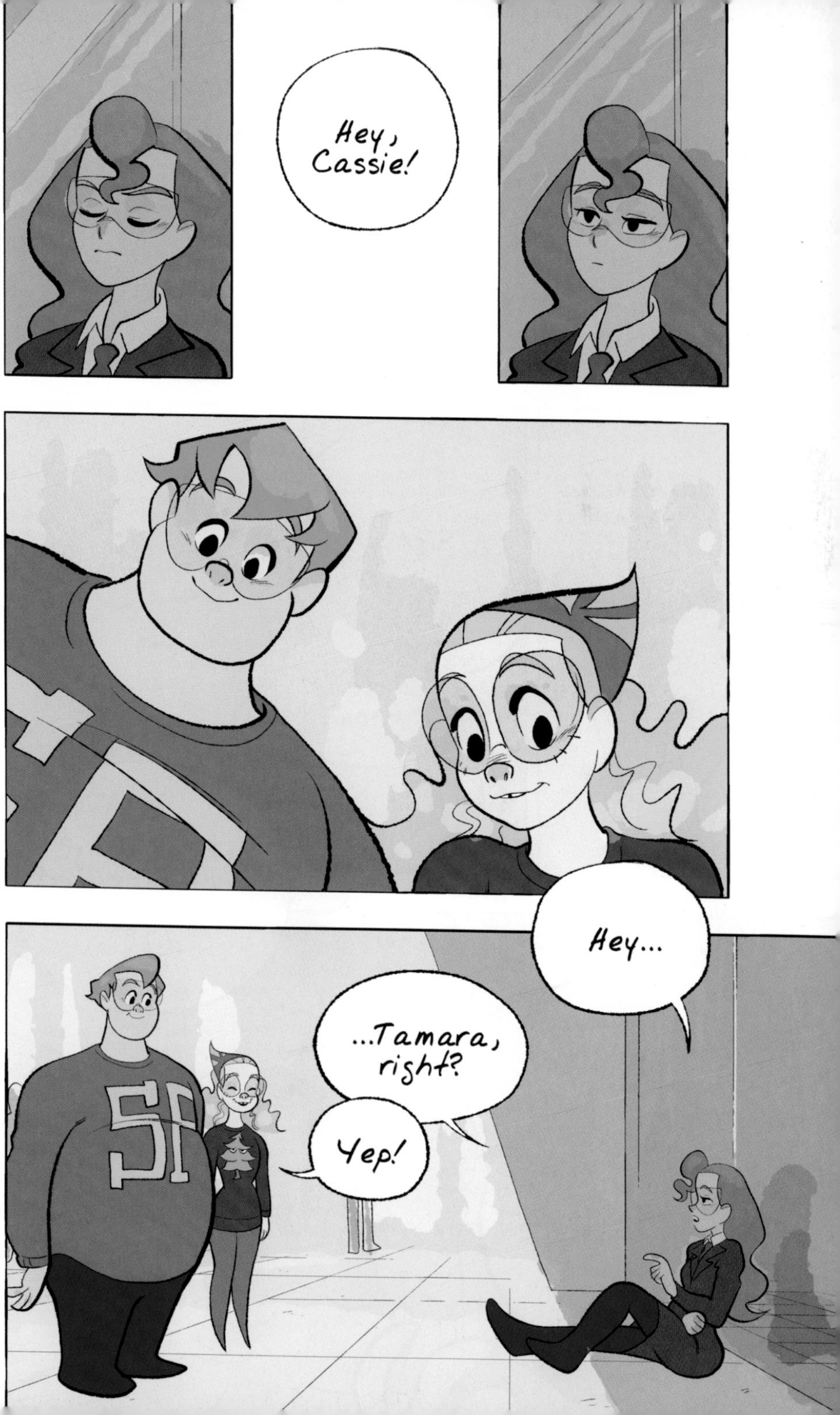
Hey, Cassie!
Hey...
...Tamara, right?
Yep!

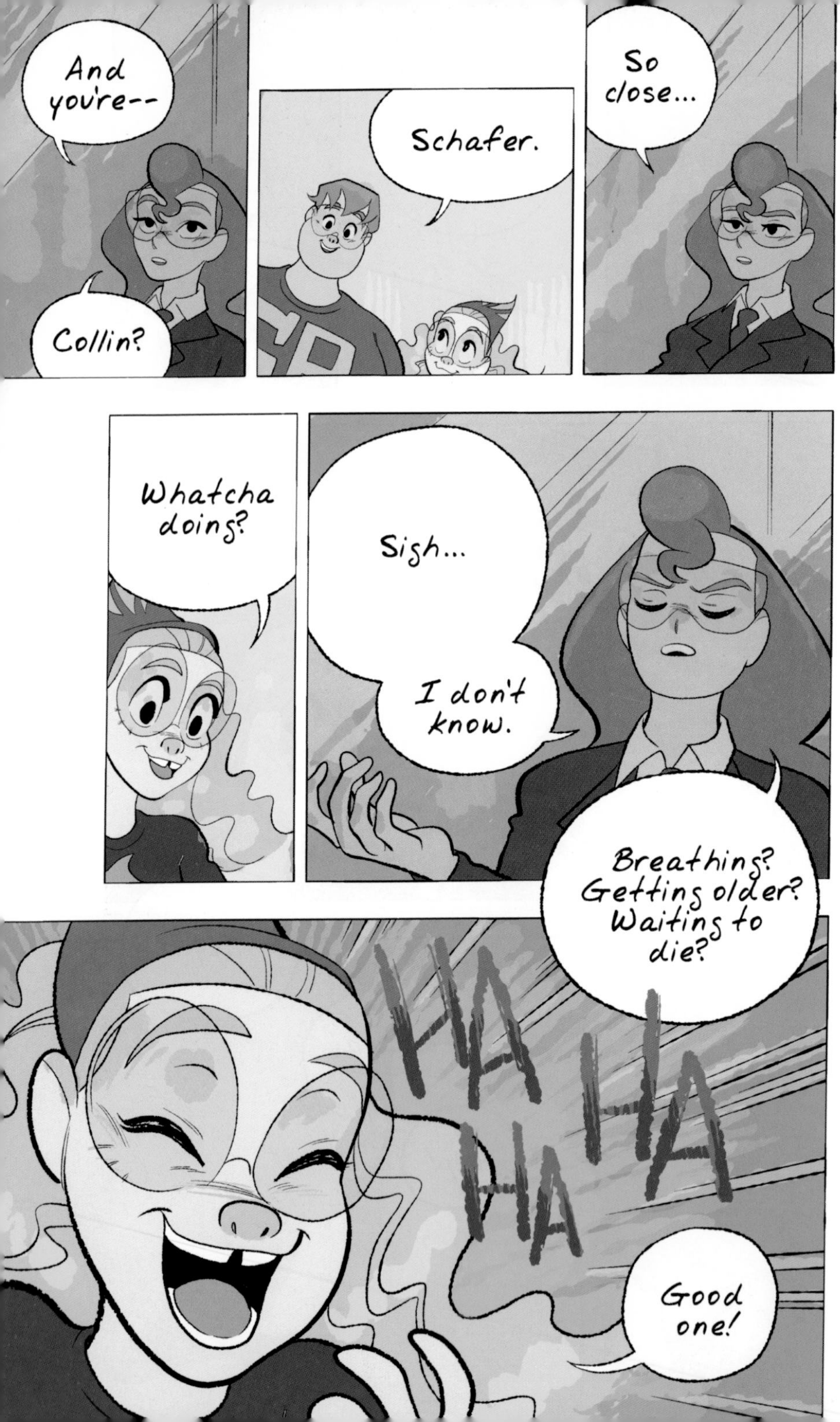
And you're--
Collin?
Schafer.
So close...
Whatcha doing?
Sigh...
I don't know.
Breathing? Getting older? Waiting to die?
HA HA HA
Good one!

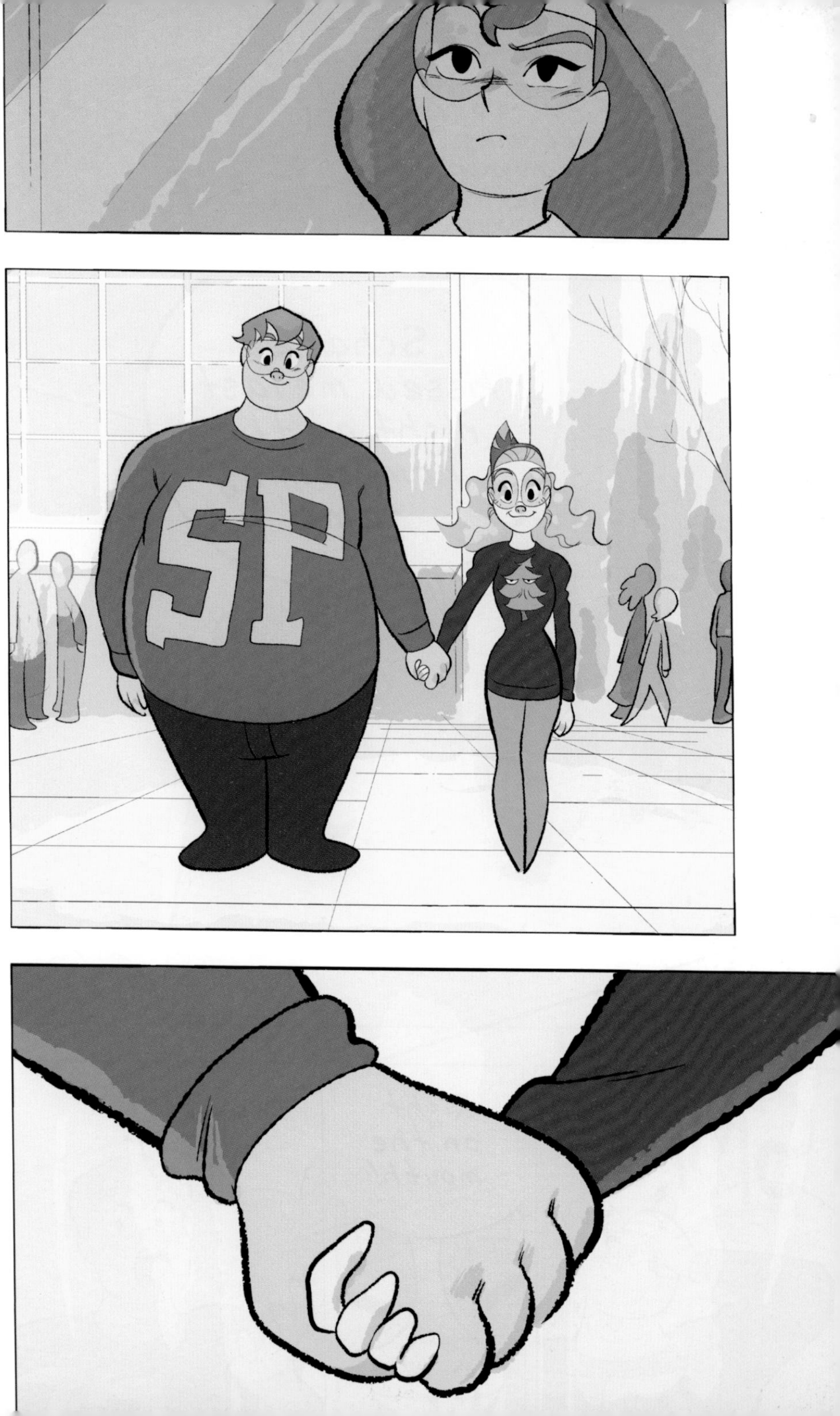
SP

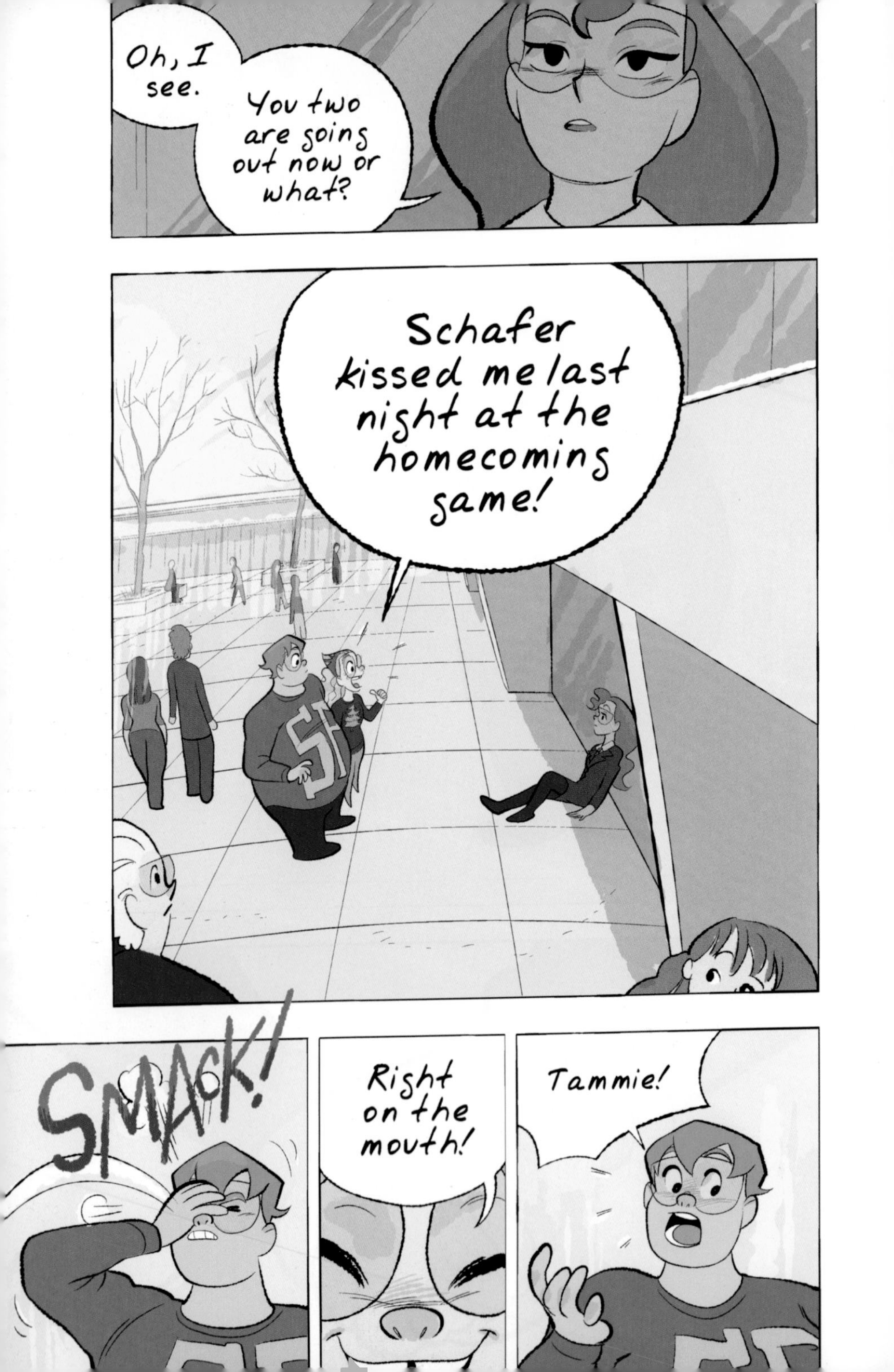
Oh, I see.
You two are going out now or what?
Schafer kissed me last night at the homecoming game!
SMACK!
Right on the mouth!
Tammie!

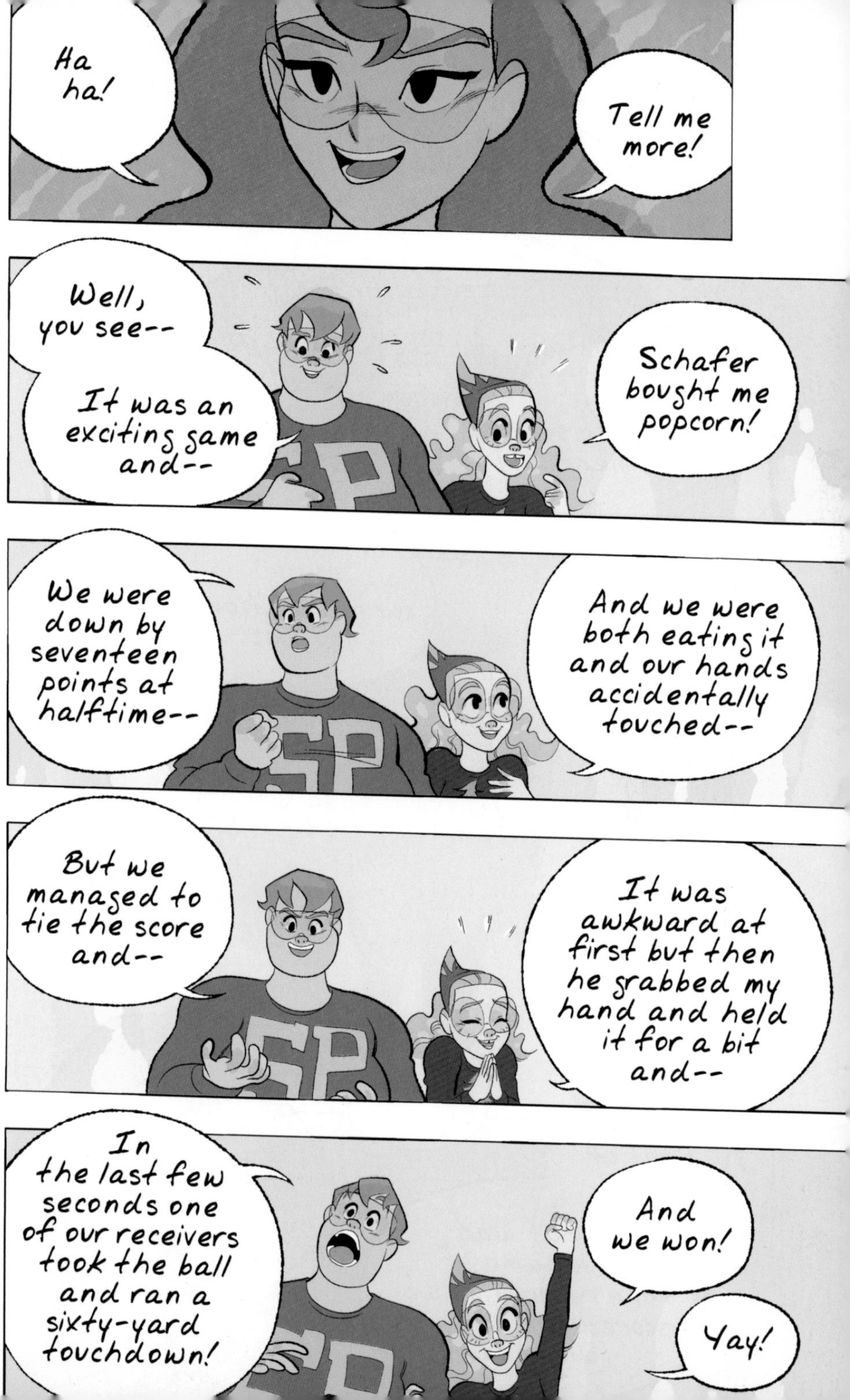
Ha ha!
Tell me more!
Well, you see--
It was an exciting game and--
Schafer bought me popcorn!
We were down by seventeen points at halftime--
And we were both eating it and our hands accidentally touched--
But we managed to tie the score and--
It was awkward at first but then he grabbed my hand and held it for a bit and--
In the last few seconds one of our receivers took the ball and ran a sixty-yard touchdown!
And we won!
Yay!

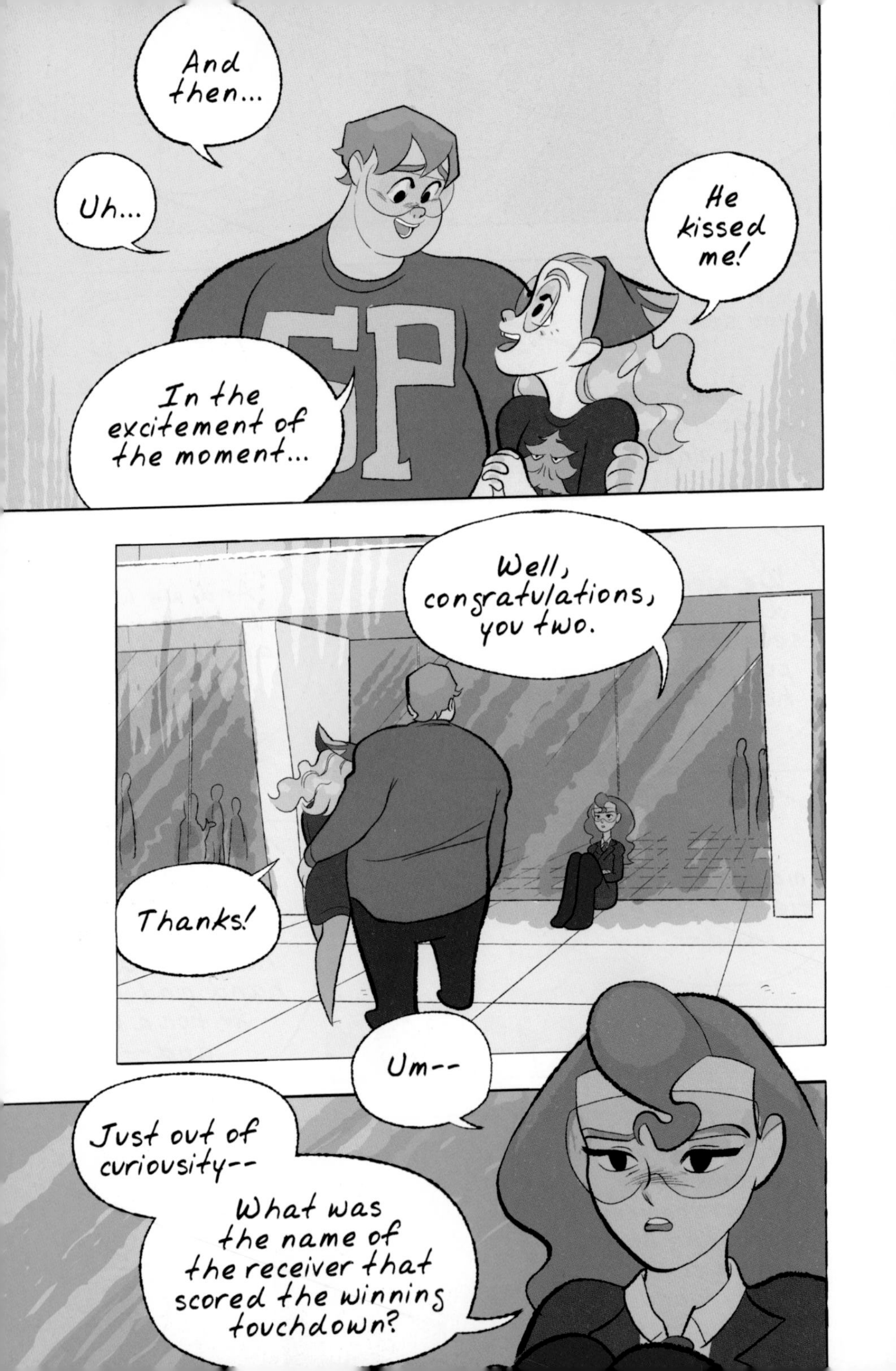
And then...
Uh...
He kissed me!
In the excitement of the moment...
Well, congratulations, you two.
Thanks!
Um--
Just out of curiousity--
What was the name of the receiver that scored the winning touchdown?

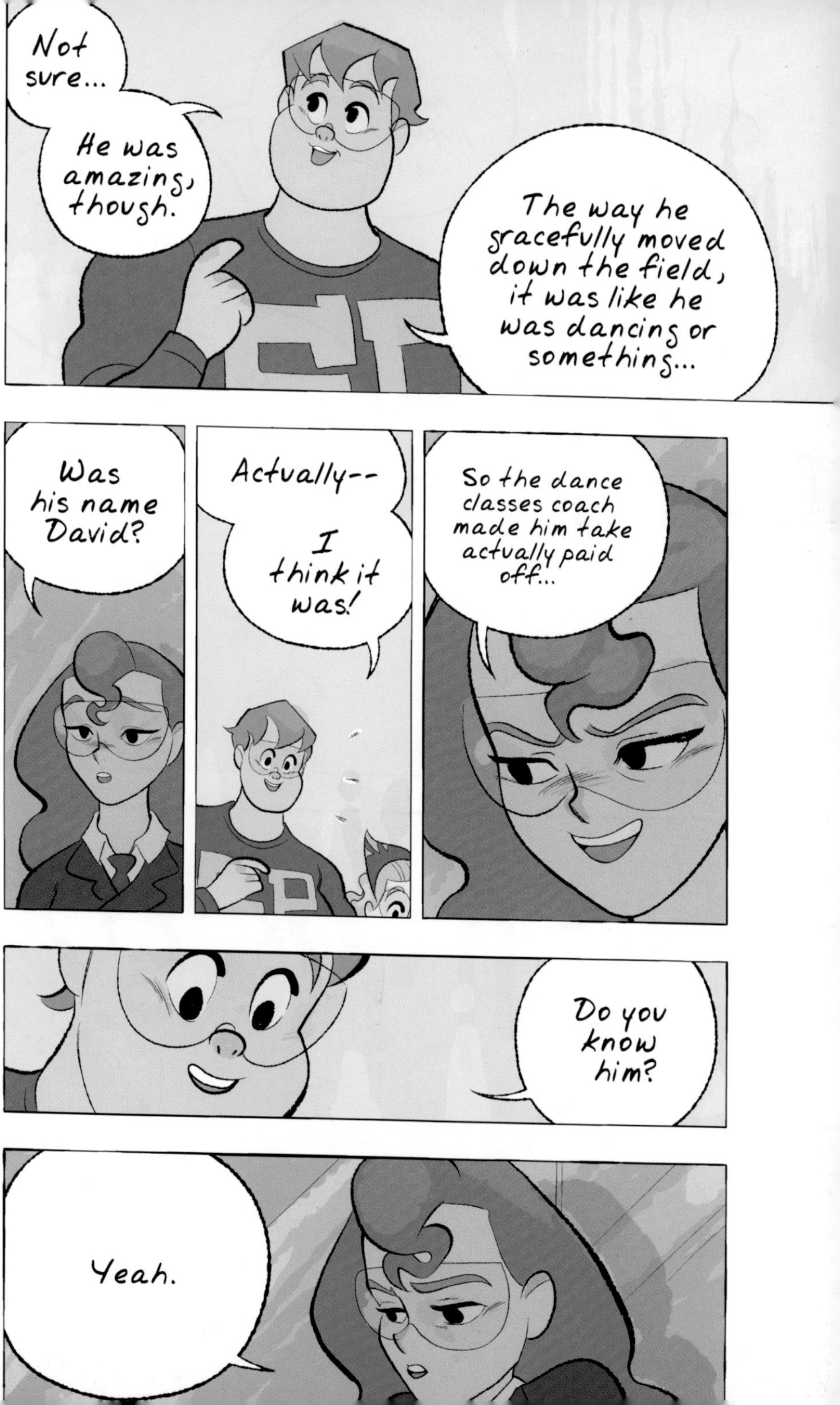
Not sure...
He was amazing, though.
The way he gracefully moved down the field, it was like he was dancing or something...
Was his name David?
Actually--
I think it was!
So the dance classes coach made him take actually paid off...
Do you know him?
Yeah.

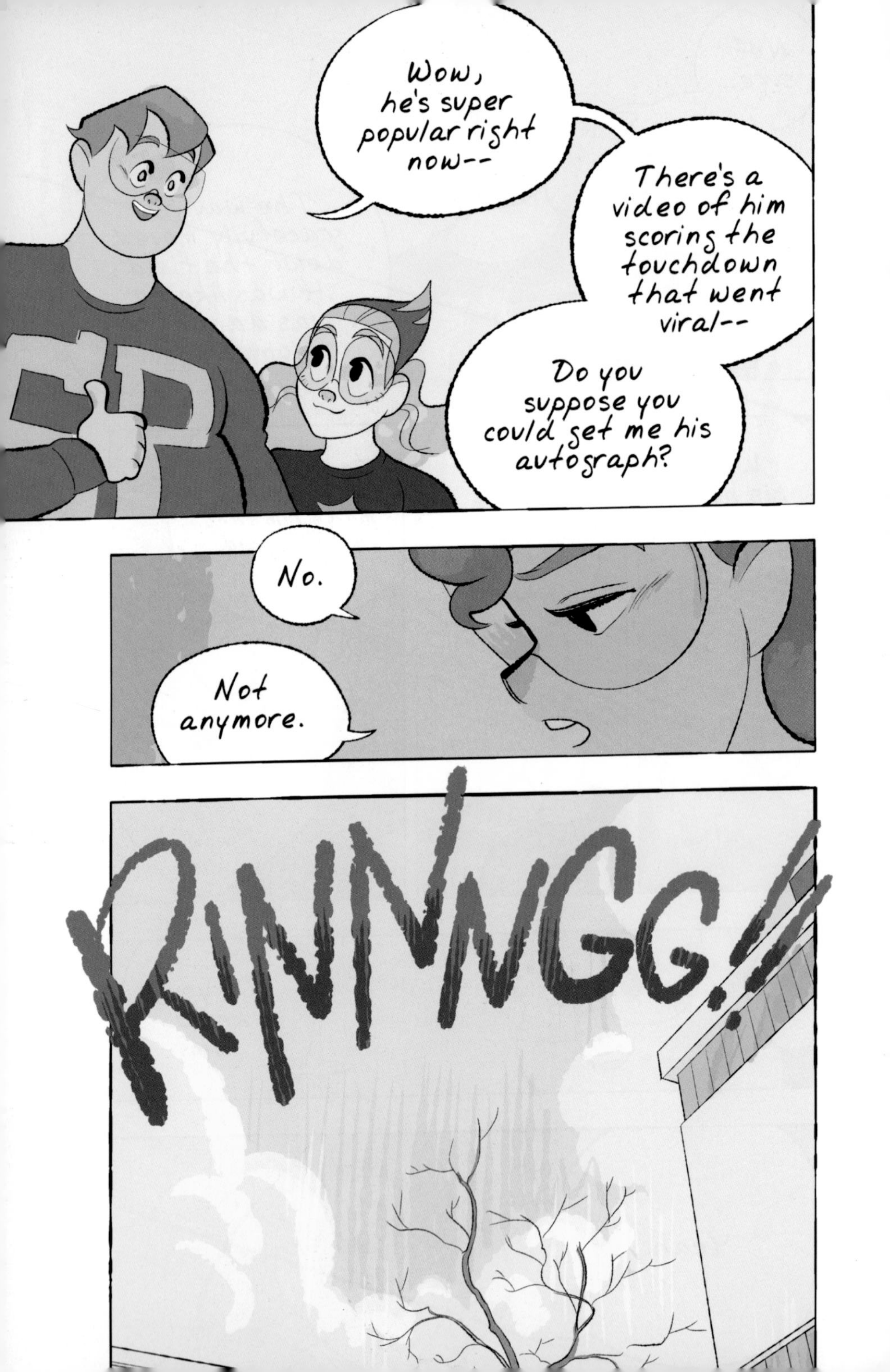
Wow, he's super popular right now--
There's a video of him scoring the touchdown that went viral--
Do you suppose you could get me his autograph?
No.
Not anymore.
RINNNGG!!

SMOOCH!!

See you guys at lunch!

Bye, Schafer!

B--

Bye...

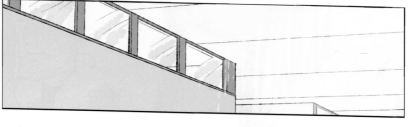

Excuse me...

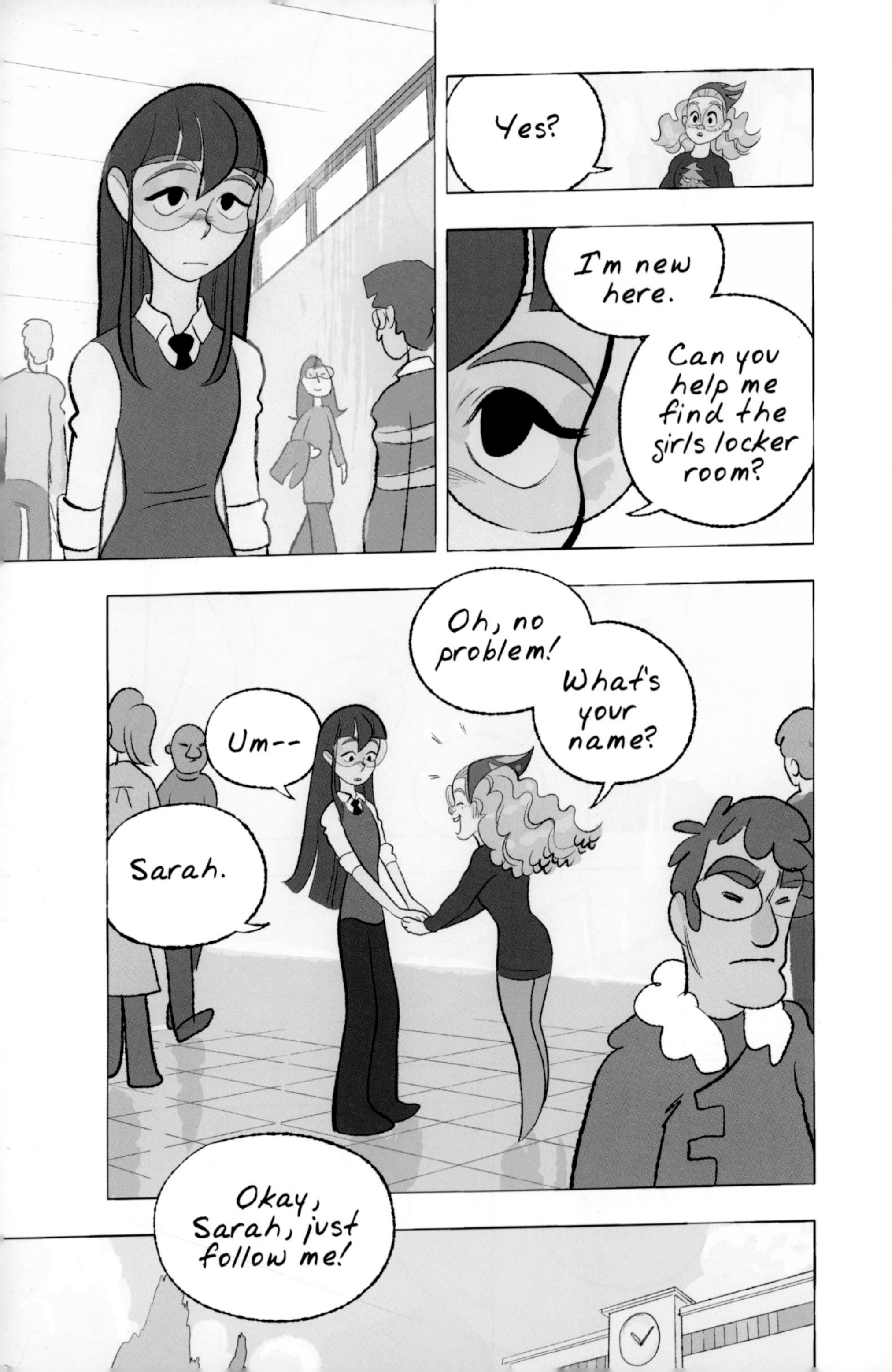
Yes?
I'm new here.
Can you help me find the girls locker room?
Oh, no problem!
What's your name?
Um--
Sarah.
Okay, Sarah, just follow me!

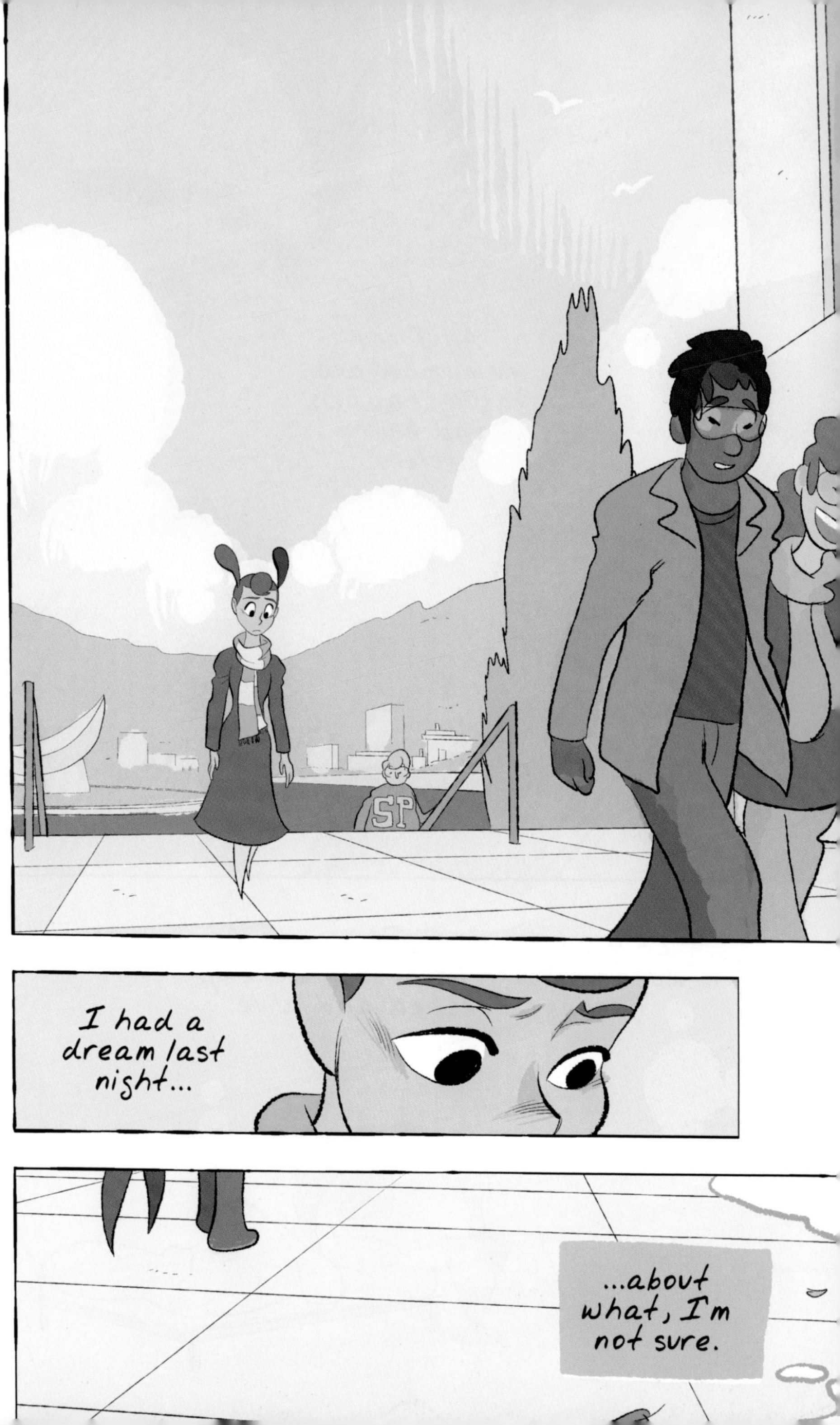
SP
I had a dream last night...
...about what, I'm not sure.

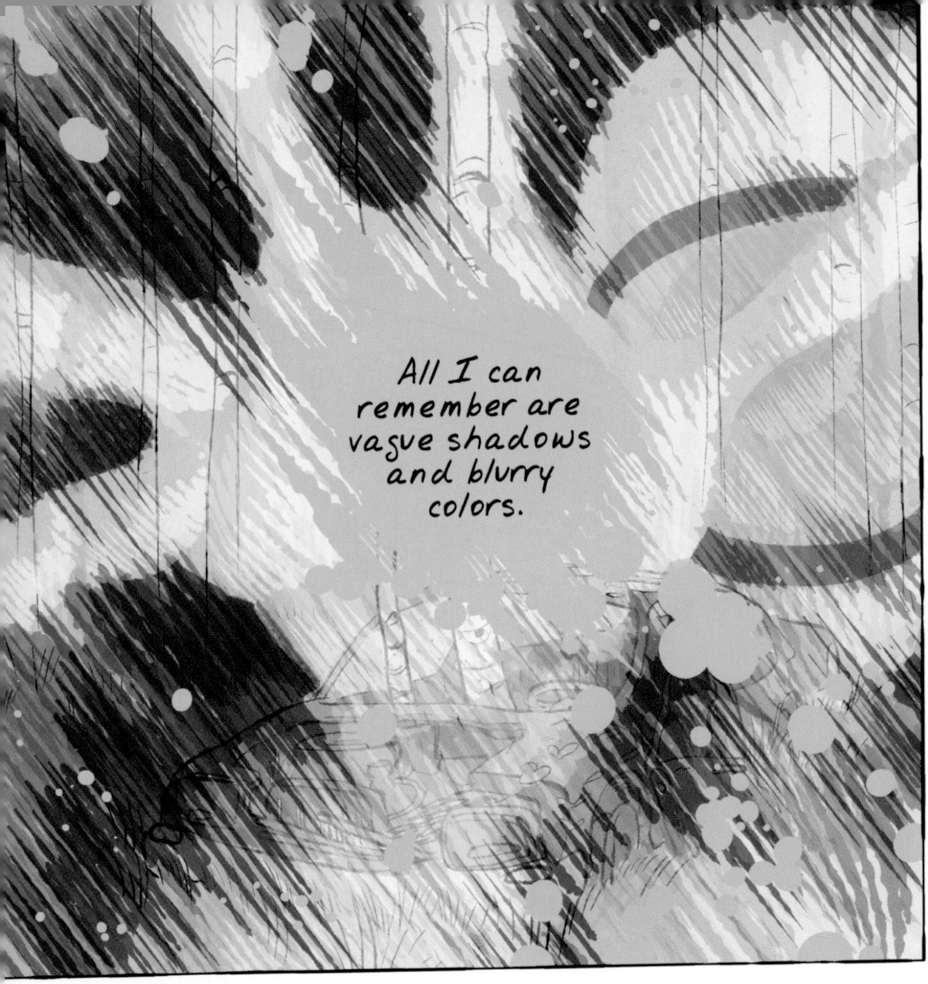
All I can remember are vague shadows and blurry colors.

It must have been a wonderful dream though because I woke up feeling refreshed and alive.

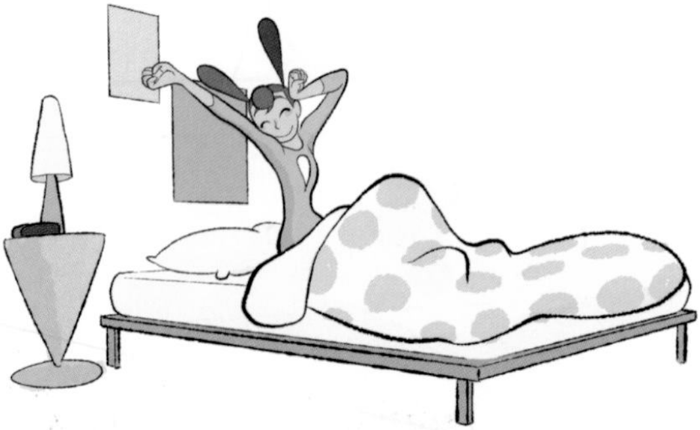

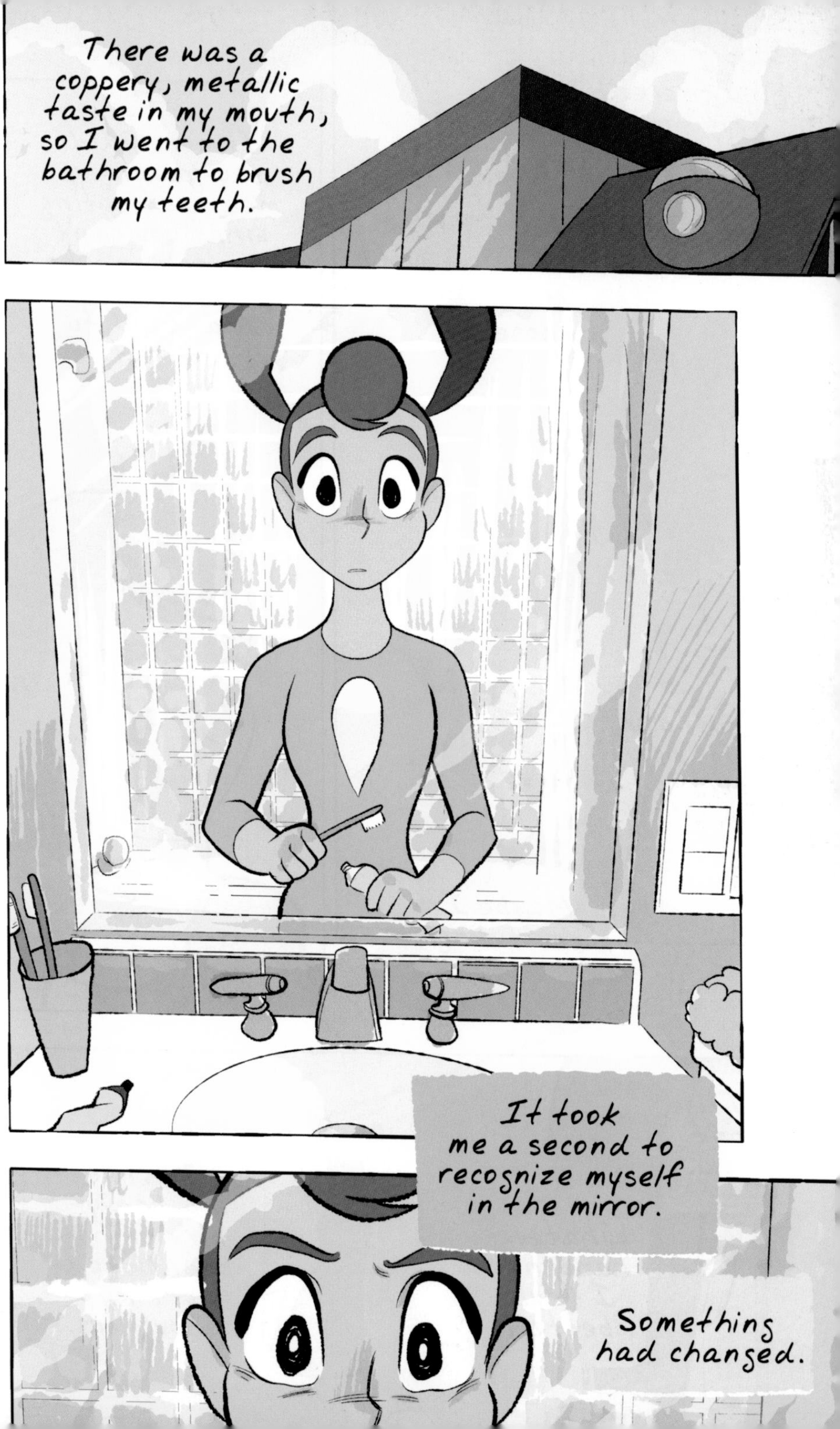
There was a coppery, metallic taste in my mouth, so I went to the bathroom to brush my teeth.
It took me a second to recognize myself in the mirror.
Somethins had chansed.

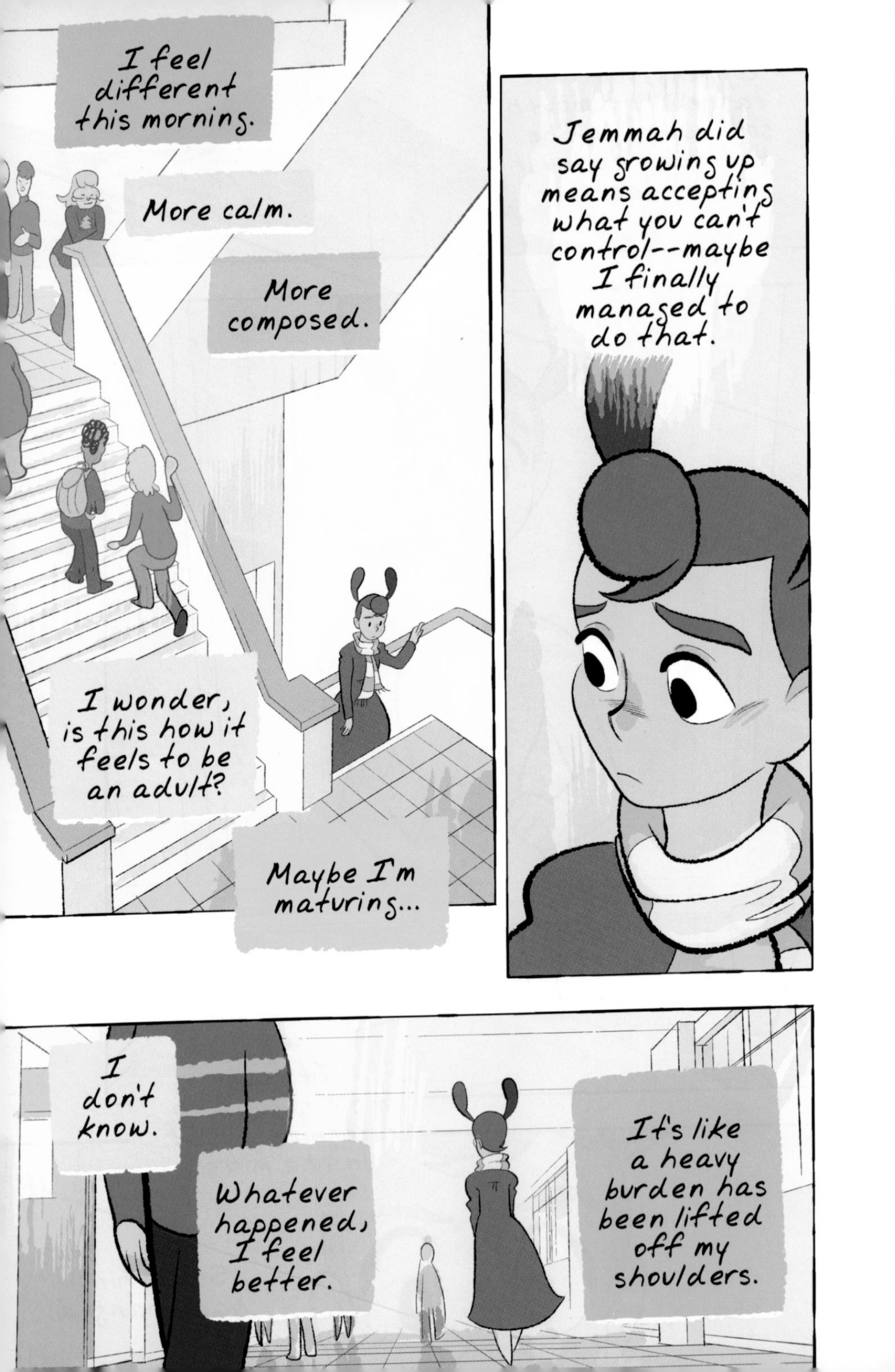
I feel different this morning.
More calm.
More composed.
I wonder, is this how it feels to be an adult?
Maybe I'm maturing...
Jemmah did say growing up means accepting what you can't control--maybe I finally managed to do that.
I don't know.
Whatever happened, I feel better.
It's like a heavy burden has been lifted off my shoulders.

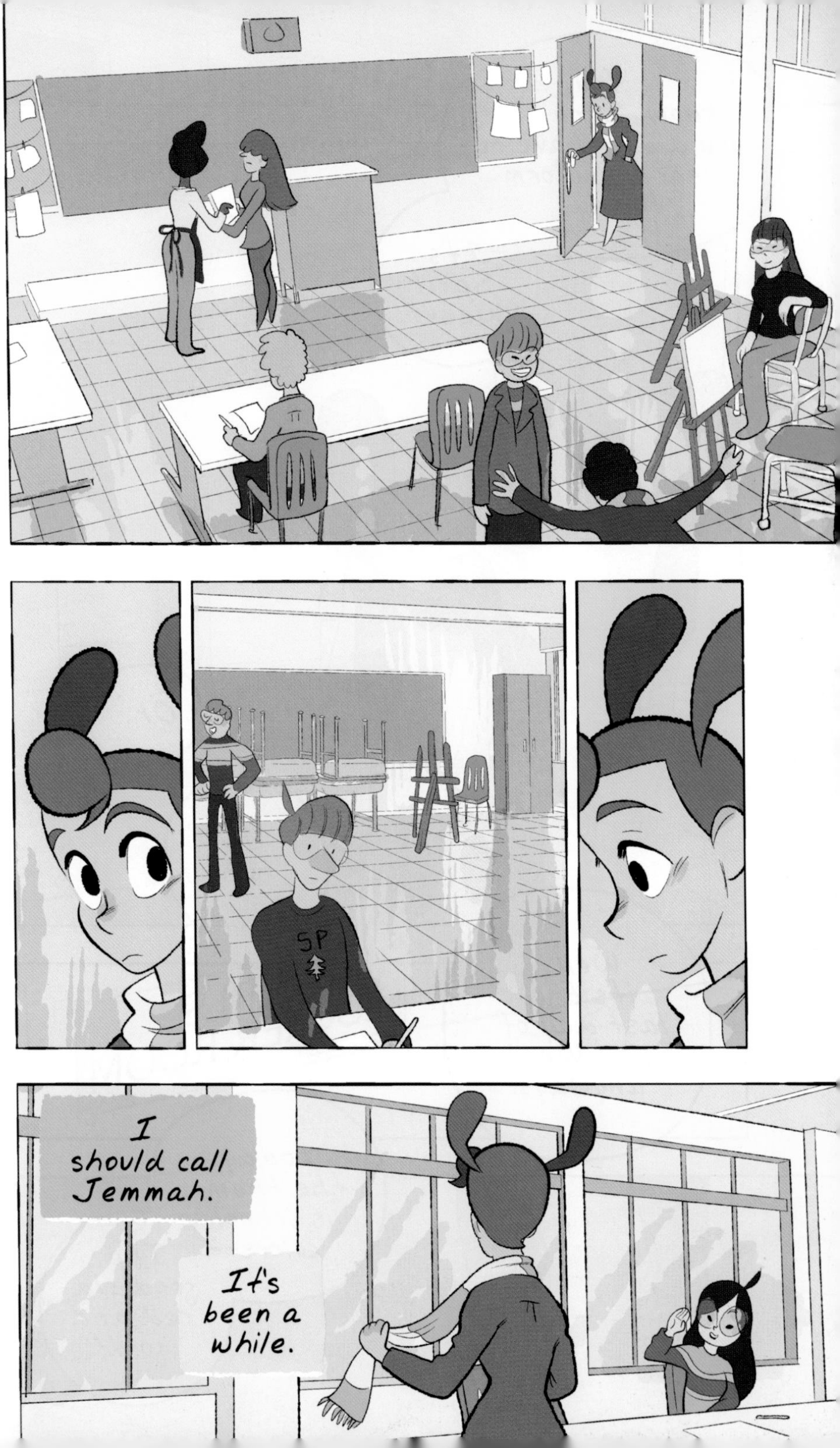

I should call Jemmah.
It's been a while.

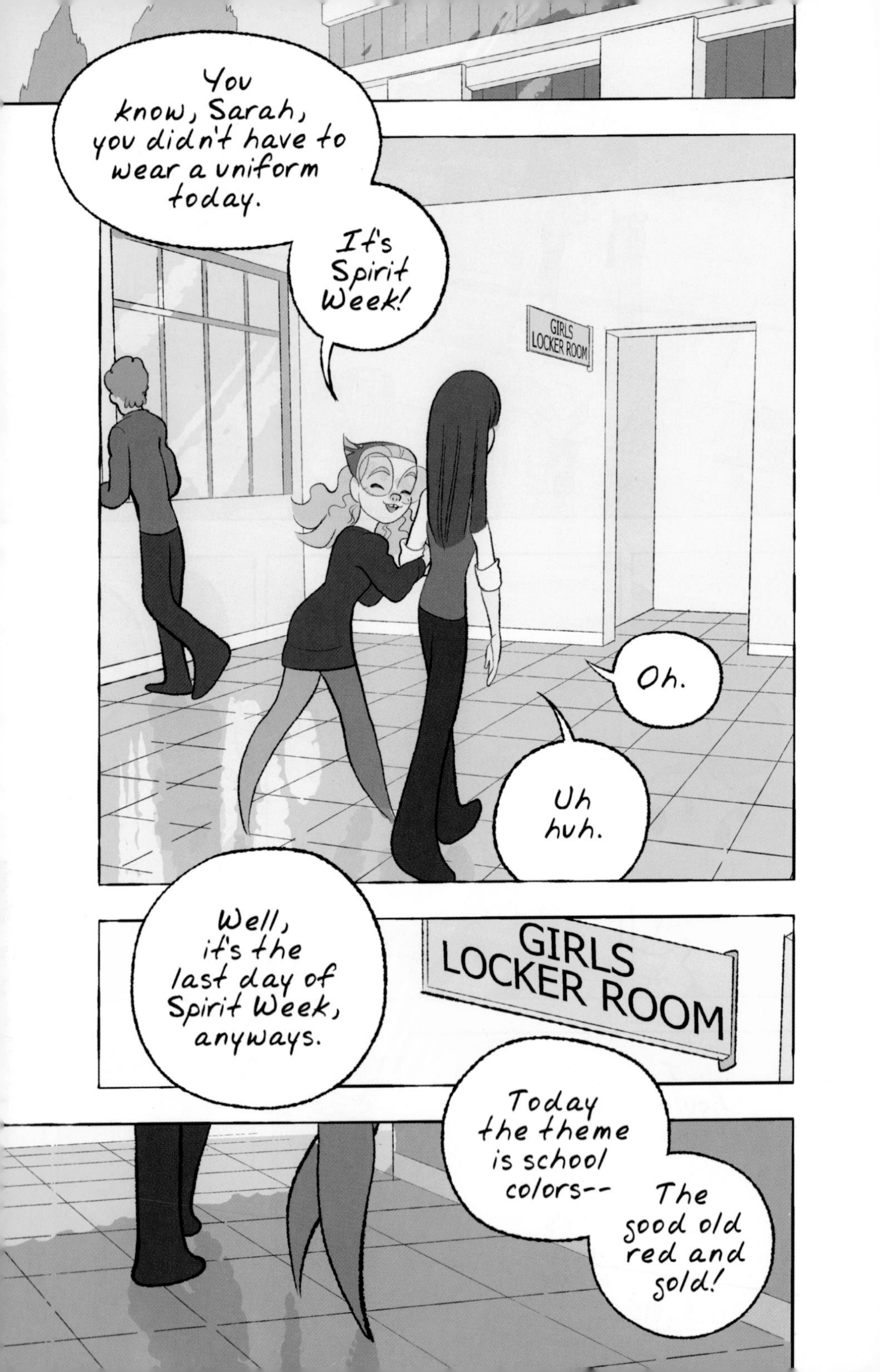
You know, Sarah, you didn't have to wear a uniform today.
It's Spirit Week!
GIRLS LOCKER ROOM
Oh.
Uh huh.
Well, it's the last day of Spirit Week, anyways.
GIRLS LOCKER ROOM
Today the theme is school colors--
The good old red and gold!

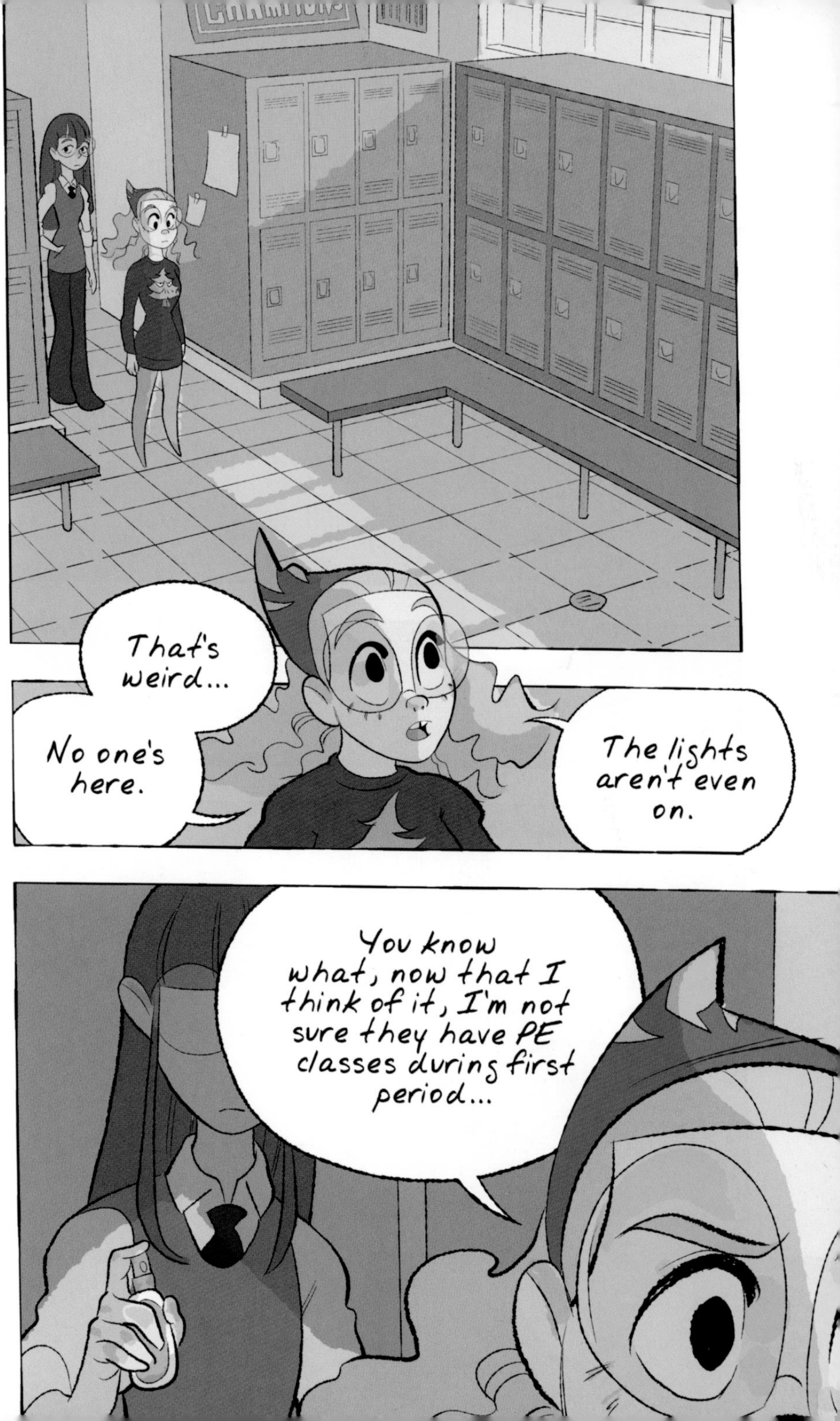
That's weird...
No one's here.
The lights aren't even on.
You know what, now that I think of it, I'm not sure they have PE classes during first period...

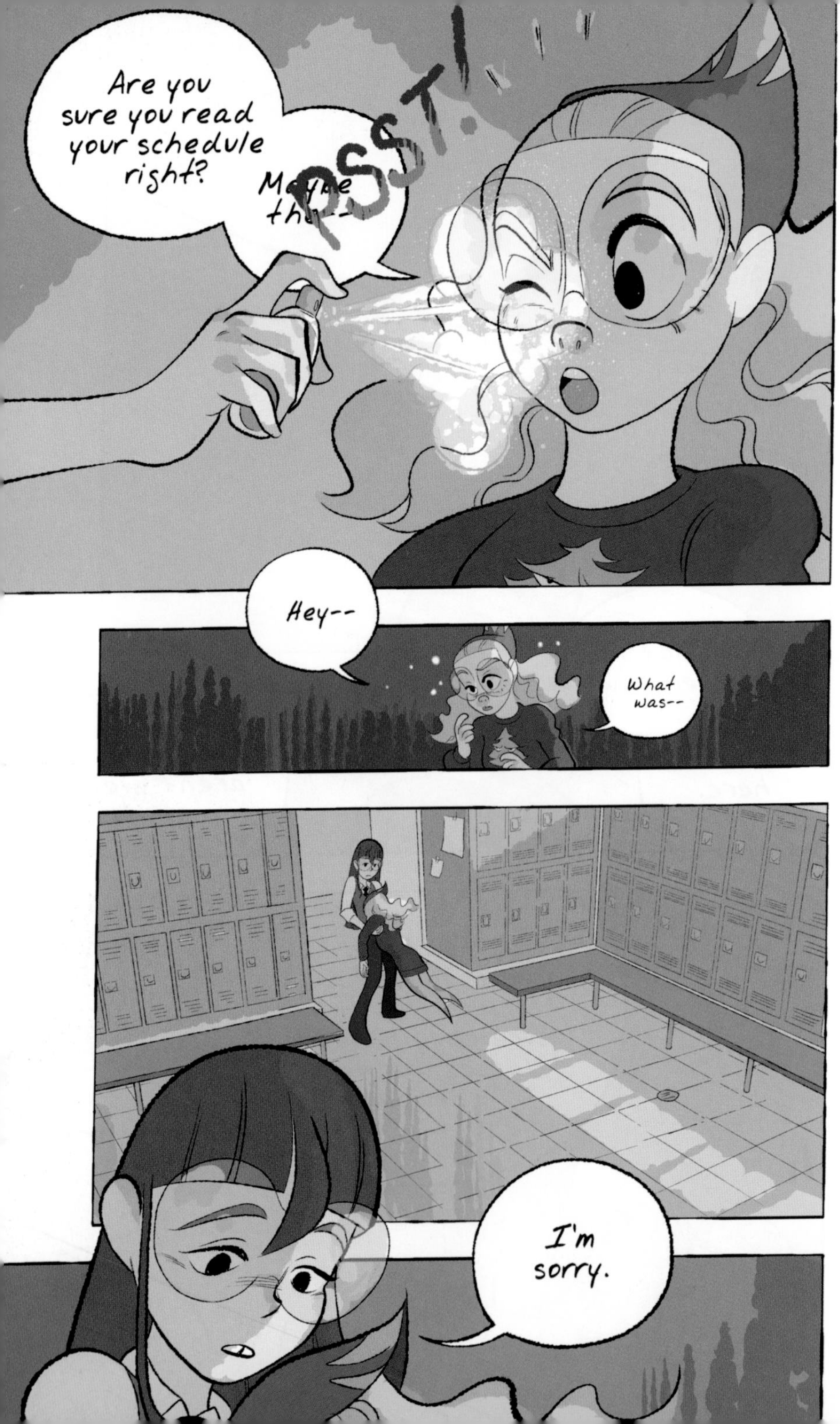
Are you sure you read your schedule right?
Maybe th--
PSST!
Hey--
What was--
I'm sorry.

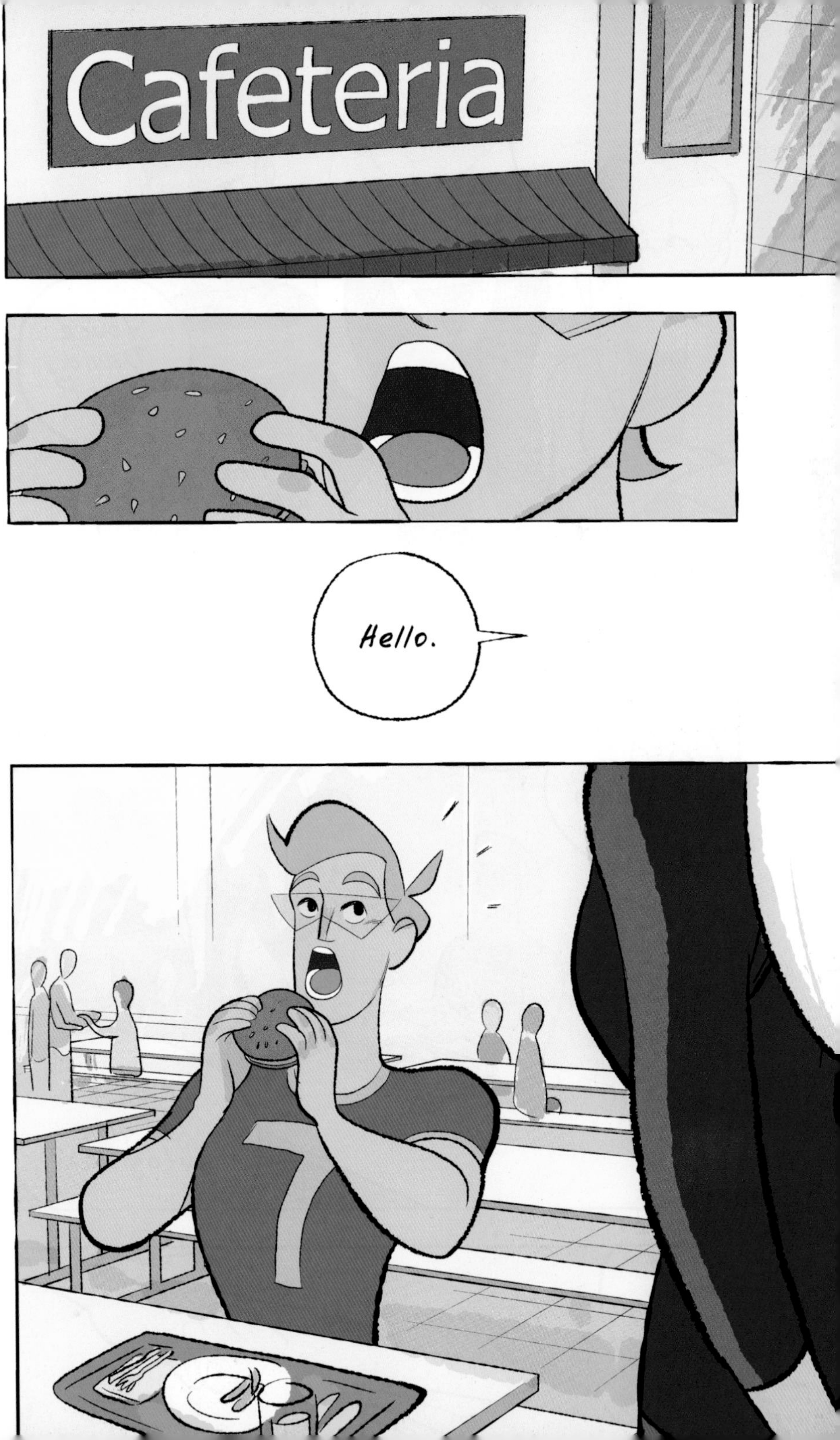
Cafeteria
Hello.
7

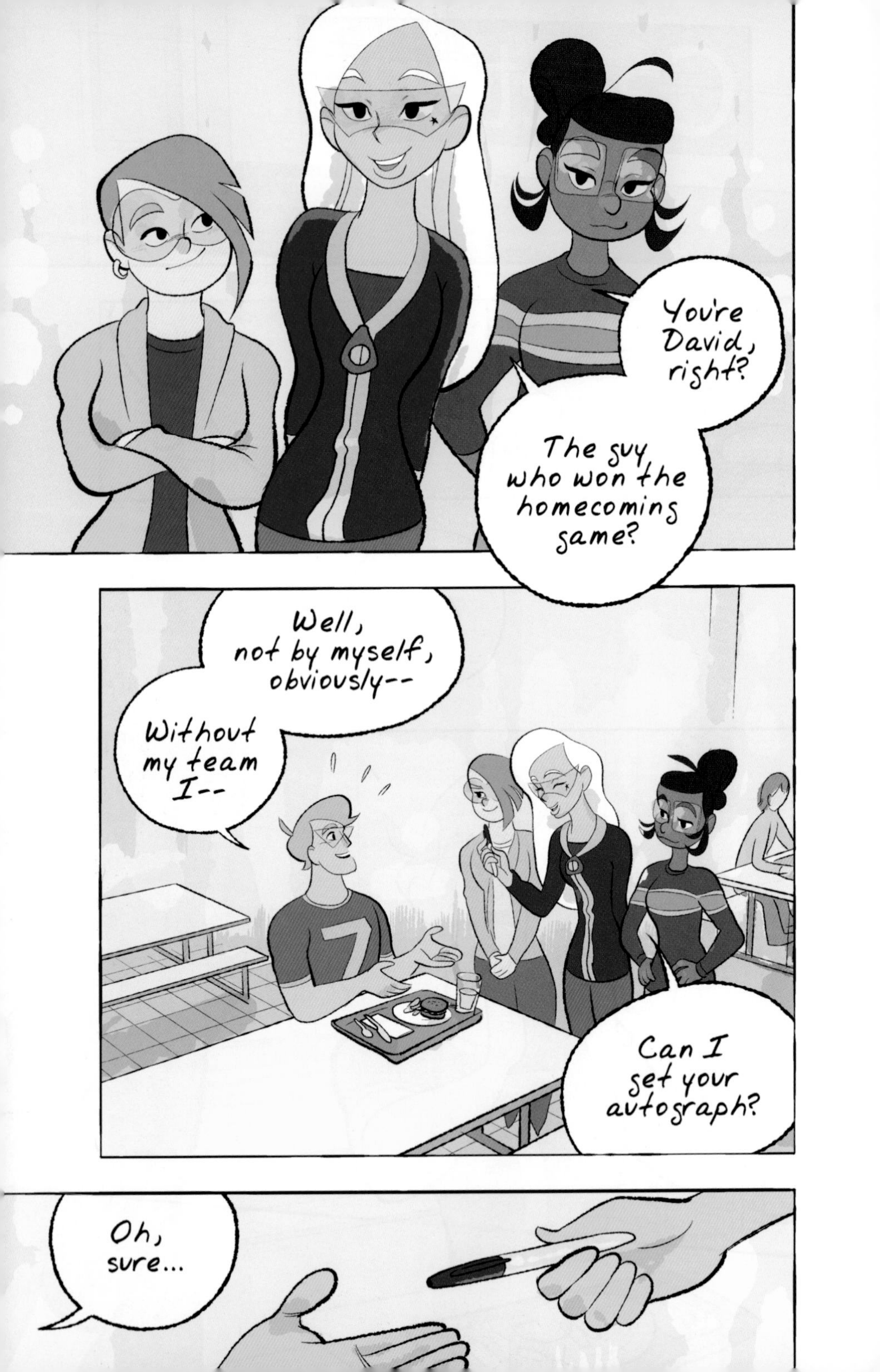
You're David, right?
The guy who won the homecoming game?
Well, not by myself, obviously--
Without my team I--
Can I get your autograph?
Oh, sure...

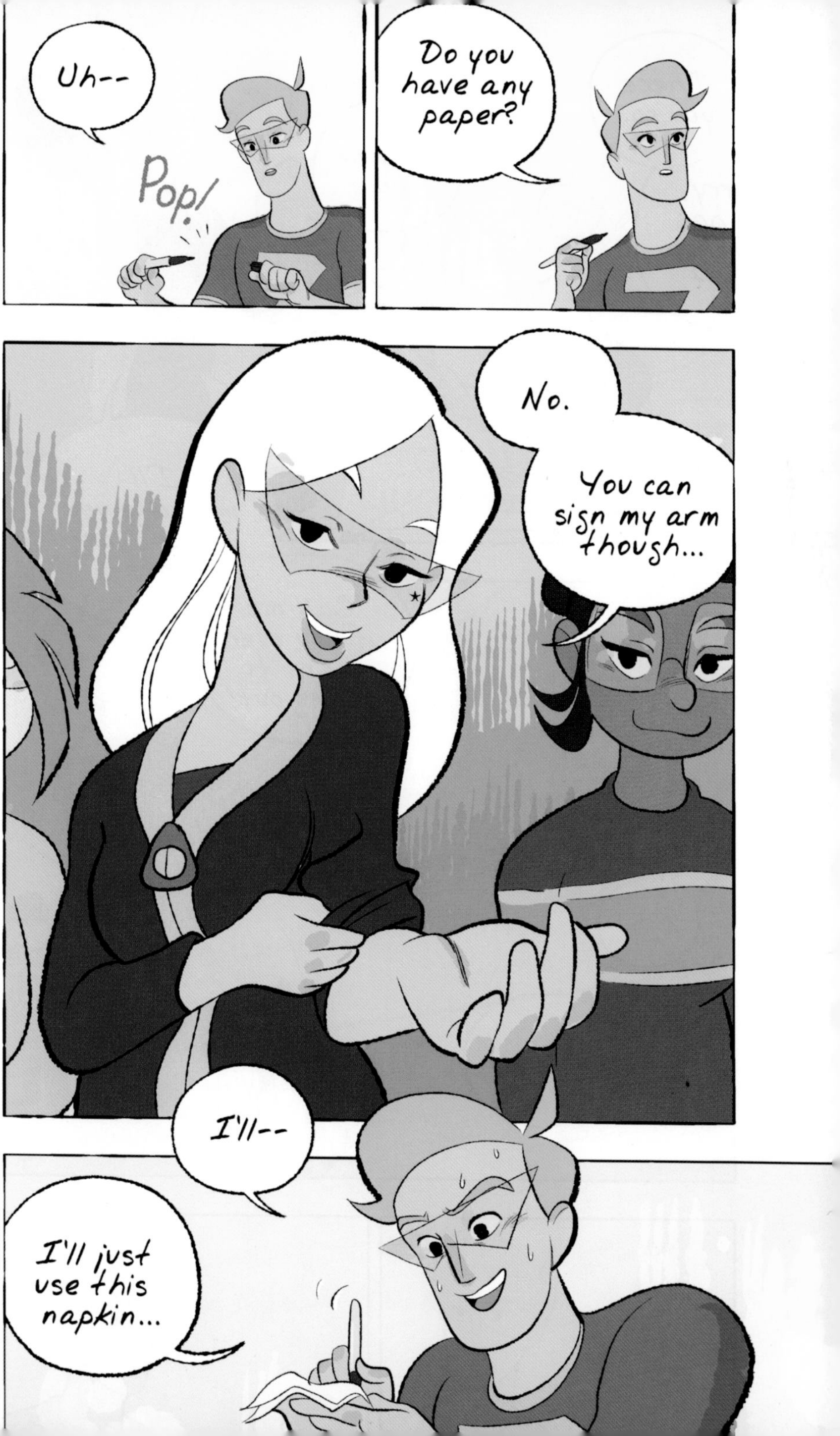
Uh--
Pop!
Do you have any paper?
No.
You can sign my arm though...
I'll--
I'll just use this napkin...

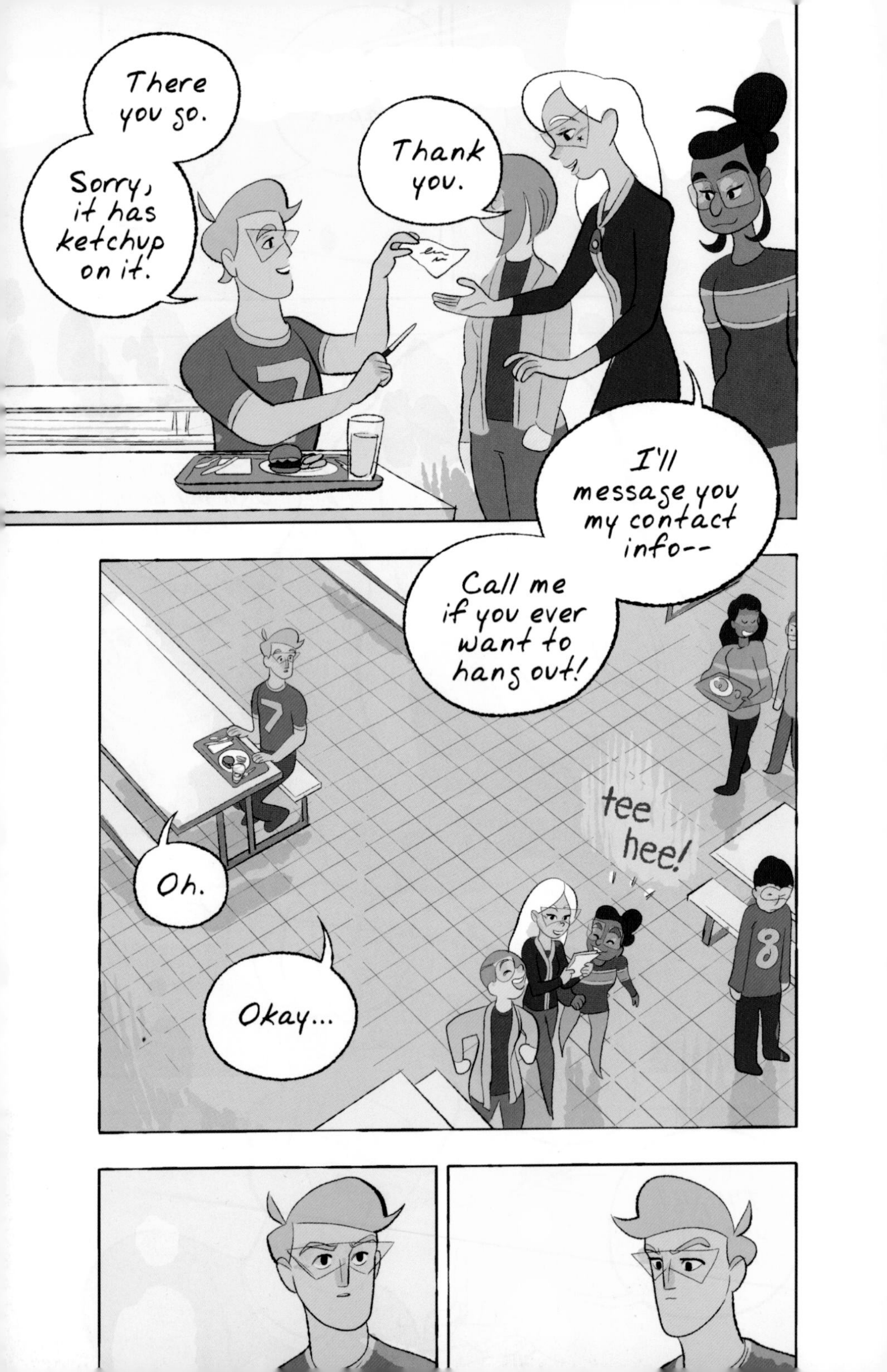
There you go.
Sorry, it has ketchup on it.
Thank you.
I'll message you my contact info--
Call me if you ever want to hang out!
Oh.
tee hee!
Okay...

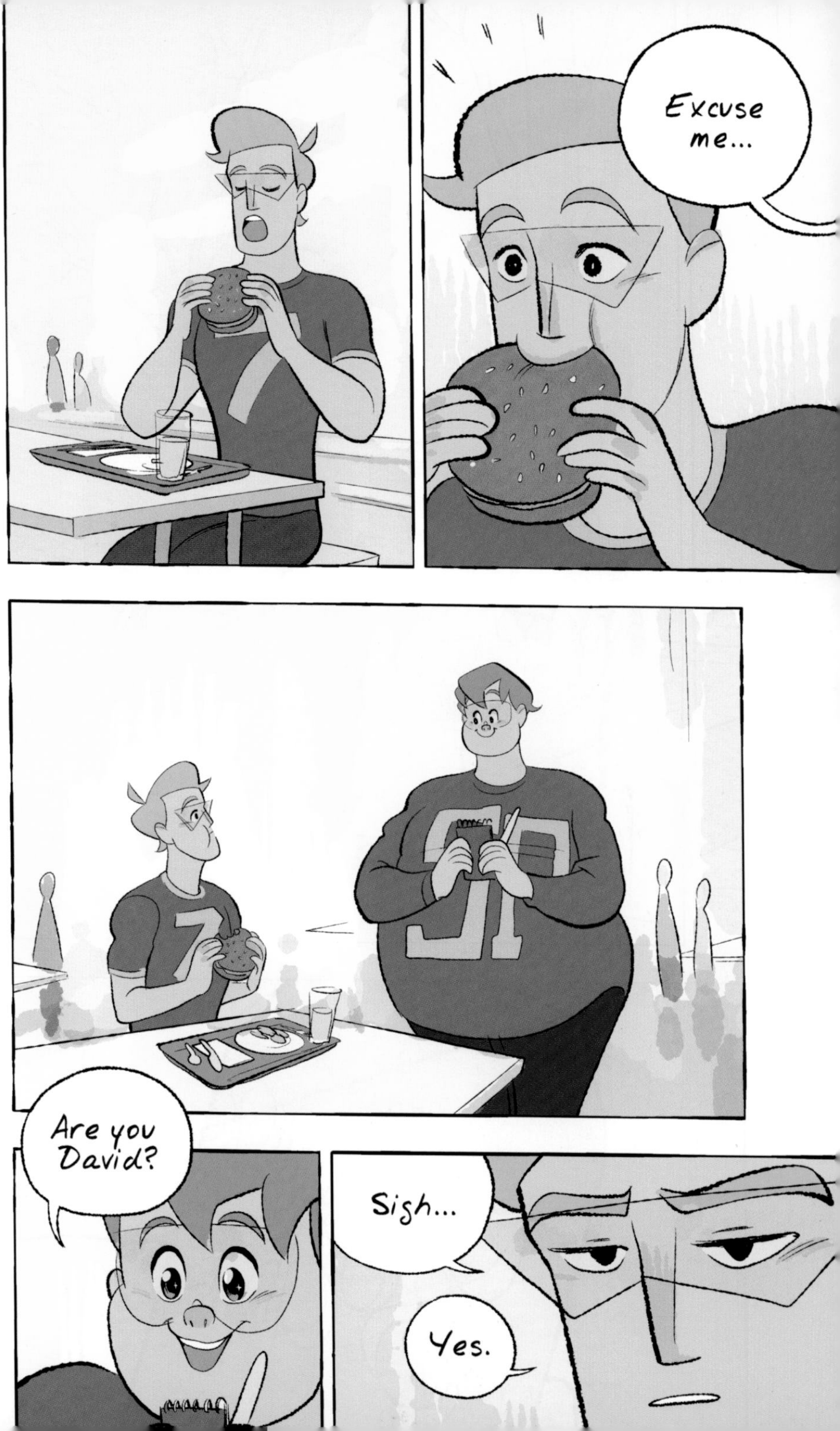
Excuse me...
Are you David?
Sigh...
Yes.

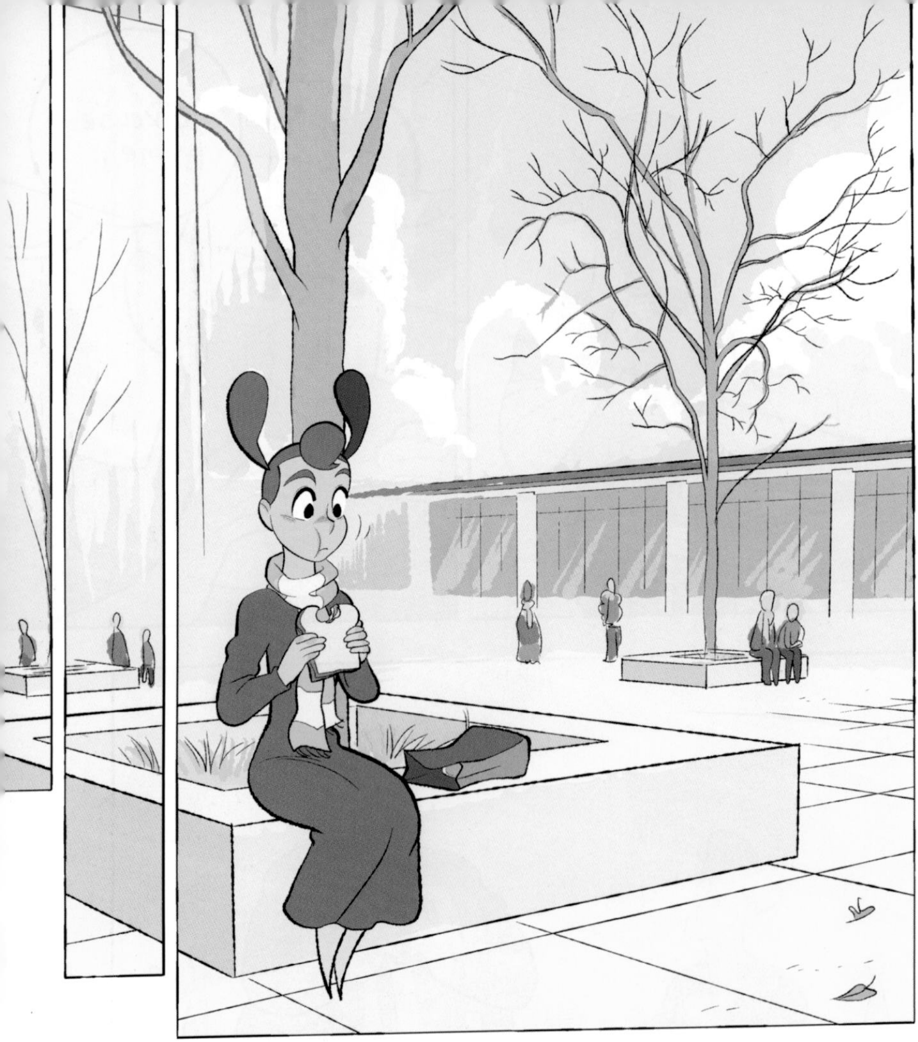

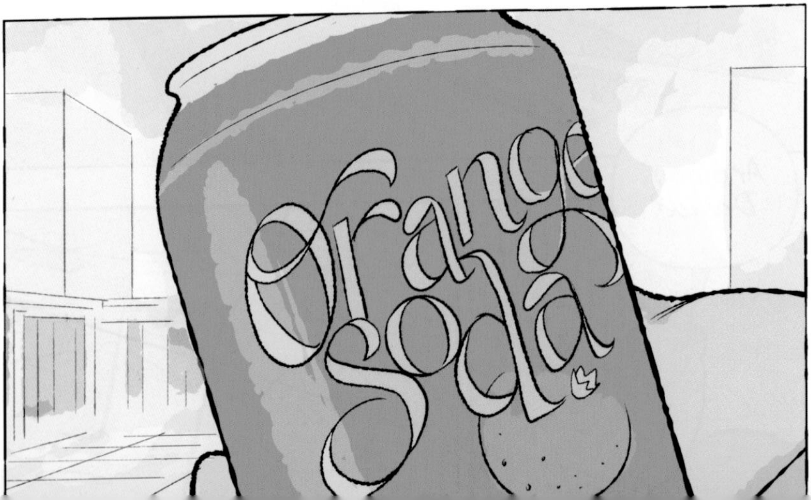
Orange
Soda

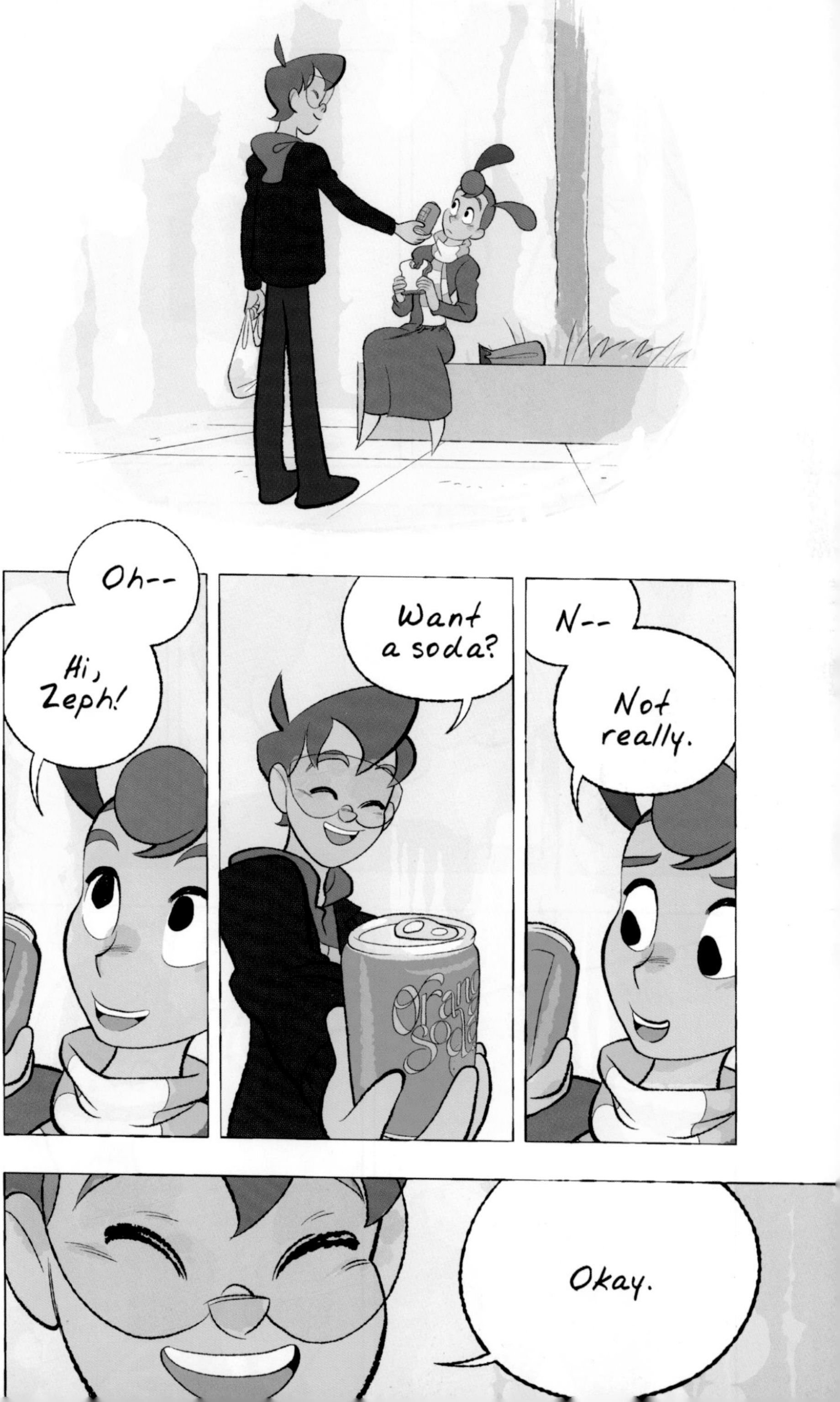
Oh--
Hi, Zeph!
Want a soda?
Orange Soda
N--
Not really.
Okay.

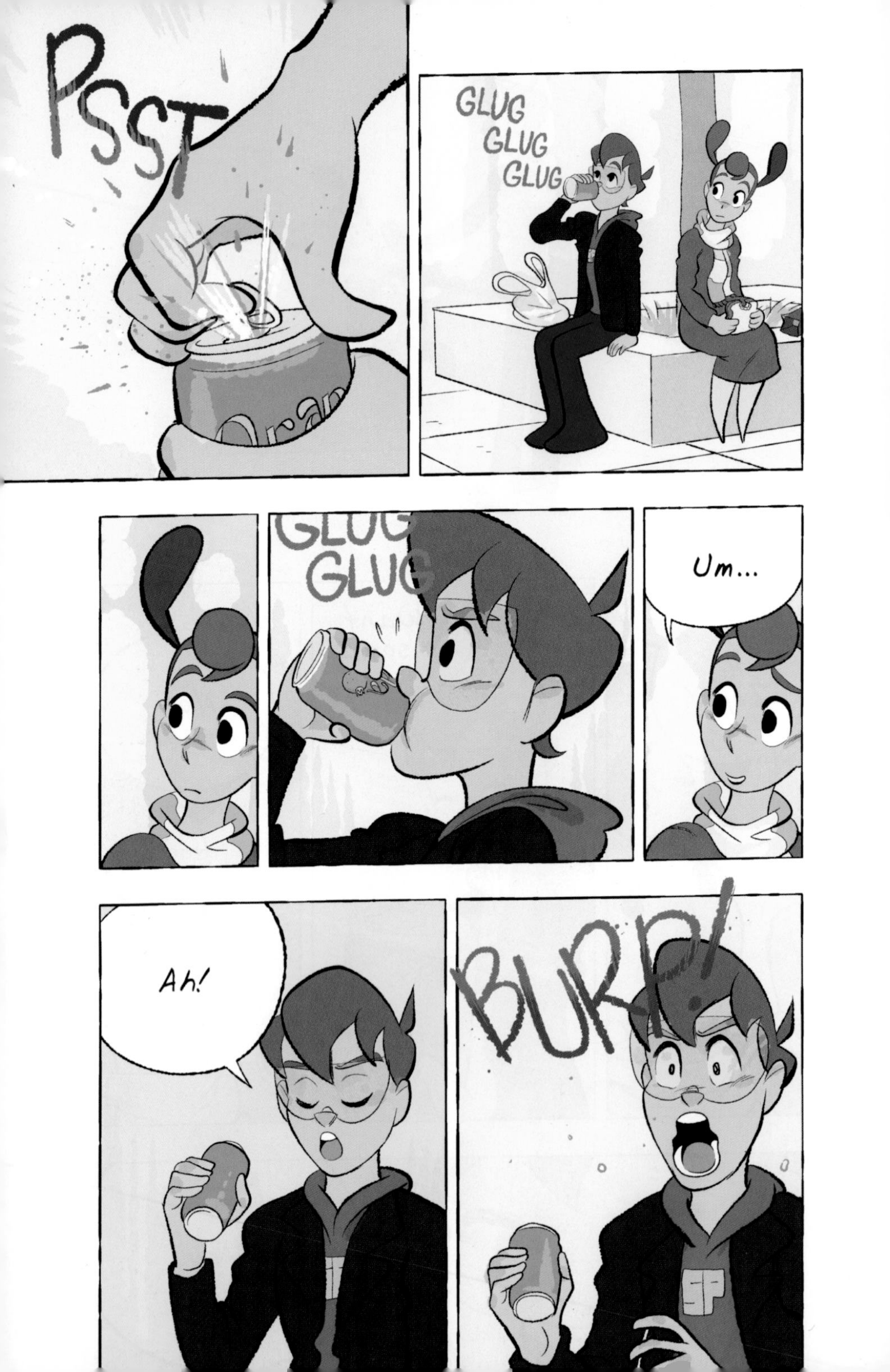
PSST
GLUG
GLUG
GLUG
GLUG
GLUG
Um...
Ah!
BURP!

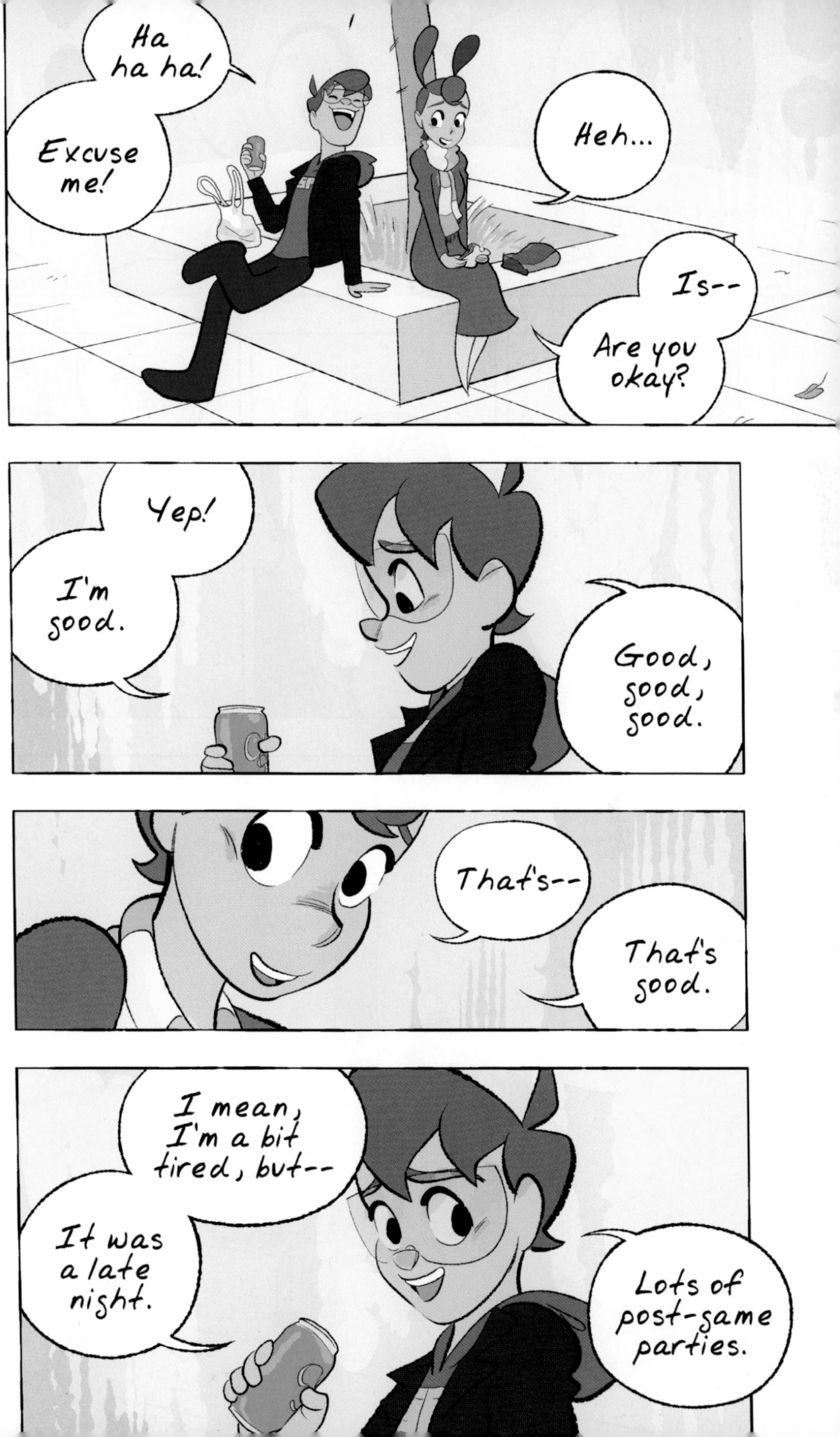
Ha ha ha!
Excuse me!
Heh...
Is--
Are you okay?
Yep!
I'm good.
Good, good, good.
That's--
That's good.
I mean, I'm a bit tired, but--
It was a late night.
Lots of post-game parties.

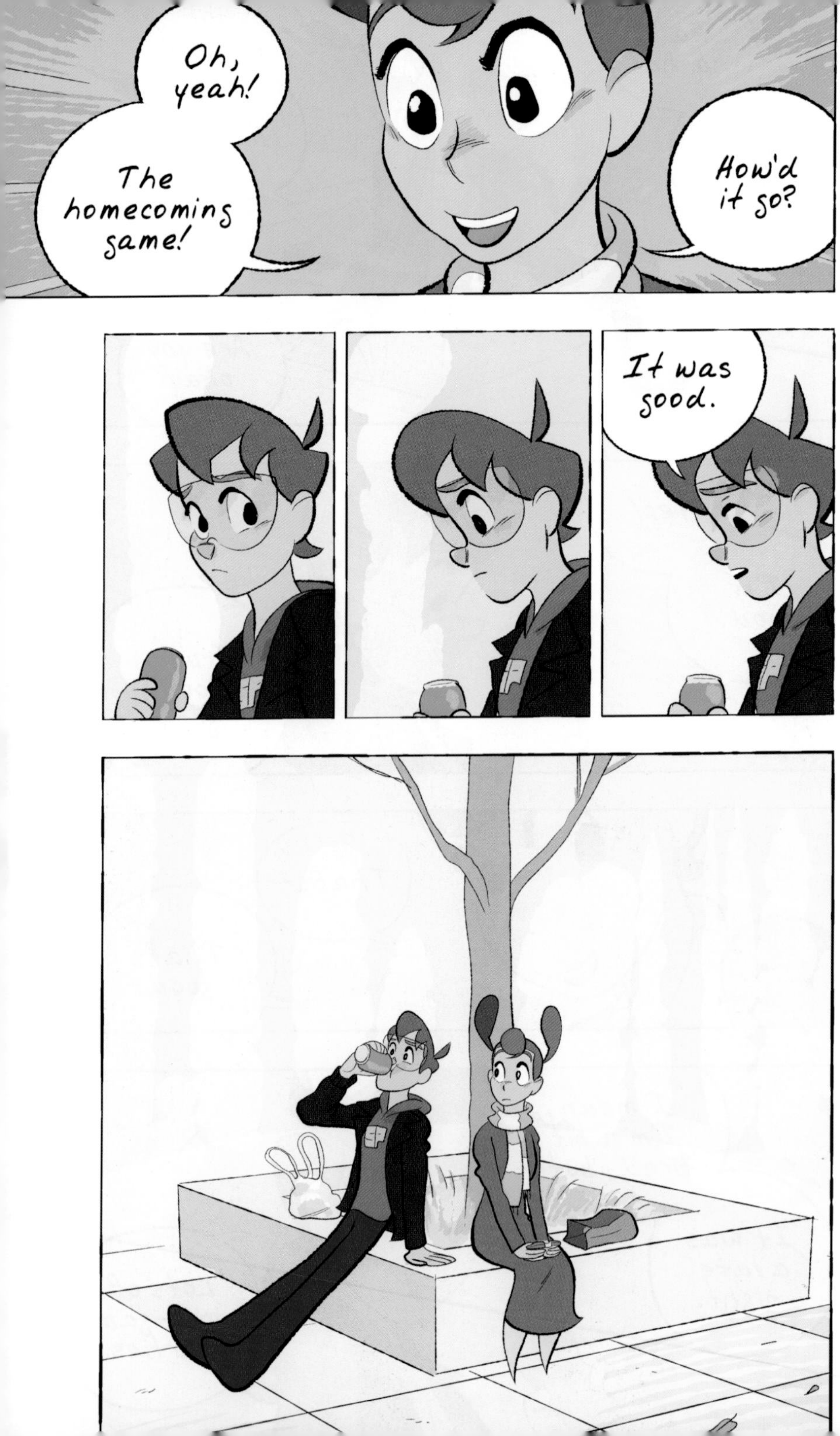
Oh, yeah!
The homecoming game!
How'd it go?
It was good.

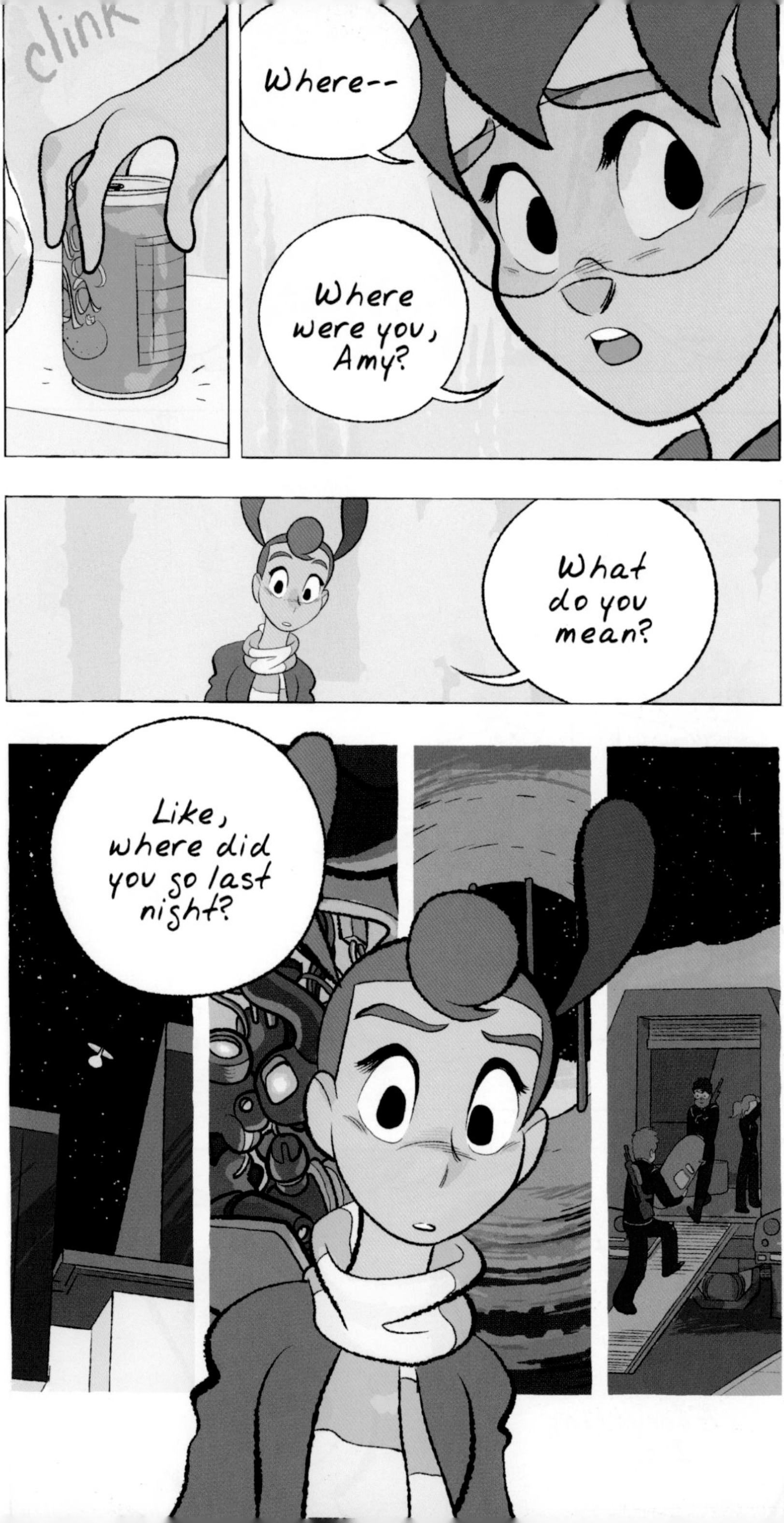
clink
Where--
Where were you, Amy?
What do you mean?
Like, where did you go last night?

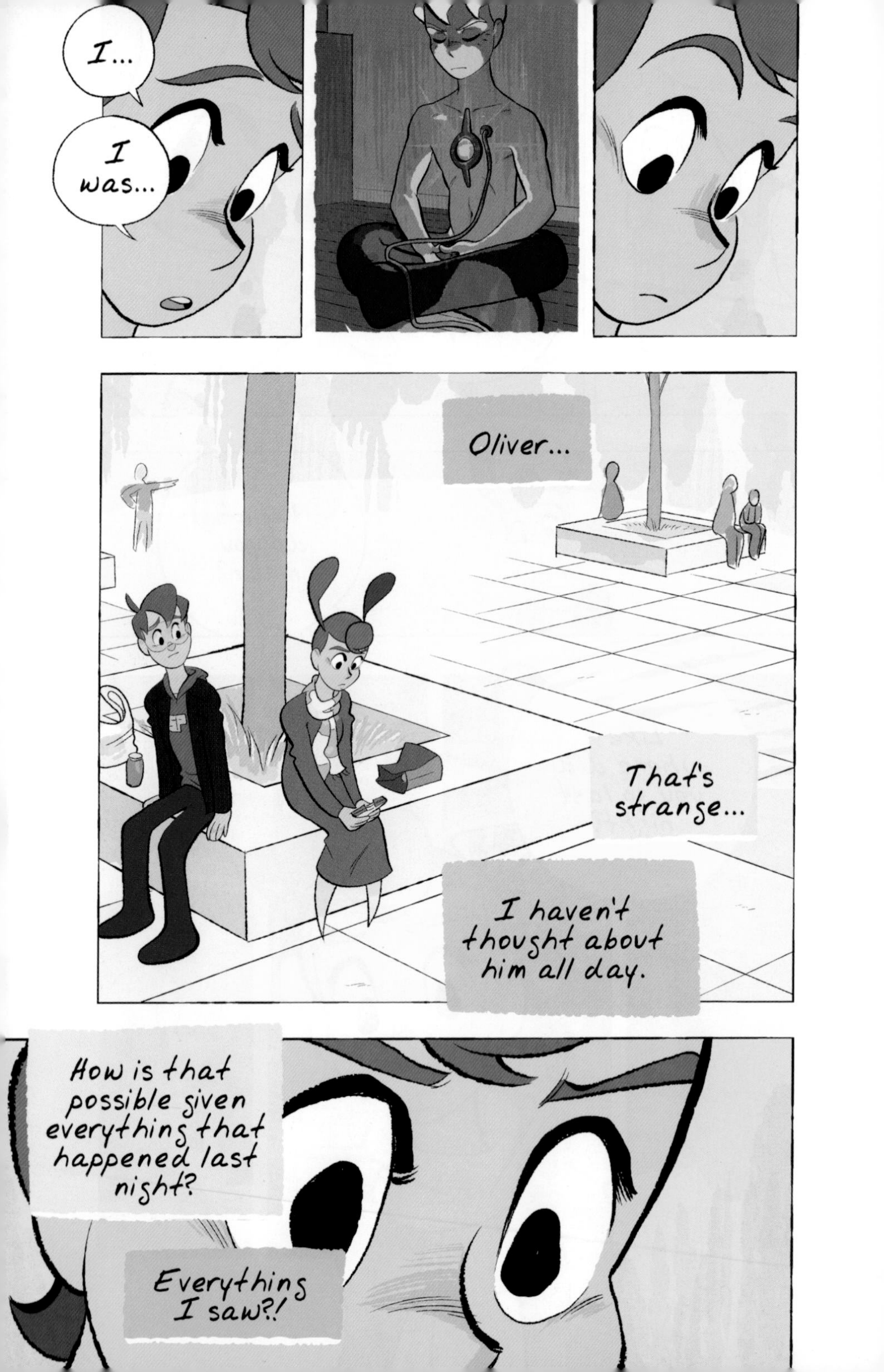
I...
I was...
Oliver...
That's strange...
I haven't thought about him all day.
How is that possible given everything that happened last night?
Everything I saw?!

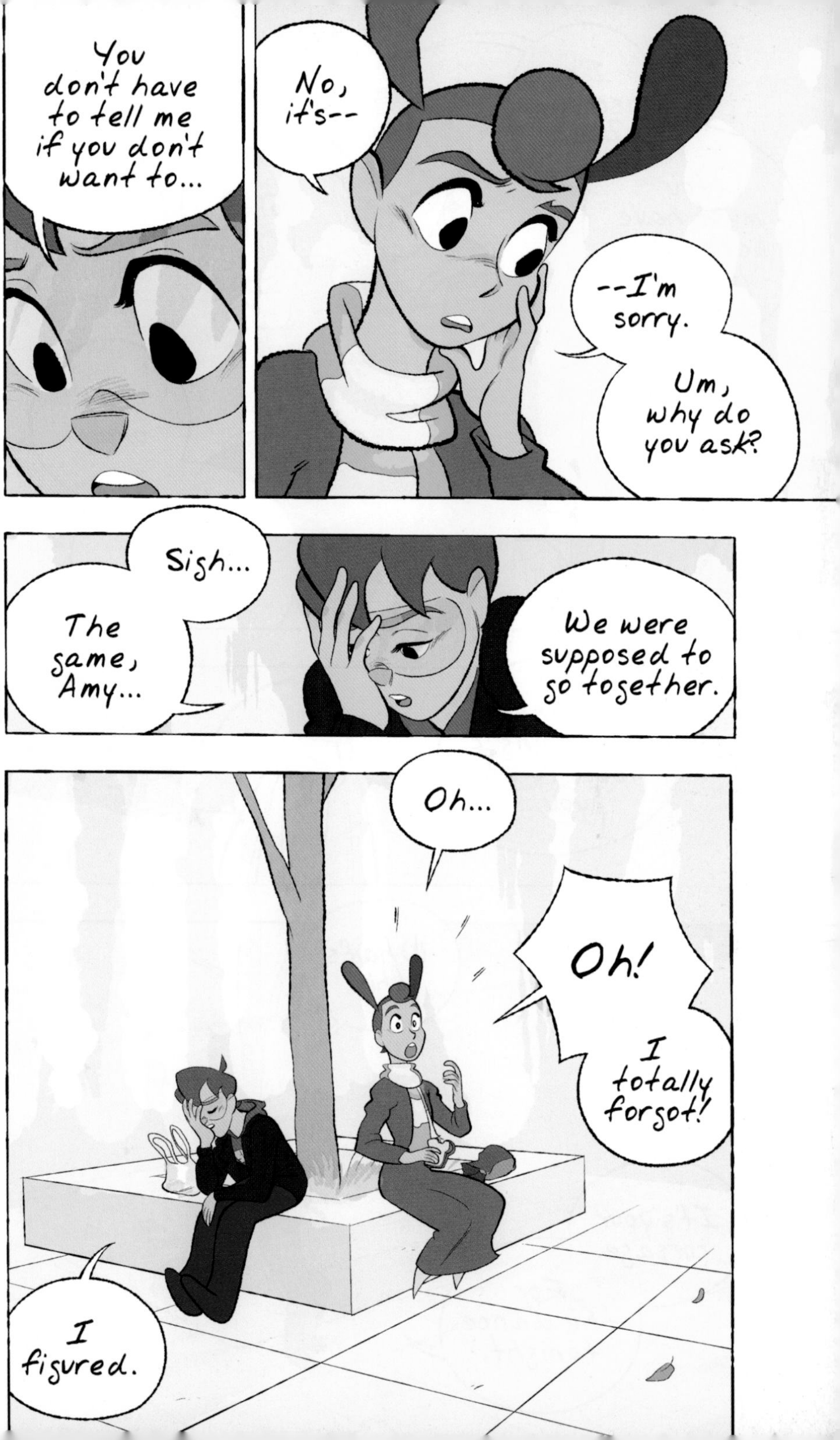

You don't have to tell me if you don't want to...
No, it's--
--I'm sorry.
Um, why do you ask?
Sigh...
The same, Amy...
We were supposed to go together.
Oh...
Oh!
I totally forgot!
I figured.

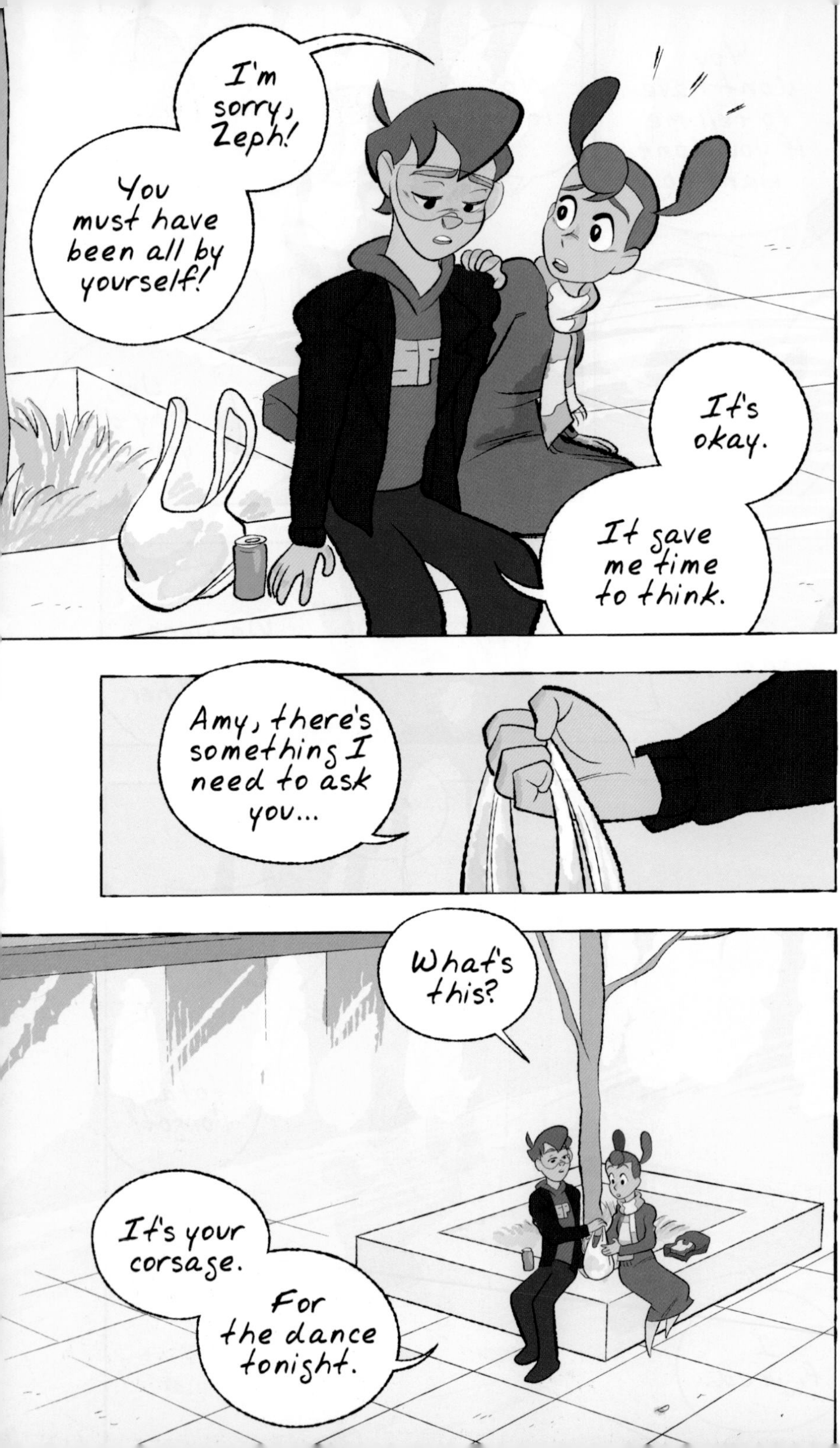
I'm sorry, Zeph!
You must have been all by yourself!
It's okay.
It gave me time to think.
Amy, there's something I need to ask you...
What's this?
It's your corsage.
For the dance tonight.

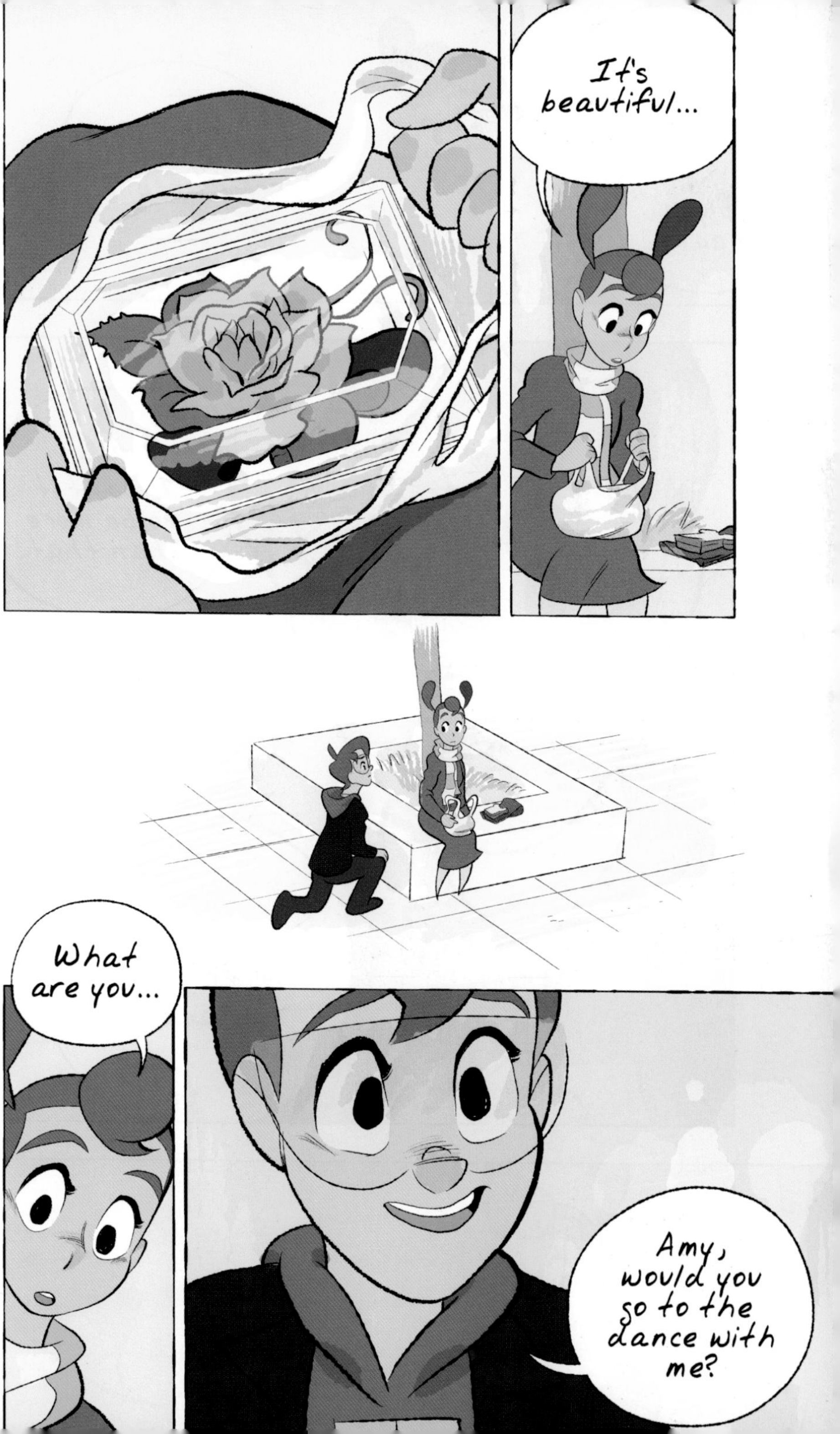
It's beautiful...
What are you...
Amy, would you go to the dance with me?

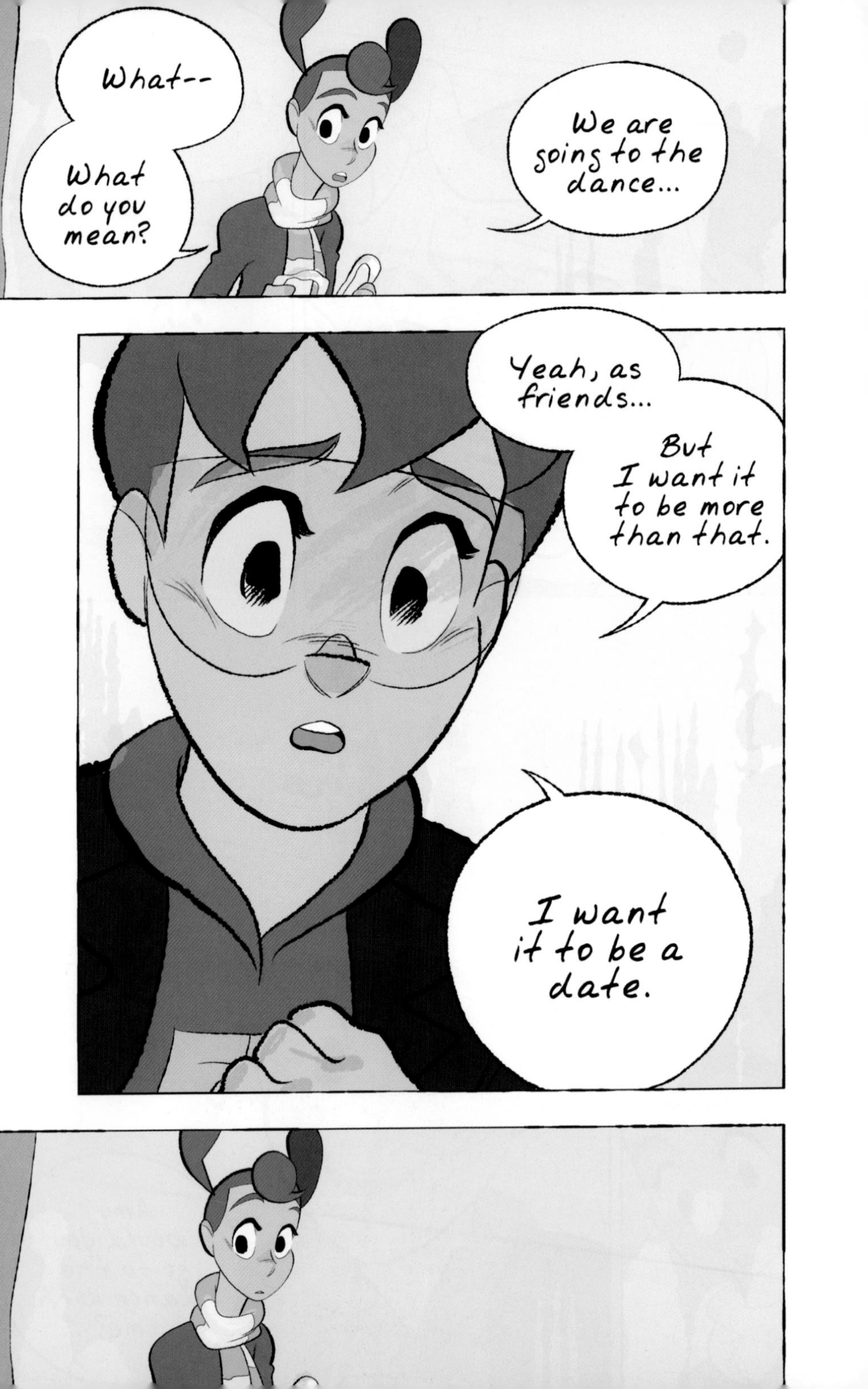
What--
What do you mean?
We are going to the dance...
Yeah, as friends...
But I want it to be more than that.
I want it to be a date.

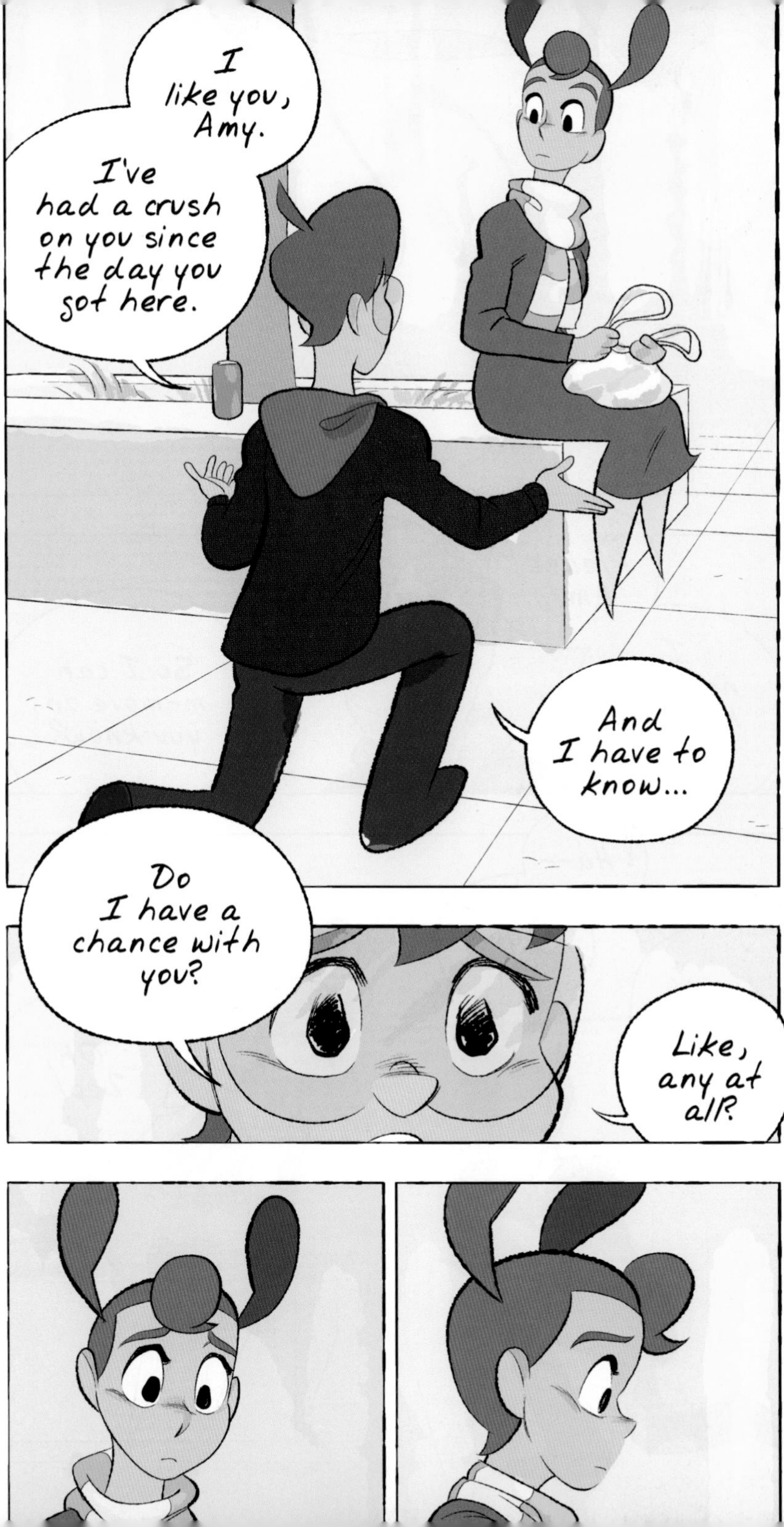
I like you, Amy.
I've had a crush on you since the day you got here.
And I have to know...
Do I have a chance with you?
Like, any at all?

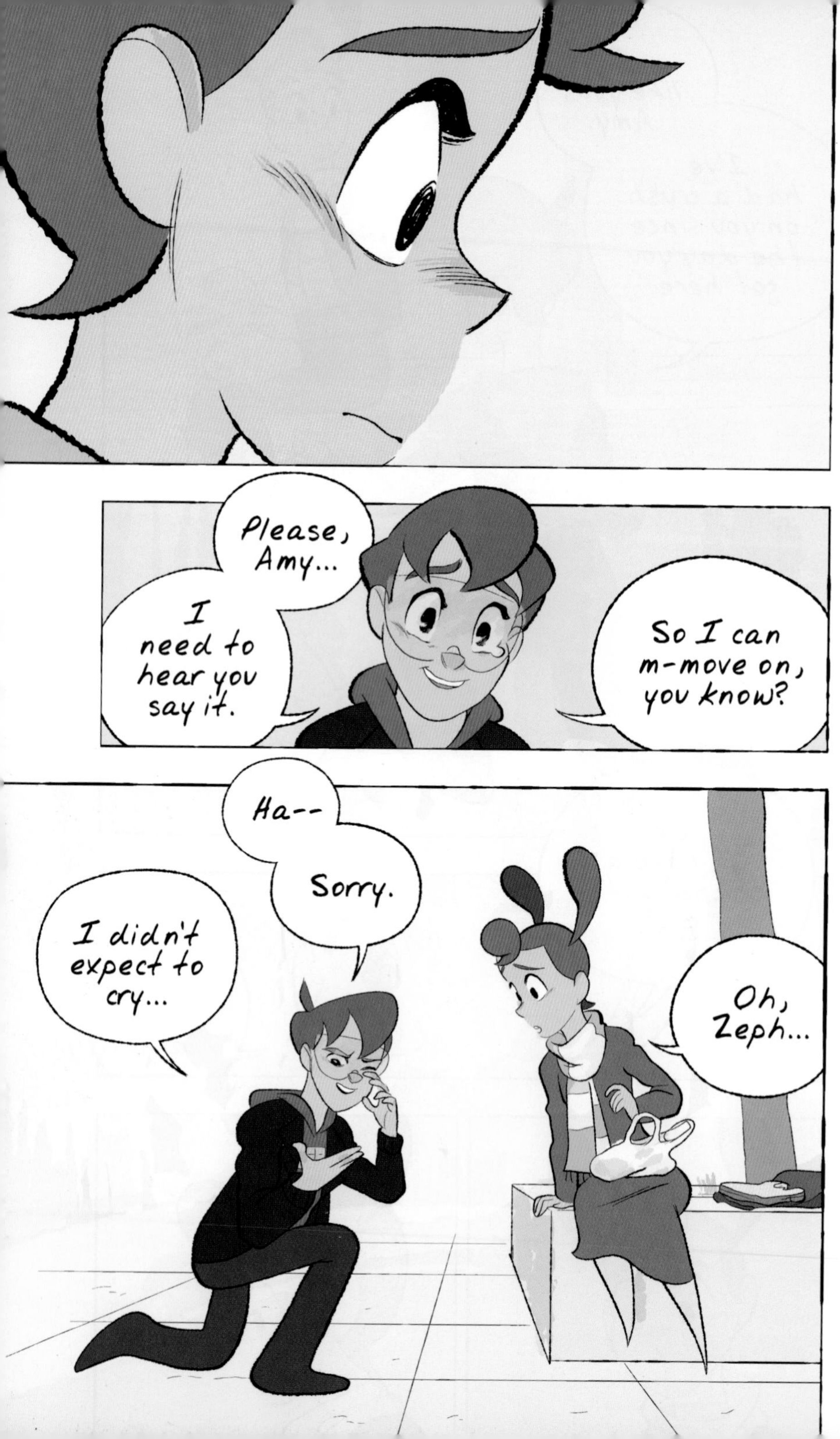
Please, Amy...
I need to hear you say it.
So I can m-move on, you know?
Ha--
Sorry.
I didn't expect to cry...
Oh, Zeph...

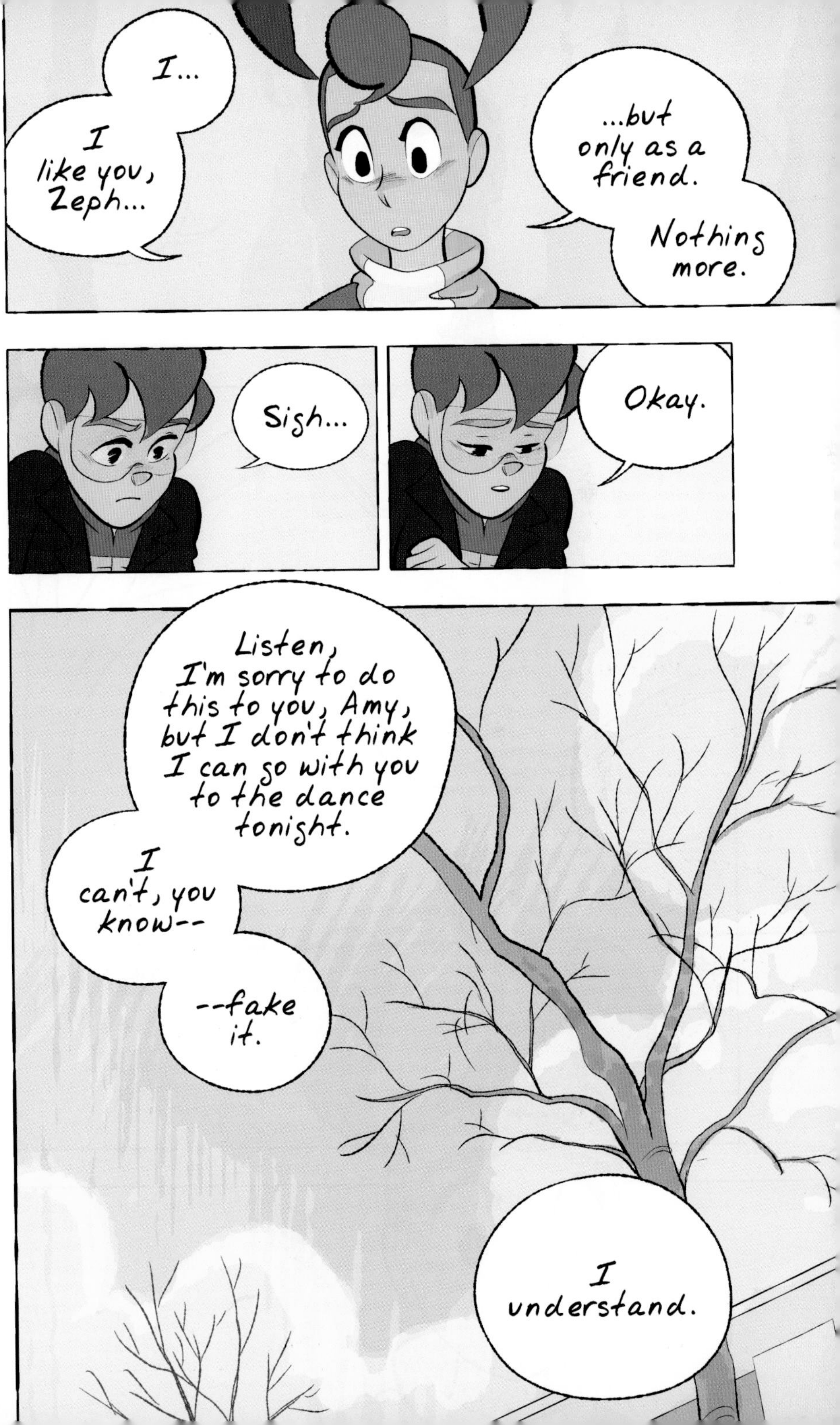
I...
I like you, Zeph...
...but only as a friend.
Nothing more.
Sigh...
Okay.
Listen, I'm sorry to do this to you, Amy, but I don't think I can go with you to the dance tonight.
I can't, you know--
--fake it.
I understand.

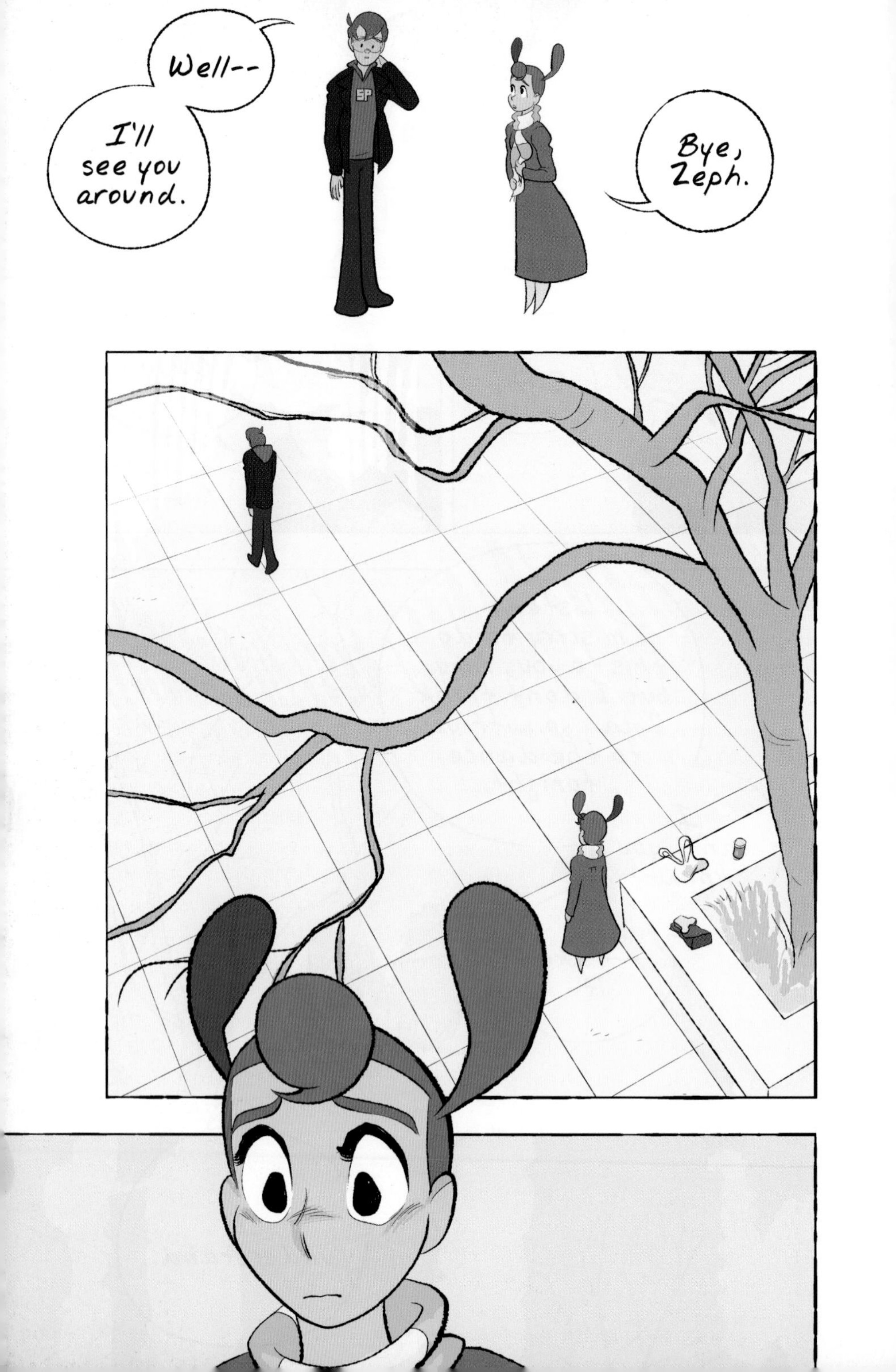
Well--
I'll see you around.
Bye, Zeph.

# COMING SOON . . .

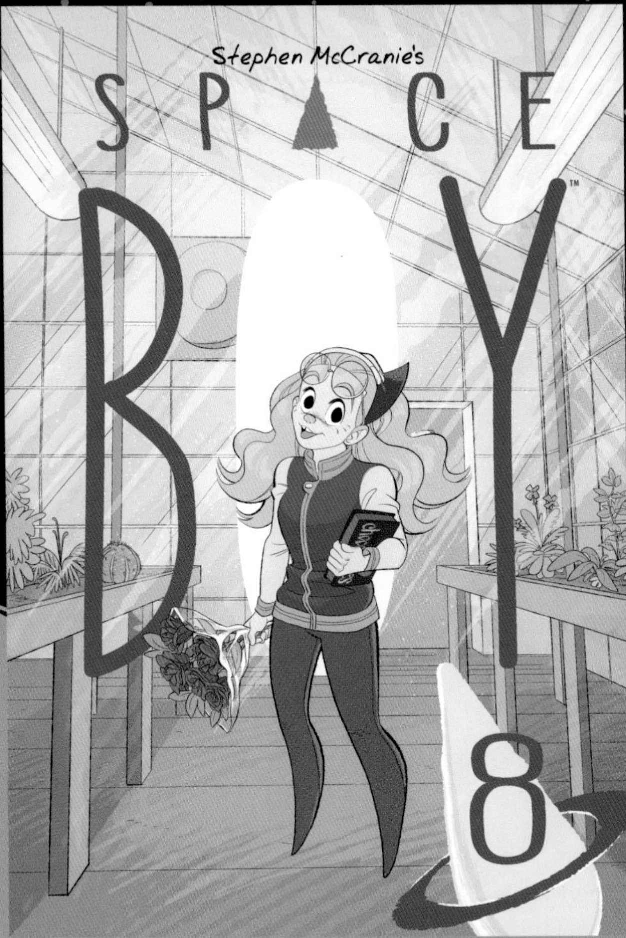

Stephen McCranie's
SPACE BOY
8


Amy's suspicions over Oliver are put on hold when she goes to the homecoming dance with Cassie, but once there she takes an unexpected detour alone, and discovers the secret she has been looking for may have been in plain view all along. However, her discovery brings new dangers, confusion, and excitement along with it! Find out more in the next volume, available October 2020!

YOU CAN ALSO READ MORE SPACE BOY COMICS ON WEBTOONS.COM!

# HAVE YOU READ THEM ALL?

**VOLUME 1**
$10.99 • ISBN 978-1-50670-648-1

**VOLUME 2**
$10.99 • ISBN 978-1-50670-680-1

**VOLUME 3**
$10.99 • ISBN 978-1-50670-842-3

**VOLUME 4**
$10.99 • ISBN 978-1-50670-843-0

**VOLUME 5**
$10.99 • ISBN 978-1-50671-399-1

**VOLUME 6**
$10.99 • ISBN 978-1-50671-400-4

# MORE TITLES YOU MIGHT ENJOY

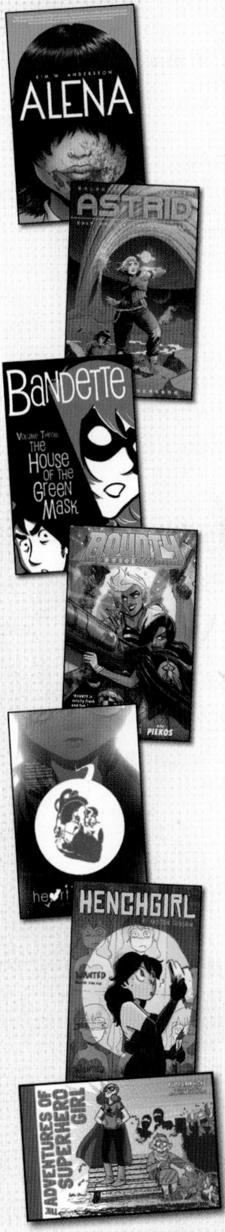
ALENA
ASTRID
BANDETTE
Volume Three: The House of the Green Mask
BOUNTY
PIEKOS
HENCHGIRL
WANTED
THE ADVENTURES OF SUPERHERO GIRL

## ALENA
***Kim W. Andersson***

Since arriving at a snobbish boarding school, Alena's been harassed every day by the lacrosse team. But Alena's best friend Josephine is not going to accept that anymore. If Alena does not fight back, then she will take matters into her own hands. There's just one problem . . . Josephine has been dead for a year.

$17.99 | ISBN 978-1-50670-215-5

## ASTRID: CULT OF THE VOLCANIC MOON
***Kim W. Andersson***

Formerly the Galactic Coalition's top recruit, the now-disgraced Astrid is offered a special mission from her old commander. She'll prove herself worthy of another chance at becoming a Galactic Peacekeeper . . . if she can survive.

$19.99 | ISBN 978-1-61655-690-7

## BANDETTE
***Paul Tobin, Colleen Coover***

A costumed teen burglar by the *nome d'arte* of Bandette and her group of street urchins find equal fun in both skirting and aiding the law, in this enchanting, Eisner-nominated series!

$14.99 each

Volume 1: Presto! | ISBN 978-1-61655-279-4

Volume 2: Stealers, Keepers! | ISBN 978-1-61655-668-6

Volume 3: The House of the Green Mask | ISBN 978-1-50670-219-3

## BOUNTY
***Kurtis Wiebe, Mindy Lee***

The Gadflies were the most wanted criminals in the galaxy. Now, with a bounty to match their reputation, the Gadflies are forced to abandon banditry for a career as bounty hunters . . . 'cause if you can't beat 'em, join 'em—then rob 'em blind!

$14.99 | ISBN 978-1-50670-044-1

## HEART IN A BOX
***Kelly Thompson, Meredith McClaren***

In a moment of post-heartbreak weakness, Emma wishes her heart away and a mysterious stranger obliges. But emptiness is even worse than grief, and Emma sets out to collect the pieces of her heart and face the cost of recapturing it.

$14.99 | ISBN 978-1-61655-694-5

## HENCHGIRL
***Kristen Gudsnuk***

Mary Posa hates her job. She works long hours for little pay, no insurance, and worst of all, no respect. Her coworkers are jerks, and her boss doesn't appreciate her. He's also a supervillain. Cursed with a conscience, Mary would give anything to be something other than a henchgirl.

$17.99 | ISBN 978-1-50670-144-8

## THE ADVENTURES OF SUPERHERO GIRL, SECOND EDITION
***Faith Erin Hicks***

What if you can leap tall buildings and defeat alien monsters with your bare hands, but you buy your capes at secondhand stores and have a weakness for kittens? Faith Erin Hicks brings humor to the trials and tribulations of a young, female superhero, battling monsters both supernatural and mundane in an all-too-ordinary world.

$16.99 each | ISBN 978-1-61655-084-4

Expanded Edition | ISBN 978-1-50670-336-7

---

DARK HORSE BOOKS

DARKHORSE.COM AVAILABLE AT YOUR LOCAL COMICS SHOP OR BOOKSTORE • TO FIND A COMICS SHOP IN YOUR AREA, VISIT COMICSHOPLOCATOR.COM

For more information or to order direct, visit DarkHorse.com

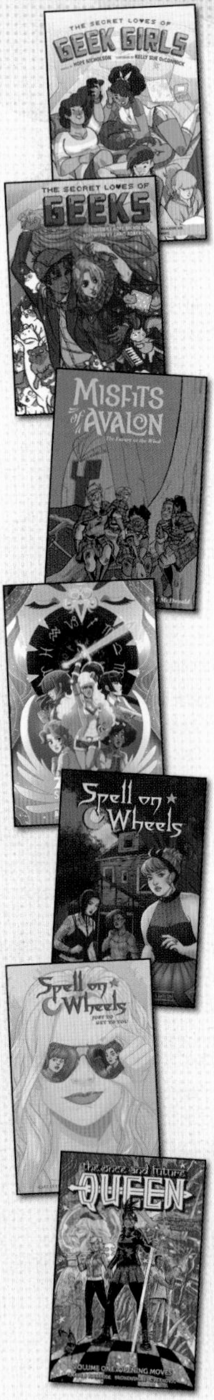
THE SECRET LOVES OF
GEEK GIRLS
THE SECRET LOVES OF
GEEKS
Misfits of Avalon
Spell on Wheels
Spell on Wheels
QUEEN

## THE SECRET LOVES OF GEEK GIRLS

***Hope Nicholson, Margaret Atwood, Mariko Tamaki, and more***

*The Secret Loves of Geek Girls* is a nonfiction anthology mixing prose, comics, and illustrated stories on the lives and loves of an amazing cast of female creators.

$14.99 | ISBN 978-1-50670-099-1

## THE SECRET LOVES OF GEEKS

***Gerard Way, Dana Simpson, Hope Larson, and more***

The follow-up to the smash hit *The Secret Loves of Geek Girls*, this brand new anthology features comic and prose stories from cartoonists and professional geeks about their most intimate, heartbreaking, and inspiring tales of love, sex, and dating. This volume includes creators of diverse genders, orientations, and cultural backgrounds.

$14.99 | ISBN 978-1-50670-473-9

## MISFITS OF AVALON

***Kel McDonald***

Four misfit teens are reluctant recruits to save the mystical isle of Avalon. Magically empowered and directed by a talking dog, they must stop the rise of King Arthur. As they struggle to become a team, they're faced with the discovery that they may not be the good guys.

$14.99 each

Volume 1: The Queen of Air and Delinquency | ISBN 978-1-61655-538-2

Volume 2: The Ill-Made Guardian | ISBN 978-1-61655-748-5

Volume 3: The Future in the Wind | ISBN 978-1-61655-749-2

## ZODIAC STARFORCE: BY THE POWER OF ASTRA

***Kevin Panetta, Paulina Ganucheau***

A group of teenage girls with magical powers have sworn to protect our planet against dark creatures. Known as the Zodiac Starforce, these high-school girls aren't just combating math tests—they're also battling monsters!

$12.99 | ISBN 978-1-61655-913-7

## ZODIAC STARFORCE: CRIES OF THE FIRE PRINCE

***Kevin Panetta, Paulina Ganucheau***

A new Big Bad has come out to play and demons are overrunning the town! The UK team's secrets are causing a rift in the Zodiac alliance, and divided they may fall!

$17.99 | ISBN 978-1-50670-310-7

## SPELL ON WHEELS

***Kate Leth, Megan Levens, Marissa Louise***

A road trip story. A magical revenge fantasy. A sisters-over-misters tale of three witches out to get back what was taken from them.

$14.99 | ISBN 978-1-50670-183-7

## SPELL ON WHEELS: JUST TO GET TO YOU

***Kate Leth, Megan Levens, Marissa Louise***

As they make their way along the highway toward the strange presence possessing Claire, the witches find you can't go home again. And they're running out of time.

$19.99 | ISBN 978-1-50671-477-6

## THE ONCE AND FUTURE QUEEN

***Adam P. Knave, D.J. Kirkbride, Nick Brokenshire, Frank Cvetkovic***

It's out with the old myths and in with the new as a nineteen-year-old chess prodigy pulls Excalibur from the stone and becomes queen. Now, magic, romance, Fae, Merlin, and more await her!

$14.99 | ISBN 978-1-50670-250-6

---

DARK HORSE BOOKS

DARKHORSE.COM AVAILABLE AT YOUR LOCAL COMICS SHOP OR BOOKSTORE • TO FIND A COMICS SHOP IN YOUR AREA, VISIT COMICSHOPLOCATOR.COM
For more information or to order direct, visit DarkHorse.com